"Before you kn

you didn't want

You said you don't want a PA. But
it's clear you need one. So obviously
there's a reason you're fighting having
someone work for you."

He sighed.

Fine. Don't tell me. Because I don't care. What I *do* care about is earning my keep."

He sighed again. "You are a pregnant woman who needs a rest. Just take the time here with me to have some fun."

She raised her chin. "No. If you won't let me work I won't take your charity. I'm going home."

"You don't have a home to go back to."

"Then let me stay here for two weeks as your assistant. If you don't like what I do, or still feel you don't need someone at the end of two weeks, I'll take another two weeks to rest and then go home."

When they'd first begun arguing, before he'd known she was pregnant, his eyes had been sharp. Glowing. She could have sworn he wanted to kiss her. It was as if he had been daring her to step closer—

Had he been daring her to step closer?

HER BROODING
ITALIAN BOSS

BY
SUSAN MEIER

Published in Great Britain 2015
by Mills & Boon, an imprint of Harlequin (UK) Limited,
Eton House, 18-24 Paradise Road, Richmond, Surrey, TW9 1SR

© 2015 Linda Susan Meier

ISBN: 978-0-263-25109-8

23-0215

Harlequin (UK) Limited's policy is to use papers that are natural, renewable and recyclable products and made from wood grown in sustainable forests. The logging and manufacturing processes conform to the legal environmental regulations of the country of origin.

Printed and bound in Spain
by CPI, Barcelona

Susan Meier is the author of over fifty books for Mills & Boon. *The Tycoon's Secret Daughter* was a RITA® finalist and *Nanny for the Millionaire's Twins* won the Book Buyers' Best award and was a finalist in the National Readers' Choice awards. She is married and has three children. One of eleven siblings, she loves to write about the complexity of families and totally believes in the power of love.

CHAPTER ONE

LAURA BETH MATTHEWS sat on the rim of the old porcelain tub in the New York City apartment she had to vacate by the next morning. Her long brown hair had been swirled into a sophisticated French twist. Her lilac organza bridesmaid gown was an original Eloise Vaughn design. A pregnancy test shook in her right hand.

Tears pooled in her eyes. There was no question now. She was going to have a baby.

"Laura Beth! Come on!" Eloise called from the hall as she knocked on the bathroom door. "I'm the bride! I should at least get ten minutes in the bathroom to check my makeup."

"Sorry!" She swiped at her tears and quickly examined her face in the medicine cabinet mirror. No real mascara smudges yet, but the day was young.

For the first time since she, Eloise and their third original roommate, Olivia Prentiss Engle, had decided to spend the night before Eloise's wedding together and dress together, Laura Beth regretted it. She was pregnant. The father of her child, one of Olivia's husband's vice presidents, had called her a slut when she'd told him she was late and they might be parents. And now she didn't just have to smile her way through a wedding; she had to hide a pregnancy test in a tiny bathroom.

She glanced around. "I'll be two more seconds." Out of time, she wrapped the stick in toilet paper and tossed it in the little wastebasket. Satisfied neither Olivia nor Eloise would rummage through the trash, she sucked in a breath, pasted on a happy smile and opened the door.

Eloise stood before her, glowing, a vision in her original Artie Best gown, designed specifically by her boss, the one and only Artie Best. Smooth silk rode Eloise's feminine curves. Rhinestones sparkled across the sweetheart neckline. And real diamonds—enough to support the population of a third-world country for a decade—glittered at her throat.

Tears pooled in Laura Beth's eyes again, but this time they were tears of joy for her friend. Eloise, Olivia and Laura Beth had moved to New York City with stars in their eyes. Now Olivia was a married mom. Eloise would be married in a few hours. And Laura Beth was pregnant, with a deadbeat for her child's father and twenty-four hours to vacate her apartment.

She was in deep trouble.

Antonio Bartulocci studied his shoulder-length curly black hair in the mirror. He'd gotten it cut for Ricky and Eloise's wedding, but he still debated tying it back, out of the way. He looked to the left, then the right, and decided he was worrying over nothing. Eloise and Ricky were his friends because they liked him just as he was. They didn't care that he was a tad bohemian. Most artists were.

He straightened his silver tie one last time before he walked out of the bedroom of his suite in his father's Park Avenue penthouse and headed for the main room.

Comfortable aqua sofas faced each other atop a pale gray area rug, flanked by white Queen Anne chairs. A gray stone fireplace took up the back wall, and a dark walnut wet bar sat in the corner. The view of the New York City skyline from the wall of windows in the back had taken Antonio's breath away when he first saw it. Since his wife's death, it barely registered.

"Hurry up, Antonio," his father called from the bar as he poured bourbon into a crystal glass. He wore a simple black suit, a white shirt and yellow striped tie that would be replaced by a tuxedo for the reception later that night. Though he was well into his seventies and a few pounds overweight, Italian billionaire Constanzo Bartulocci was a dashing man. A man whose looks spoke of money and power, who lived not in an ordinary world, but in one he could control. Unlike Antonio's world, where passion, inspiration and luck ruled.

"I'm right behind you."

Constanzo jumped and faced his son, his right hand over his heart. "You scare me."

Antonio laughed. "I'll bet I do."

After downing his drink in one long swallow, Constanzo pointed at the door. "Let's get going. I don't want to end up in a crush of reporters like we did the last time we went somewhere."

Antonio straightened his tie one more time. "Hey, you made me the paparazzi monster I am today."

"You are not a monster." The lilt of an Italian accent warmed his father's voice. "You could be one of the most important painters of the twenty-first century. You are a talent."

He knew that, of course. But having talent wasn't what most people imagined. He didn't put his gift away in a shiny box and take it out when he needed it. Talent, the need to paint, the breathtaking yearning to explore life on a canvas, were what drove him. But for the past two years he hadn't even been able to pick up a brush. Forget about painting, accepting commissions, having a purpose in life. Now, he ate, drank, slept—but didn't really live. Because he'd made millions on his art in the past few years, and, with his savvy businessman father's help, he'd parlayed those millions into hundreds of millions through investments, money wasn't an issue. He had the freedom and the resources to ignore his calling.

The private elevator door silently opened. Antonio and his father stepped inside. Constanzo sighed. "If you had a personal assistant, this wouldn't have happened."

Antonio worked to hide a wince. He didn't have to ask what his father meant. He knew. "I'm sorry."

"I wanted you to be the artist who did the murals for Tucker's new building. Those works would have been seen by thousands of people. Ordinary people. You would have brought art to the masses in a concrete way. But you missed the deadline."

"I don't have a brain for remembering dates."

"Which is exactly why you need a personal assistant."

Antonio fought the urge to squeeze his eyes shut. What he needed was to be left alone. Or maybe to roll back the clock so far that he hadn't married the woman who'd betrayed him. But that wasn't going to happen. He was stuck in a combination of grief and guilt that paralyzed him.

Constanzo's limousine awaited them on the street. They walked under the building portico without speaking. Antonio motioned for his father to enter first.

When he slid in behind him, soft white leather greeted him. A discreet minibar sat near the media controls. His father hit a few buttons and classical music quietly entered the space.

The driver closed the door and in less than a minute the limo pulled onto the street.

"A PA could also handle some of the Gisella problems that remain."

Antonio's jaw twitched.

Constanzo sighed. "Well, you don't seem to want to handle them." He sighed again, more deeply this time. "Antonio, it's been two years. You cannot grieve forever."

Antonio glanced at his father. He let his lips lift into a small smile. Pretending he was grieving had been the only way he'd survived the years since his wife's death. Beautiful Gisella had burst into his life like a whirlwind. Twenty-four hours after they'd met they'd been in bed. Twenty-four weeks after that they were married. He'd been so smitten, so hopelessly in love, that days, weeks, months hadn't mattered. But looking back, he recognized the signs he should have seen. Her modeling career hadn't tanked, but it had been teetering, and marriage to the newly famous Italian painter had put her in the limelight again. Her sudden interest in international causes hadn't cropped up until she found a way to use them to keep herself, her name, in the papers and on everybody's lips. She'd even spoken at the UN. He'd been so proud…so stupid.

"My son, I know adult children don't like nagging, meddling parents, but this time I am correct. You must move on."

Without replying, he looked out the window at the hustle and bustle of New York City in the spring. Bumper-to-bumper traffic, most of it taxicabs. Optimistic residents walking up and down the sidewalk in lightweight coats. The sun glittering off the glass of towering buildings. At one time he'd loved this city more than he'd loved the

Italian countryside that was his home. But she'd even ruined that for him.

"Please do not spoil Ricky and Eloise's day with your sadness."

"I'm not sad, Dad. I'm fine."

The limo stopped. They exited and headed into the enormous gray stone cathedral.

The ceremony was long and Antonio's mind wandered to his own wedding, in this same church, to a woman who hadn't really loved him.

No, he wasn't sad. He was angry, so furious some days his heart beat slow and heavy with it. But he couldn't ruin the reputation of a woman who'd used him to become a cultural icon any more than he could pretend she'd been the perfect wife she'd portrayed.

Which meant he couldn't have a PA digging through papers in his office or documents on his computer.

The ceremony ended. The priest said, "I now introduce Mr. and Mrs. Richard Langley."

His best friend, Ricky, and his beautiful new wife, Eloise, turned and faced the crowd of friends and relatives sitting in the pews. A round of applause burst through the church and Ricky and Eloise headed down the aisle. Matron of honor Olivia Engle and best man Tucker Engle, also husband and wife, followed them out of the church. Antonio walked to the center aisle to meet his partner, Laura Beth Matthews.

Laura Beth was a sweet young woman he'd met and had gotten to know fairly well over the years when she'd visited Olivia and Tucker at their Italian villa, and every time there was a baptism, birthday or holiday party at the Engle penthouse on Park Avenue. Unfortunately, she had usually been with an annoying boyfriend, someone who didn't fit into Tucker Engle's world or Ricky Langley's, but who desperately tried to.

Laura Beth slid her hand to Antonio's elbow and he smiled at her before they walked down the aisle and out of the church.

As Ricky and Eloise greeted the long line of guests filing through the vestibule, Antonio turned to Laura Beth. "You look lovely."

She glanced down at the pale purple dress. "Eloise designs the most beautiful gowns."

"Ah, so she did this herself."

Laura Beth nodded. When she brought her gaze back to his, though, her green eyes were dull. Not sad for the change in her life that the marriage of her last roommate would bring, but lifeless.

He caught her forearm to bring her attention to him. "Are you okay?"

She suddenly brightened. "Sure. Yes. I'm fine. Wonderful. It was just a stressful morning."

"Tell me about it. Have you ever tried traveling with a billionaire who expects everybody and everything to be at his fingertips?"

Laura Beth laughed. "Oh, come on. I love your father! He's not a prima donna."

"You've only dealt with him when you were on vacation or at a party for one of Tucker and Olivia's kids. Just try flying across the Atlantic with him."

She laughed again and something lightened in Antonio's chest. With her dark brown hair and bright green eyes, Laura Beth was much too pretty to be so—

He paused, not able to put a label on her mood. Nervous didn't quite hit the mark. Unhappy wasn't it either. She seemed more like distant. As if she were preoccupied.

Seeing Ricky and Eloise still had a line of guests filing out of the church, he said, "So what's up?"

Her head snapped in his direction. "Up?"

"You're here one minute, but your mind is gone the next. You're obviously mulling something over. Or trying to figure something out."

"I...um...well, I have to be out of my apartment tomorrow before noon."

His eyebrows rose. "And you're not packed?"

"No, I'm packed. I just don't have anywhere to go."

"You could stay at Constanzo's penthouse. We leave tomorrow morning."

She blushed. "Yeah, I could stay at Tucker and Olivia's, too." The red of her face deepened. "I'm always taking advantage of other people's goodwill."

The greeting line for wedding guests suddenly ended. Ricky and Eloise headed outside. Antonio caught Laura Beth's hand and led her to the side door. "Let's go. We want to be outside to toss confetti when they come out."

When Antonio took her hand and guided her out into the warm spring day, Laura Beth's heart tugged. With his shoulder-length curly black hair and penetrating dark eyes, he was the epitome of the sexy artist. But that wasn't why her heart skipped a beat. His very casual way of making her feel a part of things, when her brain kept dragging her away, lifted her spirits. He was a good man, with a big heart and so much talent she almost couldn't fathom it.

She'd had a crush on him from the day she'd met him. But she'd been dating Bruce. Then Antonio had gotten married, and two short years after that he was mourning the loss of his beautiful, equally talented, dedicated wife. So though she'd crushed on him, she'd never even let the thought of flirting with him fully form. And now, pregnant, she only let the thought flit through her brain. She absolutely wouldn't act on it.

She should just get off her self-pity train and help Antonio enjoy the wedding, not expect him to help her.

So she made light, happy conversation while they posed for pictures as members of the wedding party, and hours later in the ballroom of the Waldorf, while they ate dinner. Antonio laughed in all the right places, but Laura Beth could see the glimmer of sadness in his eyes. As much as she wanted to be able to entertain him, she was failing. Her own troubles weighed her down, just as his dampened his mood. They'd both run out of jokes and neutral topics and even fun-filled facts. Worse, every time he turned his dark, brooding eyes on her, she wanted to flirt. Flirt! He had troubles. She had troubles. And she wanted to flirt? Ridiculous. So after the wedding party dance, she shuffled off to the ladies' room.

She sat on the cushioned sofa along the back wall and took several deep breaths. She might be able to hide out in her apartment one more night, but then she seriously had to decide where she'd sleep tomorrow. In Tucker and Olivia's penthouse? Or Constanzo Bartulocci's? Once again accepting charity.

How long could she live like this? She did not have a home. She did not have a full-time job. She was *pregnant* by a man who thought her a slut. She was a failure.

Tears filled her eyes.

Oh, great. Now she'd upset herself.

She sucked in a breath, brushed away her tears and rose from the comfortable sofa. She might not be able to pretend she wasn't in financial trouble, but for the next few hours she still had to feign happiness and fulfill her bridesmaid responsibilities.

In the plush hall outside the ladies' room, she straightened her shoulders and drank in another fortifying breath. She could do this.

The first person she saw as she entered the ballroom was Antonio, so she walked in the other direction. The pull of her attraction to him was so strong today she could have melted in his arms when they danced, and that was just wrong. He was grieving a wonderful woman whom he'd adored. And Laura Beth herself had problems to solve before she could even consider flirting with someone, let alone melting into his arms.

Walking past laughing entrepreneurs, happy socialites and waiters serving champagne, she had a strange epiphany, or maybe a rush of reality. She was only here because of her roommates. In the four years since she'd been invited into this rarified world by Olivia and Eloise, they had not only found their true callings, but they had fallen for the loves of their lives—while she hadn't found squat. Rubbing elbows with executives, she hadn't been able to prove herself enough to anyone to get a full-time job. And despite being in front of all these gorgeous eligible bachelors, she hadn't yet found a man who wanted her.

Maybe her problem wasn't that there was something wrong with her. Maybe she was in the wrong class of people. After all, she'd grown up blue-collar. Why did she believe that just because her friends fit into the glitzy, glamorous world of billionaires, she should fit in, too?

Maybe this whole mess—her inability to get a full-time job, her inability to keep her apartment and her pregnancy—was a wake-up call from the universe. *Hey,*

Laura Beth, you're in the wrong crowd. That's why you're failing!

It made so much sense that she stopped short, not quite at the open bar.

The answer was so obvious it stunned her. Though she would always be friends with Olivia and Eloise, she didn't belong in this part of their world. She was common. Normal. Not that there was anything wrong with that. It was more that a common person, someone who didn't fit in this world, would always come up short. But if she were to jump off her high horse and get a normal job, she would probably be very happy right now.

If only because she would get to be herself.

Antonio almost groaned when his dad sidled up to him at the bar. "So have you given any thought to my suggestion about a personal assistant?"

As much as Antonio loved his dad, he did have moments when he wished the old billionaire would just get lost.

"Dad, how about letting this go?"

"I think it's the answer to your problems."

Out of the corner of his eye, he saw his partner for the wedding, Laura Beth, walk up beside him and order a ginger ale from the bartender. He would only have to tap her arm and snag her attention to get himself out of this conversation. But how fair was that? Not only did he need to put his foot down with his dad, but Laura Beth obviously wanted to be left alone. It wouldn't be right to drag her into his drama.

He sucked in a breath and smiled at his dad. There was only one way to stop Constanzo—pretend to agree. Albeit temporarily. "You know what? I will think about the PA." It really wasn't a lie. He would *think* about hiring a PA, but that was as far as it would go. There was no way he wanted a stranger in his house. No way he wanted someone going through his things. No way he wanted a stranger to accidentally stumble upon any of his wife's deceit when rummaging through papers or files or phone records while trying to organize him.

Constanzo's face lit. "You will?"

"Sure."

"And maybe start painting again?"

He stole a glance at Laura Beth, suddenly wishing he could capture that faraway look in her eyes, the expression that was half-wistful, half-sad. She was so naturally beautiful. High cheekbones gave her face a sculpted look that would serve her well as she aged. And her bounty of hair? He could see himself undoing that fancy hairdo and fanning his fingers through the silken strands to loosen it, right before he kissed her.

What? Where had that come from?

He shook his head to clear it, deciding it was time to get away from his dad before he had any more crazy thoughts.

He faced Constanzo. "I'll paint when I paint. Now, I need to get mingling again."

As he walked away from the bar, he noticed his dad bridging the gap between himself and Laura Beth and sighed with relief. This meant his dad wouldn't follow him. Besides which, it would help Laura Beth get her mind off her troubles. When he wasn't hounding Antonio about something or another in his life, Constanzo Bartulocci could be a very funny guy.

Laura Beth glanced at Constanzo and pasted a smile on her face. Now that she recognized she didn't belong in this crowd, that she was pretending to be someone she wasn't, she knew exactly what to do: enjoy the rest of the wedding, then get busy finding a normal job and some new roommates. Whoever she chose couldn't ever replace Olivia and Eloise—no one would ever replace her two best friends—but she'd make it work.

"You seem sad tonight."

Laura Beth nodded and smiled at Constanzo. He was like everybody's rich uncle. But he didn't flaunt his money. He made people laugh. He'd made *her* laugh at more than one of Olivia and Tucker's family events. It wasn't unusual or out of line for her to confide. She simply wouldn't tell him everything.

"My second roommate got married today," she said, taking advantage of the obvious. "I'm not exactly an old maid, but I'm on the road."

Constanzo laughed. "You Americans. What is this old maid thing? Can't a woman mature and enjoy life without being married?"

She laughed lightly. That was exactly the attitude she needed to cultivate. "Actually, yes, she can."

"Good. A woman doesn't need a man. She should *want* a man in her life. But he should complement her, not define her."

She toasted him with her glass of ginger ale. "Wise words."

"So, now that we've settled the old maid issue, what else has made you sad?"

"I'm fine."

He studied her face, then shook his head. "I don't think so."

"Jeez. You're as perceptive as Antonio."

"Where do you think he gets it?"

"I thought it was the artist in him."

Constanzo shook his head sadly. "Unfortunately,

since his wife's death, I think the artist in my son is withering and dying."

His gaze drifted to Antonio, and Laura Beth followed his line of sight. Antonio was stunning in his tuxedo, with his hair a little wild. Every woman he passed eyed him with interest. The spark of her crush lit again, the desire to walk over and suggest another dance rising up in her. But that was wrong. Not only did she have troubles she had to solve before she got involved with another man, but as every woman around him drooled, Antonio didn't seem to see anybody.

"The death of a spouse is difficult."

Constanzo accepted that with a slight nod of his head. "I don't want him to lose his entire life over this."

"He'll come around."

"He needs a nudge."

Laura Beth laughed. "A nudge?"

Constanzo sucked in a breath. "Yes, he needs to hire help. An assistant. Somebody who can live with him and get him on track."

"Sounds like a tall order."

"I don't think so. We've been talking about him hiring a personal assistant, and he's finally agreeable, which means he's finally ready to heal and get back into life. I think once an assistant gets rid of the two years of junk he's let accumulate in his office, Antonio will be able to see his future—not his past."

Laura Beth mulled that over for a second. "Oddly, Constanzo, that actually makes sense."

Constanzo laughed. "I like that you understand us. It's part of why I find you to chat to at parties."

She smiled. "There's not much to understand. You're a dad who loves his son. He's a son who appreciates having a dad. All the rest is just stuff."

He laughed again. "I wish I could hire you to be his PA."

Laura Beth paused her ginger ale halfway to her lips.

"But I'm sure you wouldn't want to live in Italy. And then there's matter of the job itself. I'm sure you're accustomed to much loftier employment."

She sniffed a laugh. "My degree has gotten me nothing but temp jobs."

His eyebrows rose. "So you're interested?"

She thought that through. A real full-time job, that came with room and board? In a country away from her family and friends, so she could think through what to do about her pregnancy before she announced it?

"Yes. I'm interested."

CHAPTER TWO

THE NEXT MORNING, as instructed by Constanzo, Laura Beth took a taxi to Tucker Engle's private airstrip. She pulled her measly suitcase out of the backseat and paid the driver one-fifth of the money she had, leaving her a mere pittance. If this job didn't pan out, she'd be penniless. But since she was already in trouble, and knew Antonio and Constanzo well, taking work as Antonio's personal assistant wasn't much of a risk.

A swirl of April air kicked up dust on the tarmac as she walked to the plane. Two pilots stood beside the lowered stairway, comparing information in logbooks. As she approached, one of the men saw her and smiled. He said something in Italian and she winced.

"Sorry. I don't speak Italian."

The pilot laughed. "I speak English. What can we do for you?"

"I'm Laura Beth Matthews. Constanzo told me he would call you to add my name to your passenger list."

The pilot looked down, then back up again. But the second pilot pointed at the list.

"Ah, *sì*. Here you are." He reached for her pathetic suitcase. "I will take care of this."

Fear ruffled through her as a man she didn't know

took the entirety of her possessions out of her hand and walked away. But the second pilot pointed up the steps.

She sucked in a breath. She needed to get away. She needed time to think. She needed a job. She climbed the stairs.

At the doorway she stopped and gasped. The main area looked more like a living room than a plane. Rows of seats had been replaced by long, comfortable-looking sofas. Tables beside the sofas provided places for books, drinks or food. A desk and wet bar in the back filled the remaining space.

She eased toward the sofas, wondering where the heck Constanzo and Antonio were. Sitting on the soft leather, she leaned back, enjoying the feel of it against her nape. She'd been so nervous the night before she hadn't slept, and part of her just wanted to nod off. Before she got too comfortable, though, a commotion sounded outside. She jumped up and looked out the window.

A big white limo had pulled up. Antonio got out and held the door for his dad. She tilted her head, watching them.

Dressed in jeans and an open dress shirt over a white T-shirt, Antonio looked totally different. She usually saw him in tuxedos at gallery openings or formal events, or trousers and white shirts at parties for Olivia and Tucker's kids. Seeing him so casual sent a jolt of attraction through her. Especially with the way the breeze blew through his long curly hair, making her wonder if it was as soft as it looked.

She shook her head at her stupidity and raced back to her seat. She'd just gotten settled when Constanzo boarded the plane.

"*Carissima*. You made it."

She rose, just in case she was sitting in the wrong place. "I did."

Antonio entered behind his dad. He stopped when he saw her, his brow wrinkling. "Laura Beth?"

Though Antonio had been raised in the United States, he'd spent the past five years in Italy. Speaking Italian had changed the timbre of his voice. Her name rolled off his tongue sensually. A shiver breezed along her skin. And another thought suddenly hit her—this man was now her boss. She wouldn't just be working to organize him. They'd be living together.

Oh, wow. No wonder her thoughts ran amok. *She was going to be living with the guy she'd had a crush on for five years.*

Right. Plain Jane Laura Beth would be living with a famous artist, who still grieved his equally gorgeous, equally wonderful wife. Common sense plucked away her fear. She had nothing to worry about.

She smiled and said, "Hello."

Constanzo ambled to the back of the plane. "Can I get you a drink?"

She turned to watch Constanzo as he approached the bar. "No. Thanks."

Antonio stopped in front of her. With his windblown hair and sun-kissed skin, he looked so good, so sexy, that her mouth watered. Especially when his dark eyes met hers.

"What are you doing here?"

Reminding herself Antonio wouldn't ever be attracted to her and she had to get rid of this crush, she peeked back at Constanzo again.

He batted a hand. "I hired her. She's out of her apartment and had no permanent job. It was perfect timing."

Antonio's lips lifted into a smile that would have

stopped her heart if she hadn't known he was off-limits. "Oh. That's great."

The pilot announced they'd been cleared for takeoff. Antonio pointed at the leather sofa, indicating Laura Beth should sit, then he sat beside her. Close enough to touch. Close enough that if they hit turbulence, they'd tumble together.

She squeezed her eyes shut. *Stop!*

She had to get ahold of these wayward thoughts or she'd drive herself crazy living with him! She was not in this guy's league. She'd figured all this out yesterday. She was common, pregnant and needed a job more than a crush.

They both buckled in. The little jet taxied to the runway of the small airstrip and took off smoothly. It climbed for a few minutes and leveled off before the fasten-seat-belts light blinked off and the pilot announced they anticipated an uneventful flight, so they could move about the cabin.

To settle her nerves and maybe waylay the attraction that zapped her every time she looked down and saw Antonio's thigh mere inches away from hers, Laura Beth pulled a book from her purse.

"Ah. I loved that novel."

She glanced at the book, then at Antonio. "I never took you for a science fiction fan."

"Are you kidding? Some of the best art is in science fiction. The imaginations and imagery required are magnificent."

Laura Beth smiled, glad they had something normal to talk about, but her stomach picked that exact second to growl. Her face flushed.

Antonio laughed. "You skipped breakfast."

She hadn't been able eat breakfast. It seemed that

now that she knew she was pregnant, morning sickness had kicked in.

"Um, I wasn't hungry when I got up this morning."

Antonio unbuckled his seat belt. He reached for her hand. "Come with me."

She undid her seat belt and took the hand he'd offered. Her fingers tingled when his warm hand wrapped around them. As he pulled her up to stand, she reminded herself to stop noticing these things and followed him to the back of the plane.

The area she'd believed was a wet bar was actually a small kitchenette. She gaped at it. "You have to be kidding me."

Antonio nudged his head in the direction of his dad, who had fallen asleep on the sofa across from the one where Antonio and Laura Beth had been sitting.

"Anything my dad could possibly want is always stocked on the plane. When we arrive at our destination, any food not eaten will be donated to a charity." He laughed and opened the small fridge. "How about eggs and toast?"

Her stomach didn't lurch at the thought, so she nodded.

Antonio studied her. "Hmm. Not very enthusiastic. So let's try French toast."

"I love French toast." And she hadn't had it in forever.

He motioned for her to sit at one of the bar stools, obviously needing her out of the way in the tiny space. He hit a button and what looked to be a grill appeared.

"This is so cool."

"This is the life of a billionaire."

She glanced around. Remembering her thoughts from the night before, she didn't look at the plane as somebody who someday wanted to own one. She counted her blessings that she was here and had a job and a place to stay.

"It's kind of fun getting to see things that I wouldn't normally see."

He frowned. "I don't understand."

"Well, I'm never going to be a billionaire. So I'm never going to own a plane like this."

"Ah." He broke two eggs in a bowl, added milk, vanilla and a dash of what appeared to be cinnamon, beat the mixture, then rummaged for bread. When he found it, he dipped two slices into the egg mixture and put them on the small griddle. They sizzled.

She sniffed the vanilla. "Yum."

"You really must be hungry."

"I am."

He turned to flip the two pieces of French toast. She tilted her head, taking in the details that made him who he was. Sexy dark hair. Wide shoulders. Trim hips. But his face was the showstopper. Dark, dark eyes in olive skin. A square jaw. High cheekbones.

Something soft and warm floated through her. She was just about to curse herself for looking at him again when she realized she'd never felt like this with Bruce. She'd liked Bruce—actually, she'd believed she'd loved him. But she'd never felt this odd combination of attraction and curiosity that mixed and mingled with the warmth of their friendship and turned her feelings into something more…something special.

She cleared her throat. What was she doing? Fantasizing again? This guy was her boss! Not only that, but he was a widower. Someone who'd lost his wife and still grieved her so much he no longer painted. What would he want with her? Plain, simple Laura Beth Matthews, who—oh, by the way—was also pregnant with another man's child. Her job was to organize him back to the land of the living, not drool over him.

He made eight pieces of French toast, divided them onto two plates and handed one to her.

Her stomach rumbled again. "Thanks."

He passed the syrup across the bar. She slathered it on her French toast, but waited for him to pick up his fork before she picked up hers. If there was one thing she'd learned from her years of attending Olivia and Tucker's baby events and Ricky and Eloise's elaborate parties, it was to follow the lead of the host and hostess.

He took a bite of his French toast, then smiled at her. "So getting a job where you get to live in was a pretty nifty way to handle the apartment problem."

She reddened to the roots of her hair. "Does it seem sleazy?"

"No. It's smart. After I rotated out of the foster-care system, I'd have killed for a job that got me off the streets."

"Yeah, but then you wouldn't have scrounged your way to Italy, where your dad found you."

"Scrounged." He grinned. "I love American words."

"Hey, you're half-American!"

"Yes, I am. And proud of it. I use both worlds." He frowned. "Or did." Then he brightened. "Never mind. How's the toast?"

"I love it." She pushed her plate away having eaten only two slices. "But I'm full."

Antonio took her plate and his and set them in a metal drawer, which he closed. "Staff will get this when we land."

She laughed. "Wow."

"Hey, you better get used to living like this."

Though she didn't think Antonio was as persnickety or as pampered as his dad, she decided not to argue the point. Especially since she'd had a sleepless night, agonizing over her problems. With her tummy full and the lull of the plane, she just wanted to curl up on one of the sofas.

She wandered back to her seat, buckled herself in—in case they hit turbulence—and almost immediately fell asleep.

She awoke to the feeling of someone shaking her. "Laura Beth…we're here."

She snuggled into the blanket someone had thrown over her. "We're where?"

"In Italy."

Her eyes popped open. When she found herself staring into the gorgeous face of Antonio Bartulocci, it all tumbled back. They were on a plane to Italy. His dad had hired her. She didn't have an apartment. She was pregnant.

Her stomach dropped.

She was pregnant. In a foreign country. Starting a new job. Working for Antonio, who needed her. But she was attracted to him. She thought he was the sexiest, most gorgeous man alive and she would be living with him. But he didn't feel the same way about her.

That relaxed her. It could be a good thing if he only saw her as a friend. As long as she hid her crush, there'd be no problem. Plus, being on call twenty-four-seven to help him get his life back would keep her from dwelling on her problems.

That was the real silver lining. Not just the money. Not just a place to live. But someone to take care of, so she could forget about herself.

She pushed aside the soft cover. Her days of daydreaming she belonged in this world as anything other than an employee were over. She could take this job and run with it, create a halfway decent life for herself and her baby. Everything would be fine.

"Thanks for the blanket."

Antonio smiled. "My pleasure."

She found her purse and tucked her science fiction novel inside. Two gentlemen, Antonio and Constanzo waited for her to exit first.

Constanzo paused to say something to the pilots, but quickly joined them on the tarmac below the steps.

She glanced around. The sky was blue, as perfect as any she'd seen in Kentucky. Tall green grass in the fields surrounding the airstrip swayed in a subtle breeze that cut through the heat. "Another private airstrip?"

"You don't think my dad's going to have a plane and suffer the torment of going to a real airport and waiting to take off and land, do you?"

Pushing a strand of her hair off her face, she laughed. "Right. Spoiled."

"Incredibly spoiled. You're going to need to remember that."

She frowned. It was the second time he'd said something odd about her getting accustomed to his dad. Still, he was her boss now. They might have been able to relate like friends on the plane, but here on Italian soil, his home turf, her role kicked in. She was his assistant. Basically, a secretary. But this was better than anything she'd even come close to finding in New York.

This was her life now.

Constanzo walked over. "Bags are on their way to the limo."

Laura Beth said, "Wow. Fast."

Antonio laughed. "So much for you to get used to

about my dad." He nudged his father's shoulder. "Exactly how do you intend to explain to Bernice that you hired someone to help her?"

Laura Beth's brow wrinkled.

Constanzo's face reddened.

Laura Beth gasped as she faced Antonio. "You think Constanzo hired me to work for *him*?"

This time Antonio's brow wrinkled. "You're not working for my dad?"

Constanzo's face reddened even more as both Laura Beth and Antonio turned to him.

"I did not hire her to help my PA. I hired her to be yours."

Antonio's mouth fell open at his father's audacity. Anger whispered across his skin, causing his temper to bubble. He took a minute to pull in a breath and remind himself that his father hiring a PA was nothing compared to his deceased wife's handiwork.

Still, when he spoke, his voice was harsh, angry. "Why are you meddling in my life?"

Constanzo headed for the limo again. "I'm not meddling." He strolled across the quiet tarmac. "You said last night that you were thinking about this. When Laura Beth and I struck up a conversation and I realized she'd be perfect for the job, I did what I do best… I anticipated."

He almost cursed. "You meddled!"

Laura Beth touched his arm to get his attention. Her fingertips warmed his skin, caused his breathing to stutter.

"I didn't realize he didn't have your permission."

Constanzo bristled. "I did not need my son's permission. He said last night he was agreeable. I *anticipated*."

Antonio stayed outside the limo, unable to get himself to move into the car with his dad and Laura Beth, who had hesitantly climbed inside. Confusion and resentment clamored inside him. He wasn't just angry about his dad hiring someone for him; his reactions to Laura Beth were wrong.

He'd always liked her. And, yes, he supposed there was a bit of an attraction there. But suddenly, today, maybe because they'd had such an intimate chat on the plane, he was feeling things he shouldn't feel. Good God, she was a sweet girl trying to find her way in life. And he was an angry widower. He did not want to be attracted to her, and if she were smart she wouldn't want to be attracted to him. Worse, they should not be living together.

He had to fire her.

No...*Constanzo* had to fire her.

Behind him, the chauffeur wheeled their luggage to the rear of the limo. One scruffy brown bag stood out.

It had to be Laura Beth's.

Just one bag. And it was worn. So worn he would consider it unusable. But that was her best.

He scrubbed his hand across his mouth as a picture formed in his brain. Her two roommates hadn't just found the loves of their lives, they'd made careers for themselves and she was still working temp jobs.

Damn it.

He couldn't embarrass her by refusing to let her work for him. But he didn't want to be living with an attractive woman—the first woman to stir something inside him since Gisella. Worse, he didn't want someone rifling through his things.

He'd give Laura Beth a few days to rest in his country house, then gently explain that he didn't want a PA.

Since he was essentially firing her, he'd send her back to the US with a good-sized severance check and the codes for his dad's penthouse so she'd be okay until she found a new job.

But today, once he had her settled, he intended to have this out with his dad.

CHAPTER THREE

LAURA BETH WATCHED Antonio climb into the limo. He didn't say a word the entire drive to his father's house.

Nerves skittered along her skin. He didn't want her. It seemed he didn't want a PA at all…*Constanzo* did. And the second he got out of the car, Antonio would fire her.

They reached Constanzo's beautiful country home and he unceremoniously got out. Angry, too, he didn't say a word to his son. When the limo began moving again, she couldn't take the quiet.

"I'm so sorry."

Antonio stared out the window. "Not your fault. As I told you on the plane, my dad has the mistaken belief that everything he wants should be there when he wants it. Sometimes that translates into a belief that everyone in his life should do what he wants when he wants it done."

With that the car got quiet again. Any second now she expected him to apologize and fire her. But he didn't. The twenty-minute drive was extremely quiet, but with every mile that passed without him saying, "You're fired," her spirits lifted a bit. They drove up to his gorgeous country home and he got out as if nothing were amiss.

Exiting the limo, she glanced around. Antonio's

home was nestled in a silent stretch of Italian country-side. Hills and valleys layered in rich green grass with a spattering of wildflowers surrounded the new house. A smaller, much older house sat at the end of a stone path.

As if seeing the direction of her gaze, Antonio said, "That's my studio."

She tilted her head as she studied it. In some ways the old stone house was more beautiful than the big elaborate home that had obviously been built within the past few years—probably for his wife.

Her face heated as envy tightened her chest, so she quickly reprimanded herself. This man she thought so handsome had had a wife, someone he'd adored. She'd been hired to be a glorified secretary. She was pregnant with another man's child. *And* she'd also decided the night before that she was no longer going to try to fit herself into a world too grand for her. Being jealous of Antonio's dead wife, being attracted to a famous artist slated to inherit the estate of one of the world's wealthiest men…that was foolishness that she'd nip in the bud every time it popped into her head, until it left for good.

Antonio motioned to the door and she walked before him into the grand foyer of his home. A wide circular stairway and marble floors welcomed her. To the right, a painting of what looked to be the field outside his house brightened the huge foyer with its rich greens and striking blues of both the flowers and sky.

"I've seen this before."

He laughed. "In Tucker and Olivia's Montauk mansion."

She faced him. "That's right!"

"I bought it back from them."

"I can see why. It's beautiful."

"It was the first thing I painted when I rented the run-down shack I now use as a studio."

He walked up behind her. Little pinpricks of awareness danced up her spine. "The second I set foot on Italian soil, I knew this was my home, that the time I'd spent in foster care in America was an aberration. An accident." He pointed at the painting. "This picture captures all the happiness of that discovery."

"I see it."

He sniffed a laugh. "Tucker did too. Made me pay him a pretty penny to get it back." He motioned to the stairs. "Let me show you to your room."

Taken aback by the abrupt change of mood, she almost didn't follow him. Her skin was prickly and hot from his nearness, her breathing shallow. Still, she smiled and started up the steps, reminding herself that he was off-limits and she should be paying attention to the layout of the house rather than the nearness of her boss.

At the top of the staircase, Antonio directed her down a short hall. A glance to the left and right showed her the upstairs had been designed in such a way that private hallways led to individual rooms. And each wall had a painting. Some stark and stunning. Some warm and rich with color.

They finally stopped at a closed door. Antonio opened it and directed her inside. She gasped as she entered. Thick white carpets protected golden hardwood floors. A white headboard matched the white furniture, which was all brightened by an aqua comforter and bed skirt and sheer aqua curtains that billowed in the breeze of the open window.

"It's beautiful." She'd tried not to sound so pedestrian

and poor, but the simple color scheme in the huge room with such beautiful furniture took her breath away.

"Thank you. I did this room myself."

"You did?" She turned with a happy smile on her face, but her smile died when she saw him looking around oddly. "What?"

He shook his head. "It's nothing. Foolish."

"Come on." She used the cajoling voice she'd use with her older brother when he had a secret. If they were going to be working together—and she hoped his recent change in mood was an indicator that they were— she needed to get him to trust her. "We're friends. You can tell me."

He sucked in a breath, walked a bit farther into the room. "Most men let their wives decorate, but mine was away—" He caught her gaze. "Traveling. She also showed no interest in the samples the designer sent to her, and one day I just decided to look at the whole house as a canvas and—" he shrugged "—here we are."

"Well, if the rest of the rooms are as beautiful as this one, I can't wait to see everything."

He smiled slightly. "I'll give you a tour tonight."

She said, "Great," but her heart sank. Talking about his wife had made him sad. He might give her the tour, but it would be grudgingly. The disparity of their stations in life and the reality of her situation poured through her. She might be trying to get him to trust her, but if she were simply a new assistant not a friend of friends, he wouldn't give her the tour of his house. She might not even get such a grand bedroom. He probably wouldn't have told her the tidbit about decorating it himself. And he wouldn't be sad.

Maybe it was time to put herself in her place with him—*for* him.

"You don't have to." She laughed lightly, trying to sound like an employee, not a friend. "This is your home. There might be areas you wish to keep private."

He faced her, his expression filled with sadness. "People in the public eye quickly realize there is no such thing as privacy. If you sense hesitancy about my showing you the house, it's because the house reminds me of better times."

She struggled to hold back a wince at her stupidity. Of course, memories of his dead wife affected him more than the oddness of having a friend working for him. "I'm sorry."

"I'm sorry too." He glanced around at her room again. "I'd love to have my inspiration back. I'd love to paint again." He drew in a breath, as if erasing whatever memories had come to mind and faced her. "I need to go to my father's for an hour or so. But it's already late. Especially considering we're five hours ahead of New York here. You may just want to turn in for the night."

"Are you kidding? I had a seven-hour nap! Plus, I'm still on New York time."

"Maybe you'd like to read by the pool? Or make yourself something to eat. The staff doesn't return until tomorrow, but the kitchen is all yours."

He left her then and she fell to the bed, trepidation filling her. So much for thinking he'd changed his mind about keeping her. He was going to Constanzo's to confront him about hiring her. When he came back, he'd probably tell her that her services were no longer needed.

She wanted to stay. Not just because she needed a job, loved getting room and board and wanted some time away from everyone to figure out her life, but also because Antonio was so sad. Somebody needed to help him.

Empathy for Constanzo rippled through her, total understanding of why he desperately wanted to do something to lift his son out of his sadness. Antonio was a good man. Life had treated him abysmally by taking away his beloved wife. He deserved to have someone nudge him back into the real world. And having someone to help actually gave her a way to forget about her own troubles. It could be the perfect situation for both of them.

Except Antonio didn't want her.

Her stomach rumbled and she rose. Might as well find the kitchen and make herself something to eat. Because this time tomorrow she'd probably be on a plane back to New York.

A failure again.

But on her way to the kitchen, the beauty of the house superseded her need for food as it lured her from one room to the next. She hadn't expected a stuffy, formal house. Antonio was too creative for that. But she also hadn't expected to be so charmed by paintings and sculptures that added life and energy to brightly colored sofas, or the eclectic dining room that had a long wood table and sixteen different-styled chairs around it.

Eventually she found herself at the door of a room with a desk and a tall-backed chair, which fronted a huge office with an enormous window through which she could see the pool and the field of flowers behind it.

His office?

With an office in front? For an assistant?

Had he had an assistant before? Could Constanzo be right? Was he ready for someone again?

She entered hesitantly. Stacks of papers littered the first desk, the desk she believed would belong to an assistant. But his room was empty, his desk dusty though free of clutter.

She walked in slowly, ran her fingers through the dust on his desk, curious again. From the coating of dust alone, she'd swear he hadn't been in this room since his wife died.

At the wall of glass, she stopped. The window was actually a series of doors, which she slid aside. A warm breeze fluttered in, bringing the scent of the pool not more than twenty feet away. When forced to do paperwork, Antonio could be poolside.

Sheesh. The rich really knew how to live.

With a sigh, she closed the doors. But as she walked into the outer office, she saw all those papers piled high on the assistant's desk. A film of dust dulled the white of envelopes. Dust covered the arms of the desk chair. But that was nothing compared to the sheer volume of untouched paperwork, unopened mail.

Glancing around, she combed her fingers through her hair. It was no wonder Constanzo wanted his son to hire a PA. He clearly needed some assistance.

And, technically, helping him straighten this mess was her job—

If she kept it.

She walked to the desk, lifted a piece of paper and realized it was a thank-you from a fan. Reading it, she lowered herself to the chair. Obviously, Antonio didn't know the letter's author. So a simple note to express appreciation for his kindness in writing would suffice as a reply.

She leaned back. A box of fancy letterhead caught her eye. A beautiful script *A* on Antonio linked with the

B in Bartulocci. What fan wouldn't want to get a thank-you on the actual letterhead of the artist he admired?

The desire to turn on the computer and write a quick thank-you tempted her. She faced the monitor that sat on the side arm of the desk. She could press the button that would turn it on...

No. She couldn't. It wasn't right.

Still, somebody had to help him, and she needed a way to prove herself.

She lifted her hand to the start button again, but paused halfway and bit her lip. The computer software would probably be in Italian—

Though Antonio had been raised in the US—

She shook her head. It was one thing to look at a few pieces of mail, quite another to actually write letters for him without his permission.

But how else would she prove herself?

Antonio stopped his motorcycle at the front door of his father's country house. He didn't knock. He just entered the foyer and walked back to his father's game room. Sure enough, there he was, playing pool.

"I see the nap you had on the plane gave you energy too."

He set down his cue stick. "Antonio! Why aren't you home?"

"With the PA you hired for me?" He shook his head. "Because I don't want a PA and because your meddling in my life has to stop."

"I don't meddle. I anticipate."

Antonio groaned. "You meddle, Dad. And I can't have it anymore. Not just because it infuriates me, but because this time you're hurting an innocent woman. She's going to be devastated when I send her home."

"So if you're the one sending her home, how can you say that I'm the one hurting her?"

"Because you're the one who brought her here under false pretenses!"

"I did no such thing. You need her."

Antonio groaned again. "There's no reasoning with you. You always see what you want to see."

"True. But that's also why I win so much." He walked to the wall of pool sticks, chose one and offered it to Antonio. "Here is a place you sometimes beat me."

Antonio snatched the stick away from his dad. "If you win, I keep her. If I win, she goes home after a few weeks of rest. But you pay her severance and you let her stay in your penthouse in New York."

Constanzo grinned. "You're on."

They decided on best out of three. Constanzo played pool constantly in his spare time, and was very, very good. But Antonio needed to prove a point, to get it across to his dad that he couldn't take every matter into his own hands. He didn't just want to win. He had to win. In the end, he beat his dad by one shot.

Constanzo sighed. "This is a big mistake. You need her. And she needs a break."

Antonio headed for the door. "That's why I'm going to let her stay a few weeks. It'll give her time to relax enough that she can think through her problems." He turned and faced his dad. "And *you* pay her a big enough severance that she can get a decent apartment."

Constanzo sighed. "It is wrong to send her home. But I lost the bet and I agree. If she must go, I'm the one who owes her severance."

Antonio got back on his bike feeling only slightly better. He didn't want to hurt Laura Beth, and he didn't like the fact that he'd had to gamble to get his way in a situation that his father shouldn't have interfered with. But he'd won.

Revving the bike's engine, he shot along the hills, past the green fields to his house, the wind blowing his hair and teasing his face. By the time he got home, darkness had fully descended and he noticed a light coming from his office. Confused, he parked in the garage and entered through the series of doors that took him from the garage, through the butler's pantry and kitchen to the main living area.

Because there were no lights in the pool area, he thought Laura Beth must have been more tired than she'd thought and retired to her room. Glad he didn't have to face her until the next day, he headed back to the office to turn off the light.

But when he stepped inside, he stopped dead in his tracks. There, behind the stacks of unopened mail and the wide computer monitor, was Laura Beth.

He raced to the desk. "What are you doing?"

She looked up at him. "I've been sitting here fighting the temptation to read your mail." She pointed at one open fan letter. "I know you well enough that I could answer that for you. And any letter like it."

Fear collided with anger. But the stacks appeared to be untouched. The computer hadn't been turned on. She couldn't have seen anything.

His head began to pound anyway. Still, he calmed his voice before he said, "You went into my office without permission."

"I didn't touch anything but this one letter that was already open." She met his gaze. "Plus, it's my job to get you organized."

He sucked in a breath. Memories of finding his wife's itineraries and the matching itineraries of her lovers swam through him, making him shake with anger. Not at Laura Beth, but at his wife. At her shameless audacity. And his just plain stupidity. Add to that the abortion information. The appointment on the calendar. The payment in her check registry. The way she hadn't even tried to hide the fact that she'd taken his child from him.

How the hell could he face that? How could he face another person knowing that his wife hadn't even told him of the pregnancy?

It took great effort for him to soften his voice, but he did it. "I'm not ready for this."

She pointed at the stacks of papers again. "You don't have to be ready. If most of this is fan mail, I can answer it. I can create lists of requests for charitable events. I can coordinate your schedule with Olivia," she said, referring to her friend, who was also his manager. "And I think that's Constanzo's point. A smart PA could do a lot of this work for you."

"I don't want you in here! I don't want anybody in here!"

His shout echoed off the walls of the quiet office. Laura Beth shrank back, her big green eyes round and frightened.

He ran his hand along his nape. "I'm sorry. But this will not work for me." He motioned for her to rise. "Please come out from behind the desk."

She rose and stepped away from his desk.

"You are welcome to stay for the next two weeks. Rest in the sun. Be a tourist. Hell, I can take you around to see the sights. But I do not want a PA."

To his great dismay, her lower lip trembled.

"Seriously. When you return to New York, you can stay in Constanzo's penthouse. And Constanzo is writing a check for a huge severance."

The lower lip stopped trembling as fire came into her green eyes. "What?"

"This is Constanzo's mistake. He will pay for it."

"I don't want your severance! I want a job. I'm insulted by your charity when it's pretty clear I could earn my keep, and even more clear that you need me."

To his surprise, she propelled herself toward him and stood directly in front of him. The tinge of flush in her cheeks matched the glitter of anger in her green eyes. Heat poured from her, triggering his attraction. He'd always loved the way she could stand up for herself.

"I don't want to go home! I want this job. I need this job!"

She stepped closer. The raw power in her glittering eyes hit him like a punch in the gut. He hadn't seen this kind of passion in years. Hadn't felt it himself in forever. It was everything he could do not to pull her to him and kiss her senseless to capture it.

He stepped back. "You think you want this job. You think living in Italy will be a grand adventure. But trust me. You will miss your city and your family."

She eliminated the distance between them again. The fire in his belly spiked. He caught her gaze. Was she daring him to kiss her?

She didn't back down. She stood toe to toe with him. Fire matching fire. "And you can trust me when I tell you that I will not regret being thousands of miles away from my family. I need to be here. I want this job!"

He snorted in derision. He was feeling passion. She was talking about a job. He must really be tired to be so far off base, thinking a woman was daring him to kiss her when she was simply fighting to keep her job.

He turned away, started walking to the door.

Quiet, but close, as if she'd followed him, her voice

drifted to him. "Antonio, I need to be away from my family and friends. For a while. I have more than job troubles to figure out." She said nothing until he faced her again, then she caught his gaze. "I'm pregnant."

CHAPTER FOUR

"PREGNANT?"

Laura Beth watched Antonio, her heart chugging, her nerve endings glittering. Her announcement might have settled him down, but while they'd argued, she'd seen something in his eyes. She'd expected anger and had been prepared to deal with it, but the smoldering gazes? Sweet, considerate Antonio had been replaced by sexy Antonio, a man who looked as though he wanted to kiss her.

The only way she could think to deal with it was to tell him the truth, and now here they were, talking about something she wasn't even ready to announce.

She stepped back. "I'm only two months along, but pregnant all the same."

He rubbed his hands across his eyes, as if confused. Whatever had been happening with him in that argument had disappeared, and he was back to being sweet Antonio, her friend.

"I'm a man. Right now I have no idea if it's appropriate to say congratulations or offer sympathy. I mean, I know this is trouble for you, but babies are wonderful." He shook his head. "And my dad? He goes bananas over babies. Boy or girl. It doesn't matter. He's a cuddler."

A laugh bubbled up. Not just from relief. He'd made

her think about the baby as a baby. A little girl. Or a little boy. She wasn't just going to be a mother; she was getting a baby.

"Congratulations are what I want."

"So the father's on board?"

She swallowed hard, not sure what to say. But she'd be answering this question for the remaining seven months of her pregnancy, so she might as well get used to it.

"No." She cleared her throat. "Let's just say his response was less than enthusiastic."

"And there's no wedding in your future?"

"He doesn't want to see me again or see the baby at all."

Antonio pointed a finger at her. "With my dad's lawyers, we can force him to be part of the baby's life."

She shook her head. "I don't want him to. He said he would send child support, but only if no one knows it's coming from him."

"I think you just blew that by telling me."

She paced away. "If he doesn't want to be part of our baby's life, then I don't want him to be. I think an angry dad would do more harm than good. And I don't want his money."

Thankfully, Antonio refrained from pointing out the obvious: that she needed money too much to turn any down. Instead, he asked, "What do you want?"

She shrugged and spread her hands. "Time. I have to tell my conservative parents that their little girl is about to become a mom with no father for her child. Ultimately, I'll need a job that supports not just me, but me and a baby. So working for you kind of solved all my problems."

He winced. "You can stay."

Hope blossomed in her chest. Being here was the perfect opportunity for her. But she couldn't take charity. "And be your assistant?"

"You're my friend. You don't have to work for your keep."

She stormed over to him. "Yes! I do! I can't be a charity case. Don't you see?"

He sighed and shook his head. "All I see is a woman with a lot of pride."

"Oh, yeah?" She crossed her arms on her chest. "What I see is a man with a lot of pride. You're fighting with your dad about hiring one measly assistant—whom you need—and you won't budge an inch! Why won't you let me work for you?"

"We're friends. I should be able to let you stay in my home as a guest, not an employee."

"That's not why you're fighting Constanzo."

He gaped at her. "Now you're telling me how I feel?"

"Before you knew I was pregnant, you didn't want me working for you. You said you don't want a PA. But it's clear you need one. So obviously there's a reason you're fighting having someone work for you."

He sighed.

"Fine. Don't tell me. Because I don't care. What I do care about is earning my keep. And just from the glance I got at your mail, it was clear that I could at least answer your fan letters. I minored in accounting, so I could also keep track of your money. Anything else in your office, in your life, in your world, I wouldn't care about."

He sighed again. "You are a pregnant woman who needs a rest. Just take the time here with me to have some fun."

She raised her chin. "No. If you won't let me work,

I won't take your charity. Not even your offer of Constanzo's penthouse. I'm going home."

"You don't have a home to go back to."

"I'll think of something."

"If I tell Constanzo you're pregnant and refusing a few weeks of rest, he won't let you use his plane."

"Then I'll fly commercial."

He raised his hands in defeat and slapped them down again. "You can't afford that."

"I know. But I'll be fine."

"No. You won't!"

"Then let me stay here for two weeks as your assistant. If you don't like what I do or still feel you don't need someone at the end of two weeks, I'll take another two weeks to rest and then go home."

He stalled, as if unaccustomed to someone compromising. His brow furrowed. His expression and demeanor were so different than five minutes ago that confusion billowed through her. When they'd first begun arguing, before he'd known she was pregnant, his eyes had been sharp. Glowing. She could have sworn he wanted to kiss her.

Her eyes narrowed again. He might have been seductive Antonio, but he hadn't made a move to kiss her. It was as if he had been daring *her* to step closer—

Had he been daring her to step closer?

He might have been. But to what end? She'd been close enough to kiss, yet he hadn't kissed her.

She swallowed just as he said, "Really? If I let you work for me for two weeks then you'll spend another two weeks resting and not arguing about going home?"

"Yes, I'll get out of your hair if you let me work for two weeks and rest for two more. But that's if you still want me to go home." Her voice shook a bit as she considered that he might have actually been attracted to her. If she hadn't told him about being pregnant…he might have kissed her. Just the thought almost made her swoon.

Telling herself it was foolishness to deal in *what if*s, she said, "But who knows? You might—" she swallowed again "—like me."

Her heart thrummed as their gazes met. He didn't seem to get the double meaning.

He broke their connection and stepped back. "Constanzo can help you find a job in New York."

She smiled sadly. Before he'd discovered she was pregnant he might have found her attractive, but he didn't now. Though something in her heart pinched, it was okay. It had to be okay. She had bigger worries than disappointment over being wanted one minute and discarded the next. After all, why would a man who'd been married to a supermodel want a pregnant commoner?

She took a step back too. "I'd have to make a ton of money to be able to live in New York on my own, especially with the added expense of a baby. If I couldn't make it as a single woman, it's pretty far-fetched to think I could make it as a single mom. At the wedding, I thought about finding new roommates, but I now realize it might be impossible to find two women who want to share the small amount of space we could afford with an infant. I think, in the end, I'm going to have to go back to Kentucky. Live with my parents until the baby is born and then hope I can find a job."

The sadness in her voice sat on Antonio's shoulders like a cold, wet coat. Two minutes ago, she'd been so fiery he'd wanted to kiss her. But suddenly she'd become meek, docile.

Not that he wasn't glad. Now that he knew she was pregnant, everything inside him had frozen with a new kind of fear. The last thing he needed in his life was someone who would remind him of the child he had lost. He might be able to keep her in his home for the four weeks of rest she needed, four weeks before her pregnancy showed…but he couldn't handle watching another man's baby grow when he knew his own child had been cast aside.

She pointed behind her to the door. "If you don't mind, I'd like to go to the kitchen to make a sandwich."

"I'll show you—"

She waved a hand to stop him. "I'm fine. I really do need some time by myself."

She turned and walked out of the room, and he fell to the tall-backed chair behind the desk and rubbed his hands down his face. The man who loved peace and quiet now had a constantly hungry pregnant woman in his home. Pregnant. As in with child. Here was a single woman with no money who was willing to beg and sacrifice to figure out what to do with her life so she could keep her child—and his wealthy wife, who could have hired all the help in the world, had aborted his baby.

He squeezed his eyes shut. He had to get her out of his house before her pregnancy showed, before the constant reminder drove him insane with sadness and anger.

But he wouldn't do it at the expense of her feelings. She'd left his office believing she'd done something wrong, when she had done nothing wrong. His jumbled emotions had caused him to react poorly.

He should apologize tonight, before she went to bed,

so she didn't take the weight of this job loss on her shoulders like one more mistake.

He bounced out of his chair and headed for the kitchen, but when he got there it was empty. And clean. Not even a bread crumb on a countertop.

Regret tightened his stomach. He hoped to God he hadn't upset her so much she'd decided not to eat. Thinking that she might have gone outside for some fresh air before making her snack, he waited in the kitchen for twenty minutes. But she never came in.

Irritation with himself poured through him. Of course he'd upset her by telling her she couldn't stay. She was pregnant and sensitive. Right now she was probably taking responsibility for everything that happened to her.

Knowing he had to apologize and make her see it wasn't her fault that he couldn't keep her, he headed upstairs to her room. The strip of light below the white door to her bedroom indicated she was inside, and he knocked once.

"Laura Beth?"

There was no answer, but the light told him she was still awake, probably reading the science fiction novel she'd had on the plane.

He knocked again. "Laura Beth?"

This time when she didn't answer, he sighed heavily. She might want her privacy, but he didn't want a sleepless night, angry with himself for being the cause of her anxiety and going to bed hungry. And he didn't want her upset with herself.

He twisted the knob. "I'm coming in."

As soon as the door opened, he knew why she hadn't answered. Sprawled across the bed, wrapped in the bath towel she'd used after showering, lay his houseguest.

Her toes hung off the side. Her hair fell down her long, sleek back. The towel cruised across her round buttocks.

The fact that she was angry with him disappeared from his brain like a puff of smoke as interest and curiosity fluttered inside him. He told himself to get out of her room. She was sleeping. Obviously exhausted. And tiptoeing closer was not a very gentlemanly thing to do.

But right at that moment, he didn't feel like a gentleman. The artist in him awoke and cautiously eyed the smooth lines of her back, the long sweep that spoke of classic femininity, the perfect milk-white skin interrupted by dark locks of hair that shimmered when she sniffed and shifted in her sleep.

Longing to paint coiled through him. Swift and sharp, it stole his breath. His fingers twitched, yearning for the slim wooden handle of a paintbrush, and also pulling him out of his trance.

Oh, dear God.

He squeezed his eyes shut. *He'd wanted to paint her.* For real. At the wedding he'd wanted to capture the expression in her eyes, but that had been more like a wish.

What he'd just felt was a genuine yearning to see her form on a canvas, to bring her essence to life.

Excitement raced through him and he studied her back, her hair, her peaceful face against the soft white pillow. His unwanted attraction to her blossomed, but the desire to paint didn't return.

Anguish filled him, but he brushed it off. He couldn't explain the fleeting moment of wanting to paint her, but it was gone and that might be for the best. His decision to let her go was a good one. Even if his ability to paint returned, he could not paint her. It could take weeks to get the image of her he wanted and by that time she'd be showing and he'd experience all the sadness of the loss of his child a hundred times over.

He quietly tiptoed backward toward the door and left her as she lay.

The next morning, Laura Beth awakened to the bright Italian sun peeking in through the blinds behind the sheer aqua curtains. She stretched luxuriously on the smooth, cool sheets that felt like—terry cloth?

Her brow furrowed and she looked down with a gasp as the events of the night before tumbled back. She'd been too tired to make herself something to eat but had forced herself to shower, then she'd fallen asleep before she could even get into pajamas. Pregnancy was full of surprises.

But that was fine. Today was the second day of her life as a realist. No more dreaming or rhapsodizing for her. She had a child to consider. She might have told Antonio the night before that she envisioned herself going back to Kentucky, but that wasn't the optimal plan. Her parents would eventually come around and love the baby, no matter that it didn't have a participating father and that their daughter wasn't married. But there weren't a lot of jobs for IT—information technology—people in Starlight, Kentucky, the small town in which she'd grown up. If she was going to earn a decent living, it would be by getting a job where she could use her degree. And that was what she needed to consider while she had this one-month reprieve. She had to think about exactly what kind of job she could do and in what city she would find it.

She dressed in her best jeans—which were nonetheless worn—and a pink tank top, then ambled downstairs feeling a little better. Because she'd slept later than she

normally did, her morning sickness was barely notice-
able. Antonio might not be giving her a shot to prove
that she could be a good assistant, but she needed time
to really think through her options. And he was giving
it to her. In beautiful Italy.

Technically, she was lucky.

Very lucky.

When she opened the door to the huge stainless-steel
kitchen, the noise of shuffling pots and chatting servants greeted her. Antonio's staff hadn't been around
the day before. He'd mentioned giving them time off
while he was in New York for the two weeks for Eloise and Ricky's wedding. But today they were in the
kitchen, going about what looked to be typical duties.

"Good morning!"

The three women froze. Dressed in yellow uniforms,
with their hair tucked into neat buns at the backs of
their heads, they could have been triplets, except the
woman at the stove appeared to be in her seventies.
The woman at the table was probably in her thirties.
And the woman with the dust cloth looked to be in her
early twenties.

The oldest woman said, "Good morning," but it
sounded more like *"Goot* morning."

Laura Beth eased a little farther into the room. "I'm
a friend of Antonio's. I'm staying here for a few weeks.
Hopefully, I'm going to be helping him clean his outer
office."

The youngest woman smiled. Her big brown eyes
brightened. *"Sì."*

The oldest woman batted a hand. "Her English isn't
good. God only knows what she thought you said." She
walked from behind the huge center island that housed

the six-burner chef's stove. "Would you like some coffee?"

"She can't drink coffee." Antonio's words were followed by the sound of the swinging door behind Laura Beth closing. "She's pregnant."

The eyes of all three women grew round, then bright with happiness.

Caught like a child with her hand in the cookie jar, Laura Beth spun around. Antonio's usually wild hair had been tied back, and the curve of a tattoo rose above the crew neck of his T-shirt, teasing her, tempting her to wonder what an artist would have chosen to have drawn on his shoulder. Rumor had it that he had a huge dragon tattooed from his neck to his lower back and that it was magnificent.

Interest turned to real curiosity, the kind that sent a tingle through her and made her long to ask him to take off his shirt.

Their gazes caught and her stomach cartwheeled. The attraction she felt for him rippled through her, reminding her of the look he'd given her the night before. She told herself she wasn't allowed to be attracted to her boss—even if he was gorgeous and sexy with his dark eyes that seemed to hold secrets, and the unruly hair that framed the strong face of an aristocrat. But after their encounter in the office the night before, everything about him seemed amplified.

He'd wanted to kiss her. She was just about positive of it. So why hadn't he?

Her curiosity spiked. Something soft and warm shivered in the pit of her stomach.

Oh…that had been a bad question to ask.

The oldest housekeeper's excited voice broke the trance. "We will have a baby here!"

"No." Antonio faced his staff and said, "We will have a pregnant woman here for about four weeks."

"Ah. *Sì*."

Antonio pointed at her. "This is Rosina. She supervises Carmella and Francesca."

Laura Beth stepped forward to shake their hands. "It's nice to meet you."

They giggled.

"They aren't accustomed to guests shaking their hands."

"But I'm an employee, just as they are." She turned to Antonio. Her gaze met his simmering brown eyes and her stomach fell. Good grief, he was hot.

She took a step back, but swayed. She hoped her morning sickness was back because she'd hate to think she'd actually faint over a good-looking guy.

He caught her elbows and kept her upright. "Let's get you to the dining room and get some food in that stomach."

As he led her into the ultramodern dining room, dominated by the large rectangular table with mismatched chairs, her skin prickled from the touch of his fingers on her arm.

She reminded herself that he was only a friend helping her because she'd swayed. And she was pregnant—with another man's child. She didn't know how Italian men were about these things, but lots of American men would think long and hard before they took on the responsibility for another man's child. And Antonio was half-American.

Damn it! Why was she even thinking about this?

He pulled out her chair and helped her sit, but immediately excused himself. "I'll need five minutes. By the time I get back, the staff will have breakfast ready."

She nodded and he left. Nervous, she shifted on her chair, until the pool beyond the wall of glass caught her eye. Past the shimmering water were lush gardens, and beyond that, the blue sky. She'd been to Italy before, but this place, the place Antonio had chosen, was so perfect it seemed to have been carved out of heaven. The peace and quiet of it settled over her.

The door swung open and Antonio returned to the table. "I'm sorry about that."

As he spoke, Rosina entered behind him, carrying two plates of eggs, bacon and toast. She served their breakfasts and exited. Antonio opened his napkin and picked up his fork.

"I trust eggs and bacon are good for you this morning."

She nodded eagerly, her stomach rumbling from the scent of warm bacon. "It's great. I'm starving."

His fork halfway to his plate, he paused. "You should be. You didn't eat last night. I went into the kitchen ten minutes after you said you'd be getting a snack, but you weren't there."

"Too tired. Honestly, Antonio, everybody talks about things like morning sickness, but nobody ever mentions the exhaustion."

He fussed with the silverware beside his plate. "When I told Rosina you had fallen asleep last night without even changing into pajamas, she said women are very tired for the first three months and fall asleep often."

She heard everything he said as a jumble of words. Her brain stalled then exploded after he said he knew she'd fallen asleep without changing. For him to know that, he had to have checked up on her. Which meant he'd seen her lying naked across her bed. Her face blossomed with heat.

"What?"

She sucked in a breath. "You came looking for me last night?"

"Yes."

She groaned.

He frowned. "What?"

"You saw me naked."

He busied himself with his silverware again. "No. I saw you lying on the bed with a towel wrapped around you. You weren't naked."

"Oh, way to split hairs."

"Americans are prudish."

She squeezed her eyes shut. Was she making too much of this? "You're half-American!"

He laughed. "What are you worried about? You have a beautiful, long, sleek back. I'd love to paint you, but I'd replace the towel with a swatch of silk—" He stopped. His brow furrowed.

This time she frowned. "What?"

He picked up his napkin. "It's my turn to say nothing."

"Really? Because I wouldn't mind sitting for a portrait."

He sniffed a laugh. "Then you'd be sitting for a long time. I haven't painted for two years."

Since his wife died. She knew that. And knowing he'd grieved for two long years, a smart person wouldn't push, wouldn't question any further. She reached for her toast.

Rosina walked into the dining room. "Excuse me, Mr. B. Your package has arrived. I sent it back to the office as you requested."

He rose. "Thank you, Rosina."

Laura Beth looked from Antonio to Rosina and back again. But the oldest maid smiled and walked away. Antonio set his napkin on his plate. "That would be your computer."

"My computer?"

"Yes. I ordered you a new one, since you insist on playing secretary for two weeks. Come back to the office whenever you're ready. I'll have it set up."

An odd feeling stole through Laura Beth as he walked out of the room. Why had he gotten her a new computer when there were two perfectly good computers in his office? She remembered the software might have commands in Italian and she didn't speak Italian, and went back to eating.

She finished her breakfast, wishing she could eat more. Not because she was hungry but because she simply wanted more food. But in the end, she knew if she didn't soon get ahold of her appetite, she'd be big as a house when this baby was born.

After washing her hands and brushing her teeth in her room, she made her way to the office.

As she entered, she gasped. "Wow. Look at this." Everything on the desk had been stacked in neat piles. The old computer had been removed and sat on the floor in a corner.

He pointed at his office behind her. "Everything in that room is to be left alone." He motioned to the piles on the smaller secretarial desk. "This fan mail you can answer."

"What about the other stacks?"

"Some are requests for portraits or for me to paint specific scenes or commissioned work for someone's home or office. Those we will answer together."

She nodded. Obviously considering the conversation over, he walked to the computer sitting in the corner, picked up the monitor and took it into his office. He returned and did the same with the computer tower and the keyboard. When he was done, he pulled the office door closed and locked it.

She tried to catch his gaze, but he avoided her by keeping his attention on the keys he shoved into his pocket.

"I have some errands in town. I'll be back at noon to read any letters you've drafted."

She nodded and said, "Yes," but before the word was fully out of her mouth he was gone.

She sat at her desk, glancing at the new computer, which he'd set up while she finished breakfast. When she saw that everything was in English, she reminded herself that was why he'd bought a new computer.

But that made her frown. If the computer had instructions and menus in a language she didn't speak, why would he feel the need to hide it behind closed doors?

Why hide it at all?

CHAPTER FIVE

ANTONIO RETURNED A little after three. Angry with himself for being so obvious about hiding the computer, he'd avoided his office. But he couldn't stay away any longer.

With a resigned sigh, he walked down the long quiet hall. About two feet before he reached the door, he heard the click, clack of the computer keys. He sucked in a breath and stepped inside. Laura Beth immediately looked up.

Her green eyes sparkled. Obviously, she loved to work, and he had to admit she looked right sitting behind the long, flat computer screen, her brown hair knotted away from her face and held together by two pencils.

"Love your hair."

She laughed and stretched her arms above her head, revealing her perfect bosom to him. Her pink tank top expanded to its limits. The long lines of her slender neck all but outlined themselves for him. The slope of her breasts above the pale pink material made his fingers twitch.

The desire to paint her tightened his chest and he had to fight to stop a groan. She was the last woman in the world he needed to have in his house right now. He didn't want to give their attraction the chance to grow when he knew there was no future for them. Not only did he not want to hurt her, but he also could not handle seeing her pregnancy.

But, oh, how he wanted to paint. How he longed for brushstrokes. For the joy of finding just the right light, just the right angle…and he could see all of it with her.

She pointed at her head. "I forgot that my hair gets in my way. So I had to improvise."

She lowered her arms and his vision of painting her crumbled like the walls of the Coliseum. One second the urge to paint was so strong he could see the brushstrokes in his mind's eye; the next minute it was gone and in its wake was a cold, hollow space.

He wanted to curse. He'd finally gotten adjusted to not painting. He'd lost the hunger. He didn't awaken every morning trembling with sorrow over losing himself, his identity, his passion.

And she'd brought it all back.

He fought the impulse to turn and walk out of the office, telling himself anything to do with painting wasn't Laura Beth's fault. These were his demons, left behind by the betrayal of a narcissistic wife and his own stupidity in tumbling into a disastrous marriage with her. He couldn't take any of this out on Laura Beth.

As casually as possible, he said, "Well, your hair is certainly interesting." He motioned to the stacks of letters. "I see you made headway."

"It's fun pretending to be you, thanking people for adoring my work."

He sniffed a laugh and leaned his hip against the corner of the desk. "Give me a pen and I'll sign them."

Like a good assistant, she rummaged for a pen. When she found one, she handed it to him along with the first stack of replies to fan letters. He looked down only long enough to find the place for his signature, then began writing.

He'd signed three letters before she grabbed the stack and pulled it away from him.

A look of sheer horror darkened her face. "You're not reading them!"

"I don't need to read them. I trust you."

"That's nice, but aren't you at least a little curious about what I'm telling people?"

"No. I assume you're saying thanks, and that you homed in on some detail of their letter to me, some comment, and you addressed that to make each letter sound personal."

She fell back to her chair. "Yes. But you should still want to read them."

He took the stack of letters from her again. "One would think you'd be happier that I trust you."

She crossed her arms on her chest. "One would, except I don't think you trust me as much as you're disinterested."

"I'm not sure I see the difference."

"I did a good job!"

"Oh, you want me to read them so I can praise you?"

She tossed her hands in the air. "You're impossible."

"Actually, I'm very simple to understand. None of this interests me because I was a painter. Now I'm not."

She frowned. "But you said this morning that you'd like to paint me."

He had wanted to paint her. Twice. But both times the feeling had come and gone. Now that he had a minute of distance from it, it was easy to see the urge was unreliable. Not something to take seriously. Certainly not something to change the stable course of his life. Given that he was attracted to her and she was pregnant—while he still wrestled with the loss of his own child—that was for the best.

"A momentary slip."

She frowned at him. "Really? Because it might actually be your desire to paint coming back, and like I told you, I wouldn't mind sitting for a portrait."

He chuckled at her innocence. "Trust me. You wouldn't want to sit for a portrait."

She rose and came around the desk to face him. Leaning on the corner, he didn't have to look down to catch her gaze. They were eye level.

"I have the chance to be painted by the most sought-after artist in the world. How could that not be fun?"

He licked his suddenly dry lips. She stood inches away. Close enough that he could touch her. His desire to paint her took second place to his desire to kiss her. If wanting to paint a pregnant woman was a bad idea, being attracted to that woman was a hundred times worse. Spending the amount of time together that they'd need for a portrait would be asking for trouble.

"I didn't say it wouldn't be fun. But it wouldn't be what you think."

Her eyes lit. "That's what makes it great. I have no idea about so many things in life. I might have lived in one of the most wonderful cities in the world, but I was broke and couldn't experience any of it. Now, here I am in gorgeous Italy and I feel like the whole world is opened up to me." She stepped closer, put her hands on his shoulders. "Paint me, Antonio."

Her simple words sent a raging fire through him and the desire to paint reared up. Having to turn down the chance to get his life back hurt almost as much as the betrayal that had brought him here. But though his attraction to her was very real, there was no guarantee this yearning to paint was. He could take her to his studio, risk his sanity, feed his attraction to her, and then be unable to hold a brush.

"I told you. It wouldn't be what you think."

"Then tell me." Her eyelids blinked over her incredibly big, incredibly innocent green eyes. "Please."

Attraction stole through him, reminding him that his desire to paint her and his attraction to her were somehow knitted together, something he'd never felt before, adding to the untrustworthiness of his desire to paint. He refused to embarrass himself by taking her to his studio and freezing. And maybe it was time to be honest with her so she'd know the truth and they wouldn't have this discussion again.

"Last night, seeing your back, I might have wanted to paint you, but the feelings were different than any other I'd had when I saw something—*someone*—I wanted to paint."

Her head tilted. "How?"

He'd always known, even before he'd studied painting, that the eyes were the windows to the soul. With his gaze connected to Laura Beth's, he could see the naïveté, see that she really didn't understand a lot about life. How could he explain that the reasons he wanted to paint her were all wrapped up in an appreciation of her beauty that tipped into physical desire, when he wasn't 100 percent sure he understood it himself?

When he didn't answer, she stepped back. The innocent joy on her face disappeared. "It's okay. I get it."

"I don't think you do."

"Sure, I do. It's been two years since you've painted and suddenly you're feeling the urge again. It's not me. It's your talent waking up."

He should have agreed and let it go, but her eyes were just so sad. "It is you."

"Oh, come on, Antonio. Look at me. I'm a green-eyed brunette. A common combination. I've never stood out. Not anywhere. Not because of anything."

He stifled a laugh, then realized she was serious. "You don't think you're beautiful?"

She sniffed and turned away. "Right."

Pushing off the desk, he headed toward her. He pulled the pencils from her hair, tossed them beside the computer and watched as the smooth brown locks swayed gracefully to her shoulders. He turned her to face the mirror on the wall by the door. "Still don't think you're beautiful?"

Her mouth went dry. Her gaze latched onto his, and the heat she saw in his eyes made her knees wobble. "What are you doing?"

"I want you to see what I see when I look at you." He watched his finger as it traced along her jaw, down her neck to her collarbone. A thin line of fire sparked along her skin.

"You think you're common. I see classic beauty." His dark eyes heated even more. Anticipation trickled through her, tightening her chest, stealing her breath.

"A woman on the verge of life, about to become a mother. With everything in front of her. The painting wouldn't be simple. It would be as complex as the wonder I see in your eyes every time I look at you. And it would take time. Lots of time." His gaze met hers. "Still want me to paint you?"

Good God, yes.

The words didn't come out, but she knew they were in her eyes. She couldn't tell if he wanted to paint her because he saw something in her eyes, or if he saw something in her eyes because he wanted to paint her. But did it matter? Right at that second, with her attraction to him creating an ache in her chest…did it really freaking matter?

She waited. He waited. The electricity of longing passed between them. He longed to paint. She suddenly, fervently, wished he liked her.

Finally, her voice a mere whisper, she said, "You said this doesn't happen often?"

He shook his head. "It's never happened at all."

She swallowed. "Wow."

He spun around and stepped away. "Oh, Lord! Don't be so naive! I have no idea what this feeling is, but it's powerful." He met her gaze again. "And it could let me down. We could spend hours in my studio and I could freeze. Or your portrait could be the most exciting, most important of my life."

"Antonio, if you're trying to dissuade me, you're going at it all wrong. What woman in the world wouldn't want to hear that?"

"You shouldn't!" The words were hot, clipped. "This feeling could be nothing but my talent tormenting me." He picked up the stack of letters. "Go freshen up for dinner while I sign these."

She stayed where she stood, frozen, suddenly understanding. To him she wasn't an opportunity, but a torment.

"Now!"

She pivoted and raced from the room, but even before she reached the stairs she'd decided Antonio was wrong. He couldn't know that he would freeze unless he tried to paint her.

She might have lost tonight's fight, but the next time they had this discussion, she wouldn't lose.

They managed to get through dinner by skirting the elephant in the room. He feared picking up a brush and she longed for him to paint her. Or maybe she was just curious. After all, Bruce dumping her had made her feel worthless. She'd spent every moment of every date trying to get Bruce to say something special, something romantic, and she'd failed. But Antonio wanted to paint her. He thought she was classically beautiful. That her painting might become the most important of his life.

She knew he hadn't meant it as romantic, but she was so starved for affection that it felt romantic. And she was supposed to ignore it? Not want it? Not be curious?

But that night in her bed, she scolded herself for being such a schoolgirl. Yes, she'd never had a man think her beautiful enough to be a work of art. And, yes, she'd never been attracted to anyone the way she was to Antonio…but was that good? Or bad? She was a pregnant woman with responsibilities to think about. She shouldn't be daydreaming. Fantasizing.

She spent an almost sleepless night, and in the morning groaned when she knew she had to get up. The truth was Antonio would probably like it if she slept in and didn't do any work. They both knew the job was temporary. She was going home in a few weeks. He didn't want the feelings that he had around her, and her going home would settle all that for him.

But like it or not, Antonio needed a PA and she had a baby to support. She should have been able to prove herself and keep this job, but that crazy feeling or need he had to paint her had ruined everything.

She pulled a pair of old, worn jeans and a big gray

T-shirt from her closet. The staff might wear uniforms, but Antonio wore T-shirts—

An idea came and her eyes narrowed as she thought it through. She dug through her clothes until she found her three skirts, three pairs of dress trousers and a few tops that she typically wore for work. This might be Italy, and Antonio might dress like a beach bum, but she was supposed to be a PA. Maybe if she dressed like one, he'd stop wanting to paint her and see her as the worker she was supposed to be.

She slipped into a gray skirt and white blouse that looked like a man's shirt, pulled her hair back into a bun at her nape, sans pencils this time, and slid into gray flats. Instead of her contacts, she wore brown-framed glasses.

Antonio wasn't at breakfast that morning, so she ate quickly and headed for the office. He wasn't there either. But that was fine. She still had plenty of fan letters to answer. She ate lunch alone, fighting the urge to ask Rosina if she knew where Antonio was. She was a secretary, not his girlfriend. Or even his friend. If she wanted to keep her job, then she couldn't see herself as his friend anymore. She had to work the job correctly. Not insinuate herself into his life.

Not secretly long for a relationship with him.

But when he wasn't there at supper time or for breakfast the next morning, she got nervous, antsy. What if his plan was to avoid her for two weeks, tell her the PA thing hadn't worked out and give her another two weeks of alone time to rest? What if she was working to prove herself when there really was no possibility of her keeping this job?

In the office, she lifted the final three fan letters. In an hour, she'd have nothing to do. She answered the last pieces of fan mail and set the letters on top of the stack she'd generated the day before.

He hadn't even come in to sign the letters.

Where was he?

Was she going to let him avoid her so he could take the easy way out? Just send her off with a pat on her head?

She straightened her shoulders. She'd be damned if yet another man would send her off with a pat on her head. And if she had to drag him into this office by the scruff of the neck, he would see that one of two things was going to happen here. Either he would let her work for him—really work—or she was going home. She did not take charity.

Still, she needed the job more than her pride. She was not going to let him slide out of giving her a chance to prove herself by avoiding her. He was going to answer the requests for commissioned paintings with her. He was going to do his job, damn it!

All fired up, she marched out of the office and into the kitchen. "Rosina?"

The maid looked up. *"Sì?"*

"Where is Mr. Bartulocci?"

She frowned. "He say not to tell you."

She shoved her shoulders back even farther. "Oh, really? Would you like me to tell his father that you stood in the way of him getting the help in his office that he needs?"

"No, ma'am."

"Then let me suggest you tell me where he is."

Rosina sighed. "Mr. Constanzo might be bossy, but Antonio is my boss."

She spun on her heel. "Fine. Then I'll simply find him myself."

"Okay. Just don't go into his studio."

Her hand on the swinging door, Laura Beth paused, turned and faced Rosina. "His studio?"

Rosina went back to kneading her bread. "I said nothing."

Laura Beth's lips rose slowly. "I wasn't even in the kitchen."

His strong reaction to painting her had led her to believe his studio would be the last place he'd want to be. So it confused her that he'd be in the old, crumbling house that reminded him he couldn't paint.

But whatever. The plan was to find him, no matter where he was, and force him to see she could be a good employee for him.

It took a few minutes to locate the door that led to the studio. The old stone path had been repaired, but appeared to be the original walkway. The house's door was so old the bottom looked to have been gnawed by wild animals. She tried the knob and it moved, granting her entrance.

The cluttered front room held everything *but* canvases and frames. Paint cans—not artist's paint, but house paint—sat on the floor. Strips of fabric lay haphazardly on metal shelves. She recognized one of the swatches as the fabric for one of the chairs in his dining room.

She glanced around. Most of this stuff corresponded to something in his house. He'd stored leftovers and castoffs here.

He'd said he hadn't painted since his wife's death. But if the items in this room were any indicator, it had been longer than that.

She stepped over a small stack of lumber and around some paint cans and walked through a door that took her into the huge back room, empty save for Antonio, who sat on a stool, staring at a blank canvas.

Light poured in from a bank of windows on the back wall and set the entire room aglow. She didn't know much about painting, but she imagined lots of light was essential.

"Think of the devil and look who appears."

She walked a little farther into the room. "Are you calling me Satan?"

"I'm telling you I was thinking about you."

In a room with a blank canvas.

Because he wanted to paint her.

Because he thought she was classically beautiful.

Tingles pirouetted along her skin. She told herself to ignore them. He didn't want what he felt for her and she did want this job. Acting like a PA had jarred her out of her feelings, so maybe forcing him to see her as a PA would jar him out of his.

She cleared her throat. "I have nothing to do."

He sucked in a long breath and said, "Fine," as he turned on the stool. But when he saw her, he burst out laughing. "Trying to tune in to my librarian fantasy?"

She pushed her glasses up her nose. "I'm trying to look like a PA so I get a fair shot at working for you."

He rose from the stool and walked toward her, stopping mere inches in front of her. "You still want to work for me?"

Her heart jumped. The pirouetting tingles became little brush fires. A smart girl might take Constanzo's severance and run. But though Laura Beth prided herself on being smart, she was also a woman who didn't take charity and who liked a long-term plan. This one, working for Antonio, living in Italy, was a good one.

She couldn't afford New York. She didn't want to burden her parents. Keeping this job was the right move.

Instead of stepping back, she stepped forward, into his personal space, showing him he couldn't intimidate her. "Yes. I still want to work for you."

"You're a crazy woman."

"I'm a desperate woman. Your confusion about painting me isn't going to scare me."

He out and out laughed at that. "Fine."

She motioned to the door. "So let's get back to the office and tackle those letters requesting commissions."

He almost followed her to the door, but hesitated. He'd been thinking about painting her. Imagining it. Mentally feeling the sway of his brush along the canvas. The ease of movement of his arm and hand as they applied color and life to a blank space.

But his hand had shaken when he'd reached for a brush. His heart had pounded. His fingers refused to wrap around the thin handle.

"Come on, mister. I don't have all day."

He laughed. Dear God, how he wished he could get *that* on a canvas. Sensuality, sass and sense of humor. A few years ago, capturing that wouldn't even have been a challenge. It would have been a joy. Today, he couldn't pick up a brush.

He ran his shaky hand along his forehead as sadness poured through him. This place of being trapped between desire to paint and the reality that he couldn't even pick up a brush was as hot and barren as hell.

And maybe she *was* Satan.

He glanced at her simple skirt, the shirt made for a man, the too-big glasses. Or maybe she was right. Maybe she was just a single woman looking to make a life for herself, and *he* was Satan—depriving her because he worried that he couldn't endure seeing her pregnancy, watching another man's child get the chance for life his child hadn't. Watching her joy over becoming a mom.

"I'm not ready to answer the letters about commissions yet." He wasn't sure why he'd said that, except that turning everything down really was like telling the world his career was over. "But maybe it's time I looked at some of the invitations."

"Invitations?"

"To parties and galas and gallery openings." He caught her gaze. "Maybe it's time for me to get out into the world again."

Who would have thought it would be running from a pretty girl that would force him back into the world he didn't want to face? If it weren't for his fears around her, he'd be staying right where he was—hiding.

Instead, he was about to face his greatest fear—getting back into the public eye.

CHAPTER SIX

ANTONIO MANAGED TO find a gallery opening for that weekend. He called Olivia, his manager, putting his phone on speaker, and Laura Beth heard the astonishment in her friend's voice when Antonio told her he would be leaving for Barcelona that evening and would be at the event on Saturday night.

"I hadn't planned on going myself," Olivia said, her voice the kind of astonished happy that made Laura Beth stifle a laugh, since Olivia didn't know Laura Beth was in the room, or even that she was in Italy, working for Antonio. "But I can be on Tucker's plane tomorrow morning. In fact, my parents can stay with the kids and Tucker and I will both come. We'll make a romantic weekend of it."

Laura Beth glanced at Antonio, who quickly looked away. "You know I'd love to see you, but I'll be okay on my own."

"Oh, no, you won't!" Olivia immediately corrected. "You'll probably start telling people you never want to paint again, and all those great commission offers will be off the table. I'm going."

He laughed and Laura Beth watched him, a mixture of curiosity and admiration tumbling around inside her like black and white towels in a dryer. *She* saw a dark, unhappy side of Antonio when he talked about painting. But with Olivia he could joke about it. So who was he showing the real Antonio? Her or Olivia?

He disconnected the call and rose from his desk. "I will be gone for the next few days. You have two choices. Enjoy the pool or sightsee."

Watching him walk to the door, she swallowed. Had he just used work to get out of work? Maybe to show her she wasn't needed?

When she didn't answer him, Antonio motioned toward the door. "Come on, missy. I don't have all day."

Knowing she had no right to question him, she rose from her chair. "No fair using my own lines against me."

He followed her out the door. "All's fair."

In love and war.

She knew the quote. She just didn't know if he thought wanting to paint her was love or war.

Sitting alone in the huge, echoing dining room two nights later, Laura Beth felt like an idiot. She gathered her dish and silver and carried them into the kitchen.

Rosina about had a heart attack. "You are done? You barely ate two bites!"

"I'm lonely. I thought I'd come in here for company."

"Francesca and Carmella are gone."

She walked to the table and set down her plate. "But you're still here."

Rosina winced. *"Sì."*

"Then I'll talk to you."

"You are a guest! You shouldn't be in here and we're not supposed to talk to you."

"Did Antonio tell you that?"

"No. It's good manners."

"I'm not a guest. I'm an employee, like you. I should be eating in here. I *would* be eating in here with you if it weren't for my friend Olivia, who is Antonio's manager."

Rosina eased to the table, slowly took a seat. "*Sì*, Miss Olivia."

"I'm actually an IT person." At Rosina's frown, she clarified. "Information technology." She took a bite of ravioli and groaned. "This is great."

"You should eat lots of it."

Laura Beth laughed. "And get big as a house?"

"You're pregnant. You don't need to worry about gaining a little weight."

"Thanks."

"You're welcome."

They chatted a bit about Rosina's grandchildren. But the whole time they talked, Rosina looked over her shoulder, as if she was worried Antonio would arrive and scold her for fraternizing with his guests.

Respecting Rosina's fear, Laura Beth ate breakfast by herself Friday morning, but by lunch she couldn't stand being alone another second. She wandered into the kitchen long before noon and actually made her own sandwich, which seemed to scandalize Carmella.

She tried to eat alone at dinnertime, but the quiet closed in on her, and she took her plate and silver into the kitchen again.

Rosina sighed but joined her at the table.

"I'm sorry. I just hate being alone."

Rosina shook her head. "This isn't the way it works in a house with staff."

"I know. I know. But I still say we're both employees and we should be allowed to talk."

The sound of the doorbell echoed in the huge kitchen.

Rosina's face glowed with relief as she bounced off her chair. It almost seemed as if she'd been expecting the interruption. Maybe even waiting for it.

"I will get it."

As Rosina raced away, Laura Beth frowned, unable to figure out who'd be at the door. It was a little late for a delivery, though what did she know? She was in Italy, not the US. The country might be beautiful, but it was unfamiliar. Antonio had run from her. Rosina was afraid to talk to her.

This wasn't working out any better than New York would be. Though Italy offered her a way to raise her child in the sunny countryside, rather than being stifled in the kind of run-down New York City apartment she could afford, what good would it do to be raised in a home where people ignored him or her?

The kitchen door swung open. *"Cara!"* Constanzo boomed. Dressed in a lightweight suit, he strode over to her. "What are you doing here when your boss is in Spain?"

She shrugged. "He never asked me to go with him."

"You are his assistant. He needs you." He tapped her chair twice. "Go pack."

She gaped at him. "Go pack? No way! Antonio will be really mad at me if I just pop up in Barcelona!"

"Then you will go as my guest. You can't sit around here moping for days."

She'd actually thought something similar sitting by the pool that afternoon.

"And since you're in Europe, why not enjoy the sights? If you don't want to find your boss, we'll make a weekend of it. I will show you Barcelona, then take you to the gallery opening myself."

Her heart thrummed with interest. She'd never seen

Spain. Still, she was in Italy to work, not race around Europe with her boss's dad. "I can't. I'm supposed to be working."

"And did my son leave you anything to do?"

She winced.

"I didn't think so."

The pragmatist in her just wouldn't give up. "It really sounds like fun, and part of me would love to go, but I didn't pack for vacation. I packed to work. I shipped most of my fun clothes home to my parents. I don't think I have anything to wear."

"You have…what you call it…a sundress? Something light and airy? Something pretty?"

"Won't women be wearing gowns at the gallery opening?" She frowned. "Or at least cocktail dresses?"

Constanzo waved his hands. "Who cares? You will be with me. No one will dare comment. Besides, you will look lovely no matter what you wear. If they snipe or whisper, it will be out of jealousy."

She didn't believe a word of it, but in desperate need of that kind of encouragement, she laughed. "You're good for my ego."

"And you laugh at my jokes." He turned her to the door. "We make a good pair. Go pack."

She quickly threw two sundresses, jeans and tops, undergarments and toiletries into her shabby bag. Trepidation nipped at her brain, but she stopped it. Antonio had left her alone with nothing to do and a staff that was afraid of her. At least with Constanzo, she'd be doing something.

With her suitcase packed, she took a quick shower, put on her taupe trousers and a crisp peach-colored blouse and headed downstairs.

She walked to the foyer, suitcase in hand, and was

met by Constanzo's driver, who took her bag and led her to the limo. When she slid onto the seat, Constanzo was talking on the phone. "Yes. The Barcelona penthouse, Bernice. And don't forget that other thing I told you." He disconnected the call. "Ready?"

She laughed. "Sure. Why not?"

Traveling with Constanzo, Laura Beth quickly learned that Antonio was right—his dad was a pain in the butt. His plane left on his timing. Cars had to be waiting for him, drivers ready to open the door and speed off, and his favorite bourbon had to be stocked everywhere.

They arrived in Barcelona late and went directly to the penthouse—a vision of modern art itself with its glass walls, high ceilings and shiny steel beams and trim.

She gasped as she entered. "Holy cow."

Constanzo laughed. "That's another reason I like you. You remind me not to take my good fortune for granted."

The limo driver set Laura Beth's bag on the marble floor and silently left in the private elevator.

Constanzo reached for the handle of her bag. "I will take this to your room."

"No. No! I'll do it." She picked it up. "See? It's light."

"Okay. Normally the gentleman in me wouldn't let you, but for some reason or another I'm very tired tonight." He plopped down on a white sofa. "Your room is the second door on the left. I'll check to see if the cook is here yet. We'll have a snack."

She almost told him she was more sleepy than hungry, but she finally realized he'd invited her along on this jaunt because he liked company too. So she headed for her room, intending to wash her face and comb her hair, then spend some time with him while he snacked.

Corridors with steel beams, skylights and glass walls took her to the second door on the left. She opened it and stepped inside.

She loved her room in Antonio's house, but this room was magnificent. Beiges, grays and whites flowed together to create a soothing space like a spa. She could almost hear the wind chimes and sitar music.

She put her suitcase on the bed and walked toward the bathroom, desperate to freshen up before her snack with Constanzo.

With a quick twist of the handle, she opened the door and there stood Antonio, wiping a white terry cloth towel down his chest, as if he'd just gotten out of the shower.

His eyes widened and he instantly rearranged the towel to cover as much of himself as possible.

But it was too late. She'd seen the dark swatches of hair covering his muscled chest, and—wrapped around the side of his neck—the black ink of the webbed wing of the rumored dragon tattoo.

He gaped at her. "What are you doing here!"

"Me?" Too shocked to monitor her responses, she yelled right back, "What are you doing here!"

"This is my dad's penthouse. Why would I not use it when I'm in Barcelona?"

She couldn't argue that, so she said, "Fine. Whatever." Lifting her chin, she began backing out of the marble-and-travertine bathroom, embarrassed not just by the fact that she'd walked in on him naked, but also because her mouth watered for a look at his tattoo. From his muscled arms, broad shoulders and defined pecs, she knew his back was probably every bit as spectacular. The right tattoo would make it sexy as hell. "I'm only here because your dad said this was my room."

"I always use this room when I stay here."

"Great. Peachy."

Her face hot, her mind reeling, she pivoted out of the bathroom and walked to the bed. Grabbing her suitcase, she headed for the main living area. Unfortunately, Antonio was right behind her.

Not about to be intimidated, she tossed her suitcase on a white sofa and made her way to the kitchen.

Constanzo sat on a stool at the center island, dipping bread into olive oil. "Come, *cara*. Eat."

Then Antonio walked in behind her and Constanzo's smile grew. "Antonio!"

He scowled at his dad. "What are you doing here?"

Constanzo laughed. "I live here."

"You live in a country house in Italy! This is a spare house."

He smiled. "It's still mine."

Antonio tossed up his hands in despair and walked to the center island. And there, on his back, was the glorious dragon.

Prickly heat crawled all over Laura Beth. The man was a god. Not only was the dragon perfect, crafted in reds, greens and blacks, but his shoulders were wide, and behind the ink of the dragon, well-defined muscles linked one to another. Every time he moved his arm, the dragon seemed to shift and shimmer as if alive.

Of course. What did she expect from an artist but a tattoo that was a work of art itself?

Oh, this was bad. Every time she learned something new about her boss, she liked him a little bit more. Deciding the best thing to do would be to pretend everything was fine, she strolled to the center island, sat on a stool and took a piece of the crusty bread.

Constanzo motioned for her to dip the bread in the olive oil. "So you and I, we go to see the sights tomorrow?"

She nodded as she slid the bread into her mouth. "Oh, this is wonderful."

From her peripheral vision, she watched Antonio's eyes narrow, as she and Constanzo behaved as if nothing was wrong, then he shook his head and stormed out.

When she was sure he was gone, she caught Constanzo's gaze. "I hope you have another bedroom for me."

He laughed. "There are five bedrooms. Suites, really. You don't even have to bump into him accidentally if you don't want to."

She sucked in a breath. Considering how much he didn't want to see her, she imagined Antonio would pack and move to a hotel the next morning, but she wasn't about to explain that to Constanzo. She sent him a smile. "Good."

But the next morning when she entered the dining room, Antonio and Constanzo sat at the long cherry-wood table, as if nothing had happened. Both rose. "Good morning!"

Constanzo's greeting was a little cheerier than Antonio's, but at least he wasn't scowling. What was with these two that they could argue one minute and be best friends the next?

Was that why she couldn't get along with Antonio? Because she wanted resolutions to arguments, when he seemed perfectly happy to ignore conflict?

Antonio surreptitiously watched Laura Beth walk to her seat. She looked girl-next-door pretty in a coral-colored

T-shirt and jeans that were so worn she was either really, really poor or really, really in fashion.

He watched her all but devour a plate of French toast as his father rambled off a long list of places he wanted to show her that morning, including the Museum of Modern Art and the Picasso Museum.

His pulse thrummed. He never came to Barcelona without a trip to the Picasso Museum. But should he risk spending time with her when she pushed all his attraction buttons?

Without looking up from the morning paper, his father said, "Would you care to join us, Antonio?"

He wanted to, but he also didn't. He'd come on this trip to get away from the temptation of his assistant, the longing to paint, when he knew it was off, wrong somehow. She was a nice girl and he was a bleak, angry man who was as much attracted to the idea of painting again as he was attracted to her. No matter how he sliced it, he would be using her.

And, if nothing else, he knew *that* wasn't right.

"I'm thinking about—" He paused. His brain picked now to die on him? He was the king of excuses for getting out of things. Especially with his father. But he wasn't at home, where he could cite a million nitpicky things he could do. He was in his father's home, in a city he didn't visit often.

His father peered at him over his reading glasses. "Thinking about what? Going to the museum? Or something else?"

He couldn't make an excuse Constanzo would see right through. It would only make the old man more curious, and when he was curious, he hounded Antonio until he admitted things he didn't want to admit. If he gave his father even the slightest hint he was avoiding

Laura Beth, his dad would either get angry or he'd figure out Antonio was attracted to her.

Oh, Lord! With his nosy dad, *that* would be a di-
saster.

It was the lesser of two evils to just give in and join
Laura Beth and Constanzo. He could always go his own
way in the museum.

"Actually, I'd love to go to the museum with you."

Constanzo's face split into a wide grin. Laura Beth
looked confused. Well, good. She certainly confused
him enough.

An hour later, he strolled into the main room of the
penthouse, where Laura Beth perched on one of the
parallel white sofas, awaiting his father. Though Constanzo had said they'd leave at ten, his dad didn't really
keep to a schedule.

"He might be a minute."

She laughed. "Really? I'm shocked."

Antonio lowered himself to the sofa across from her.
He didn't want to be attracted to her, hated the fleeting
longing to paint she inspired, if only because it always
flitted away, but she was a guest and it was time to
mend fences. Even if she returned to New York tomorrow, he'd see her at Olivia and Tucker's parties. They
needed to get back to behaving normally around each
other. Small talk to show he wanted to be friends was
exactly what they needed.

"That's right, you flew here with him last night.
You've experienced the joy of traveling with my dad
when he doesn't fall asleep."

She winced. "He wasn't too bad. He just wants what
he wants when he wants it."

"Precisely."

He tried a smile and she smiled back. But it was a

slow, awkward lift of her lips. Discomfort shimmied around them. And why not? He'd told her his thoughts. His desire to paint her. The fact that he thought she was classically beautiful. Right before he'd chased her out of his office and then arranged to be away from her. She probably thought he was just shy of insane and might never be comfortable around him again.

She rose from the sofa and walked to the wall of windows. "The ocean is pretty from up here."

He swallowed. Her little coral-colored top hugged her back. Her threadbare jeans caressed her bottom. In his mind's eye he didn't merely see her sensual curves; he saw the breakdown of lines and color.

Longing to paint swooped through him. But he answered as calmly as he could. "The ocean is always pretty."

She conceded that with a shrug and didn't say anything else, just gazed out at the sea, looking like a woman lost, with no home…because that's what she was. Lost. Alone. Homeless.

And pregnant.

Emptiness billowed through him, like the wind catching a sail, when he thought of the loss of his own child. But his conscience pricked. As much as he'd like to pretend everything between him and Laura Beth was okay—the way he and his dad always handled conflict—she was his friend. No matter that he couldn't paint her because he didn't trust the artistic urges she inspired; he'd treated her abysmally the night before.

Heat washed through him as he remembered her walking in on him in the bathroom. Her eyes had grown huge with surprise, but he'd seen the interest, too. And her interest had fed his. Two steps forward and he could have taken her into his arms, kissed her senseless.

That's why he'd gotten angry. It had been a defense mechanism against the temptation to take advantage of what he saw in her eyes.

He should say, "I'm sorry," and apologize for yelling. He nearly did, but that might take them into a discussion of his attraction, which would lead to a discussion of him wanting to paint her and they'd already gone that route. It didn't solve anything. It actually made things worse between them.

So maybe the just-gloss-over-what-happened-and-pretend-everything's-okay technique he and Constanzo used was the way to go? Some arguments didn't have conclusions, and some conflicts simply weren't meant to be faced.

He rose, walked beside her, and said the most non-romantic, nonconfrontational thing he could think of. "So how are you feeling today?"

She cast a quick glance at him. "I'm pretty good. No morning sickness, but I think that's because your dad keeps feeding me."

"Have you told him you're pregnant?"

She grimaced. "Still working on figuring out how to tell people."

"Well, my dad would be thrilled." He would have been even more thrilled with Antonio's child, but Gisella had stolen that from both of them. "I told you. He loves babies."

"Which is why he spends so much time with Tucker and Olivia?"

"Yes. That's part of it. But Olivia and Tucker also go out of their way to make sure he's a part of things. They think of him as family and he loves that."

"That's nice."

"It is, and it works for me, too. Because any week they're in Italy entertaining him is a week I don't have to."

"Oh, really?"

Antonio pivoted away from the window to see his dad standing in the entry to the main room.

Red blotches had risen to his cheeks. His eyes narrowed condemningly. "You think you have to entertain me?"

Antonio grimaced. "I didn't mean that the way it sounded, Dad."

"I'm perfectly clear on what you meant." His chin lifted. "And if I'm such a burden, then perhaps I'll just go back to my room and wait for the soccer game." He turned on his heel and headed down the hall.

"Dad, really!" Antonio started after him. "Wait!"

Constanzo spun around. "No, you wait. I'm tired today. Very tired. But I was happy to spend the day with you anyway. If you don't like having me around, then I'll do what *I* want to do—rest in my room with a good soccer game." He turned and headed down the hall. "It's not a big deal."

Antonio watched his father walk away and turn to the right to go to his room. Constanzo backing out of plans made no sense. His dad never turned down an opportunity to be out and about, doing things, seeing things, especially when he had somebody like Laura Beth to play tour guide for.

Antonio shoved his hands into his jeans pockets and walked back to the main room to see Laura Beth standing by the window, waiting for him.

"He isn't going. Says he wants to rest."

"Oh." Laura Beth hesitantly walked toward him. "Is he okay?"

"Yeah, he just seemed—" *Odd. Unusual. Confusing.* "Tired."

"I get that. He didn't sleep on the flight. We got in late. Then we stayed up another hour or so eating." She winced. "The man's going to make me huge."

He laughed. "He prides himself on being a good host."

She smiled, then glanced around. "So what now?"

He sucked in a breath. "I usually go to the Picasso Museum when I'm here."

She brightened. "Then let's go. I don't have anything else to do until the gallery opening tonight."

He wasn't surprised she and his father planned on going to the opening. When Constanzo butted in, he went full tilt. Maybe that was why he wanted to rest?

Antonio glanced back down the hall that led to his dad's suite. The gallery opening started late and ended in the wee hours of the morning. Constanzo wasn't as young as he used to be, and he might have realized he couldn't waste his energy today if he intended to be up until three. Maybe he knew he couldn't spend the day sightseeing and also go to the gallery opening? And maybe the whole nonargument they'd just had was his way of getting out of sightseeing so he didn't have to admit he needed the rest.

The crazy old coot hated admitting shortcomings. Even if they were a normal part of life.

With that settled in his mind, he glanced at Laura Beth, with her bright, expectant face. He should tell her no. He'd sort of gotten them back to being friends. Spending the day with her was like tempting fate—

Or he could turn it into a day to cement their friendship. He could show her around, acting like a friend, and maybe his attraction would go away.

Actually, that idea was perfect.

He hoped.

CHAPTER SEVEN

PRAYING HIS PLAN to get them back behaving like friends worked, Antonio pointed to the elevator and Laura Beth followed him into the plush car, through the ornate lobby and then to the street. The doorman tossed him a set of keys. He motioned to a shiny red sports car. Low and sleek, with the black top retracted, the Jaguar hit the sweet spot of luxury and fun.

"Oh, nice!"

"It's my dad's, of course." He paused halfway to the car as guilt unexpectedly nudged him. His dad shared everything he had, gave Antonio anything he asked for, and he shouldn't have made that remark about being glad that Tucker and Olivia sometimes entertained him. But as quickly as the thoughts came, Antonio shoved them aside. His dad hadn't been insulted by his comment as much as he'd been looking for a way to bail on a day of sightseeing. Antonio was positive he had nothing to feel guilty for.

Laura Beth ambled to the Jag. Her eyes lit with joy as she took in the stunning vehicle. "Your dad has the best taste."

"Yes. He does." He opened the car door for Laura Beth and motioned for her to step inside.

She slid in, immediately glancing behind her at the

nonexistent backseat. "Maybe it's a good thing Constanzo bailed. I'm not sure how we all would have fit in this."

Walking around the hood of the car, Antonio laughed. "No worries. My dad has a limo here. There could have been space for everybody if he'd really wanted to come along."

He jumped inside. As he slipped the key into the ignition, he could feel the heat of her gaze as she studied him. This was the closest they'd been since the day he'd explained why he wanted to paint her. Hot and sharp, his attraction to her tumbled back. The temptation to touch her was so strong, he fisted his hands.

"My mom does that, you know."

Expecting something totally different from her, he frowned and peered over at her. "Does what?"

"Tells me she isn't upset when I know she is. Especially when I'm home for a holiday and I want to go somewhere without her. It's not really passive-aggressive behavior. It's more like she sees I'm an adult, and, though it's hard, she has to give me some space. So she says she's not mad and lets me go alone." She caught his gaze. "Sometimes it makes me feel guilty. But I know it's her choice. Almost like a gift."

He frowned. If Laura Beth had picked up on his exchange with Constanzo, maybe it hadn't been so innocent after all. "A gift?"

"Yes. Time alone with my friends is a gift."

He scrunched his face in confusion. "Why would Constanzo think we needed alone time when we just spent several days together?"

She shrugged. "I don't know."

"Well, whatever he's doing, it's weird, because until today Constanzo's never dropped back."

"Maybe this morning he finally got the message that you don't want him around so much?"

The guilt rolled back. It tightened his chest and clenched his stomach. He looked out over the hood of the car, then faced her. "It's not like that. The only time I freak is when he meddles."

She shook her head. "No. You're pretty much always grouchy with him. But I get it." She put her hand on his forearm, as if what she had to say was supremely important and she wanted to listen. "You're an adult who lives twenty minutes away from a retired wealthy man who adores you and has nothing to do but dote on you."

He laughed.

"When he first found you, all this attention was probably fun. Now you want to be yourself."

"I suppose." Except without painting he had no idea who he was. And maybe that's what made him the most angry with Constanzo's meddling. He wanted to be able to say, *Let me alone so I can paint, or feed the hungry, or gamble, or read, or sit on the beach.* But he couldn't. He had no interest in anything. And having Constanzo around always reminded him of that.

Not wanting to think about *that* anymore, he hit the gas and propelled them into the street, ending the discussion.

The wind ruffled through their hair, and Laura Beth laughed with glee. "This is great!"

He hit the clutch and shifted into the next gear, working up some speed before he shifted again, and again, each time sending the little car faster as he wove in and out of lanes, dodging traffic.

She laughed merrily, shoving her hands above her head to feel the air.

Something about her laugh soothed him. She hadn't

been right about Constanzo giving him space. Never in their history together had his dad ever dropped back, unless Antonio pushed him. But suddenly it didn't matter. With the wind in his face and the sun beating down on him, it was just nice to be outside. To be away from his dad. To be away from two years' worth of requests for paintings. To be away from the studio that reminded him he couldn't create.

He sucked in the spring air, let her laugh echo around him and felt the tightness of his muscles loosen as he drove to the Picasso Museum.

Laura Beth followed Antonio to a back entrance of the pale stone museum. Glancing around, she said, "So, are you a friend of the curator or is your dad a donor?"

He said, "Both," then pulled his cell phone from his jeans pocket. "Carmen, we're here."

They waited only a few seconds before a short dark-haired woman opened the door for them. Antonio said something to her in Spanish, then she smiled and disappeared down a hallway.

The power of a billionaire would never cease to amaze Laura Beth. "Nice."

"It is nice. I don't like having to work my way through crowds or wait in lines."

"Nobody likes to work their way through a crowd or wait in a line."

"Which makes me lucky that I can come in through a back door."

She shook her head. "Right."

He led her through a maze of corridors until they entered the museum proper. Paintings dominated the space. Color and light flowed like honey. A true fan, Antonio stopped, closed his eyes and inhaled.

Laura Beth stifled a laugh. Not because it wasn't funny, but because he was home. *This* was where he loved to be.

He didn't say anything, just walked up to a painting and stood in front of it. She ambled over, sidling up to him to see the picture. Her eyes narrowed as she looked at the odd shapes, the out-of-proportion dimensions, the unexpected colors.

"Isn't that something?"

She fought not to grimace. "Yeah, it's something, all right."

It took only ten minutes and two more paintings for her to realize she didn't just dislike the first piece of art. She didn't like Picasso. Still, she smiled and nodded in all the right places, if only because she didn't want to look like a bumpkin.

Finally, she couldn't take it anymore. "I'm sorry, but these paintings are weird."

He spared her a glance and said simply, "You don't like abstracts."

She winced. "I don't."

"Why didn't you say something sooner?"

"I thought you liked this museum."

"I do." He glanced around, as if the ten minutes had filled his desire and now he was fidgety. "But today I feel odd being here—"

She didn't think that was it. As casual and calm as he tried to be about his dad backing out of their plans, she knew it had upset him. Or maybe it nagged at him. If it really was the first time Constanzo had canceled plans with him, there was a reason. And Antonio was too smart of a guy not to know that.

So why did he keep pretending he didn't care?

He looked around. "Maybe I just don't want to be inside a building?"

"Maybe." And maybe he needed a little time in the good, old-fashioned outdoors to think things through. "We've got a pretty fancy car out there. If you wanna take a ride through the city, I'm game."

Antonio cast a longing look at a painting and another thought suddenly struck her. What if his edginess wasn't about his dad but about the paintings? Picasso might be his favorite artist and he might have visited this museum every time he came to Barcelona, but she'd bet he hadn't been here since he stopped painting.

He definitely needed to get out of here.

So she gave him an easy way out. "Please. I'd love to see the city."

"Then I will take you to see the sights."

She caught his arm. "Are you missing what I said about the fancy car? I don't want to walk through museums or cathedrals. I wanna ride. Besides, I think I could get a better feel for the city if we drove."

"Barcelona is beautiful." He sucked in a breath. "Actually, a drive might be a good idea."

They climbed into the little red sports car again. Within seconds Antonio eased them into traffic. Cool air and scenery—a mix of old buildings and new, leafy green trees standing beside palms, and a sea of pedestrians—whipped by as he shifted gears to go faster and faster and swung in and out of lanes.

Air ruffled her hair. The sun warmed her. But it was the power of the Jag that put a knot in her chest. For all her intentions to stop lusting after the wonderful toys and lives of her rich friends, she loved this car.

Longing rose up in her, teasing her, tempting her. Her fingers itched to wrap around the white leather steering wheel. Her toes longed to punch the gas to the floor. For twenty minutes, she constrained it. Then suddenly she couldn't take it anymore.

She leaned toward Antonio. Shouting so he could hear her above the wind and the noise of the city, she said, "Would you mind if I drove?"

He cast her a puzzled frown, as if he wasn't sure he'd heard correctly.

She smiled hopefully. "Please? Let me drive?"

"Oh!" His voice vibrated in the wind swirling around them. "Can you drive in a city you don't know?"

She nodded eagerly. "I've driven in New York."

He frowned. "Can you drive a stick?"

"Are you kidding? I was driving my granddad's old farm pickup when I was thirteen."

He eased the car over to a space on a side street between two tall stucco buildings with black wrought-iron balconies that looked to belong to apartments. "Thirteen was a long time ago for you. Are you sure you remember how to use a clutch?"

She playfully punched his arm.

"Okay, I get it." He shoved open his car door. "Let's see what you can do."

It took a minute for them to switch seats. When she got settled, she caressed the soft leather steering wheel before she turned the key in the ignition, depressed the clutch and punched the gas.

They jolted forward and he grabbed the dash for support. "Careful, now."

She laughed, hit the clutch and shifted to a better gear. "This car is like heaven." When the engine growled for release, she hit the clutch, shifting again. "Holy bananas. It's like driving the wind."

He laughed, but he still clung to the dash. "You're going to kill someone!"

She depressed the clutch and shifted a final time, reaching the speed she wanted, barreling through yellow lights, weaving in and out of traffic.

"I never knew you were a daredevil."

His eyes weren't exactly wide with fear. But they were close. Still, she was good. She knew she was good. Driving was in her blood. "I'm not. I just like a good car."

"Really? I'd have never guessed."

"What? You think women can't appreciate a powerful engine?"

"No, you just seem a little more tame than this."

She shook her head. Yet another person who thought she was dull Laura Beth. "Right. I guess we all have our secrets." She spared him a glance. "Our passions."

He tilted his head.

She shrugged. "You like to express yourself through art. I want to be free." She took her eyes off the road to catch his gaze. "And maybe a little wild."

He laughed. "You? Wild?"

"Thank you for underestimating me."

"I don't underestimate you."

"Right. That's why you refuse to paint me. You all but said you don't think I can handle it."

"I said *I* can't handle it."

"Oh, sure you could. I can see in your eyes that you could. You just don't want it to happen."

"Sitting for a portrait can be long and boring."

She shrugged. "So?"

Antonio shook his head, but didn't reply. Laura Beth suddenly didn't care. With the wind in her hair, the sun pouring down on her and the engine in her control, for once in her life she experienced the joy of total power. She soaked it up. Swam in it. She was so sick of everybody underestimating her, thinking they knew her, when all they knew was the shadow of the person she could be with no money, no opportunities.

She suddenly wondered if that's what Antonio saw when he thought of painting her. The longing to be something more. The hidden passion.

Hope spiked through her, then quickly disappeared. He might see it, but he didn't want it.

Saddened, she slowed the car. Palm trees and four-lane streets nestled into Old World architecture gave the city a timeless air but she barely noticed it. Something inside her ached for release. She didn't want people to pity her or dismiss her. She wanted to be herself. She wanted to be the woman Antonio saw when he looked at her.

And she honest to God didn't know how to make that happen.

The more she slowed down, the more Antonio relaxed in the passenger's seat. He forgot all about her little tantrum about him underestimating her when he realized how much she truly loved driving. A passenger on Laura Beth's journey of joy, he saw everything in squares and ovals of light that highlighted aspects of her face or body. The desire to paint her didn't swell inside him. Longing didn't torment him. Instead, his painter's mind clicked in, judging light and measuring shapes, as he watched the pure, unadulterated happiness that glowed from her eyes as she drove.

But something had happened as she slowed the car. Her expression had changed. Not softened, but shifted as if she were thinking. Pondering something she couldn't quite figure out.

He tapped her arm. "Maybe it's time to head back?"

She quietly said, "Yeah."

Curiosity rose in him. She was the second person that day to do a total one-hundred-eighty-degree turn on him. Happy one minute, unhappy the next. Still, he'd made a vow to himself not to get involved with her, and he intended to keep it.

He pointed at his watch. "We have a gallery opening tonight."

She nodded, and at the first chance, she turned the car around. He thought she'd stop and they'd switch places, but she kept driving, and he leaned back. Surreptitiously watching her, he let the images of light and lines swirl around in his brain. Normal images. Calculations of dimension and perspective. They might be pointless, but at least this afternoon they weren't painful. She was a passionate, innocent woman who wanted to love life but who really hadn't had a chance. And that's what he longed to capture. The myriad emotions that always showed on her face, in her eyes.

Eventually, she pulled into a side street and turned to him. "I'm a little bit lost."

He laughed. "I think you are."

"So you don't mind taking over?"

"No."

She fondled the steering wheel, then peeked at him. "Thanks."

The sudden urge to gift her the car almost overwhelmed him. Watching her drive might have been the first time he'd seen the real Laura Beth. And he knew that was the person she wanted to be all the time. The woman who wasn't afraid. The woman who grabbed life and ran with it.

"You looked like you enjoyed it."

Her gaze darted to his. "Maybe too much."

The desire to lean forward and kiss her crept up on him so swiftly it could have surprised him, but it didn't. The woman who'd pushed that gas pedal to the floor piqued his curiosity. Not just sexually, but personally. She was as complicated as his desire to paint her.

He moved closer, watching her eyes darken as she realized he was about to kiss her. His eyelids drifted shut as his lips met hers and everything inside him froze, then sprang to glorious life. She was soft, sweet and just innocent enough to fuel the fire of his need to learn more. His hands slid up her arms to her shoulders, pulling her closer as his mouth opened over hers and she answered. His lips parted. Her tongue darted out enough for him to recognize the invitation.

Raw male need flooded him. The powerful yearning to taste and touch every inch of her rose up. But when his hormones would have pushed him, his common sense slowed him down. It was as if kissing her made him believe they could have a real relationship. No painting seduction of an innocent, but a real relationship.

The thought rocked him to his core. Dear God, this woman was pregnant. A relationship meant watching her grow with another man's child, sadly realizing he'd lost his own.

Worse, the last woman he'd been in a relationship with had made a mockery of their marriage. She'd broken his heart. Stolen his ability to paint. He'd never, ever go there again. He'd never trust. He'd certainly never give his heart. And whether she knew it or not, that was what Laura Beth needed.

Someone to trust her. Someone to love her.

He broke the kiss. But he couldn't pull away. He stared into eyes that asked a million questions he couldn't answer.

"I'm sorry."

She blinked. "Sorry you kissed me?"

He stroked her hair as the truth tumbled out. "No."

Her voice a mere whisper, she said, "Then...what are you sorry for?"

"Sorry that this can't go any further. There can't be anything between us."

"Oh. Okay."

But she didn't move away and neither did he. Confusion buffeted him. If he knew it was a bad idea to get involved with her, why couldn't he move away from her?

"We should go."

"Yeah."

Grateful that she wasn't bombarding him with questions about why there couldn't be anything between them, he opened his door and got out, and she did the same. She rounded the trunk. He walked in front of the car to get to the driver's side. He slid behind the wheel, started the car, made a series of turns and headed toward Constanzo's penthouse.

Still rattled by their kiss, he wanted to speed up and get them the hell home so he could have a few minutes alone. But he slowed the car and let her admire the architecture, the town square, the street vendors and shops.

When they returned to the penthouse, she took one last look at the Jag before shoving open her door and stepping out onto the sidewalk.

Joining her, he tossed the keys to the doorman and led her to the elevator. Neither said a word. A strange kind of sadness had enveloped him. For the first time since he'd met Gisella, he found a woman attractive, stimulating. But he was so wounded by his marriage he knew it was wrong to pursue her.

He walked through the entry to the main room of Constanzo's penthouse, and saw a huge white sheet of paper propped up on a vase on the coffee table.

He ambled over, picked up the note written in Constanzo's wide-looped script and cursed.

"What?"

"My dad has gone."

Her brow wrinkled. "Gone?"

"He took the jet and went home." Realizing this ruined Laura Beth's trip, Antonio faced her. "I'm sorry."

She bit her lower lip. "I think that little tiff with your dad this morning was bigger than you thought."

"Seriously? Do you really believe he was angry that I said I was happy to have someone else entertain him every once in a while?" He tossed his hands in disgust. "I tell him that four times a week."

She shrugged. "That might be true, but he seemed a little more sensitive than usual this morning." When Antonio groaned, she added, "Why else would he leave?"

He crumpled the paper, annoyance skittering through him. What did his dad expect him to do? Race after him? Apologize, again? He'd apologized already and Constanzo had blown him off, told him he was tired. He'd given him more reason to believe he wasn't angry than to believe he was.

"Don't worry about it." He certainly refused to. If Constanzo wanted something, expected something, then maybe he needed to be forthright and not sulk like a sour old woman. "It's not a big deal. It just means you'll have to—" *Go to the gallery opening with me.* He almost said the words, but snapped his mouth shut as the truth finally hit him.

That meddling old man!

That's why he'd left him and Laura Beth alone that morning. He wasn't mad. He must have seen something pass between them, and he'd left so they'd be forced to interact.

No. They wouldn't just be forced to interact. They'd have fun, as they'd had driving that afternoon. And they'd connected. He *kissed her.*

Oh, Constanzo was devious.

Antonio shrugged out of his jacket and tossed it on the sofa, his blood boiling. As if making him feel guilty wasn't bad enough, matchmaking was the ultimate insult.

Still, just because Constanzo had played a few tricks, that didn't mean he had to roll over and be a victim.

His voice crisp, casual, he said, "The real bottom line to this is that he took the plane. But even that's not a big deal. If he doesn't send it back for us, I have a friend I can call."

She bit her lip again, took a few steps back. "I don't want to be a burden."

He sighed. When he saw Constanzo again he intended to let him have it with both barrels, if only for scaring Laura Beth. He'd left a shy, broke, single woman in a city where she didn't even speak the language.

"You're not a burden." But he also wasn't going to let Constanzo set them up this way. As much as he would like to take her to the gallery, to have her on his arm, to laugh with her he couldn't do it. It had been wrong for him to kiss her. Equally wrong for him to be interested in her. She deserved so much more than the broken man he was. He wouldn't be a bad host, but Constanzo's plan ground to a halt right here. They'd eat something, then he would retire to his room until it was time to dress for dinner and the gallery opening—for which he had plans with Olivia. Because this was business, he didn't even have to make an excuse for not inviting Laura Beth along. His plans were already set.

He glanced around. "So, lunch?"

"We're past lunch and jogging toward dinner."

"Oh, you want to wait for dinner?"

"Are you kidding? I'm pregnant and I haven't eaten since breakfast. I'm starving. I need something now."

"That's fine. We'll have Cook make whatever you want."

Antonio led her to the kitchen, but as soon as he opened the door, he knew Cook was also gone. The place wasn't just empty. It appeared to have been buttoned down, as if Cook had stowed everything away until Constanzo's next visit.

The prickle of anger with his dad heated his blood again. Now the old coot wanted him to take Laura Beth to dinner? Well, he had another thought coming, because Antonio had plans.

Strolling toward the pantry, Laura Beth said, "I can make something for us to eat. It'll be fun."

He winced. "I can't eat now. I have dinner plans with Olivia."

She stopped and faced him. "Oh."

"I'm sorry. We haven't had a real meeting in weeks, and she likes to give me pep talks…check in with me." He shrugged. "It's a working dinner."

She waved her hand in dismissal. "No. No. I get it. This is a business trip for you."

Feeling like a first-class heel, and not able to completely ditch her, even though he knew getting involved with her would only hurt hert, he halfheartedly said, "You can come—"

But Laura Beth knew she couldn't. It would be one thing to go to dinner and the gallery with Constanzo. People would look at her and assume she was his assistant. It wouldn't matter what she wore, how much she ate, if she laughed at all the wrong places. But with Antonio and Olivia and Tucker? They would look like a foursome. Olivia would be dressed to kill, and Laura Beth would be in an old sundress, looking foolish.

"No. Thanks." She caught his gaze. "I'm tired. It's better for me to stay in. I'll fix myself a little something to eat and probably go to bed."

"You're sure?"

The relief in his eyes rattled through her, confirming her worst suspicions, filling her with disappointment. He didn't want her to tag along. They'd been fine in the car, chatty even. She'd admitted things she normally didn't admit and he'd listened. But just as he didn't want to give in to the urge to paint her, he didn't want to like her, to get to know her. He'd made that clear after their kiss when he said there could be nothing between them.

And now here she was, like Cinderella, being told she couldn't go to the ball. Even though she knew damned well she didn't belong there, it still hurt.

So she smiled. "Sure. I'm fine."

He took a few steps backward. "If you're sure."

"Antonio, stop being so polite and go."

"Okay." He turned around and walked out of the kitchen.

She leaned against the center island, disappointment flooding her. She didn't know why she was upset. So what if he'd kissed her? The moment had been right. For all she knew she could have looked like a woman issuing an invitation. He'd taken it...but regretted it. And she was wise enough not to want a man who didn't want her. She'd already had a guy like that and she was smarter than to want to get involved with another. Her current overload of emotions had to be hormonal, brought on by her pregnancy.

So why did being left behind feel like such a huge insult?

Because, deep down, she knew he liked her. Damn it.

That's what had been simmering between them all along. Not her desperate need for a job or his unexpected desire to paint her. But attraction. Maybe even genuine affection.

She pulled away from the center island and straightened her shoulders. She had to stop thinking about this. She was hungry. She needed to rest. She also needed Antonio's plane or his friend's plane, or his help, at least, to get back to Italy. She couldn't get upset because he refused to admit he liked her.

She made herself some eggs and toast and ate them on the balcony, listening to the soothing sounds of the ocean. Finished eating, she set her plate on the table beside her outdoor chair and let herself drift off to sleep.

The sound of Antonio calling for her woke her. "Laura Beth?"

She snapped up on her seat. Her heart leaped, and for a second she let herself consider that he might have changed his mind about her coming along. Lord knew she could eat a second dinner. And though she hadn't liked Picasso, a gallery opening didn't usually show-case only one artist. She'd probably see lots of paint-ings she'd like.

Filled with hope, she pushed off the patio chair and slid the glass door aside to enter the main living area, and there stood Antonio, so gorgeous in a black tux that her breathing actually stuttered.

"Look at you!"

His hair tied back off his face highlighted the sharp angles and planes of his chin and cheeks and made his large brown eyes appear even larger. His crisp white shirt and sleek tux weren't just sexy. They made the statement of just how refined, how wealthy, he was. Even his shiny shoes spoke of pure elegance.

"It's the first time I'll be in a gallery in over two years. I figured I couldn't look like a slouch."

"Oh, trust me. You do not look like a slouch."

He laughed, but extended his right arm toward her. "I can't get this cuff link to close."

She walked over. "Let me see."

The cuff link in question was black onyx with a di-amond stud.

"I can get it."

She smiled up at him and he gazed down at her, his beautiful dark eyes shiny with anticipation. Her heart tugged. He really wanted to be back in his world. Back with his peers. His people.

And here she stood in threadbare jeans, an old top and flip-flops. Her longing for him to ask her to come to dinner and the opening with him morphed into shame. Humiliation. Even if he begged, she had nothing to wear.

But he wasn't begging.

His phone rang and she quickly fastened his cuff link so he could grab it from the coffee table. "Olivia, what's up?"

She heard the sounds of her friend's voice, though she couldn't make out the words. But Antonio laughed.

"That's perfect. I love that restaurant." He headed for the elevator. "I've got my dad's limo. I can be at your hotel in twenty minutes." He pressed the button and the door magically opened. Listening to Olivia, he turned and waved goodbye to Laura Beth as the door closed behind him.

And she stood in the glamorous main room, alone, listening to the sounds of silence.

Tears threatened but she stopped them. She wasn't upset. She was angry. It didn't matter that she didn't have a dress to wear or shoes. Antonio hadn't been glad to ditch her because she was penniless. He'd been glad to leave her behind because they'd connected that afternoon. They'd talked about Constanzo. He'd let her drive. He'd kissed her, for heaven's sake. Then they came upstairs to the penthouse and he'd gotten—distant?

She glanced around.

Why would he suddenly become cold? The only thing that had happened was finding Constanzo's note—

No. He'd become cold when they'd discovered they were alone.

And he didn't want to be alone with her.

Part of her understood. She was a pregnant woman. What rich, eligible bachelor would want to be alone with a pregnant woman?

But he had no reason to fear her. She'd never made a pass at him. If anything, he'd made a pass at her. He'd kissed her—

She tossed her hands in the air in frustration. Why was she thinking about this!

To get her mind off it all, she took a shower and washed her hair. With nothing better to do, she heated the curling iron she found in a drawer and made huge, bouncy curls out of her long locks. Before she could comb them out and style her hair, her stomach growled.

With fat, uncombed curls and dressed in pajama pants and a huge T-shirt, she walked to the kitchen. Just as she opened the refrigerator, the building doorman rang up. Though she answered the phone, she winced when a bounty of Spanish bombarded her. With a grimace, not even sure she'd be understood, she said, "I don't speak Spanish."

He said something else, then disconnected the call.

Shaking her head, she headed back to the refrigerator to find a snack, but she heard the elevator doors open, and she walked to the main room.

There in the elevator was the doorman, package in hand, grinning at her.

She walked over. "Oh, a package. That's what you were saying. We had a package."

He nodded, handed it to her and left as quickly as he'd arrived, apparently deciding she was a poor candidate for a tip, and he was right, because she didn't have any of the local currency.

She started for the coffee table to leave the big box somewhere Antonio would see it, assuming it was something for him, only to see her name on the label.

She frowned. Who would send her something here? Who even knew she was here?

Slowly walking back to her room, she examined the label one more time to make sure it really was for her.

She closed her bedroom door behind her and opened the box to find a simple black dress and black spike heels.

Confused, she pulled the dress out of the box. The material was sinfully soft, rich in texture, like a chiffon or organza. A card sat in the crinkled tissue paper that had caressed the dress. She grabbed it, opened it and read, *"Cara, go to the opening. Constanzo."*

She stared at the card, then burst out laughing. This was just too weird. How did he know she wasn't going to the opening? Unless he'd realized that she'd refused to go to the opening with Antonio because she had nothing to wear? She had mentioned that to him—

What difference did it make? Antonio was gone. She didn't have money for a taxi. Antonio had taken the limo. And she couldn't get the doorman to bring the Jag around because she didn't speak Spanish. Constanzo might want her to go, but the dress had arrived an hour too late. Which was too bad. She'd really like to go to that opening and show vain, conceited, jumping-to-conclusions Antonio he had nothing to worry about from her.

She tapped the note against her palm, then glanced at it again and smiled. It was printed on Constanzo's stationery and had his cell number on it.

She glanced at the dress, glanced at the card, glanced at herself in the mirror with her hair curled but not combed. She might look like a street person right now, but Antonio had been the one to say he wanted to paint her. Considered her classically beautiful. Kissed her. She hadn't been the one to make passes at him. So why was he acting as if she were someone to be afraid of?

Anger bubbled in her stomach. How dare he behave as if *she* was the one with the crush on him and insultingly leave her behind when he was the one who'd kissed her?

The shy Kentucky girl in her filled with fire. She raced to the kitchen and picked up the phone the staff probably used to order groceries.

It took three rings before Constanzo answered. "Hello?"

"I need a coach."

"Excuse me."

"You sent me a Cinderella dress but it came too late for me to go to the opening. Antonio's long gone with the limo. I can't go with him to the gallery."

"I will call the driver and have him come back for you."

"I want the Jag."

Constanzo laughed. "Excuse me."

"I want the Jag. If I'm going to go to the trouble of getting all dolled up…I'm making an entrance."

Constanzo laughed with glee. "That's my girl. I'll call the doorman and tell him to have the keys waiting for you when you get downstairs."

"You better also get my name on the guest list for the opening. I'm pretty sure a fancy gathering like this one is by invitation only."

"I'll have Bernice call."

"Thanks."

"You're welcome. Go knock his socks off."

CHAPTER EIGHT

STANDING IN THE main room of the gallery, pressed in by art aficionados, Antonio glanced at his watch. His return to the world of art had been a subtle, almost disappointing, one. Olivia had other clients—working clients—she was schmoozing right now. Tucker had found two business acquaintances he was talking up. And Antonio stood by a gallery owner from Madrid who desperately wanted him to do a showing.

Half of him had gone breathless at the prospect. The other half wanted to run in terror.

The screech of a car grinding to a stop stabbed into the noise of the gallery. He looked up, past Juanita Santos to the wall of windows behind her. A red Jag had pulled up to the curb for valet parking. His eyes narrowed. That looked just like Constanzo's car.

The driver's door opened. A spike heel emerged, connected to one long, slim leg.

His eyebrows rose. The crowd outside the gallery turned to the newcomer. Men smiled. Women gave her the once-over.

Antonio's mouth fell open as Laura Beth tossed the keys to the valet.

With her hair pulled up, piled high on her head, and looking luscious in the slim black dress, she walked the cobblestone path like a model working the catwalk. The dress rode her curves, accenting her womanly figure, but the black color gave her a sleek, sophisticated air. In her worn jeans and goofy librarian work clothes, she was an all-American girl. In this dress, she was a woman.

And all eyes were on her.

His heart caught and his breathing faltered, but he ignored them. He wasn't in a position to get involved with her. Though looking at her in that dress, he was again tempted. Still, for all he knew, Constanzo had set this up. But even if he hadn't, his reasons for staying away from Laura Beth were sound. Responsible. He feared watching her belly swell with child, but his first marriage had also made him jaded, angry. She was absolutely too nice for him. And right now she was about to be rejected at the door.

A gentleman, he couldn't let that happen. He turned to Juanita. "If you'll excuse me."

"Of course."

He headed for the door, his heart thundering in his chest with fear that she'd be embarrassingly refused entrance. Instead, the young man smiled and motioned for her to enter.

She dipped her head in thanks and glided into the crowd.

He stopped and waited for her to see him. When she did, she approached him.

"Well, look at you."

She smiled slowly. "You've got to stop stealing my good lines."

He laughed. "I'm glad you're here, but I'm afraid I'm—"

He was about to say *busy*, when Olivia raced over. "Laura Beth?"

She raised her hands. "In the flesh."

Olivia squealed with joy. "What are you doing here?"

"I'm spending a few weeks with Antonio, helping him try to clear out his office."

One of Olivia's eyebrows rose as she looked at Antonio, who clearly hadn't mentioned that her best friend was living with him.

Laura Beth laughed. "Don't worry. Constanzo hired me. Antonio didn't. So he's not really cooperating."

Olivia tilted her head at him. "Pity."

Then Laura Beth totally surprised him by squeezing Olivia's hand and saying, "I'd love to chat. But Antonio was just telling me that he's busy. I'm assuming you've got people for him to meet, so I'm going to walk around the gallery and, you know, browse."

Olivia gave her a quick hug. "Have fun. I do have a few people I'd like Antonio to meet. But maybe we can catch up tomorrow."

Laura Beth smiled mysteriously. "Maybe."

Then she turned and walked away.

Antonio watched the slight sway of her hips, the long curve of her spine, as she moved away from him.

"Wow. She looked happy, huh?"

Antonio faced Olivia. "Happy?"

"Yeah. Lately she's been a little glum." She slid her hand into his elbow and turned him toward the crowd again. "I guessed she was a bit upset about being room-mateless, but she wouldn't talk about it. She won't take a thing from me or Tucker. Not even a job offer. She wants to make her own way in the world." She paused and frowned. "How'd Constanzo talk her into working for you?"

He blinked. Obviously, she didn't know Laura Beth was pregnant. So he shrugged. "I think losing her apartment really brought home the fact that she couldn't be choosy about who offered her a job."

"Yeah, well, if you really don't want her, Tucker does. He has an opening for an IT person who would work directly with him, somebody he can trust with his secrets."

"Sounds perfect for her."

"It is perfect for her. He was going to make the offer after the wedding, but she disappeared. Now at least we know where she went."

"Yes, you do." And Tucker wanting to hire Laura Beth was like a blessing from heaven. A relief.

Really.

There was no reason for the odd feeling in his stomach, the fear of losing her, the reminder of how empty his house was without her.

He peered around into the crowd but couldn't see Laura Beth. Then he caught a fleeting glimpse of her as she moved between two conversation circles. The men in each cluster smiled at her and she innocently smiled back.

Jealousy catapulted through him.

"Ready to mingle?"

Thanking God for a reason to take his eyes and his attention off Laura Beth, he smiled at Olivia. "Desperately."

He spent an hour with Olivia introducing him to gallery owners, art dealers and collectors. His former charm came back to him as if he hadn't lost it. If he'd had anything new to display or sell, he would have made a killing.

But he didn't have anything new to display or sell,

and he wasn't yet entertaining commissions, so everyone drifted away. The futility of his situation roared through him, frustrating him, making him wonder why the hell he was even here.

He faced Olivia. "I'm going to get a drink. Would you like one?"

"I think I better find Tucker."

Perfect. He could go to the bar, drink himself stupid with scotch and be driven back to the penthouse, where he could pass out and forget he was a has-been.

Shifting to the side, he slid through the throng of happy people and to the discreet glass-and-marble bar set up in a corner.

"Scotch." The bartender turned to go and he caught his arm. "Three of them."

The young man nodded, apparently thinking he was getting drinks for friends, and that was just fine with Antonio. He angled himself against the marble, but when he did he saw Laura Beth, standing alone, staring at a painting.

He studied the tilt of her head, the way it clearly displayed her interest in the picture, saw the light and shadows he'd use if he painted her, so everyone would see what he saw. A newcomer falling in love.

Damn it! What was he doing imagining painting her again!

"Here you are, sir."

The bartender set three crystal glasses of scotch on the bar. Antonio took the first one and downed it. He set the empty glass on the bar, then dug through his pockets for a good tip.

He walked away with a scotch in each hand, deliberately heading away from Laura Beth, but apparently she'd moved too, because there she stood, in front of another display. This one she seemed to like about as much as she liked the Picassos.

Watching her, he sipped the second scotch. The desire to capture her slithered through him again, just as Jason Ashbury stopped in front of him.

"I wanted to give you a card."

Antonio set his second scotch on an available tray with a wince. "Sorry."

Jason laughed. "Never apologize for enjoying a good scotch." He handed the card to Antonio. "I know you're accustomed to bigger galleries, but we'd love to have you in Arizona."

And he'd love to be in a gallery in Arizona. He'd love to have a showing anywhere. If he could just freaking paint again.

His gaze strolled to Laura Beth.

Jason shook his hand. "Come visit us. Maybe we'll inspire you."

He walked away and Antonio's eyes sought Laura Beth again. She all but shimmered in the sophisticated dress, but she couldn't hide that innocence. And maybe that's what drew him. She was his deceased wife's polar opposite. And if her innocence was the medicine he needed to paint again, maybe he shouldn't fight it.

He strolled over. "Are you okay?"

"What? You think a woman can't be on her own in a gallery?"

"No. You're pregnant and it's been a long night and you still have a bit of a drive home."

She winced. "Saw me in the car, did you?"

He took a step closer. "Saw you getting out of the car."

This time she laughed. "That was fun."

"You looked like you were enjoying it."

"Oh, I was." She took a long drink of air. "I'm going to miss this."

"Barcelona?"

"No. The dressing up tonight and playacting."

He raised one eyebrow in question. "Why? You've got a few more weeks in Italy. You can do all the dressing up and playacting you want."

She shook her head. "No. I can't. Walking around here tonight, I remembered something I'd thought at the wedding. I took what I believed was a real job because I'm not an executive or a trust-fund baby or even employable in New York City." She faced him. "But you don't want me and I don't really belong here. It's time for me to go home."

Panic swirled through him. "Home New York or home Kentucky?"

"Kentucky." She raised her gaze to meet his. "I know there's not much work for an IT person there, but I'm going to have a baby. I need my mom for moral support." She sucked in a breath. "But looking at one of the pictures, I also realized I had a pretty good childhood."

He frowned. "Which picture?"

She ambled to a picture a few feet away. "This one."

It was a painting of three dogs running through the dead brush around a pond in late fall. The colors were cool, dismal. The sky so dark it was almost charcoal gray.

"*This* reminds you of home?"

Gazing at the painting, she said, "Yes."

Hoping for the best, he said, "You had a dog?"

She laughed. "No. We had ugly Novembers. The cold sets in and lingers. But some of my best life things happened in fall."

She faced him with a light in her eyes that flicked

the switch of his longing to paint. But in a different way than the day he'd found her lying on her bed wrapped in a towel, a different way even than the technical visions of dimension and light that had overtaken him various times that day. This was a serious, quiet need, something that didn't hurt him or fill him with angry longing. This one was normal.

Breathlessly afraid to lose this feeling, he quietly said, "What sort of things?"

"Well, my birthday's in the fall, so there's the whole being born thing."

He laughed.

"And every fall we returned to school." She smiled at him but her eyes were distant, as if she were thinking back to the past. "Going to school meant seeing my friends, getting new clothes, football games, school play tryouts."

"Sounds like fun."

"It was."

"And that's why you're going home?"

She moved her eyes up to meet his gaze. "I just keep thinking I'd like to be around my mom when I actually have the baby. But I also had a great childhood. I want my baby to have that, too."

He whispered, "It makes sense," not sure why the moment felt so solemn, except it meant that their time together was ending. Or maybe because he knew he needed to at least try to paint her and if he didn't ask in the next few seconds he wouldn't get the chance.

"I still think about painting you."

"I know." She stepped away. "You told me it annoys you to think about painting me."

He laughed. "Tonight's feelings are different."

She faced him. "Really?"

"Yeah. Tonight it all feels real, doable."

"Well, that's…something."

He breached the space between them. "Actually, it is. The uncontrollable urge might have been a first step, but just as your feelings about becoming a mom are shifting, growing, so are my feelings about painting you."

Her breath caught. "You're serious?"

He glanced around. "Yes. But this feeling is so new and it's only cropped up around you." He caught her gaze. "Can you spend the next few weeks with me? Let me see if I can paint again?"

"Only if you also let me work as your assistant."

Her persistence made him laugh and long to kiss her. In that very second, the need was so strong he doubted his ability to resist it. Her face tipped up to him. Her earnest eyes held his. It would be so easy.

But he'd kissed her once and it had only reminded him that he couldn't have her.

Because he couldn't.

"I want the painting to be our focus."

"Can I earn my keep by answering the rest of your mail?"

He laughed. "No. I want to do this right."

She cocked her head. Understanding flitted across her face. "Okay."

And something wonderful sprinted through his blood. Acceptance. She had needs of her own. Troubles of her own. But instead of bargaining with him, she would simply help him.

"You know, Tucker wants to hire you when you get home."

Her eyes widened. "He does?"

"He needs someone to work directly with him."

"Oh my God. That might mean I could work from Kentucky."

Her eyes glittered with happiness and the lure of her lush mouth was as strong as an aphrodisiac. He wondered about his strength, his endurance, if he really could paint her without touching her.

But his fears melted away when he remembered he couldn't watch her pregnancy. And now he knew she was going home to her mom and a job from Tucker.

She would not be around forever. His endurance didn't have to last a lifetime. Only a few weeks. He had nothing to worry about.

CHAPTER NINE

WHEN THEY ARRIVED at Antonio's country home the next day, everything had a different feel to it. They were no longer adversaries. They were partners in his plan to paint again. The feeling of being on even ground was heady stuff for Laura Beth. She'd always been second-best, plain Laura Beth. Today they were equals.

Standing in the foyer, she faced him with a smile. "So? Ready to go to the studio?"

"It's Sunday."

"I thought artists had to work while they were inspired. Do you want to lose your momentum?"

She could tell from the expression that flitted across his handsome face that he didn't. Still, he said, "How about lunch first?"

She caught his hand and tugged him in the direction of the back door that led to his studio. "How about work first?"

He laughed. "Wow. I have never known you to turn down food."

"I had a peanut-butter-and-jelly sandwich while you took that catnap on the plane."

She turned the knob on the ratty door of the cottage and it gave easily. Surprise almost had her turning to ask why he didn't lock the door, then she realized he was totally comfortable here in the Italian countryside. Which was probably part of why it drove him so crazy not to be able to paint. This was his sanctuary, and it was letting him down. Since his wife's death, everybody and everything seemed to be letting him down. She would not.

Pride billowed through her. She might make nothing else of her life, but helping him to paint again would be her crowning accomplishment. Even if she never told another soul, to protect his pride, she would know simple Laura Beth Matthews had done something wonderful.

They wound their way through the maze of old paint cans, broken furniture and fabrics to the last room. His studio.

Happy, she faced him with a smile. "So where do I sit? What do I do?"

He ran his hand down his face. "We just got off a plane. Give me a minute to adjust."

His hesitancy filled the air. He wanted this so much and he'd tried and failed before. She knew that trying again, he faced disappointment again.

She stepped back, giving him space. "Sure."

He glanced around, then rummaged through stacks of paper in the drawer of a metal desk so old it didn't even have accommodations for a computer. He pulled out two tablets. One was huge. The other was the size of a spiral notebook. He set the large pad of paper on the top of the desk, and opened the smaller one.

"We'll do sketches first."

"What do you want me to do?"

"First, I just need to warm up, get the feel of your features, the shape of your body."

She nodded eagerly.

"So, I'll sit here." He leaned his hip on the corner of the desk. "And you sit there." He pointed at a ladder-back chair about ten feet away.

She frowned. "There?"

"Yes. These are preliminaries. Warm-ups. Something to get me accustomed to your shapes."

Her gaze involuntarily rippled to the chaise near the windows. That would have been more comfortable. She wanted to sit there.

But he pointed at the ladder-back chair again.

She smiled hesitantly. Though she understood what he was saying, something really drew her to that chaise. Still, she sat on the ladder-back chair. Antonio picked up a simple number-two pencil.

"Really? A pencil? You're not going to use charcoal or chalk or anything cool like that?"

He sighed and dropped the tablet to his lap. "I'm warming up!"

She waved her hand. "Okay. Okay. Whatever."

By the time Antonio had her seated on the chair, his anxiety about drawing had shimmied away. Praying that she would stop talking and especially stop second-guessing his choices, he picked up his pencil and began sketching quickly, easily, hoping to capture at least five minutes of her sitting still.

When she wrinkled her nose, as if it was itchy, he stopped and stretched. He'd drawn small sketches of her eyes, her nose, her lips, her neck, her eyebrows, the wrinkle in her forehead, the side view of her hair looping across her temple and one sketch of her entire face.

"If you need to scratch your nose, scratch."

She pulled in a breath and rubbed her palm across her nose. "Thank God."

"What? You were sitting for…" He glanced at his watch. "Wow. Ten minutes. I guess you do deserve a break. For someone unaccustomed to posing, ten minutes is a long time."

She popped off the chair. Shook out all her limbs. "I know I've sat perfectly still for more than ten minutes at a time, but sitting still without anything to think about or do? That's hard."

"I'd actually hoped to break you in with five-minute increments."

"Meaning?"

"You'd sit for five minutes a few times in our first two settings, then ten minutes in our third and fifteen in our fourth…that kind of thing."

"So we're skipping a step?"

"Which could be good."

"Can I see what you've done?"

He handed her the tablet.

She smiled. "These are great."

"That's just me messing around until I get a good feel for drawing your features. Then we move on to sketches of what I think a painting of you should look like."

She beamed at him and everything inside him lit up. He told himself he was happy that she was enjoying the process, happy that he hadn't yet had an anxiety attack, and motioned her back to the chair.

"If you can keep doing ten-minute sessions, we'll do two more, then break for the day."

"You're only working a half hour?"

He laughed. "Yes. I'm not just indoctrinating you into the process. I'm easing myself in too."

She sat on the chair, straightened her spine and lifted her face. "Okay."

He sketched for ten minutes, gave her a break,

sketched for ten more, then they had lunch. Later, while she sat by the pool, he paid his dad a visit. He expected them to argue like two overemotional Italians about Constanzo stranding them in Barcelona. Instead, his father quietly apologized, told Antonio he was tired and retired to his room.

The next day, Laura Beth easily graduated to sitting for fifteen minutes at a time. The day after that, she had a bit of trouble with sitting for twenty minutes, but eventually got it.

He drew her face over and over and over again. He sketched her arms, her feet, the slope of her shoulder. Feeling the rhythm of those shapes in his hand as it flowed over the paper, he felt little bits of himself returning. But he didn't push. Fearing he'd tumble into bad territory, he didn't let himself feel. He simply put pencil to paper.

On Sunday, with Ricky and Eloise in Italy on the last leg of their honeymoon, he forced Laura Beth to take the day off to visit with them.

Monday morning, though, she arrived in his studio, bright and eager to begin.

Trembling with equal parts of anticipation and terror over the next step of the process, he busied himself with organizing his pencils as he said, "This week we're doing potential poses for the painting."

"So now I don't just have to sit still? I have to sit still a certain way."

He glanced up. Her eyes were bright. Her smile brilliant. Enthusiasm virtually vibrated from her body.

"Basically, yes."

Knowing how uncomfortable the ladder-back chair had been, he walked her to the wall of windows in the back of the room. He posed her feet, positioned her shoulders, placed her hands together at her stomach and strode back to the old metal desk to get his pad and pencil.

He worked for twenty minutes, trying again and again to make her come to life in a sketch, but failing. He knew what he wanted. That faraway look. And though he saw snatches of it in her eyes, it didn't stay and he couldn't catch it when it was only a glimpse.

With a sigh, he said, "Let's take a break."

"Wow. Was that a half hour already?"

"Twenty minutes. I can't seem to get what I want from this pose, so I figured we'd stop, give me a bit of rest and try again."

After a bathroom break and a few sips of water, Laura Beth was ready to go again. Antonio picked up his pencil and tablet. She positioned herself and Antonio started drawing. After only a few seconds, he said, "The light is wrong."

She deflated from her pose. "Bummer."

He shook his head. "It is a bummer, but we can come back to this tomorrow morning. Right now..." He glanced around. "Let's try one with you sitting on the chaise."

She walked over and sat down. Without waiting for instructions, she angled herself on the chair with her back to him, then looked over her shoulder at him.

The vivid image of her lying wrapped in the towel on her bed popped into his head, quickly followed by the pose he'd so desperately wanted to paint. Her wrapped in silk, one shoulder and her entire back bare, the swell of her hip peeking out at him, her face a study of innocence.

His finger itched to capture that. But he was sure the urge was a leftover of an aberration. Watching her at the gallery, he'd envisioned several compelling poses, expressions, little bits of humanity that would result in a painting every bit as compelling. He did not need to go *there*.

"That's not how I want you."

"Okay."

"Let's try this." He wasn't entirely sure how to position her. He had facial expressions in his mind. Images of her hair falling just the right way. And he couldn't seem to get it right as he shifted her from one side to another, one pose to another.

"Okay. How about this? Lie down and pretend you're daydreaming."

"Oh! I get to lie down!"

He stopped in midstep toward the metal desk and faced her. "If you're tired or anything, I don't want you to overdo."

She stretched out on the sofa. "I'm fine."

Her inelegant movement struck a chord in him again and he eagerly grabbed the notebook. That was part of the essence he was trying to grasp. Beautiful yet impish. Troubled but still hopeful. With the image fresh in his mind, he began sketching. But after ten minutes he realized that pose didn't work either.

Neither surprised nor disappointed—today was all about trying and failing—he gave her a break, then sat her on a chair.

Backing away from her, he said, "Think deep thoughts."

Her face scrunched. "How deep?"

"I don't know." Remembering the feelings he'd had in the gallery and their subsequent conversation, he said, "Think about going home."

She nodded, and he watched the change come to her

eyes. Almost a sadness. Something tweaked inside him. But he didn't say anything. Though he wanted to comfort her, they weren't supposed to become friends from this. He wanted to paint her. She wanted to go home.

It made him sad. Almost angry. But he got the best sketches of the day.

After that they stopped for lunch. Rosina had prepared salads and bread, but Laura Beth skipped the bread, insisting she could *feel* herself getting fat.

He watched her single out and then dig in to her tomatoes with gusto and had to stifle a laugh. Feeling light and airy because he counted that morning as a success, he didn't want to upset her in any way, shape or form. But the look in her eyes as he'd sketched her haunted him.

Casually, as if it were the most natural question in the world, he asked, "Do you not want to go home?"

Her head popped up. Her gaze swung to his. "I need to go home."

"There's a wide gulf between need and want."

"I need my mother. Aside from Tucker and Olivia's kids, I've never been around a baby. And I can't really count Tucker and Olivia's kids because I've never changed their diapers, never fed one of them and most certainly never walked the floor."

"Ah. I get it. You need your mother's assistance."

"More her advice...her knowledge. Which means, since I need her so much, I *want* to go home."

He laughed. "That's convoluted at best."

She shrugged. "It is what it is."

But the faraway, sad expression came to her eyes again. He should have yearned to grab his pencil. Instead, that odd something tweaked inside him again.

Only this time, he recognized it. It wasn't a worry that they would get close. He hated to see her sad.

"What if you got a nanny?"

She gaped at him for a few seconds, then laughed out loud. "Right. I can't even afford an apartment. Hell, Tucker hasn't officially offered me a job yet, and you want me to hire a nanny?"

"But if he does offer you a job with a good enough salary, it would mean you could live where you want. That you wouldn't have to go back to a small town that clearly makes you sad."

"The town doesn't make me sad. I told you before. I want my child to be raised there."

He frowned. "So what makes you sad?"

Laura Beth fumbled with her napkin. For fifty cents she'd tell him the truth. She'd look him right in the eye and say, "I like being with you. I like the person I am with you. And I am going to be sad when I leave because I know I'll only ever see you at parties where we'll be polite like strangers."

But then he'd draw back. Then he wouldn't paint her. He might even put her in Constanzo's plane and ship her home so he didn't have to deal with her feelings.

So she'd handle them alone.

"I think it's just hormones."

"Ah." He nodded. "I seem to recall hearing a bit about them from Tucker when Olivia was pregnant."

And that was it. He totally believed her. He didn't even like her enough to say, "Are you sure?" He didn't dig deeper. Proof, again, that he didn't have the same kinds of feelings for her that she had for him.

In bed that night, she cautioned herself about getting so close to him—wouldn't let herself pretend there was any chance they'd be together—and the next morning she forced herself to be as chipper and happy as any woman posing for a portrait should be. She couldn't have him forever, but that didn't mean she couldn't enjoy what she had now. In fact, a wise woman would accept what she could get and make memories.

After breakfast, Antonio took her outside. She'd asked him a million times if there was anything special he wanted her to wear and every time he'd said, "Your jeans are fine."

But his attempts at capturing an outside pose failed. When the next day's poses also resulted in balled-up paper and strings of curses in Italian, Laura Beth had to hide several winces. On Friday, when his temper appeared—a real, live temper that went beyond curses and balled-up paper and resulted in explosions and tablets tossed into the trash—fear trembled through her.

Not fear of Antonio. She knew he would never hurt her. His anger was never directed at her, but always at himself. His lost focus. His inability to capture what he wanted. She also saw his volatility as part of his larger-than-life personality, very much like his dad's. What scared her was that he might quit trying and ask her to leave.

The very thought caused her chest to tighten. So Saturday after breakfast she suggested she meet him in the studio. He frowned and asked why, but she only smiled and raced off.

She styled her hair as it had been the night of the gallery opening, put on makeup and slipped into the black dress and the high heels Constanzo had bought her.

When she walked into the studio, Antonio had his back to her. She straightened her shoulders, lifted her chin and sashayed over to the wall of windows.

When he saw her, Antonio's face fell. He gaped at her for a good twenty seconds, then grabbed the tablet. Not knowing if the lighting was good or bad, she simply stood there. She thought deep thoughts, trying to get that faraway look he always talked about catching. She knew that the sooner the painting was done, the sooner she'd be going home, but she didn't care that dressing in the way that had inspired him would result in her going home. She longed to help him. This wasn't just about her doing something important with her life anymore. This was about him. About wanting him to get his life back.

And if the way he frantically scribbled was any indication, she was succeeding. Finally giving her man what he needed.

Her man.

She struggled with the urge to close her eyes. He was her man. She could feel it in her bones. And she was his muse. But he would let her go. Because he believed he'd had his woman, the love of his life, and even though Gisella was gone, he didn't want another love.

What she felt for him was pointless.

Antonio put down his pencil forty minutes later, belatedly realizing he'd made her stand stiff and silent way beyond her limitations.

"I'm sorry, *cara.*"

She shook her shoulders loose, then smiled. "It's fine. Did you get what you wanted?"

"Yes." The desire to kiss her rose strong and sure. It wasn't just her pretty face and her bright personality that drew him. Her unselfish gestures never ceased to amaze him. For almost an hour, she'd stood stiff and straight, barely blinking. Even more, though, she'd realized what he needed when he didn't. The dress, the hair, even the shoes had brought back the feelings he'd had in the gallery, and his artistic instincts hadn't merely appeared. They'd jumped to full-blown life.

Because she'd made all the connections he couldn't seem to.

Still, he fought the urge to kiss her by turning away, puttering with his tablets, pretending interest in old sketches that had no value now that he'd found what he wanted. "Thank you for thinking of the dress."

She displayed her spike heels. "And let's not forget the shoes and hair."

She said it lightly, but an undercurrent of melancholy ran through her voice. All of this was about him. Nothing they'd done in the past ten days helped her. She still had her troubles.

He walked over and caught her hands. Fear of getting too close, of longing to kiss her, had to be shoved aside. He owed her. "You look so pretty. Let me take you to lunch."

She shook her head. "Nah. You don't have to."

"I insist. Give me ten minutes to clean up."

"It's okay. There's no need to thank me."

He smiled. "I'll let you drive."

Her eyes widened. "Do you have a Jag?"

"I have a Lamborghini."

"Oh, dear God." She pressed her hand to her chest. "How can I turn *that* down?"

He motioned for her to precede him out of the studio and up the cobblestone path, then headed to his room to change. Considering her attire, he slid into beige slacks and a short-sleeved white shirt, which he left open at the throat.

When she saw his car, she squealed with delight and

raced to get behind the wheel. He tossed the keys at her. She caught them like a left fielder for the Yankees. The engine rumbled to life and she shifted into reverse to get them out of the garage, then shoved the pedal to the floor when they reached the road.

The noise from the wind swirling around the open roof prevented conversation, so he pointed to give her directions to the nearest small town. He motioned with his hand to let her know she needed to slow down as they drew closer.

They entered the village and their speed decreased. The noise of the wind diminished. He heard the appreciative sigh that told him she was pleased with his choice of village, with its cobblestone streets, old houses, street vendors and sidewalk cafés.

"Park here."

She pulled the car into a little space. They both got out and he directed her to walk to the right.

The way she looked at his little town was like nothing he'd ever seen before. Her lips kicked upward into a smile of pure joy, but not like a person surprised by what she saw. More like a woman who'd found a place she loved.

Mesmerized by her excitement, he caught her hand and led her down the street to the outdoor seating of his favorite local restaurant.

They ordered salads and once again she refused bread. He shook his head. "You are supposed to gain weight."

"Yeah, but I'm not supposed to turn into a tub of lard."

He laughed. "The way you talk reminds me of my childhood."

Her gaze rose to meet his. "Really?"

"Yes. Everybody I know either speaks Italian or they're a bigwig in the art world or in one of Dad's former companies. You speak like a normal person."

"I am a normal person."

"And most of my foster parents were normal."

Her eyes softened. "Did you have a rough time?"

He shook his head. "Tucker had a rough time. I think that's because he was actually in New York City. I was in a quiet city in Pennsylvania. I had a bit of trouble with being angry about not knowing my dad, but my foster parents were always simple, normal people with big hearts."

She said, "Hmm," then cocked her head. "Pennsylvania's not so different from Kentucky."

He chuckled. "You have a twang that Pennsylvanians don't."

She frowned. "Hey, I worked really hard to get rid of that twang."

"And you've mostly succeeded."

Laughing, Laura Beth glanced across the table at Antonio. The blue sky smiled down on them. A light breeze kept everything cool. The hum of life, of street vendors, cars and chatting passersby, filled the place with life and energy. She totally understood why Tucker and Olivia spent several months a year in Italy. If she could, she would, too. But in a few days she'd be going home. Back to her blue-collar roots. Back where she belonged.

Emotion clogged her throat. She wouldn't just miss Antonio. She would miss his world. Italy. Art. Interesting people. Sun that warmed everything.

Still, she swallowed back her feelings. She'd already decided her future was in her small town with her parents. Because she loved that world, too. She loved crisp autumns. Sleigh rides and skating in the winter. The love of people she knew. A quiet, humble place to raise a child.

It just seemed so unfair that she had to choose. But, really, she didn't have a choice. She was broke. Longing to live in two worlds was the last resort of a foolish woman. And she knew it was time to get sensible. The best way to do that would be to take the focus of this conversation off herself and get it back on him.

"Tell me more about your childhood." Changing her mind, she waved her hand to stop his response. "No. Tell me about Constanzo finding you. I've only ever heard bits and pieces of that story from Olivia. I'd love to hear it from your perspective."

He grinned sheepishly and glanced down at his empty salad plate. A waitress strolled over and said something in Italian before she poured him a second glass of wine and took his empty plate.

He sucked in a breath. "Imagine being exactly where you are right now financially, taking your last pennies and getting on a plane to another continent and literally swapping a painting every month for your rent."

She sighed dreamily. "It sounds romantic."

"It was terrifying."

"Yes, but at least you had something to barter. You had paintings that your landlord obviously wanted."

He sniffed a laugh. "Don't think he was being altruistic. I'm sure he's made a bundle off me."

"Maybe. But you still had something to trade."

"Right. After I bought the canvases and paint." He shook his head. "I was always scrambling for odd jobs, in a country I didn't know, as I learned to speak the language."

The breeze lifted the hair around his shoulders and

she saw the tip of the webbed wing of his dragon tattoo, the sexy contrast to the quiet, calm man before her. Totally captivated by his smooth voice and his cool sophistication in the white shirt that accented his olive skin, she put her elbow on the table and her chin on her fist. "So what happened?"

He lifted his wineglass. "Constanzo bartered Tucker into paving the way for us to meet."

"So he'd already found you?"

Antonio nodded. "Yes. But he was clumsy about it. He'd chased my mom out of his office when she told him she was pregnant and she'd disappeared, gone to America without even telling her family where she was going. Humiliated, she clearly didn't want anyone to find her." He swirled the wine in his glass. "Her family didn't even know I existed. But Constanzo knew that somewhere in the world was a child he'd rejected and he knew our getting to know each other wasn't going to be easy."

"Wow."

"So Constanzo enlisted Tucker's help, but it was actually Olivia who brought me into the fold."

"I don't understand."

"Tucker is like a bull in a china shop. Very much like my dad. Olivia appealed to me as a person. We connected immediately."

She smiled. She could see Olivia and Antonio connecting. She saw signs of their closeness every time they were together. Until he'd stopped painting, they'd been totally in sync about his career. They connected like friends, not romantically, the way Laura Beth was drawn to him. But that was probably why it had been so easy for Antonio and Olivia. They were friends only, while she and Antonio had an attraction flipping back and forth between them, a longing to be close that actually somehow kept them separated.

"So how did they spring it on you that you were the long-lost son of a billionaire?"

"My cousin Maria had apparently figured everything out." He laughed. "Maria makes bulls in china shops look tame. So rather than risk that she'd bulldoze the information into a conversation, they told me at my first showing here in Italy."

She winced. "Yikes."

"It was weird. But Constanzo had been involved in the preparations for the showing right from the beginning as backer. So I'd gotten to know him a bit, and when they told me he was my dad, instead of that resulting in confusion, it just sort of pulled everything together."

The warm breeze ruffled past again, drawing her gaze to the square, the tourists and street vendors. "That's nice."

"What about you?"

Her gaze snapped over to his. Asking about his dad was supposed to keep the conversation off her. Now, here he was, bringing it back to her again. "Me?"

"Any odd stories in your life?"

"Unless you count the story of me getting pregnant, my life has been simple. Uncomplicated." She shrugged. "Which is why I'm simple, silly Laura Beth."

"Have you ever thought that being simple, being honest, being kind is a good thing?"

Her breath stuttered into her lungs. This was why she was falling head over heels in love with him. He didn't just like her as she was. He made her feel that who she was was more than enough. It was special. And she was so hungry to be special that she gobbled up his compliments like gelato.

"I used to."

"You should start believing it again." He took her hand and she froze. The way he touched her always sent a zing of excitement through her, but it also always felt right. Natural. As if the two of them had been created to touch and love and talk.

"To me, you are wonderful."

If she still had a sliver of her heart left, he took it with those words. And the horrible truth hit her. She wasn't falling in love with Antonio. She was already totally gone. So in love with him that when she had to leave, her heart would dissolve into a puddle of sadness.

CHAPTER TEN

GETTING READY FOR bed that night, she once again forced herself to face reality. She truly loved Antonio, and she believed he loved her too. Not the head-over-heels way she loved him, or the way he'd loved Gisella, but in a quieter, gentler way.

But he didn't *want* to love her. She saw the hesitation in his eyes every time he pulled his hands back, stepped away from her, turned away rather than kiss her. His wife might be dead, but she was very much alive in Antonio's heart. If he loved Laura Beth, and she believed he did, it wouldn't be the same way Tucker adored Olivia or Ricky worshipped Eloise. It would be a quiet, simple, you-are-second-best kind of love.

She let that realization wash over her because it would dictate every decision she made from now until she boarded a plane and left him…left this beautiful place.

Knowing that he had feelings for her, she could push him to admit them. She could promise him the one thing he truly wanted—his ability to paint. She could be his muse forever.

She would win him. Win a place in his life.

But even if he asked her to marry him, she would always be second-best.

Was winning the object of her love, getting to be with the man she loved, worth never being in first place in anyone's life?

She didn't know. Right now, just the thought of leaving him, or only seeing him at friends' functions, where he'd be distantly polite to her, shattered her heart. She wasn't even sure she could walk away. As much as she needed her mom's help, she also needed Antonio. She needed to hear him say she was special. She needed the feeling of purpose he'd inspired in her.

But she also needed to be someone's one true love.

And Antonio had had his one true love.

Antonio refused to work on Sunday, so it was Monday morning before they headed to the studio again. Knowing they would be working, she'd worn the black dress and spike heels, wound her hair into the fancy hairdo and put on makeup.

He raced down the cobblestone path. "Today is the day I get you on canvas."

She laughed. "Really? All in one day?"

"I'll do a slight pencil drawing today and from here on out you won't need to pose every day, just when I want to be reminded of something."

"Sounds good."

It really didn't sound good. It sounded like the beginning of the end. Still, she kept up the happy facade as he chose canvas, found pencils and went to work.

But he cursed at his first attempts to sketch her. He took digital pictures and studied the light, the angle of her head, shoulders and torso. But nothing pleased him. By noon, he was annoyed with himself, and they quit for the day.

Tuesday, he got angry. He'd drawn plenty of versions

of her, had captured the look he wanted in his initial drawings, but none of the sketches on canvas caught the look he wanted to show the world.

On Wednesday, she tried talking. So what if her face was moving? He wasn't getting anything he liked anyway. And when she talked, she usually calmed him or inspired him. But that day it didn't help.

As he ran an eraser over the shadowy pencil lines he'd made, her purpose shivered through her. The one thing she really wanted out of life—the one memory she wanted to hold in her heart to prove her time had meant something—was to pull him out of his anger, his funk, and get him painting again, and she was failing.

So she asked about Constanzo and let Antonio relax as he talked about his dad, about the success of his first showing and his rapid rise in the world of art. But he still sighed heavily and tossed that morning's canvas out the back door as if it were trash.

She wondered if sweet, wonderful Gisella had ever seen his little fits of temper, and had to hold back a gasp. They'd never spoken about his wife! They'd never even brushed against the real reason he didn't paint. And she suddenly saw the mistake in that. By ignoring that they were, in effect, trying to put a bandage on an open wound. She'd brought him this far by being someone he wanted to paint, but what if that was only half the battle? What if he needed to talk out some of his pain? What if he needed to face the sadness inside him before he could actually use his talent to the fullest?

As he set another canvas on the easel, she swallowed. Sucked in a breath. Prayed for strength. And finally said, "So is this what happened when you stopped painting?"

He peered over. "Excuse me?"

"Did you try canvas after canvas and toss them aside?"

He bristled. "Yes."

"So tell me about it."

"No."

She sighed. "Look, I get it that you can't paint because you lost the love of your life. I just lost a boyfriend who didn't really like me and it hurt like hell. But you lost the love of your life. You need to address that."

His expression shifted from angry to confused. Twice, he opened his mouth to say something. Twice, he stopped himself.

"What?"

He licked his lips and turned away. "Nothing."

Purpose rattled through her again. She needed to get him to admit he'd quit painting because without his wife his art had no meaning. He needed to say the words. Needed those words to come out into the open so he could face them. "It's not nothing. It's *something*. Tell me."

"I don't want to talk about it."

"Look, this…me posing for you…is all about you getting your mojo back. So we've hit an impasse." She glanced down at her black dress and heels, then smiled up at him. "I helped you through the last one by recreating the look that inspired you. Now I'm sensing that it's your wife—your love for your wife—that's holding you back. I don't think I'm wrong. You need to talk about it."

He tossed his pencil to the metal desk, massaged his forehead, then laughed slightly. "No."

A minute went by in complete silence, but eventually he picked up a pencil and began drawing a light outline on the canvas.

Desperation filled her, but so did a realization. In

falling for him so quickly, she'd forgotten his real pain. Maybe the first move was actually hers. "I don't think I ever told you I was sorry."

He peeked away from his work, across the room at her. "For what?"

"That you lost your wife." She paused a second. Though forcing him to talk about his wife was the right thing to do, it hurt. Gisella was the reason he would never love her. And she gave herself a space of time to acknowledge that pain before she said, "She was beautiful."

He turned his attention back to the canvas. "Yes. She was."

Laura Beth swallowed hard. "And special."

He said nothing.

"Please. I think you need to talk about her."

"No."

"My gram told me one of the hardest things about losing my pap was that after a few weeks people stopped talking about him. She longed to remember him, to keep his memory alive, and people seemed to forget him."

"Laura Beth, please. That's enough."

"I just want you to know that you can talk about her with me."

He stepped away from the canvas, his spine stiff, his eyes narrow. Irritation vibrated from him across the room to her. "Dear God! Will you just let it drop?"

She snapped her mouth shut. She knew he might not be eager to talk about Gisella, but she hadn't expected him to get angry. "I'm sorry. I just desperately want this for you. I want you to be able to paint again."

Antonio's fingers tightened on his pencil. He realized she was trying to help him relax by what she considered to be a logical method, but she had no way of knowing her comments about his wife were actually doing more harm than good.

Still, it wasn't her fault. No one knew the real story, his real pain, and though he would die before he would admit his failings, he could at least let Laura Beth know she wasn't at fault.

"Look, my wife wasn't exactly what everyone thought."

"Okay."

Again a soft word filled with regret. He shifted a bit, putting himself solidly behind the canvas. He hated the self-loathing in her voice. Hated that he was responsible for it. He might not be able to tell her the whole story, but he could tiptoe around enough facts that she'd stop feeling bad.

"I'm not angry with you. I've simply never spoken about my wife with anyone."

"I still think you should."

He sniffed a laugh. "Honestly, *carissima*, I don't know what I'd say."

"Why don't you just tell me the truth?"

The truth would probably scandalize her. But he suddenly noticed that his pencil was moving with easy efficiency. The image he captured was perfect. His vision. Exactly what he wanted.

He didn't know if it was the pose or the distraction of talking or even the power of the topic, but he was working…effortlessly. And he couldn't break the spell, ruin the moment or lose the opportunity.

"I wish I could tell you the truth." As the words spilled out and the picture before him began to take shape, something inside his chest loosened. A weird kind of excitement nudged his heart, and he wondered if she was right. Did he need to talk about his wife to let his anger with her go?

His pencil paused. He glanced over at Laura Beth. He might need to talk, but was Laura Beth—was anyone—ready to hear what he had to say? "The story of my marriage is not a happy one."

She frowned and the look he'd been trying to capture flitted over her features, filled her eyes. A longing so intense it shifted every muscle in her face, darkened her eyes.

His pencil began to move again, feverishly, desperate to get that expression.

"You weren't happy?"

"Is anybody ever really happy?"

"Don't talk in abstracts when you know the truth. Olivia and Tucker are happy. Content. Eloise and Ricky are happy. You know happy. You know what it looks like. So you know if you were happy or not."

Absorbed in his work, more grateful that he was succeeding than antsy about the conversation, he said, "Then we were not."

"Then I'm sorry." She waited a beat before she said, "Want to tell me what happened?"

As his pencil captured the fine details that made Laura Beth who she was, he weighed his options. Sunlight pouring in from the wall of windows gave the quiet room the feel of a sacred space. A time and place he could be honest. Having been left by the father of her child, if anyone could understand his situation, it would be Laura Beth.

And if telling her the truth was what he needed to do to rid himself of the demons that tormented him, then so be it.

He cut right to the chase, didn't mince words, but

was as honest, as open, as she'd asked him to be. "My wife ran around on me and aborted my child."

The words that sounded so simple, so reasonable, in his head leveled him. His wife had gotten rid of his baby. Made a mockery of his naive love for her. Made him a fool. And now the words were out in the open, hanging on the air.

Behind the canvas, he squeezed his eyes shut, ran his angry fingers along his forehead. What was he doing?

He heard a soft swish, then saw Laura Beth's long legs approaching before she appeared at his side.

"I am so sorry."

A piece of her dark hair had fallen loose from its pins and framed her face. Her green eyes filled with sadness.

"I shouldn't have told you."

"What? That your marriage was a mess?"

"That my marriage was a lie. And I was a fool."

She stepped closer, examining his face. "All this time, I thought you were mourning her." She shook her head as if confused. "Everybody thought you'd been so sad these past years because you mourned her."

"Not her, my child. To the world she was an icon. But I lived the truth. She was a narcissist, who did everything she did not out of love or compassion but to make herself look important." He caught Laura Beth's gaze. "For two years I've been trapped. I couldn't tell the world who or what she was and yet I couldn't live the lie."

Her face softened. "Oh, Antonio."

Turning away from her, he grabbed a cloth and wiped his hands.

"You should talk about this with Olivia. She knows all about being forced to live a lie."

He shook his head. "I don't really want anyone to know."

"I know."

He sniffed a laugh.

"So maybe, since you started opening up, you should keep going." She paused, waited for him to look at her. "Get it off your shoulders."

Her honest eyes beckoned. The feeling of something loosening in his chest shuddered through him again and he knew she was right. He'd started the story. He needed to finish it.

"A year after we were married, she scheduled a trip for her charity. I'd lost her itinerary, so I went into her computer to find it and what I found was an identical itinerary for a man. She had an explanation, of course, so I felt foolish for accusing her."

He walked away from the easel. "Dear God, she held that first accusation over my head every time I questioned something she said or did. She'd remind me of how bad I felt over that mistake and I'd back off. For months, I believed lie after lie. Then she began to get careless. Her lies weren't as tight. Newspaper pictures of her with one man became commonplace. I saw the smiles that passed between them. I *saw* the intimacy. Until eventually I got so angry I went through the documents in her computer in earnest and that's when I found the abortion."

Laura Beth squeezed her eyes shut. "I'm so sorry, Antonio."

"She denied it. But I told her I had seen the appointment on her calendar, the check that paid the clinic. She told me that her life was her charity and she didn't want any time taken away from that for any reason. She said she wasn't cut out to be a mom. I exploded and told her

I wanted to be a dad and she laughed. That's when I knew our marriage was over." He tossed a rag to the table. "I don't believe she ever loved anyone as much as she loved herself. The fact that she didn't even give me an option with our child proved she never thought beyond herself."

"I'm so sorry."

"You needn't be. She taught me some valuable lessons. People change. Love doesn't last." He sniffed a laugh. "Trust no one."

The room grew quiet. Antonio heard the click of her heels again. When he turned she was right behind him.

"She didn't deserve you."

He sniffed a laugh.

"I'm serious."

"I have my faults."

"Oh, don't I know it. But I still think you're special." She caught his gaze. "Wonderful."

The magnetic pull of her innocent green eyes drew him to her. An inch. Then two. Then his hands were close enough that he could lay them on her warm shoulders. His mouth was close enough that he could touch his lips to hers.

As if thought gave birth to action, he closed the distance between them and brushed his lips across hers. Laura Beth edged closer too. Her lips were warm and sweet. The way she kissed him, answering the moves of his mouth slowly, hesitantly, then completely, spoke of submission. Honesty. A change in the way she felt about him, the way she related to him. She was taking the step that would shift them from friends to so much more.

He slid his tongue along the seam of her lips and when she opened to him he deepened the kiss.

CHAPTER ELEVEN

LAURA BETH SURRENDERED to the urgent prodding of Antonio's mouth. Desperate, shivering with need, she pressed into him as he pulled her closer.

He didn't mourn his wife.

He did want her.

She could be the love of his life.

Except he didn't trust.

The cell phone in his pocket began to chime out a happy beat. Antonio pulled away. Their gazes caught and held.

The phone rang again.

Antonio quietly said, "That ringtone is Bernice, my father's assistant. She never calls unless it's an emergency."

Laura Beth whispered, "You should take it."

As if in a trance, he nodded, retrieved the phone from his pocket and clicked the button to answer it. "Bernice? What's up?"

Because he'd put his phone on speaker, the voice of Constanzo's assistant erupted in the room. "Oh, Antonio! It's awful! Just awful!"

Laura Beth walked a few feet away. Her head spun—the truth about his life, his marriage, had shaken her to the core. It gave her a crazy kind of hope, even as it dashed her hopes. How could she expect to build a life with a man who couldn't trust?

Antonio said, "Hey. Calm down. Whatever my dad did, we can fix it."

"This isn't about a mistake." A sob escaped. "The ambulance just left. Your dad is on his way to the hospital. They think he had a heart attack."

Antonio stumbled to the chaise and collapsed on it. "A heart attack?"

Laura Beth gasped. "Oh, my God." All her other thoughts and troubles flitted away in a surge of worry about Constanzo.

"Yes! Hurry! Get to the hospital!"

He disconnected the call as Laura Beth walked to the door. "You give me directions and I'll drive."

Antonio raced out of the studio toward the house for keys. "*I'll* drive."

She didn't follow him, but ran to the garage. In less than a minute, Antonio joined her with his car keys. He jumped into the Lamborghini and Laura Beth climbed in too.

As he sped along the winding roads of the hills between his country house and Bogodehra, she wasn't sure it was wise for him to drive. But she was as desperate to get to the hospital as he was, and simply held onto the dashboard for support as they raced to the city.

When they finally arrived at the stucco building with loops of arches and fancy pillars, they jumped out and dashed inside.

Laura Beth's gaze winged from side to side as she took in the surroundings that were both familiar and unfamiliar. Department names were in Italian, but most of the words were close enough to English that she could translate. Still, the chatter of doctors, nurses, patients and patients' families in the area best described by an American as the emergency room was in Italian. Even Antonio spoke Italian when he reached a nurse's station.

Using the universal language of pointing, the nurse obviously told him to have a seat.

He sighed and faced Laura Beth. "We can't see him."

She caught his arm frantically. "We can't?"

He squeezed his eyes shut and Laura Beth realized she wasn't helping by panicking.

"They haven't yet gotten the word that he's stable."

Her heart dipped. Fear crept into her limbs and froze them. It was impossible for her to picture an event for one of Tucker and Olivia's kids without big, boisterous Constanzo Bartulocci, the man everyone thought of like a favorite uncle.

If she was this upset about Constanzo, she couldn't imagine Antonio's fright. Constanzo was his *father*. If her father was the one in this hospital right now, she'd be a basket case.

She tugged lightly on his arm and got him to a plastic seat. As if in a daze, he lowered himself to the chair. She sat beside him, but took his hand, keeping the connection, so he'd know he wasn't alone.

"My father and I haven't really spoken since we got back from Barcelona. When I did stop by, he said he was sorry for stranding us, but didn't want to talk about anything else. I never went over after that."

She smiled weakly, acknowledging that. "We've been busy."

He put his head back and rubbed his hand across his mouth. "I should have gone to see him again. I should have forced him to talk about that fight, or at least let him know I wasn't angry." He sighed. "Why are we always squabbling?"

She squeezed his hand and again her sense of purpose, of destiny, with Antonio filled her. All she had to do was listen to the easy way he confided in her, talked about such personal things, to know that he trusted her. He might not realize it, but she did.

"It's how you show love."

He sniffed a laugh. "Right. Either that or he hates me."

That admission further bolstered her belief that there was more between them than friendship, more between them than a few kisses. And she knew she was the person to help him through this crisis.

"He doesn't hate you. If he did, he wouldn't meddle."

Antonio shut his eyes. "He always meddles."

"Yeah, but I think his intentions are good. I'm sure Tucker and Olivia were glad he forced them to come to Italy together to find you."

He sniffed a laugh. "Such a matchmaker and a do-gooder."

"Lots of people would be glad their dad looks for ways to help other people."

"I am. Most days I'm proud of him." He sighed and closed his eyes. "I wish I'd told him that."

She tightened her hold on his hand. "I'm sure he knows."

"By my yelling at him?"

"By the fact that you're honest with each other." She thought of her parents back in Kentucky. "I wish I could be so open with my parents."

He turned his head and studied her. "You're not?"

"I haven't yet told them I'm pregnant." She shrugged. "I'm afraid of their reaction. I don't think you and Constanzo hold important things back. Even if you do sometimes get loud when you talk."

Antonio's eyes softened. "Have you even called your parents?"

Knowing the distraction of a different topic might be good for him, she said, "Yes. Once. I let them know I was here in Italy."

"Why haven't you told them?"

"I guess deep down I'm afraid of what they'll say. They'd wanted me to become a doctor or a lawyer and start a practice in our small town." She sighed. "But I wanted something more."

"Something more?"

Knowing she was doing a good job of keeping Antonio occupied, she decided to be honest, to continue the conversation that held his nerves at bay. "That's the bad part. I couldn't even give them a description of what I wanted. All I could tell them was I had this feeling in my soul that I was meant to do something wonderful with my life."

He winced. "But you couldn't tell them what."

"No. And now I'm returning educated but not employable." She shook her head.

"Hey, Olivia says Tucker has a job for you."

"But what if he doesn't? There aren't a lot of jobs for IT people in Starlight, Kentucky. So I'll end up being somebody's glorified secretary. I'll be coming back a failure and pregnant."

His gaze slowly met hers. "Some people would consider a child a blessing."

She swallowed. Caught in the fierce light in his dark eyes, she could almost read his thoughts. He had lost a child because his wife hadn't thought beyond her own needs. Antonio himself was born to an unmarried mother, the product of the same kind of mistake Laura

Beth had made. It was important that Antonio know she did not consider her baby a mistake.

"My child is a blessing. I don't know why I got pregnant, but I believe in destiny. This little boy or girl has a purpose."

"What if his or her purpose is only to sweep streets?"

She laughed. "Destiny is about more than a job."

"You should tell that to yourself some time."

She frowned.

"You're so concerned that without a law degree or medical license your parents will consider you're a failure. What if your destiny is to be the mother of the surgeon who makes the next great medical advancement or the architect who builds the next Sistine Chapel? What if your destiny is simply to be this child's mom?"

As she thought about that, a smile bloomed. "I get it."

"And even if his destiny isn't to be great—even if his destiny is to sweep streets—he's still important."

She squeezed Antonio's hand. "I know. All along there's been something inside me that happily responded to the idea of raising a child. I won't let him down."

Antonio ran his free hand down his face again. Though the conversation had distracted him for a few minutes, his nervousness had returned.

A doctor in green scrubs walked to the nurse's station. The same nurse who'd relegated Antonio to a plastic seat pointed at him again. The doctor walked over.

Still clinging to Laura Beth's hand, Antonio rose.

The doctor began to speak in Italian. Antonio quickly cut him off. "English for my friend?"

The doctor nodded. "My English not perfect." He

smiled at Laura Beth. "But good enough. Your father's heart attack was mild, but we'll be running some tests. If all goes well, in a few days he will go home with medicine."

"If all doesn't go well?"

"Probably a bypass." The doctor smiled. "And a diet."

Antonio shook his head. He said, "Lucky old coot," but Laura Beth could feel the tension draining from him. "Can we see him?"

Making some notes on a chart, the doctor said, "Yes. I'm sure it will be a few minutes before he's wheeled out for testing."

Laura Beth and Antonio walked to Constanzo's cubicle hand in hand. Even before they reached it, they could hear the rumble of Constanzo's deep voice as he barked out complaints that his bed was too hard and he wanted a sandwich.

Pushing open the privacy curtain, Antonio said, "Too many sandwiches are what got you here."

As if glad for the reprieve, the nurses scrambled out of the cubicle.

Constanzo's eyes lit. "Laura Beth," he said, turning his pleading gaze on her, "I almost died. Tell my son to be kind to me."

She laughed, but the oddest feelings poured through her. In what should be a very private moment between a father and son, she didn't feel out of place. In fact, she felt as if she belonged here. But more than that, it felt right, perfect, that Antonio held her hand. Turned to her for comfort. Gave her advice when she tried to distract him. Liked her.

Her heart stumbled a bit as he released her hand and walked to the head of Constanzo's bed. Even though neither of them had said it, she and Antonio loved each other. Not in the way they'd loved Bruce or Gisella. But in a deep, profound way.

She was the real love of his life and he was hers.

And as soon as Constanzo was better, she would prove it to him.

With Constanzo safe in the hospital, his private doctors on the scene and a battery of tests ordered, Antonio's stress level fell. By the time they left the hospital, the sun had set. The air had cooled, but not so much that they had to put the Lamborghini's top up. He and Laura Beth didn't talk, but they didn't need to. She'd pushed him to tell the truth about Gisella and he'd forced her to admit why she'd really run to Italy. She might want to return to Starlight to raise her child, but she wasn't looking forward to the conversation she had to have with her parents. She didn't want to return to her home-town a failure.

Still, they were both on the road to recovery in their respective life crises. Now they could get on with their lives.

Already he felt strong again. Having learned his lessons about weakness, about letting anyone get too close, he'd never go through that kind of pain again. Just as Laura Beth would never again let herself be taken in by a man. She'd raise her child in her hometown and be happy.

He could picture it. He could see her in a big house with a homey kitchen and a yard full of green grass for a growing child. He smiled at the vision, but his smile quickly faded. He should have a three-year-old right now. A toddler to teach and dote on. Someone to make Constanzo smile. Someone who might grow up to be a garbageman or doctor. It wouldn't matter. He would have been Antonio's heart.

The Lamborghini roared up the driveway and, filled with indescribable pain, Antonio drove it into the garage. He and Laura Beth piled out unceremoniously. Though it was late, Rosina met them at the door to the kitchen.

"How is Mr. Constanzo?"

"He's fine."

Antonio's usually calm and collected housekeeper all but collapsed with relief.

His eyes narrowed as he directed her back into the kitchen. Her reaction had been more than a little extreme and he almost cursed the stupidity, the fruitlessness of his life. Servants who got involved in their lives like family—because they saw more of their household staff than the real world. Money. Talent. Fame. None of it mattered! He wanted his child.

"I will make sandwiches and you will tell me everything?"

He almost told her he wasn't hungry. He wanted to be alone. To lick his wounds. To roar with anger. But a glance at Laura Beth reminded him he had responsibilities. Not just to feed his probably starving guest, but to his staff. Rosina wanted information. He needed to give it to her.

"Sandwiches would be good."

Laura Beth took the stool beside his at the center island. As Rosina cut bread and assembled cold cuts, they told her everything the doctors had said. Reassured, and her job done, Rosina shuffled off to her quarters behind the kitchen.

"She likes him."

Antonio glanced over at her. "Really?"

"When your dad came to the house the night he and I flew to Barcelona, I saw looks pass between them. I got the distinct impression she'd called him and told him I was bored with nothing to do. Now I wonder if it isn't more than that."

"So all this time I thought my dad was a meddler, I actually have two meddlers in my life?"

She playfully swatted his arm. "You're missing the big picture. I think your head housekeeper is in love with your dad!"

He shook his head. "Poor Rosina."

"Why? Your dad is great. I think he and Rosina would make a cute couple."

"I think she's wishing on a star if she thinks that's ever going to happen."

His negativity surprised Laura Beth. When she peeked over at him, she saw something in his eyes she'd never seen before. She'd always known he was wounded. She'd believed the loss of his beloved wife had leveled him. Now she knew it was more than that. That he'd fallen out of love with his wife long before her death, when he'd lost a child. And something about this situation seemed to be bringing it all back for him.

Carefully, quietly, she said, "He wouldn't want anything to do with her because of her class? Because she's the maid?"

"Because he's in his seventies and he's never even slowed down, let alone settled down. The one woman who might have caught him with her pregnancy—with me—he summarily dismissed from his life. If she's in love with him, Rosina will get her heart broken, because my dad can't settle down."

She tried to make the connection. Was there something about Constanzo deserting Antonio's mom and the loss of Antonio's own child that connected? What could have made him so angry?

They finished their sandwiches and a hush fell over the kitchen. Her mind skipped back to the studio, to how they'd been kissing when Antonio got the call. With Constanzo in no real danger, would they pick up where they'd left off?

Antonio caught her hand. "You must be tired."

She swallowed. "Truthfully, I haven't had enough time to think about it today."

Their gazes met. He smiled and she could almost hear the question he wanted to ask. *Will you come to my room with me?* They'd been on the verge of making love and everything inside her wanted to go with him, to give herself to him, to take away his pain.

She waited for him to ask the question.

His eyes darkened as he studied her face.

The urge rose up to bridge the gap between them and kiss him. To make the first move.

But that silly shy fear of hers filled her. She needed to know—it had to be *clear* that he wanted her.

He released her fingers and pulled back. "I'll see you in the morning."

Confusion filled her. For all the times and ways he'd confided, telling her what troubled him tonight should be easy. They should be heading for his room together, talking things out, making love. Instead, he was walking away.

He stopped at the kitchen door and faced her. "With Constanzo having tests in the morning, maybe we could get in a few hours in the studio before we go to the hospital?"

The studio. She'd gotten him to tell her about his wife

in the studio. Whatever the cause of this new sadness, she could get it out of him tomorrow.

They ate breakfast quietly. Clearly believing his father was in good hands, Antonio ate toast while reading the paper. Laura Beth took slow, measured breaths. He wasn't upset this morning. But his dad had also had a heart attack the day before. Maybe the sadness she was so sure she'd seen while they'd eaten sandwiches had been nothing more than sadness over nearly losing Constanzo? Maybe she'd made a mountain out of a molehill?

She slipped away while he finished his second cup of coffee and raced upstairs to slip into the black dress and spike heels. The dining room was empty when she returned, so she headed for the studio.

She found him assembling brushes and paints and simply headed for the chaise.

"Ready?" He peeked from behind the canvas and laughed. "Ah. Not just ready, ahead of me."

She smiled, but her lips wobbled. Something about the mood in the room didn't feel right. How could he have been so utterly sad the day before and be almost happy today?

"Is that bad?"

"I like eagerness in a woman."

He was trying to sound light and flippant, but having spent so much time with him Laura Beth noticed the strain in his voice. Her fears came crashing back. As any child would, he'd been upset about his father the day before, but something else had happened.

"Could you straighten the fabric at your back? There's a kink I don't like."

She nodded and reached behind her to find the unwanted fold in her dress, but couldn't reach it.

"Here. Let me."

He walked over. As he pushed her long hair out of the way, she could feel his fingers skim across her back. She drew in a quick breath. Pinpricks of excitement danced along her flesh.

Looking over her shoulder at him, she raised her eyes to meet his and his fingers stopped as their gazes met.

"You're very beautiful."

And here it was. The real truth between them. He found her beautiful. He saw her in a way no man ever had. And it didn't just thrill her. It seemed to set her free. To turn her into the woman she wanted to be.

"You're very handsome."

His fingers moved from the fabric and traced a line up her shoulder. Warm and sure, his hand flattened on her back as the other went to her waist to turn her to him.

Neither waited for the other to move. His head came down as she rose up a bit to meet him and their lips met in a reunion of delicious passion. Wave after wave of heavenly delight flooded her as their kiss went on and on.

When she would have thought he'd move away, he caught her by the shoulders and deepened the kiss. She met his fierce kiss with her own fierceness. When he pulled back, his mouth fell to her neck, skimming wet kisses along the line of her collarbone.

She shuddered as her eyes closed in ecstasy. "I love you."

The words came out naturally, easily. Still, she wasn't surprised when he stopped kissing her. This was momentous for them. They might have been tumbling to this point for weeks, but neither had ever said the words. She opened her eyes and smiled expectantly. But instead of the sheen of passion or the warmth of love, pain filled his eyes.

He gazed at her longingly, as if she held the secrets to his happiness, but he said, "I don't love you."

For thirty seconds, her ears rang with the silence, then as the reality of what he'd said sank in, her heart exploded in her chest. An indescribable ache radiated to every part of her body. The words *I don't believe you* sprang to her tongue, but she cursed them. When would she ever learn she was Laura Beth Matthews, simple girl? Not glamour girl like Eloise or earth mother like Olivia. But plain Laura Beth Matthews, IT person who couldn't find a job, and who was never going to be loved with passion.

She pulled away from him. "I see."

"I don't think you do."

He reached for her but she shook him off. Thank God for good, old-fashioned American pride. Her chin lifted. Her thoughts cleared.

"I understand very well." She caught his gaze, working to hide the pain that sliced through her, cutting her to the core, making her feel like the world's biggest idiot. "A lot more than you think." She drew in a calming breath, telling herself she could scream or cry or whatever she wanted to do as soon as he was gone. But right now she had to get him away from her. "Go see your father."

He stepped back. Confusion clouded his dark brown eyes.

So she smiled. Though it physically hurt to force her lips upward and to hold back her tears, she managed because she refused, absolutely refused to look like a fool in front of another man. "I think we both need a little time to cool off before we get back to the painting, and your dad's going to be griping at the nurses." She studied the lines of his aristocratic face, the wild black hair, the set of his jaw. He would say she was memorizing him, and maybe she was. Because she knew this would be the last time she saw him.

The pain of that sliced through her, but she ignored it. She took another step back. "You better go rescue them."

He ran his hand along the back of his neck as if confused. "What are we doing?"

She had no idea what he was doing, but she was leaving. He was a brilliant but broken man, and she'd walked right into the trap of loving him, thinking she could help him when clearly she couldn't.

"We need a cooling-off period and you should be checking up on your dad." She lifted her chin again and smiled shakily. "I need some time."

"I'm sorry—"

She cut him off. "Don't make this any weirder than it already is. I'm fine. I misinterpreted what was going on between us." She shrugged. "It happens all the time. No big deal. I just need a break. And you going to see your dad is the best way for me to get myself together."

Antonio's heart seized at the loss of her as she stormed out of the studio, but he let her go. Because it was for her good. He was an angry, bitter man, mourning the loss not of a deceitful wife but a child. And she was a naive young pregnant woman who'd already gotten involved with the wrong man once.

He wouldn't tie her to him, but more than that, he wouldn't taint the experience of her first child with his wounds, his regrets.

CHAPTER TWELVE

LAURA BETH CALLED Bernice and within an hour Constanzo's plane was ready for her at the private airstrip. She climbed the steps. At the top she paused, taking one final look at the beautiful Italian countryside.

Bernice had tried to talk her out of leaving, but she'd explained that her mind was made up. She said goodbye to Rosina and drove herself to the airstrip, leaving Antonio's car to be picked up by staff.

Strapping herself into the plane seat, she remembered flying to Italy, eating French toast, falling asleep beside Antonio, who'd put a cover over her. Her heart lurched, but the memory of his rejection poured through her. Dear God. She'd never been so surprised. She'd been so sure he'd say he loved her too.

Straightening in her seat, she scolded herself for letting herself remember even one minute of their time together. She'd had warning after warning that he wasn't ready for what she needed. Twice he'd stepped back rather than kiss her. He hadn't wanted her to go to Barcelona. Yet she'd ignored every signal he sent because he was a wounded man, so desperately in need of love that, of course, she'd longed to love him. Handsome, talented and desperate for love, he'd been just a little too much to resist.

Pain threatened to overwhelm her, but she shoved it down. She had responsibilities and realities of her own, and she'd come to her senses. After one quick pass of her hand over her tummy, she snuggled into a blanket, intending to fall asleep. But tears welled in her eyes. Her chest heaved. And sobs overtook her.

Alone on a plane with no one to see or hear her, she gave in and let herself weep.

On the ground in Kentucky, she rented a car. When she used her check card to pay for it, she discovered she didn't merely have the full salary Constanzo had promised her, but Antonio's father had also ponied up the promised severance pay.

She called Bernice to have it taken back, but Bernice laughed. "Are you kidding? Constanzo is happy to be alive. He's so generous right now that I'm surprised he didn't double it. He'll never take it back. Besides, he gave orders for the money to be given to you weeks ago, when you first arrived. No matter when you left that money was going to you…so it's yours."

Though Constanzo's generosity was a bit overboard, Laura Beth understood that he felt he owed her. Helping her set up her new life was probably how he'd deal with her leaving. He needed to know she'd be okay and money was his tool. So maybe it would be best to just take what he offered. She'd fulfilled at least part of her duties to Constanzo by helping Antonio clear out his office and getting him to a gallery opening. She'd also gotten him painting again—Constanzo's real goal. So, yeah. She could understand why Constanzo had been so generous.

Plus, the money meant she could move on. Never see Antonio again.

That filled her heart with pain. She let herself feel

it as a reminder that she never wanted to be so foolish again, but she didn't really need a reminder. In her heart, she knew she'd never love another man the way she loved Antonio.

She arrived at her parents' house a little before dawn. She made coffee and pancakes, and, as she expected, the scents woke her mom and dad and her two brothers.

As hugs were exchanged, she swallowed hard. She didn't want to ruin this reunion, but she knew it was time to accept her fate and do what needed to be done.

When everyone had a few pancakes on their plates, she smiled at the group. "I have some news."

Her tall, strapping construction worker dad laughed, and said, "You're staying in Italy," as if it were a foregone conclusion.

She shook her head. "No. No more Italy. I'm actually home for good. I got a huge severance from the gentleman who'd hired me. I can afford to buy a house here."

Her mom clutched her chest. "You're back?"

She nodded. "For good."

Then her mom surprised her. "Oh, sweetie, we love you and we love the idea of you living in town with us—" she caught Laura Beth's gaze "—but you wanted so much more for yourself. A big-time career. Are you going to be happy here?"

Laura Beth swallowed as unhappiness swelled in her. Still, it wasn't the big-time career she would miss. It was Antonio. The real love of her life. But how could she explain that to her parents when she was pregnant with another man's child? Worse, how could she explain that when Antonio didn't feel for her what she felt her him?

She couldn't. Her love for Antonio would have to stay her hidden secret. Another cross to bear.

For her parents' sake, she brightened when she said,

"Yes, I'll be very happy here, because I have a child to raise."

At her parents' confused look, she said, "I'm pregnant. Bruce doesn't want to marry me, but I'm okay with that. I don't love him either." An arrow pierced her heart again when she thought of the man she did love, but she ignored it. "And with the severance pay I got from Mr. Bartulocci, I can buy a house and support myself until after the baby's born. Then I may need to take some courses, like accounting, so I can find a job around here." She squeezed her mom's hand. "But it's all good."

Nothing was good. Antonio glanced around the private suite they'd given his dad, at the rows and rows of flowers that covered every flat surface in the room, and even parts of the floor. Still, his father grumbled.

"It's hot in here."

"It's almost June. It's supposed to be hot."

"I want to see Laura Beth."

Pain squeezed Antonio's heart, but he forced himself not to show it. When he'd returned to the house the day before, her room had been empty. Rosina knew nothing, though her crying suggested otherwise. He'd had to call Bernice before he got the news that she'd taken the plane and gone to Kentucky.

"She went home."

Constanzo kicked his covers around, trying to get comfortable, but obviously failing. "I can't believe she went home. What did you say? What did you do?"

"Interesting how you assume I somehow drove her off."

"Didn't you?"

He had. He knew he had. But this was none of his father's business. Plus, there were bigger issues in Laura Beth's life than a heartbreak from a guy who hadn't deserved her love.

He sucked in a breath and faced his father. "She's pregnant."

Constanzo stopped struggling. "Oh, my God! How did I raise you to let the mother of your child go? Did you learn nothing from my mistakes?"

Antonio shook his head. "It's not my baby."

Constanzo's eyes narrowed. "Is this why she was so eager to come to Italy?"

Antonio nodded. "She needed some time to think things through and a place she could gather herself while she figured out what to do. You provided it."

"I am good that way."

Oh, how the man could turn anything to his favor! "You're a crabby old man."

"I anticipate!" Constanzo yelled, then he sucked in a long, slow breath. Antonio tensed, worried something was wrong, but Constanzo quietly said, "You are going to make me pay until the end of time, aren't you?"

Confused, Antonio caught his father's gaze. "What? What am I making you pay for this time?"

"Leaving you." He brushed his hand in dismissal. "No. That is not correct. You aren't making me pay for leaving you. You are making me pay for everything wrong that happened in your life after your mother died."

Antonio bristled. He did nothing but ask, "How high?" when his dad said, "Jump." He catered to his whims and wishes. Canceled plans. Made plans. How could Constanzo even hint that Antonio was somehow making him pay?

"That's insanity."

"Is it? You always hold yourself away. You love me but you won't give me love."

Antonio gaped at him. "Are you lying in a hospital bed, recovering from a heart attack, splitting hairs with me?"

Constanzo fussed with the covers. "Yes."

"You have got to be kidding me."

"I almost died. It gives a man clarity."

"Right."

"I am right! I want my son to love me and respect me. Not give me bits and pieces of affection."

"Maybe you should have thought of that before you kicked my mom out of your office."

"And there we have it."

Antonio shook his head and turned away from his dad. "I'm not having this conversation. I'm tired, I'm stressed and you're pushing me into saying things I don't mean."

"And why are you stressed? I'm the one who almost died."

Antonio tossed his hands in disgust. "There's no winning with you."

"There could be. All you have to do is love me like a dad, not like an enemy you're forced to interact with." When Antonio said nothing, he sighed. "Forgive me for not believing your mom."

Antonio squeezed his eyes shut.

"Then forgive Gisella for being a slut."

His eyes popped open and he spun to face his dad. "What?"

Constanzo laughed. "You think I don't know? You think my own daughter-in-law could flaunt her affairs in my favorite cities and word would not get back to me?"

Antonio rubbed his hand down his face.

"You carry the weight of betrayal like a good-luck charm. Something you're afraid to set down for fear if you do bad luck will return. Because I didn't trust your mom, you're afraid to trust me. And because Gisella humiliated you, you won't trust Laura Beth."

"If it were that simple, I think I could get beyond it."

"Then tell me the part that's complicated."

He blew out a breath. "Gisella aborted our child."

His dad blinked. "Oh."

"And Laura Beth is pregnant. I have mourned the loss of my child for two long years. I wake up most days knowing I should have a son or daughter playing in my yard. I cannot handle having a pregnant woman under my roof, and it isn't fair to subject her to my anger when she's not at fault."

Constanzo closed his eyes and shook his head. "I am so sorry."

"Why? It's not like you understand. You very easily let my mother go…then forgot her. Forgot *me*. How could you possibly understand my loss?"

"I think it's time I tell you what really happened with your mom."

Antonio slowly lifted his gaze to meet his dad's. "I'm not in the mood, Dad."

"But this is finally the right time. The only time. If you don't change now, I fear you will be gone for good."

Gobsmacked, he only stared at his dad. "*I* need to change?"

"Yes. Just listen." Constanzo cleared his throat and quietly said, "Your mother was a rebound relationship."

Antonio frowned. "I thought you'd been dating?"

"We had. I'd lost the love of my life and one day your mother happened to be at a club where I was socializing. We struck up a conversation. One thing led to another and she came home with me."

Antonio shook his head, not sure how the hell this was supposed to help him. "She was a one-night stand?"

"She was a rebound. I'd been ridiculously in love with a woman I thought loved me too. But she hadn't. She hadn't been with me for my money or for love. A rich heiress, she was simply biding time. Waiting for a better guy to come around."

"So you did the same thing with my mom."

He winced. "Yes. And after a few weeks, I let her go." He fussed with the covers. "Then a few weeks after that she came to me with the pregnancy story and I thought it was a ruse. A way to get back with me or get back at me."

"So you kicked her out of your office and forgot her because you were busy?"

Constanzo nodded. "And though it seemed like the right thing at the time, ten years later I suddenly realized what I'd done. If she really had been pregnant, I'd tossed away a child."

Antonio sniffed a laugh.

"Oh, you think you're so superior. But my loss of you is not so much different than the loss of your child. Except in my case I had a hand in things. But when a person comes to his senses and realizes he's thrown away his one chance at real happiness…" He paused, caught Antonio's gaze. "It more than hurts. Sometimes, it stops a life."

Antonio swallowed hard.

"Did you love Gisella?"

"At one time."

"But the love died?"

He glanced up at his dad. "I'm not sure she had any love for me to die."

"So you feel a fool?"

He drew in a long breath and expelled it quickly. "That sort of gets lost in the grief I feel over my child."

"And you don't see the second chance you've been handed?"

He frowned.

"You love Laura Beth."

He shook his head. "She's a very nice woman. Far too good to be dragged into my pit."

"Oh, pit, schmit."

"Excuse me?"

"Now you are splitting hairs. Maybe because you're afraid."

"Afraid? Hell, yes, I'm afraid. How do I know I won't see my baby every time I look at hers? How do I know I can be a good husband when the only chance I got to try resulted in failure?"

"Do you love Laura Beth?"

He squeezed his eyes shut. "I have feelings for her that are beyond expression. Sometimes when she's around it's comfortable. Other days, she makes me think. I can't imagine anyplace I'd go, anything I'd do that wouldn't be more fun if she was there."

Constanzo laughed. "Oh, my son. You have it bad and it scares you."

Antonio licked his suddenly dry lips. "I failed with a woman who seemed to be tailor-made for me—"

"Men like you and me, Antonio, we're not made for princesses or supermodels. We're high maintenance ourselves."

Antonio laughed.

"We are made for the Laura Beths of the world. The

women who bring sunshine. The women who make us stop and enjoy life. If you let her go, you will regret it for the rest of your days. But more than that, if you can't finally learn to forgive, the regret you have over her leaving will be nothing compared to the sadness you will find when you wake up one day and discover you created your own prison."

Antonio looked over at his dad. "You want me to forgive you?"

"For real this time. And I want you to forgive Gisella."

He sniffed a laugh. "She doesn't need my forgiveness."

Constanzo shook his head sadly. "No. But your tired soul needs the rest forgiving will give you." He patted the bed, asking for Antonio's hand. Antonio slid his hand over to his dad, who caught it and squeezed. "You lost a family, but Laura Beth is offering you another. Sometimes fate is weird like that. It cannot give you back what you lost, but sometimes it finds a replacement."

The room was quiet for a second, then Constanzo said, "If you don't take this chance, another might come along. Fate is generous. But do you want to lose Laura Beth? The real love of your life? Now that you've met her, everyone will pale compared to her. You might find happiness. But you will never again find this joy."

Antonio rose. He walked to the head of the bed, reached down and hugged his father. "I forgive you, you old coot."

Constanzo patted his back. "For real this time?"

He sucked in a breath. "For real this time."

"Thank you. Now, go get Laura Beth. I want the sound of small feet in our big houses."

* * *

Antonio drove his Lamborghini back home. He understood what his father was saying about his mom. He also felt a swell of regret for withholding forgiveness from his father. But going to get Laura Beth?

Even though he knew in his heart she was the one true love of his life, going to her with his heart in his hand was risky. He wasn't just afraid. He was unworthy. Despite his ability to forgive his dad, he couldn't trust. He didn't want to trust.

Too wired to do anything, he headed for his studio. He unlocked the old wooden door and went to the back room.

There on the easel was Laura Beth.

He hesitated as he walked to the pencil drawing that would become a painting. Her laughing eyes beckoned. He ran his finger down the line of her cheek. The problem wasn't fear that she'd hurt him as Gisella had. The problem was he feared she'd hurt him worse. What he felt for her went beyond the surface, beyond a desire for her beauty. He loved her in a way he never could have loved Gisella. With his whole heart and soul. And that's why he feared her.

Gisella could never have held that kind of power over him, which was why it was suddenly easy to forgive her.

Feeling free for the first time in years, he made his way back to the house and stepped into quiet. The kind of quiet that became an early grave if a man wasn't careful.

He walked upstairs, to his room, letting himself imagine the sounds of a child, a soothing lullaby from Laura Beth, the click of computer keys as he arranged for something totally American—a Disney vacation— and he laughed.

Maybe his dad was right? Maybe fate was giving him a second chance, with a different child. His child might be gone, but Laura Beth's baby needed a daddy.

His life would be so different with her. Noisy. Complicated. Rich.

All he had to do was get on his father's jet and find her.

Laura Beth dragged her mother to the fourth real estate appointment in as many days.

"There's no sidewalk," her mother groused. "I'm not coming to visit you if I'm going to get mud on my shoes every time I walk to your back door." She stopped, crossed her arms on her chest stubbornly. "Take pictures with that fancy phone of yours. I'll be in the car."

"Mom!" Laura Beth called after her mother, who strode back to the little blue car Laura Beth had bought the day before.

"You don't need me for this one," her mom yelled back as she opened the car door and slipped inside. "I've got a key. I'll listen to the radio and be fine."

Laura Beth sighed and turned to walk to the back door of the brand-new house. Of course it didn't have sidewalks. The contractor hadn't poured them yet. And since when was her mom so picky? For Pete's sake. She'd eagerly seen the other three houses, but it had been like wrestling a bear to get her to come with her to see this house, and when push came to shove she wouldn't even go inside.

Whatever. She was an adult now. Able to make a decision about a house without her mommy.

She marched to the back door, pushed it open and called, "Hello? Anybody here?" It was a stupid question, since the Realtor's red Cadillac was in the driveway. Of course, he was here.

Still, before she could call again, the kitchen caught her attention. Happy green wood cabinets with creamy granite countertops filled a huge room that spilled out into a family room section. She let her purse slide to the floor and walked a little farther inside. She could put a table in the area with the bay window that would let in the morning sun, and decorate the family room area with sturdy furniture to accommodate her baby.

Her baby.

Her heart fluttered a bit. In the past four days of refusing to think about Antonio, she'd spent a lot of time wondering about her baby, thinking about whether it was a boy or girl, knowing she had to get a house set up before he or she was born.

"Hello?" she called again, heading for the big formal dining room. Seeing the high ceilings, she immediately pictured Antonio painting. Not green walls or white trim. But a mural. He'd love this space.

Pain pinged through her and she shook her head, reminding herself she wasn't allowed to think about him.

"Hello?" She walked out of the dining room and into a living room with a huge stone fireplace. Her first thought was of Antonio insisting they buy some kind of funky furniture for the room, or maybe artifacts from a dig in Mongolia. She laughed and this time reminded herself more sternly that she wasn't allowed to think about him. But that only caused her to realize the reason she kept thinking about him was that the house was probably out of her price range. Constanzo had been generous, but he wasn't an idiot. He hadn't given her enough to buy a mansion. And though Tucker had called and offered her a job, she fully intended to be wise with her money and not overspend.

As she walked up the sweeping stairway to the second floor, she knew beyond a shadow of a doubt that she couldn't afford this house. Searching for the real estate agent, she knew she had to tell him that she didn't want it. The place was huge. The master bedroom alone could fit two of the New York City apartment she'd shared with Eloise and Olivia.

She ambled into the bathroom, which had brown tiles, a travertine floor and a double-sink vanity.

"Hey."

She spun around. Expecting to see her Realtor, she gasped when she saw Antonio standing in front of the open stone shower. Because he was the last person she expected to see on the outskirts of tiny Starlight, Kentucky, she opened her mouth to ask him what he was doing there, but no words came out.

He looked crazy amazing. His hair was a mess, the way it was after a day of painting, her favorite time with him—which made her wonder if she was having some kind of sadness-related hallucination.

"What are you doing here?"

The best way to end a hallucination would be to force it to talk. If he said something impossible—like that he loved her—she would know she was imagining things.

"I heard you're in the market for a house."

Now, that was an illusion if she ever heard one. Her Antonio didn't talk about commonsense, normal stuff. Still, she answered, "Yes."

"Do you like this one?"

She laughed and glanced around. "Jeez, who wouldn't? Everything is gorgeous, but I think it's too big."

He pushed off the shower wall. "Of course it's big. You're looking at it because you're thinking down the line to when you have more kids. Anticipating, like Constanzo."

She laughed out loud. Good Lord, her imagination was powerful. "I'm going to have trouble enough raising one child."

"Your mother will help."

She sucked in a breath. "I know."

He stepped toward her. "I will help."

"Okay, time to end this hallucination."

He laughed. "I wondered why you were so calm. You think I'm a figment of your imagination?"

She winced and squeezed her eyes shut. Her time with him had seemed like a dream. The four days since she'd been here in Starlight she'd sort of vibrated with confusion. Was it any wonder she was having trouble with reality?

"Okay. I'm an idiot." Her eyes popped open. "What are you doing here?"

"Constanzo forced me to talk about our relationship and to forgive him."

"Oh."

"Weird, huh?"

Not half as weird as having the love of her life in the bathroom of the house she was looking at. Tears filled her eyes as she took in his handsome face. He was everything she'd ever wanted. Even things she didn't realize she wanted. But he didn't love her. He'd said it. And by damn, she wanted to be loved.

Passionately.

Men who told you they didn't love you did not fit that bill.

She took a step back, away from him. "So what does Constanzo forcing you to forgive him have to do with you being here?"

"I looked at your Realtor's offerings and I decided this is the best house for us."

Her heart stuttered, but absolutely positive she hadn't heard correctly, she said, "For us?"

"I've done some thinking in the past few days." He walked around the big bathroom. "And my dad forced me to do even more thinking. He made me realize my problem was that I couldn't trust anyone."

She bristled. She already knew that and so did he. So what the hell was he doing talking about a house for *them*? "Are you saying you don't trust me?"

"I thought I couldn't trust anyone. You could have been the woman in the moon and I would have held myself back." He caught her gaze. "I'm sorry about that, by the way."

She sniffed. "Right."

"I am."

"So you're asking me to accept second-best? You want us to live in this house together, but only if I can accept that you'll never trust me? Wow. You're a piece of work."

He laughed, but walked closer and stopped in front of her. "I'm not a piece of work." He tapped her nose. "And if you don't let me finish this in my own way, nothing's ever going to be right between us."

She frowned. But he put a finger over her lips to silence her. "I'm not asking you to live with me. I'm not saying that I don't trust you. I do trust you. I think I have for a while. It took weeks for me to tell you my story, but eventually you got the whole thing out of me."

Her heart lifted, but she couldn't let herself dare to believe. He'd hurt her because she allowed herself to fantasize that he might love her. She would not let him hurt her again. "I think the truth is you don't trust yourself."

He shrugged. "Maybe. You have to admit it takes a pretty stupid guy to marry a supermodel and not realize she's using him."

Because he said it lightly, she almost laughed, but this conversation was too important. "You loved her."

"Yeah. I did."

Her heart felt the pinch of that. This man had been married to the woman dubbed the most beautiful woman in the world three times. Laura Beth knew Gisella hadn't been as pure of heart as the rest of the world believed, but that couldn't take away from her beauty. How could Laura Beth ever think a man like Antonio would consider *her* beautiful?

"But, Laura Beth, I love you more."

Her head snapped up. "You do?"

"Yes." He ran his finger along the line of her jaw. "You are sweet and fun and funny. You are also beautiful. So beautiful that my memories of silly women like Gisella disappear."

Her breath caught. "You don't have to say things like that."

"I say only what's true." He slid his hands to her waist. "Now, will you live with me in this house?"

Her breath shivered. Live with him? In Starlight, Kentucky? Where her mom and all her friends would see that he liked her enough to live with her but not to marry her?

She stepped back. "No."

He blinked. "No?"

"I know you're scarred. I know it took moving mountains for you to trust." Her chin lifted. "But I deserve better than living with you."

He laughed. "Oh, that is all?"

She took another few steps back. "Don't belittle what I want." Her chin lifted even higher. "What I need."

He shook his head and removed a ring box from his back pocket. "I did this all wrong. I'm sorry." He opened the box to reveal a stunning diamond. "Will you marry me?"

She pressed her trembling lips together, met his gaze.

"You are my heart and soul. You are what I've been searching for forever. My father thought things between him and me were awkward because I couldn't forgive him. The truth was our relationship was awkward because it wasn't what I was searching for. Yes, I need him in my life. But what I really wanted was love. A true love. You are that love."

Tears filled her eyes. "Oh, Antonio." She fell into his arms.

And he breathed a sigh of relief. In those seconds with her arms around him and her body pressed against his, he felt his soul knit together. He felt his mother smiling down on him from heaven. He could see the family he and Laura Beth would create and that his place in the world wouldn't be secured because he was a great artist, but because he would be a part of something bigger than himself. A family.

And he could see his dad reveling in that.

EPILOGUE

ANTONIO AND LAURA Beth waited until baby Isabella was six months old before they had their wedding. With a huge white tent in the yard of Constanzo's country home, the old billionaire about burst with pride as he greeted guests, Rosina at his side. Not as Antonio's housekeeper or even a family friend. But as his fiancé.

Laura Beth watched from the second-floor window of the room she, Olivia and Eloise used to dress for the wedding.

"He is a crazy old man."

Pinning her veil into Laura Beth's fancy updo, Olivia laughed. "He might be crazy, but he brought at least two of us together with our perfect mates."

"So maybe he's wise," Eloise said from her position kneeling between Laura Beth and a centuries-old vanity said to have been used by Marie Antoinette, as she straightened Laura Beth's train. Eloise's boss, Artie Best, had designed the pale peach bridesmaids' dresses. But Eloise herself had created Laura Beth's gown.

With her hair up and her dress fastened, Laura Beth turned to look at herself in the full-length mirror. Strapless, her dress rode her curves and flared out a few inches below her hips to become a frothy skirt with lace trim. Sequins sparkled everywhere, including in the veil that flowed gracefully from her hair along her shoulders and to the floor.

Tears filled her eyes.

Eloise clutched her chest. "You don't like it?"

"I told you in all three fittings that I love it."

Olivia said, "Then what's wrong?"

Laura Beth faced her friends. "I'm beautiful."

As Eloise collapsed with relief, Olivia hugged Laura Beth. "Of course you are. Now let's get downstairs before Isabella starts crying for her mom."

The ceremony was a quiet but loving affair. Antonio looked amazing in his black tux, with her friends' husbands as his groomsmen. The sun shone down on the white tent filled with happy friends.

Just as the minister pronounced them man and wife, Isabella began to cry and Laura Beth took her from her mother, then Antonio took her from Laura Beth. She, Antonio and Isabella walked down the aisle to the sound of Constanzo sobbing loudly.

With joy.

They hoped.

As they greeted their guests, she watched Constanzo cast a quick look to heaven. Obviously believing no one saw or heard, he quietly said, "See, *carissima*. I finally did right by our boy."

Her eyes filled with tears, but she totally understood.

* * * * *

MEET THE FORTUNES!

Fortune of the Month: Oliver Fortune Hayes

Age: 37

Vital Statistics: Blue-eyed, exceedingly handsome aristocrat and single dad. He's just a tad…uptight.

Claim to Fame: Sir Oliver is rich. *Really* rich.

Romantic Prospects: Suddenly he's got a toddler in diapers and a dog barely housebroken. Just how much are most women willing to take on?

"I can manage millions, but when it comes to my small Fortune, I haven't a clue. Shannon makes it all look so easy. She can handle baby Ollie and even get barking Barnaby to toe the line. But when Shannon and I are together, I feel as though I'm losing control all over again. She's too young for me, too exuberant, too…Shannon. The logical part of me says I should hightail it back to London before anyone gets hurt. But there's another part that says, *What if…*"

****

The Fortunes of Texas: Cowboy Country:
Lassoing hearts from across the pond!

FORTUNE'S LITTLE HEARTBREAKER

BY
CINDY KIRK

MILLS & BOON

Published in Great Britain 2015
by Mills & Boon, an imprint of Harlequin (UK) Limited,
Eton House, 18-24 Paradise Road, Richmond, Surrey, TW9 1SR

© 2015 Harlequin Books S.A.

Special thanks and acknowledgement to Cindy Kirk for her contribution to the Fortunes of Texas: Cowboy Country continuity.

ISBN: 978-0-263-25109-8

23-0215

From the time she was a little girl, **Cindy Kirk** thought everyone made up different endings to books, movies and television shows. Instead of counting sheep at night, she made up stories. She's now had over forty novels published. She enjoys writing emotionally satisfying stories with a little faith and humor tossed in. She encourages readers to connect with her on Facebook and Twitter @cindykirkauthor and via her website, cindykirk.com.

This book is dedicated to some of my favorite Facebook friends and Fortunes of Texas fans:

Pamela Lowery

Deanna Vrba

Theresa Krupicka

Caro Carson

Nancy Greenfield

Veronica Mower

Mary Spicher

Dyan Carness

Brenda Schultes Bengard

Nancy Callahan Greenfield

Jennifer Faye

Sherri Shackelford

Ann Roth

Holmes Campbell

Michelle Major

Cheri Allan

Susan Meier

Betsy Ehrhardt

Kim Thomas

Laurie Brown

Deborah Farrand

Linda Conrad

Amanda Macfarlane

Lee Ann Kopp-Lopez

Chapter One

Shannon Singleton took a sip of the Superette's medium roast coffee and exhaled a happy sigh. Since returning to Horseback Hollow several months earlier, she'd come to realize how much she'd missed the town in north Texas where she'd grown up.

The postage-stamp eating area of the Superette consisted of three orange vinyl booths and two tables, each adorned with a bud vase of silk flowers. Nice, but no comparison to the cute little coffee shop Shannon used to frequent when she lived in Lubbock.

Still, the location was bright and cheery. Thanks to a wall of glass windows, Shannon even had a stellar view of the large pothole in the middle of the street.

"I wish they'd choose one of us and get it over with." Rachel Robinson expelled a frustrated sigh and sat back in the booth.

Shannon enjoyed meeting her friend every Tuesday

morning for coffee, but frankly was tired of obsessing over—and discussing—the job they both wanted.

It was a bit awkward, being in competition—again—with her friend. The other times Rachel had bested her, it had been over inconsequential things; like the last piece of dessert at the Hollows Cantina or the pair of boots they'd both spotted at that cute little boutique in Vicker's Corners.

This time was different. *This* time the outcome mattered. Professional positions in this small town an hour south of Lubbock were few and far between. And Shannon really wanted the marketing job with the Fortune Foundation.

In the four years since graduation from Texas Tech with a degree in business, all of Shannon's experience had been in marketing. Rachel had readily admitted she didn't have experience in the marketing arena.

But that fact didn't mean squat. Just as with those pretty turquoise boots, it seemed whenever she and Rachel competed for anything, Rachel came out ahead.

"Earth to Shannon."

Shannon brought the cup to her lips and focused on her friend. She and Rachel were both in their midtwenties, had brown hair and similar interests. But that's where the comparison ended. Shannon considered herself slightly above average while Rachel was stunning. "What? Rewind."

"Wouldn't it be cool if they hired us both?" Rachel smiled at the thought and broke off a piece of scone. The woman's cheerful nature was just one of her many admirable qualities.

"I guess we'll find out…but not until the end of February." Shannon added more cream to her coffee, her tone pensive. "I don't see why it has to take that long. They completed interviews last month."

"It's probably because they're just getting this office

location up and running," Rachel said, sounding way too understanding.

Of course her friend could afford to be charitable. She had a job and was earning her way. Shannon was back living with her parents and, other than the chores she performed at the ranch for her mom and dad, had been out of work for over two months. "Just between you and me, I can't believe they're going to open a foundation branch in Horseback Hollow."

"Doesn't surprise me." Rachel laughed. "This town is turning into a Fortune family hot spot."

The Fortunes were a wealthy family with business ventures all over the world. Their largest Texas base of operations was in Red Rock, just outside San Antonio. But there were also Fortunes in Horseback Hollow. Christopher Fortune Jones, who'd grown up in the area, would be heading the foundation branch in town.

"I'm tired of worrying about a job I might not get." To soothe her rising stress level, Shannon bit into the scone. *Oh, yeah, baby—sugar and blueberries, topped with a lemon glaze.* Talk about stress eating. She could almost feel her waistline expand.

"Are you going to the party on Saturday?" Rachel asked, changing the subject.

The "party" was actually a couple's baby shower being thrown by friends. The fact it was a couple's baby shower practically guaranteed there wouldn't be any unattached men attending. After all, what single straight guy would willingly give up his Saturday night to attend such an event?

"I promised Gabi I'd attend." Shannon paused and narrowed her gaze. Outside, a sleek black car she didn't recognize pulled into the lot. "My other choice is playing cards with my parents and their friends."

Rachel gave an exaggerated shudder.

"It's not that bad." Shannon liked her parents and enjoyed the members of their card club. In fact, if she hadn't given Gabi Mendoza her word she'd show, she'd be seriously tempted to skip the shower and play cards instead.

Rachel took a sip of her chai tea. "I'm crossing my fingers there'll be some fresh meat at this little soiree."

"Don't hold your breath." Shannon could have said more but pressed her lips shut. Let the woman have her dreams…

Rachel startled her by emitting a low whistle and pointing to the window. "Get a load of that."

"I saw it." Obligingly, Shannon leaned forward for a better look. Just south of the humongous pothole sat a shiny vehicle that cost more than she used to make in a year. It was rare to see such an expensive car in Horseback Hollow. "Mercedes."

"Forget the car." Though they were alone in the café, Rachel's voice was soft, almost reverent. "Feast your eyes on him."

Shannon swung her gaze from the sleek lines and shiny black finish of the SL250 to focus on the tall, broad-shouldered man with dark brown hair exiting the vehicle.

A man obviously on a mission, he rounded the back of the car with decisive steps. When he bent over to retrieve something from the backseat, Shannon's lips curved.

"Ooh la la," Rachel breathed.

For a second Shannon forgot how to breathe as the pristine white shirt stretched tight across the breadth of shoulders, muscular legs encased in dark trousers.

Shannon's heart quivered. "If his face is half as good as his backside, we're in for a treat."

As if in answer to her prayer, the guy straightened and turned. Ooh la la, indeed. He had classically handsome features with a strong jaw, straight nose and cheekbones that looked as if they had been chiseled from granite. She'd wager his stylishly cut dark hair had never seen the insides of a Cut 'N' Curl.

Yes, indeed, the man was an impressive hunk of masculinity even with sunglasses covering his eyes.

While the set of those shoulders and confident stance said "don't mess with me," messing with him was just what Shannon longed to do. Until she saw two little legs dangling from the blanketed bundle he'd pulled from the car.

Rachel expelled a heavy sigh, apparently seeing the evidence of daddy-hood, as well. "He's got a kid."

Her friend sounded as disappointed as Shannon felt.

"Figures he'd be taken." Shannon heaved her own sigh. "The cute ones always are."

"Marriage doesn't stop some of them from sniffing around."

"My old boss Jerry was a perfect example of that." Even as she spoke, Shannon's gaze returned to the dark-haired stranger.

"You taught Jerry the Jerk not to mess with you."

Shannon just smiled and shrugged. Lately she'd begun to wonder if there was a way she could have handled the situation differently and kept her job.

Water under a collapsed bridge.

The man shut the door firmly, then stepped away, giving Shannon a glimpse of a furry head with perked-up ears, little paws braced on the dash. She couldn't stop a smile. She loved animals almost as much as she loved children. "He's got a dog, too."

Rachel looked up from the text she'd glanced down to read. Apparently discovering the stranger had a kid had turned her initial interest to indifference.

"The hot guy has a kid *and* a dog," Shannon told her friend.

"Bet you five he also has a wife with blond hair and a killer figure." Rachel's tone turned philosophical. "That's practically a given with guys like him."

Shannon grinned. "Aren't you the cynical one?"

"Realist." Rachel popped a bite of scone into her mouth. "I should have known he was too good to be single."

Shannon rolled her eyes.

"He's coming inside," Rachel hissed.

Shannon turned in her chair just as the automatic doors of the Superette slid open.

Francine, the store's lone cashier, was in the back of the store stocking shelves. Since they were the only customers, Frannie had told them to holler if someone showed and was ready to check out.

The man paused just inside the entrance and removed his sunglasses. He glanced at the empty checkout counter, impatience wrapped around him like a too-tight jacket. Shannon expected any second he'd start tapping his foot.

Shannon pulled to her feet and crossed to him, wishing she was wearing something—anything—besides jeans and a faded Texas Tech T-shirt. "May I help you?"

The man was silent for a second, staring at her. His eyes were a cool blue with a darker rim. Shannon forced herself to hold that piercing gaze.

"I find myself in need of some assistance," he said after a couple of seconds, his smile surprisingly warm and charming. "My GPS has gone bonkers. I'm looking for a ranch called the Broken R."

In addition to the killer smile, the man had a totally de-lish British accent. Shannon surreptitiously slanted a glance down but his ring finger was hidden beneath the blankets.

"Are you a relative?" Though Shannon didn't like to

pry, Rachel would kill her if she didn't get at least one or two deets.

"I'm Jensen's brother." He adjusted his stance as the child beneath the blanket stirred. "Are you familiar with the location?"

Shannon couldn't tell if the toddler was a boy or girl. The shoes were gray leather sneakers that could belong to either sex. The only thing she could see above the blanket was a thatch of slightly wavy brown hair.

"It's super easy to find." Shannon quickly gave him directions. She offered to write them down, but he told her there was no need.

"Thank you." He smiled again and his whole face relaxed. "You've been very kind."

Though she wanted to volunteer to ride with him and show him the way, Shannon resisted the temptation. Married men were not on her radar.

Still, she remained where she was and watched him stroll to the car. Once he reached the vehicle, she scurried over to where Rachel waited.

"Ohmigod." Rachel's eyes sparkled. "His accent is incredible."

"The rest of him is pretty incredible too." Shannon surreptitiously watched Jensen Fortune Chesterfield's hot brother buckle the child into the seat. The blanket around the toddler fell to the concrete but was quickly scooped up.

"He's definitely a boy," she told her friend.

"You're wrong." Rachel chuckled. "That one is all man."

"Not him. The kid. I couldn't tell initially boy or girl, but he's wearing a Thomas the Tank Engine shirt. Definitely a boy."

"Who cares about the child?" Rachel fluttered her long lashes. "Did you hear that fantabulous British accent?"

"You said that before."

"It bears repeating."

The sleek black sedan backed up and headed out of the lot, careful to avoid the asphalt crater.

"It doesn't matter." Shannon sighed and turned her attention back to her scone. "Like you said, a guy that gorgeous has a beautiful wife somewhere."

Oliver Fortune Hayes once had a beautiful wife. Then he'd had a beautiful ex-wife. Now, the stunningly beautiful blonde was gone.

"Diane was killed in a car accident two months ago," Oliver told his brother Jensen. He kept his tone matter-of-fact, tamping down any emotion. "She was in the car with a man she'd been seeing for quite some time. He also died in the crash."

The two men sat in Jensen's kitchen, having a cup of tea. Thanks to the concise directions from the pretty brunette at the grocery shop, Oliver had easily found the Broken R ranch. Jensen had been surprised to see him a full twenty-four hours earlier than expected and apologetic that Amber was in Lubbock shopping.

Oliver looked forward to meeting his brother's fiancée but appreciated the opportunity to talk privately first.

Jensen hadn't changed much since Oliver had last seen him. His brother's dark hair was perhaps a trifle longer but he was still the very proper British gentleman that Oliver remembered. Though the cowboy boots were a shock, Jensen's gray trousers were perfectly creased, and his white dress shirt startlingly white.

"This is the first I've heard of Diane's death. Why didn't you call?" Jensen was his half brother from the second marriage of Oliver's mother. Though seven years separated them in age, Oliver had always been fond of Jensen.

When Oliver had announced his intention to come to

Horseback Hollow after their sister, Amelia, gave birth, Jensen had offered to let him stay at his ranch.

"My life has been topsy-turvy since the moment I found out." He'd discovered Diane had died at a cocktail party when a mutual friend had expressed sympathy.

"I bet."

Oliver continued as if Jensen hadn't spoken. "Diane's parents didn't notify me. They took Ollie into their home even though they knew full custody immediately reverted to me upon her death. They kept my son from me."

Jensen flinched at the underlying anger in his brother's carefully controlled tone. "I'm surprised they didn't put up a fight once you found out and arrived on their doorstep to claim him."

"There would have been no point." Oliver waved a hand. "I'm the child's father."

"Given your lifestyle, taking on a child had to be difficult."

"Once I established a schedule, it went quite well," Oliver said in a clipped tone, irritated his brother could think him incapable of caring for one small boy. "The nanny I hired is excellent and believes as strongly as I do in the importance of a routine. And she fully understood why I needed to make this trip. Unfortunately she refuses to leave the country."

Jensen obviously had nothing to add. He didn't have children. Not even a wife. Not yet anyway.

Oliver glanced down, noting Barnaby had fallen asleep at his feet. He only hoped his son was sleeping as soundly as the dog. The moment he'd arrived at the ranch, Oliver had put Ollie down for a nap. After a sixteen-hour flight from London to Lubbock the day before, even the brief respite in a hotel overnight hadn't been enough sleep for a toddler.

His son had been fussy after the long flight and had kept Oliver up most of the night. Oliver had dreaded the forty-five-minute car ride from Lubbock to Horseback Hollow, but the child had fallen asleep while Oliver was strapping him into his car seat. He'd slept during the entire trip, not waking even when Oliver brought him inside and laid him on Jensen's bed.

Jensen's gaze dropped to the corgi. "What's his name?"

"Barnaby." Oliver wasn't sure who was more surprised at the fondness in his voice, him or his brother.

"You don't like dogs."

"I've never disliked them," Oliver corrected. "I simply never had time for one. Diane purchased Barnaby for Ollie when she left me. He's quite attached to the animal."

"You're going to keep him?"

"Are you referring to Ollie? Or Barnaby?"

"Both." Jensen grinned. "I've never considered you the kid or dog type."

"Ollie is my son. My responsibility. When Diane and I split up, I thought our child's needs would be better served living with her. That's the only reason I didn't fight for custody. I've already explained about the dog."

Jensen stared contemplatively at the animal that had awakened and now sat, brown eyes scanning the room, ears perked up like two radio antennae.

"Corgis are herding animals."

Oliver nodded. "I observed some of that behavior when he first came to live with me. But that's no longer an issue."

"You have the dog on a schedule, too."

"Certainly."

"Is Barnaby a dog that goes in and out?" Jensen asked in a tone that was a little too casual.

Oliver cocked his head.

"Could he be an outside dog?"

Oliver thought for a moment, considered. "He likes being outdoors, but I don't believe he's suited to roughing it."

Jensen rubbed his chin. "That presents a problem."

"How so?"

"Amber is allergic to dogs." His brother grimaced. "Come to think of it, I probably shouldn't have let the animal in the house."

Ah, now Oliver understood. "No worries. I'll stay with Mother."

"You're forgetting something, aren't you?"

"Am I?"

"Mother is also allergic." Jensen's expression was solemn. "Remember the puppy Father brought home? She got congested and broke out in hives."

Bugger. He'd forgotten all about that episode. He'd been older and away at boarding school, so the fact that the dog had to be returned to the breeder hadn't affected him.

"It appears I'll have to rent a suite at a hotel." Oliver gave a shrug. "Is there one you'd recommend?"

Jensen gave a hoot of laughter. "You saw the extent of our business district when you stopped at the Superette."

Was his brother teasing him? The way he used to when he was a bit of a boy? "I assumed the more populated area of the city was elsewhere."

"Horseback Hollow isn't a city, it's a town. There are no hotels, motels or even any B and Bs." Jensen's expression sobered. "Right now there isn't even a hotel in Vicker's Corners. You'll have to go all the way to Lubbock to find one."

Oliver pressed his lips together. There was no way he'd flown across an entire ocean and half a continent to stay an hour away. Especially not with a child. The whole purpose of this trip was to spend time with family.

"There has to be a vacant house in the area," he told his brother. "Do you have the name of a real estate broker I could contact?"

"Now?"

"Since Ollie and I don't have accommodations for this evening, time is of the essence."

His brother rose and went to a desk where he pulled out a thin phone book. "I suggest starting with Shep Singleton. He's a local rancher and I believe he has an empty house on his property. I'm not sure if it would be satisfactory or what he'll want for rent—"

"Money won't be an issue if the house is clean and nearby."

"It's in a great location." Jensen pulled his brows together as if picturing the place in his mind. "It may even have a fenced yard."

"Do you have Mr. Singleton's mobile number?" Oliver pulled the phone from his jacket, his fingers poised above the keypad. He wanted to inspect this home. One way or the other, he would secure appropriate lodging for him and his son, today.

Because Oliver Fortune Hayes was used to going after—and getting—what he wanted.

Chapter Two

Shannon swore under her breath. She and Rachel had plans to see a movie in Lubbock this evening, then check out a Mexican place that had recently opened in the Depot District. Instead she'd had to call her friend and cancel.

All because her father had gotten a call from someone interested in renting the empty ranch house on the property. Apparently that someone had to see it immediately. There was no telling how long this would take. Or who the impatient person would turn out to be.

Her father only had a name…Oliver. He wasn't certain if that was the man's first or last name, as he'd been distracted during the call. One of his prize mares was foaling.

Shep Singleton might be focused on Sweet Betsy but Shannon was still his little girl. He ordered her to take one of the ranch hands with her for safety. It made sense, but she hated to pry them away from their duties.

The odds of Mr. Oliver being a serial killer or crazed

lunatic were next to nil. Besides, she'd had self-defense training and could hold her own.

When she pulled up in front of the home and saw a dusty Mercedes, a prickle of heat traveled up her spine. Surely it couldn't be…

Even as she hopped out of her dad's rusty pickup with the gash in the front end, the man from the Superette stepped from the vehicle. Ooh la la, he looked just as good as he had several hours ago and ready for business in his hand-tailored navy suit.

Smiling, Shannon crossed the gravel drive and extended her hand. "You must be Mr. Oliver?"

"Oliver Fortune Hayes," he corrected, smiling slightly. "And you're the helpful lady from the grocer's."

"Shannon Singleton." She gave his hand a decisive shake. "Shep's daughter. My dad said you wanted to check out the house."

"Indeed." Those amazing blue eyes settled on her, warm and friendly. "I appreciate you showing it on such short notice."

What was left of her irritation vanished. "Happy to do it."

He surprised her by turning back to the car. When he opened the back door and unfastened the boy from his car seat, she realized he hadn't come alone. Once the child's feet were firmly planted on the ground, the toddler looked around, gave an ear-splitting shriek and barreled after the corgi that had just leaped from the vehicle.

"That's Ollie. My son," Oliver told her, pride in his voice.

Oliver let the boy scamper a few yards before scooping him up. Ollie giggled and squirmed but settled when Oliver said something in a low tone.

"Barnaby."

The crisp sound of his name had the corgi turning. Oliver motioned with his hand and the dog moved to his side.

He looked, Shannon thought, like a man totally in control of the situation.

Oliver gazed speculatively at the house. "Since your father knows I'm looking for immediate occupancy, I assume the home is empty."

Shannon smiled. "You assume correctly."

The entire tour of the furnished home took all of five minutes. If Shannon hadn't been looking she might have missed the slight widening of Oliver's eyes when he first stepped inside the three-bedroom, thirteen-hundred-square-foot ranch house Shannon's grandparents had once called home.

Once she'd finished the tour, she rocked back on her boot heels, feeling oddly breathless. "What do you think?"

"I'll take it." Oliver put the boy down, reached into his back pocket and pulled out a wallet. "Sixty days with an option. I'll pay in advance."

"Just like that?" Decisiveness was one thing, but he hadn't asked a single question. "Don't you have any questions?"

"You've explained everything to my satisfaction." He kept one eye on his son, who was hopping like a frog across the living room. "The fact is, I need to secure lodging close to my family."

As Shannon opened her mouth, she wondered if she might be stepping over some line. But surely the man had other options. From what she'd observed of the Fortunes, they were a tight-knit family. "You're not staying with them?"

"That was the plan. But apparently Amber—my brother's

fiancée—is highly allergic to dogs. As is my mother, which I'd very inconveniently forgotten." He gestured with his head toward the corgi, who intently watched the hopping boy. "Ollie is very attached to Barnaby."

"He's a cutie. The boy, I mean. The dog is cute, too." Shannon paused to clear the babble from her throat before continuing. "Will your wife be joining you?"

For just an instant a spark of some emotion flickered in his eyes before the shutter dropped.

"Ollie's mother and I were divorced." His tone was matter-of-fact. "Well, Ms. Singleton?"

"Please call me Shannon."

"Well, *Shannon*. Do we have a deal?" He extended his hand.

When her fingers closed over his and a hot, unfamiliar riff of sensation traveled up her spine, something told Shannon that this deal might be more than she bargained for.

To Oliver's way of thinking, money smoothed most rough patches and made life extremely manageable. Unfortunately, in the past few days he hadn't found that to be as true as in the past. There hadn't been anyone to carry in his bags or help him unpack once he'd closed the deal on the ranch house.

Oliver glanced around the small living room, smiling at the sight of Ollie playing with his A-B-C bricks, the dog supervising from his position under the kitchen table. The place was so small he could see the kitchen from where he stood. Unbelievably, there was only one lavatory in the entire structure.

Since it was just him and Ollie, even when they added a nanny, it would be workable. Not ideal, but they would make do, much the way he had on those school camping trips when he'd been a boy. He decided to view the next two months as an adventure.

Both Ollie and Barnaby seemed to like the small space. Even Oliver had to admit he found his temporary residence comfortable, quiet and surprisingly homey. Still, after two days of settling in, he was ready to get to work. For that to happen, he needed a nanny.

He'd made inquiries, as had various family members. So far, none of the women he'd interviewed had been acceptable. Oliver would also consider a manny, but when he'd mentioned that to the woman at the agency in Lubbock, her eyebrows had shot up. She informed him mannies were scarcer in Texas than rain in August.

Man or woman, Oliver didn't care. He simply needed someone he could trust to tend to his son while he worked. He ran a busy brokerage firm in London. While he trusted and valued his employees, he prided himself on being personally involved with many of the firm's larger clients.

Dealing with time zone issues was frustrating enough, but then to have Ollie call to him or start crying over his bricks tumbling down was totally unacceptable. There had to be someone suitable in the area.

His hopes of finding someone from Horseback Hollow were rapidly fading. Amber had given him a couple of names, neither of whom was willing to live in. What good would they be to him living a half hour away? With the time differences an issue, if he needed to go out or simply make a phone call, he didn't want to wait.

The head of the placement agency guaranteed she'd find the perfect person, but kept asking him to give her more time. Well, he'd given her over two days. Since she couldn't make it happen, he would take the reins.

He pulled out his wallet and removed the card Miss

Shannon Singleton had given him to use in case of emergencies.

Oliver paused, considered. As far as he was concerned, being without a nanny for forty-eight hours qualified as an emergency.

Shannon stared at the phone in her hand for a second before dropping it into her bag.

Rachel slanted a questioning glance at her as they exited the movie theater in Vicker's Corners. "Who was that?"

"Oliver Fortune Hayes."

Shannon had told her friend all about playing rental agent with Mr. Fortune Hayes. Rachel had only one question—was he married?

"Mr. Hottie from the Superette." Rachel's smile broadened. "Tell me he called to ask you out."

"I'm not exactly sure what he did."

Shannon slowed her steps as the two women strolled down the sidewalk of the quaint community with its cute little shops with canopied frontage and large pots of flowers. "He said he had a proposition for me."

A mischievous gleam sparked in Rachel's eyes. "What kind of proposition?"

Shannon swatted her friend's arm and laughed. "Not that kind."

"Don't be so sure." Rachel gave her an admiring glance. "You're a hottie, too. He'd be a fool not to be interested. And that man didn't look like anyone's fool."

"Thanks for that." Still, Shannon held no such illusions. If guys thought of her at all, it was as a buddy. She was twenty-five and had only had two boyfriends. Hardly a guy-magnet. "But remember, his home is in England. I want a nice local guy. Is that too much to ask?"

To Shannon's surprise, Rachel didn't go for the flippant

response. Instead Rachel's dark brows pulled together in thought. Her friend was a strikingly pretty woman, tall with big blue eyes and long hair so dark it looked almost black.

Though they were good friends, so much of Rachel was still a mystery. Sometimes when she turned serious and got this faraway look in her eyes, Shannon could only wonder what she was thinking.

"I love it here, too," Rachel admitted. "I can't imagine living anywhere else. So when you find that nice local guy, make sure he has a friend."

"Will do. Just don't hold your breath."

Shannon stopped short of telling Rachel if her friend was back in Austin, she'd have men beating her door down. She still didn't fully understand what had caused Rachel to leave Austin and move to Horseback Hollow. But in the five years that Rachel had been in town, she'd become part of the community.

"I'm not giving up hope. And you shouldn't either. Look at Quinn," Rachel continued. "Amelia shows up in Horseback Hollow and—boom—she and Quinn fall in love."

Amelia Fortune Chesterfield had come to Horseback Hollow last year for a wedding and had a romantic fling with cowboy Quinn Drummond. Now they were married with a baby girl. It was their baby shower that loomed on the horizon.

"That whole thing was like a made-for-TV movie," Shannon admitted. "But really, how often does that kind of thing happen, especially in a town the size of Horseback Hollow?"

"The fact is, oh ye of little faith, almost anything is possible. Hey, Mr. Oliver Fortune Hayes could fall in love with you, give up his home in London and the two of you could live happily ever after right here."

Shannon paused in front of a bakery, inhaling the scent of freshly baked chocolate chip cookies. "Have you seen a pig fly?"

"Pigs don't fly," Rachel said automatically.

"Exactly right," Shannon agreed. "Until they do, your little scenario isn't going to happen."

Oliver glanced at the Patek Philippe watch on his wrist. His new living room was so small he could cross it in several long strides, which did nothing to dissipate his agitation.

He'd asked Miss Shannon Singleton to come over as soon as possible. That was precisely one hour and forty-five minutes ago. Oliver wasn't used to his requests being ignored.

Of course, as she didn't work for him, Miss Singleton was under no obligation to comply. Still, she'd promised to come as soon as she was able.

Another full hour passed. Ollie was sitting in his high chair, eating a snack of yogurt and apple slices, when Oliver heard the sound of a vehicle coming up the gravel drive.

Barnaby's head jerked up. He let out a surprisingly deep woof, then raced to the front door, tail wagging.

Oliver tousled his son's light brown hair. "Be right back."

His hand was already on the doorknob when the knock sounded.

Looking decidedly windblown, Shannon stood on the porch, holding her flapping purse firmly against her waist as the strong breeze continued to pummel her. Her shoulder-length brown hair whipped around her pretty face and he realized her lips reminded him of plump, ripe strawberries.

He wondered if they'd taste as good as they looked.

She cleared her throat. "May I come in?"

"Of course." Pulling his gaze from her lips, he stepped back and opened the door wider to allow her to pass.

"Whew." She stopped at the edge of the living room to push her hair out of her face. "It's like a hurricane out there."

"Hurricane?" The wind couldn't possibly be over thirty knots.

She laughed. "A figure of speech. If there's a hurricane in the gulf, the only thing we get this far inland is rain. And that's usually in the fall."

Oliver found himself intrigued. Most women of his acquaintance would never think to appear at a requested meeting dressed in blue jeans and a white cotton shirt. Yet, he was oddly drawn to her. It didn't hurt that she smelled terrific, like vanilla.

Yes, the beastly day was definitely on the upswing. "I appreciate you coming on such short notice."

"I'm sorry it took so long." She smiled up at him with such charming sweetness he found himself returning her smile and taking her arm as they strolled to the kitchen.

"You're here now. That's what counts." He resisted the urge to brush back a strand of hair from her face, even as he inhaled the pleasing scent that wafted around her.

"My friend Rachel and I went to a movie in Vicker's Corners. That's where we were when you called. Then we went and got coffee at one of the little specialty shops. This time, we got ice cream, too. I told Rachel we shouldn't. I mean we had a big lunch, but—"

He did his best to process her rapid-fire speech but it was as if she was speaking a foreign language. Apparently cueing in to his glazed look, she broke off and laughed without a hint of self-consciousness.

"I'm babbling." She laughed again. "Which I sometimes do when I'm nervous."

"I make you nervous?"

A bright pink rose up her neck. "A little."

Truly puzzled now, he cocked his head. "Why?"

"You're different from the men I know, the guys in this town."

"My brothers live here. I'm not different from them."

"I'm not well acquainted with your family. At least not with the ones from England."

"Hopefully that will change." Oliver gestured to the refrigerator. "May I get you something to drink?"

"Thanks. I'm fine." She moved to Ollie's side, the dog like a little shadow at her feet. Taking a seat at the table near the child, she smiled and picked up a piece of the apple. "This looks yummy."

The toddler's fingers closed around the apple slice. Her smile flashed with delight when he put it into his mouth and began to chew.

Oliver considered offering her something to eat, but rations were in short supply at the moment. He really needed to make a trip into town to the grocery shop they called the Superette.

"You said you had a proposition for me, Mr. Fortune Hayes?"

She was direct. Oliver admired that quality. Spared all the posturing.

"I'd like you to help me find a nanny for Ollie."

Shannon leaned back in her chair and studied him for several seconds before speaking. "I thought you hired an agency in Lubbock to do that for you. That's the buzz around town."

Jensen had warned him there were no secrets in Horseback Hollow. "Their efforts so far have been disappointing."

"You've been here two days."

"It's difficult to get work done when you're caring for a child."

Unexpectedly, Shannon laughed; a delightful sound that reminded him of bells ringing. "I don't think any parent would contradict that statement."

"The fact is, Miss Singleton—"

"Shannon," she reminded him.

"Shannon." He found the name pleasant on his tongue. "My business is a demanding one. While I'm happy to come and spend time with my family, I need to stay involved."

"What is it you do?"

"I run a brokerage house." It would be bragging to say more, to tell her that his firm was one of the top ones in London. Besides, it had no relevance to the current conversation.

"Oh."

"The point is I need to find someone immediately. Of course, not just anyone will do. Ollie's happiness and welfare is paramount. The women the agency has sent so far were totally inappropriate. This has caused me to doubt the adequacy of the agency's screening process."

"How were they inappropriate?" Shannon knew he'd acquired the services of the premier placement agency in Lubbock. To hear he was dissatisfied so quickly surprised her.

"The first woman hadn't been informed this was a live-in position." Oliver snatched from the air the piece of apple Ollie had tried to fling to a waiting Barnaby. "Interviewing her was a complete waste of my time."

"Probably an oversight," Shannon said diplomatically. "What else?"

"The next woman found the accommodations—" he hesitated for a second before continuing "—substandard. That didn't concern me because I found her supercilious attitude unacceptable."

"Many live-in nannies—" Shannon chose her words carefully since the lodging they were referring to was owned by her father "—require a private bath."

"I completely understand her concern," Oliver said briskly. "I'm not looking forward to sharing the lavatory either. I'd hoped the salary I was offering and the fact that it wouldn't be a long-term placement would make that fact more palatable."

"It must be difficult living in a home that is so far below your circumstances."

He appeared to ignore her dry tone. "This home and Horseback Hollow may not be where I'd choose to live forever, but for the short term both are adequate."

Shannon knew he was being kind and exceedingly tactful. But his comment only served to remind her that Oliver Fortune Hayes wouldn't be like his sister, Amelia, or his brother Jensen, who'd come to Horseback Hollow and not only fallen in love with a local but with the town and its people, as well.

She had to keep that in mind. Despite the ooh la la factor, any relationship with Oliver would be a dead-end street.

Chapter Three

Oliver found himself enjoying his conversation with Shannon. She was obviously an intelligent woman who appeared to truly care about his situation.

"I asked Amelia for names since Amber and Jensen were fresh out of ideas." Oliver paused and tilted his head. "Are you certain I can't get you a refreshment?"

Shannon smiled. She had quite a lovely one. While her features were too strong to be considered classically beautiful, there was an arresting nature to her face that made a man—even one who'd sworn off women temporarily to focus on his son—take a second look.

Though he must admit, he couldn't recall the last time he'd seen a woman in denim and cotton. Not to mention cowboy boots. The pants hugged her slender figure like a glove, and the shirt, though not tight, hinted at underlying curves. Yes, she was striking indeed.

"I guess I could take a cup of tea, if it's not too much trouble."

He was so focused on her lips that it took him a second to process. "No trouble at all."

Oliver was putting the kettle on the stove when the doorbell rang.

"Would you like me to get that?" Even as she asked, Shannon was already rising to her feet with a fluid grace comparable to any of the ladies he knew back in London.

"Thank you, yes." Oliver pulled his gaze from her backside and gave Ollie a biscuit. His son squealed with delight.

He heard Shannon speak, then recognized his brother's voice.

Jensen strolled into the room, dressed casually—for him—in brown trousers and a cream-colored polo shirt. There was curiosity in his eyes when his brother's gaze slid between him and Shannon. "I didn't realize the two of you were acquainted."

"Shannon showed me around this lovely home," Oliver announced.

"That's, ah, correct." Shannon, who'd appeared relaxed only moments before, now appeared ready to bolt.

The fact puzzled Oliver. He'd been under the impression that while Shannon and Jensen weren't well acquainted, they were on good terms.

"Will you have a cup?" Oliver asked his brother. "I have Fortnum & Mason."

Jensen's smile gave Oliver his answer, while Shannon's brows pulled together.

"Fortnum & Mason is a popular British tea manufacturer. They have a Smoky Earl Grey blend that Oliver—and almost everyone in the family—prefers," Jensen explained before Oliver could open his mouth.

"I'm sure it's delicious, but I'll pass." Shannon

appeared to make a great show of looking at her watch. "We can talk another time, Oliver. I have plans and I'm sure you and your brother have a lot to discuss."

Oliver's heart gave an odd lurch. He surprised himself by crossing the room, taking her arm and leading her back to her seat at the table. "Nonsense. You're staying for tea."

"Down," Ollie called out. "Want down."

"I can get—" Shannon began.

Oliver held up a hand, then fixed his gaze on his son. "What do you say?"

Ollie stared at him with innocent blue eyes before his mouth widened into a grin. "Pease."

"Good man." Oliver lifted his son down from the high chair.

Jensen exchanged a look with Shannon. "Amazing."

Shannon cocked her head, but before Jensen could explain, Oliver looked up from wiping Ollie's hands.

"Nothing amazing about it. Child rearing is no different from running a successful business enterprise. Rules and order are essential." Oliver shifted his gaze to Shannon. "My brother expected me to be a bumbling feckwit incapable of rearing my son."

Oliver pulled out a bin containing an assortment of toys, placing several before Ollie on the rug within eyeshot of the kitchen table. The whistling teakettle brought him back to the stove, where he produced three cups of the steaming brew in short order.

"Surely he's seen you in action before?" Shannon cradled the "I Love Texas" mug in her hands with an unexpected reverence.

"Oliver only recently gained custody of Ollie," Jensen explained. "After Diane…"

Jensen stopped and slanted Oliver an apologetic glance.

In their family, private matters weren't usually discussed in the presence of a guest.

"Diane was my ex-wife," Oliver explained. "The divorce was already in process when Ollie was born. Because I believed a child—a baby especially—needed his mother, I didn't fight her for custody. She recently died in a car accident."

"She shouldn't have been out that night." Jensen's voice rose and anger flashed in his eyes. "She should—"

"Enough."

The quietly spoken word was enough to stop Jensen's potential tirade in its tracks.

"She was Ollie's mother." Looking back, the person Oliver blamed most was himself. He should have paid more attention. He should have known that Diane was spending more time with her new boyfriend than with Ollie. "The accident occurred fairly recently."

He felt Shannon's hand on his arm, looked up to find her soft eyes filled with compassion. "I'm sorry for your loss."

"We'd been divorced over a year."

"You were also once married to her. That means you once loved her." She gave his forearm a squeeze, then removed her hand.

Oliver nodded briskly.

Diane hadn't wasted any time finding another man once the baby was born. She'd been with yet another man when she died. That's why the sadness he'd experienced upon hearing of her passing had blindsided him. He finally accepted it was understandable, given this was a woman he'd once known and loved.

Jensen steepled his fingers and his gaze settled on Shannon. "I understand you work for your father."

"I do." She sipped her tea and her smile told Oliver she found it pleasing. "The Triple S is a large spread. I do mostly administrative work, but in a pinch I'm able to do just about anything—feed cattle, vaccinate, castrate…"

"Good Lord." The words popped from Oliver's lips before he could stop them.

"You're in the Wild West now, brother." Jensen grinned. "Oh, and before I forget, I brought you some more names of possible nannies for Ollie. These are from Amelia since you didn't appear happy with any of the ones Amber and I suggested."

"I'm very particular when it comes to my son," Oliver said without apology.

Jensen took a sip of tea, then lifted the mug higher to read the inscription—"This Ain't My First Rodeo." His lips twitched and he shook his head before taking another drink. Seconds later he reached into his pocket and pulled out a sheet of paper. "The latest list."

"Perfect," Oliver pronounced. "We'll take care of this right now."

Jensen tilted his head back. "How do you propose to do that?"

"Miss Singleton knows everyone in the area." Oliver smiled at Shannon. "She and I will go through the names over dinner and decide which ones to interview."

"I'm afraid that won't be possible." Shannon set down her mug, the flash of irritation in her eyes at odds with her easy tone. "I have plans."

"Break them," Oliver ordered. "This is more important. A child's welfare is at stake."

The men in Shannon's family often told their friends that she was a contradiction: a purring kitten and a ready-to-strike rattler. The consensus seemed to be it was best not to push her too far.

The good humor drained from Shannon's body. Did the

rich and powerful Oliver Fortune Hayes really think he could, with a cavalier wave of his hand, dismiss her plans for the evening?

There was no reason for him to know that those plans were fluid. Several friends planned to eat and drink their way through platters of nachos and bottles of Corona beer at the Hollows Cantina during happy hour. They'd told her to join them if she was free.

But as Shannon opened her mouth to reiterate she had plans, his words gave her pause. As much as she didn't want Oliver to think he could bring her to heel with a single wave of those elegant fingers, she wanted him to find a suitable nanny for Ollie.

You'd think after growing up with four younger siblings—and years spent babysitting—she should be tired of children. But she loved them. Not just the small ones. She even got a kick out of the often obnoxious teenagers from Lubbock who came out to ride horses as part of a Country Connection program.

Ollie was such a cute little guy and he'd recently lost his mother...

"Shannon." Oliver reached across the table and took her hand. "Please. I need your help." His tone was softer this time.

Heat rose up her arm. For a second she forgot how to speak. She licked her lips. When his eyes darkened, her resistance melted into a liquid pool.

"I'd love to stay and chat, but Amber is expecting me." Jensen attempted to hide his grin by raising the cup to his lips for one last swallow. "It appears you two have a lot to, uh, discuss."

Shannon flushed. "Be sure to tell Amber hello from me."

"I will give her your regards." Jensen gave a slight bow

of his head, all serious now. One hundred percent British. He turned and handed Oliver the promised list. "The names."

"Thank you." Oliver took the list in his left hand, extended his right. The two men shook.

Shannon blinked at the civilized gesture. She tried to imagine her brothers shaking hands and…couldn't. Punching each other, heck yes. That occurred on a daily basis.

Because the men were standing, she also rose to her feet. Jensen shook her hand before he left.

With a resigned sigh, Shannon turned to Oliver. She had to admit she was curious whom Amelia had recommended. She gazed pointedly at the list dangling from his fingers. "May I see it?"

With paper in hand, Shannon wandered back to the table and sat. Taking a gulp of tea, she narrowed her gaze and scanned the names.

After putting down a few more toys for Ollie, Oliver took a seat across from her.

"What do you think?" he asked when several seconds had passed. "Any good possibilities?"

Shannon laid the paper on the table and sat back. "Do you want tactful? Or honest?"

Oliver's gaze lingered on her face, and a curious energy filled the air. An invisible web of attraction wrapped around them. When he leaned forward, Shannon was sure he was going to kiss her.

Unable to move, she held her breath and stared into those brilliant blue eyes.

His lips were a heartbeat away when little Ollie let out a high-pitched squeal. Shannon turned her head just in time to see him gleefully knock down the stack of blocks.

Though he'd recently lost his mother, the child appeared happy and content, with the dog sitting upright beside him.

Right now all was well in his life, and that warmed her heart. But the little boy's world could quickly take a nose-dive if Oliver hired any of the women Amelia had sug-gested.

She shifted her gaze back to Oliver. The moment had vanished. It was almost as if it had never existed. This made Shannon wonder if it had been simply wishful think-ing on her part.

"Quinn isn't much for gossip and your sister is rela-tively new to Horseback Hollow." Shannon strove to keep her tone matter-of-fact. "I grew up here. I keep my ear to the ground."

The expression seemed to puzzle Oliver. His dark brows pulled together.

"I know everything that goes on in this town," she clari-fied. "Things your sister and even her husband might not know."

Understanding filled his eyes. "Tell me."

"Will you keep it confidential?" Though Shannon liked to have the scoop, she wasn't a gossip. Okay, not much of one. The only reason she was considering sharing what she knew with Oliver was to protect Ollie.

"Most certainly."

Based on what Shannon had observed, Oliver appeared to be an honorable man who loved his son and wanted the best for him.

Hoping she wasn't making a mistake dissing women his sister had recommended, Shannon went through the names on the list one by one. By the time they'd gone through three, Ollie had tired of his toys and was rubbing his eyes and whining. Barnaby sprawled on a nearby rug, snoring lightly.

"Let's break for a few minutes." Oliver rose to his feet.

"I need to change Ollie's nappy and put him down for a kip."

He inclined his head, and she knew what he was asking without him saying a word.

"I'll wait."

"Your dinner plans?"

"No worries." Though it was almost five and the start of happy hour was seconds away, Shannon was no longer in a hurry to leave. "While you're taking care of Ollie, I'll make us another cup of that delicious tea."

"Thank you."

When he and his son disappeared down the hall, Shannon sent a quick text to her friends, canceling her appearance, then put the kettle on. By the time he returned from the bedroom, the tea was ready.

"How is he?" She placed the two cups on the table.

"Dry and sleeping." He gestured toward the steaming tea. "Thank you for that…and for staying."

"I let my friends know I'd be late." She raised a hand when he started to protest. "I want to finish this with you. We only have two names left."

He studied her for a long moment before dropping his gaze down to the list and pointing. "What about this one?"

"Sally Steinacher drinks." When Oliver opened his mouth, she continued. "Not just socially. She has a problem. The family did an intervention last year and she went through treatment, but she's fallen off the wagon. Last week when I was in Vicker's Corners, I spotted her coming out of a liquor store with a sack."

"Perhaps she was buying for a friend or a family member," Oliver suggested.

Shannon gave him a pitying glance. "What kind of friend or relative would send an alcoholic to buy them liquor? Even if someone were that stupid, Rachel and I ran into her later on the street and we both smelled alcohol on her breath."

Oliver lined through her name with a single precise stroke of his Montblanc pen, the same way he'd done with the previous three names. "We've now reached the last person on the list. Is Cissy Jirovec a possibility?"

The hopeful look in his eye vanished when Shannon shook her head.

"She used to live in Horseback Hollow. Cissy calls Vicker's Corners home now. She's a nice person and I know she did a lot of babysitting while she was growing up."

"Then what's the issue?"

There was something about having those vivid blue eyes focused on her that Shannon found unsettling. "The problem isn't with Cissy. It's with her boyfriend."

"I wouldn't be hiring him."

"Wayne used to live in Horseback Hollow. He has a bad temper."

"What does her relationship with this man have to do with her suitability for the position?"

"Wayne has a child from a relationship with another woman in Lubbock. Several years ago he lost his temper and broke his daughter's arm. The doctors in the ER found other healed injuries when they examined the little girl. He was charged with felony child abuse. I read all about it in the Lubbock paper."

"He did this to his own child?"

"He did." Shannon nodded solemnly. "I would hope Cissy wouldn't invite Wayne over while she was watching Ollie. But if Ollie were my son, I wouldn't take the risk."

Just as he had with the previous four names, Oliver drew a line through Cissy's name. With one hand he crumpled the sheet of paper.

"I might have hired one of these women." There was a look of restrained horror on his face.

"On the surface they look good. But, don't despair. The placement agency you're working with is top-notch. They'll do a good job of screening the candidates for you." She offered him a reassuring smile. "You'll find that right someone soon."

Oliver shook his head. "I think I've just found her. I want you to watch Oliver."

"Pardon me?"

"Name your price."

"Mr. Fortune Hayes—"

"Oliver," he interrupted, offering her a smile that turned her bones to liquid. "If we're going to be living under the same roof, it makes sense to be on a first-name basis."

Her breath caught in her throat. "What are you saying?"

"We should be on a first-name basis. Don't you agree?"

"I—I suppose."

"Splendid." The smile that split his face made him look almost boyish. "Shall we shake on it…Shannon?"

Chapter Four

"Shake on what? I haven't agreed to any deal." Shannon stuck her hands behind her back. Thank goodness the words came out casual and offhand.

"Smart woman. It's always best to discuss terms on the front end." He leaned forward in a companionable gesture, resting his forearms on the table.

The gesture somehow made him seem more approachable and appealing. Although if he got much more appealing, Shannon might jump him and rip off that pristine white shirt and perfectly knotted tie.

When Shannon didn't speak, he simply smiled. "You obviously know your negotiating techniques. Okay, I'll toss out an amount."

"We're not negotiating," Shannon protested. "Look, Mr. Fortune Hay—"

"Oliver," he said, once more not playing fair by flashing that enticing smile. "We decided on first names."

"Okay, Oliver." Shannon raked back her hair with her fingers, her heart pounding. Why did she feel as if she was in a race she was destined to lose? A race that, in some ways, she wanted to lose? "I—"

Before she could say more, he tossed out a number that had her forgetting what she'd been about to say.

"I believe that's a fair offer."

"Per…?" She really didn't want to say per month if he meant every two weeks, but it was an amazing sum of money either way.

"Week."

Shannon tried to control her expression by counting to ten in her head. The amount was five times what she'd been making in Lubbock. She swallowed past her suddenly dry throat and shifted in her seat. "If you're offering to pay that much, I'm surprised you don't have women—and men—beating down the door to work for you."

"That's not the salary the agency suggested. They told me the going rate in the area and I agreed to it." His gaze searched her eyes. "I'm a businessman, Shannon. I'm willing to pay for quality. It's as simple as that."

Shannon never considered she could be bought, but then again she'd never been offered so much money for a position she knew she'd enjoy. Working for her father was fine, but he really didn't need her. Little Ollie did.

Oliver turned his head slightly to the side. "What do you say?"

Shannon wiped suddenly sweaty palms on her jeans. "Before we discuss salary any further, I'd like to know your expectations."

He nodded approvingly and studied her for another long moment.

"Timewise, London is six hours ahead of Horseback Hollow." He gestured with an open palm to the clock on the wall in the shape of a rooster. "This means that much of my business will be conducted very early in the morning. That's why living in is nonnegotiable."

"I could come first thing in the morning, say at six a.m." She'd almost said five, but that was her father's favorite time to roll out of bed, not hers.

"That won't work." Oliver tapped a finger on the table. "If I'm speaking with a client at two a.m. and Ollie starts crying and needs attention, I need someone here who can tend to him."

"He could spend the night with me at my parents' home." The words came out in a rush, before she even considered what her folks might think about having a toddler underfoot. All she knew was the idea of being under the same roof with Oliver Fortune Hayes night after night was...disturbing. "That way, you could conduct business without any interruptions at all."

When she finished speaking, Oliver shook his head. The set of his jaw said there would be no changing his mind. "I want Ollie's schedule to be disrupted as little as possible. If I hadn't already canceled other trips to see my family, I'd have canceled this one and remained in London. Ollie has experienced more changes in the past few months than any little boy should have to face."

"You care about him."

Oliver looked perplexed. "Did you think I didn't?"

Well, she wanted to say, *sometimes you treat him like just one more thing in your life you need to handle.* But she knew that wasn't being fair. Her interaction with Oliver and his son had been minimal.

"No, of course not." Shannon blew out a breath. "You're probably right about not injecting more change into his life."

He relaxed in his chair. "Any other concerns you'd like to discuss?"

Shannon cleared her throat. "What about meal preparation, laundry and housecleaning duties? Would those be something you'd expect from me?"

"Negotiable."

"I would need time off."

"I'm not a slave driver, Shannon." His lips lifted in a boyish smile before he became all business again. "At a minimum I would require you to be here between the hours of midnight to noon, Monday through Friday. However, I'd prefer that during the working week you remain on duty until six p.m. That would allow me to have some sleep knowing Ollie is safe under your care."

Though he was proposing some pretty long hours, she *would* have every evening free. Other than Rachel, most of her friends worked eight-to-five jobs, and this really would be no different. "What about weekends?"

"Those days are yours."

She tapped her index finger against her bottom lip. "It's tempting."

"I'd like you to start immediately."

"You're getting ahead of yourself, Bucko." The word, commonly used by Shannon and her sibs, slipped out before her lips could trap it and swallow it whole.

"Bucko?" Oliver raised one dark brow. "I don't believe I'm familiar with the term."

His lips twitched ever so slightly.

Sheesh, the guy was appealing. And that was part of her concern.

Shannon jerked her gaze from those lips and squared her shoulders. There was no getting around it. The elephant in the room had to be addressed. "There's one thing we haven't yet discussed. How you respond may be the difference between my accepting your offer or respectfully declining it."

Oliver's eyes turned flat. He folded his hands before him on the table, his gaze never wavering from her face. "You have my undivided attention."

The fact that Oliver was being so businesslike should have made it easier to spit out the words stuck in her throat. But somehow, having those blue eyes focused so intently on her made her feel like a schoolgirl about to admit to a crush. Dear God, what if she'd only imagined the chemistry between them?

Shannon shifted in her seat and hesitated, despite knowing there was nothing to do at this point but take a deep breath and plunge ahead.

She focused her gaze on a spot over his left shoulder. "Ever since we've met, I've noticed this crazy kind of electricity between us. That's why I think it's important we agree up front to keep things strictly platonic between us. Giving in to the attraction would only complicate the situation."

She was out of breath by the time she finished. Had he been able to understand what she was trying to say? She'd spoken so fast—too fast—the words tripping over each other in her haste to get them out.

"Electricity?"

Of course if he was going to pick one word to focus on, it would naturally be that one. But it was the twinkle in those blue eyes that had her jerking to her feet, a hot flush shooting up her neck.

"Forget it. Forget I said anything. This isn't going to work." To her horror, her voice shook slightly.

It wasn't the hint of amusement in his eyes that had gotten to her. It was the frustration of not being able to make herself heard. Of her concerns and feelings being summarily dismissed.

That's how it had been with Jerry the Jerk. No matter how many different ways she'd told him to back off—that she wasn't interested—he never heard her.

Because he didn't want to hear what I had to say. Because I didn't matter.

As emotions flooded her, Shannon whirled toward the door.

She'd taken only a step or two when Oliver grabbed her arm, his expression contrite.

"I didn't mean to wind you up." He loosened his grip but didn't let go. "You have my word as a gentleman that I will never take advantage of you while you're under my roof and in my employ."

Shannon blew out a shaky breath and swayed slightly, conscious of his hand on her arm. He stood an arm's breadth away, near enough for the intoxicating scent of his cologne to tease her nostrils and make her want to lean close.

Step back, she told herself. She needed to put some distance between her and Oliver. That way she could think. That way she could breathe.

But her feet were as heavy and unmoving as if rooted in concrete. At that moment Shannon didn't have the energy— or the desire—to move.

Instead she tilted her head back and once again found herself drowning in the shockingly blue depths of Oliver's eyes.

Oliver stepped toward her, hand outstretched.

The heat in his gaze ignited a fire in her belly.

A zillion butterflies fluttered in her chest. Shannon moistened her lips and, as she caught another whiff of his cologne, reconsidered her hardline stance of only a moment ago.

One kiss.

What would really be wrong with one little kiss?

After all, people shook hands all the time to seal a deal. How would this be any different? Even as the rational piece of her brain still capable of cognizant thought told her it was indeed *very different*, she extended her hand.

Shannon waited for him to take her fingers and tug her to him. Waited for that magic moment when he would enfold her in a warm embrace before covering her mouth with his…

Her lips were already tingling with anticipation when his hand closed over hers and he gave it a decisive shake. "To new beginnings."

Even as a tsunami-sized wave of disappointment washed over her, Shannon forced herself to breathe and made her lips curve in an easy smile.

Regroup, she told herself.

Her father always said actions spoke louder than words. By his actions, Oliver had shown he was a man of his word. A man she could trust. There was something even more important Shannon had learned today.

She had more to fear from herself than from him.

Happy Hour at the Hollows Cantina had been going for close to two hours by the time Shannon strolled through the front door. She wasn't surprised to find standing-room-only in the bar area.

Her friends tried to squeeze her in at their table, but even if she could have located a spare chair, there was no room for one more.

"That's okay." Shannon waved a hand in the direction of the bar. "I'll just mingle."

"I'm coming with you." Rachel's heels had barely hit the shiny hardwood before her chair was snatched away.

Good old Rachel, Shannon thought with a warm rush of affection. She could always count on her.

The two women wove their way through the crowd, stopping every few feet to chat with friends and acquaintances while keeping an eye out for a couple of empty spots at the bar. They finally snagged two stools when a young couple got up abruptly and hurried off, hands all over each other.

"Get a room," someone yelled, and laughter rippled through the crowd.

A bartender approached to wipe the counter and take their order.

"The nachos are my treat," Shannon announced.

Rachel narrowed her gaze. "What's got you feeling so generous?"

"Tonight is a special occasion." Shannon smiled her thanks as the bartender placed a bottle of Corona beer sporting a wedge of lime in front of her. Before he rushed off he assured her the nachos would be out shortly. "We're celebrating."

The half-finished bottle Rachel had brought with her from the table paused midway to her lips and a smile blossomed on her mouth. "You know I adore happy news. Clue me in. What are we celebrating?"

Shannon raised the beer in a mock toast. Initially she'd been hesitant about accepting Oliver's offer. But now she felt confident of her ability to withstand temptation. "My new job."

Rachel's smile froze. Then she clinked her bottle against the one Shannon held and sputtered out her congratulations.

"Thanks. I'm superjazzed." The position was all about

Ollie, she reassured herself. She had no doubt she and
the boy would get along splendidly. Shannon would not
think about the way her heart hammered whenever Oliver was near.

"When did they call you?"

The quietly spoken question came out of nowhere.
Shannon blinked and focused on her friend. "Who?"

"The person who contacted you about the Fortune Foundation job." Rachel cleared her throat. "When did you get
the good news?"

The bartender, a thirtysomething-year-old with a shaved
head, set a plate of loaded nachos in front of them.

"I never thought they'd choose someone this soon," Rachel continued before Shannon had a chance to respond.
"But, hey, if it couldn't be me, I'm happy it was you."

"This isn't the foundation job. They won't let us know
until the end of the month, remember?" Shannon picked
up a chip dripping with cheese and nibbled. "I'm going to
be a nanny to Oliver Fortune Hayes's son. It's short-term
but the position pays extremely well."

"Oh." The tightness on Rachel's face eased. "When do
you start?"

"I move in Sunday night." Shannon popped the nacho
into her mouth. "I asked him for a few days to get my stuff
together and my bags packed."

"You're moving in with him?" Rachel's voice rose.

Shannon quickly explained about the time difference
and the need to be there to watch Ollie while Oliver was
conducting business.

"How did your folks take the news?"

A twinkle of amusement danced in Rachel's eyes. Like
most Horseback Hollow natives, her friend knew Shannon's parents were a bit on the conservative side.

Shannon grimaced, not looking forward to that conversation. "They don't know. Not yet. I was at Oliver's place until I came here. All I can do is assure them it's strictly business between us."

"Easy peasy." Rachel waved a dismissive hand. "Five minutes in his presence and they'll see it couldn't be anything but business."

Shannon frowned. "What makes you say that?"

"Think about how he stands, so straight and tall. It's like he's got a poker up his a—" Rachel stopped abruptly when she saw Pastor Dunbrook two stools away. She lowered her voice. "I'm just saying that while Oliver may look smokin' hot—and sound just as good as he looks—he has that British thing going."

"British thing?"

"Stiff upper lip and all that. Jolly good and tally-ho." Rachel tapped two fingers against her lips. "Kissing him would probably be like kissing a corpse."

As if Rachel's attempt at a proper British accent wasn't hilarious enough, her describing Oliver as a cold fish made Shannon laugh.

"What's so funny?" Rachel tilted her head, and a speculative gleam shone in her eyes. "Have you already kissed him?"

"Ra-chel." The name was said with just the right touch of injured emotion and appeared to allay her friend's suspicions. "I barely know the man."

"That wouldn't stop me if I was interested in a guy."

"Well, I'm not interested in Oliver, not in that way. This is strictly a business arrangement."

"Then why did you laugh?"

"Because I don't see Oliver as being a cold fish."

"Yeah, right."

"No. Seriously. He's simply...British."

Rachel rolled her eyes and swiped a nacho off the plate.

"Okay, so maybe he's a bit uptight," Shannon admitted. "But it wouldn't take much to loosen him up."

"You go for it, sister." Rachel's red lips focused on something in the distance then curved upward in a sly smile. "In fact, there's no better time to start than right now."

"Other than I'm occupied, enjoying this scrumptious plate of nachos and—" Shannon lifted the Corona "—this ice-cold beer with you. Oliver, on the other hand, is—"

"Right behind you."

"What?"

"Turn," Rachel ordered.

Shannon swiveled on the bar stool. She inhaled sharply and her heart began pumping in time to the sexy salsa beat.

The man she'd been chatting with less than an hour earlier stood in the lobby. Ollie stood fidgeting at his side while Oliver chatted amiably with Wendy Fortune Mendoza and Marcos Mendoza, owners of the cantina. Wendy, looking as stylish as ever in a wrap dress of bright red with matching five-inch heels, clasped the hand of her three-year-old daughter, MaryAnne.

Even as Shannon's eyes were drawn to MaryAnne's adorable pink-and-white-striped dress, she couldn't help noticing the way Marcos's hand rested lovingly on his wife's shoulder or how hot Oliver looked.

He'd changed his clothes, wearing yet another dark suit but this time coupled with a gray shirt and charcoal tie. Odd he hadn't mentioned he had plans for the evening. He certainly hadn't acted as if he was in a rush for her to leave. Quite the contrary.

"Time to start warming up the iceberg," Rachel said in a low tone.

"Saying hello would be the polite thing to do," Shannon agreed, ignoring Rachel's snort of laughter.

Placing her Corona bottle down, Shannon hopped off the stool and pulled a small round mirror from her bag. Before taking a step, she touched up her lipstick, then flashed Rachel a smile. "Back in five."

Rachel lifted a nacho heavy with beef and cheese and gestured to the platter. "Just warning you, these may be all gone when you get back."

"I will return to find both the nachos *and* my seat waiting." Shannon pointed at her friend and spoke in an ominous voice suitable for any horror flick. "Or you will pay the price."

"No guarantee, Chickadee." Rachel peered over the Corona bottle at Shannon and those baby blues twinkled. "If some sexy cowboy wants that stool, those chips or me, I'm sayin' yes."

Shannon ignored the warning and turned, anticipation fueling her steps as she headed across the hardwood floor toward Oliver.

Chapter Five

Though Oliver hadn't had the pleasure of meeting Wendy Fortune Mendoza before tonight, he was well aware she was one of his Texas cousins. The minute he walked into the Hollows Cantina, she greeted him warmly. Since she and her husband owned the cantina, Oliver assumed Wendy and Marcos were cohosting the last-minute party his mother, Josephine, had organized.

But Wendy informed him that she and Marcos wouldn't be able to stay. Even though they couldn't attend, they'd made the restaurant's private room available for the impromptu dinner.

"I'm happy to have the opportunity to meet you." Marcos, a tall man in a perfectly tailored suit with piercing dark eyes, gave Oliver's hand a firm shake.

From what Oliver had heard, Marcos was a savvy businessman, yet it was clear, seeing him with his wife and daughter, that family was also important to him. A man would have to be blind not to notice the loving way Marcos's gaze lingered on Wendy.

"I don't know if you heard but I've secured lodging at a ranch house on the Singleton property. I'll be there for the duration of my stay in Horseback Hollow." Oliver dropped his gaze and shot Ollie a warning glance when the child began tugging on his hand. "Stop by sometime. Bring your daughter. Ollie seems to enjoy being around other children."

"Wonderful. I'll call you this week and we'll set something up." Wendy started to say more but shifted her attention and smiled brilliantly. "Shannon. It's been ages."

Oliver turned to see Wendy give his new nanny a quick hug. She slipped an arm through Shannon's and lifted her gaze to Oliver. "I'm not sure if you've had a chance to meet Shep's daughter—"

"Introductions are unnecessary." Oliver offered Shannon a warm smile. "Miss Singleton and I are well acquainted."

Wendy exchanged a glance with her husband.

"Just this afternoon Shannon agreed to be Ollie's live-in nanny," Oliver announced.

Astonishment rippled across his cousin's pretty face. "Why, that's wonderful."

"Live-in?" Marcos's dark eyes narrowed. "Your father approves of this plan?"

"I'm twenty-five, Marcos," Shannon said drily. "I hardly need my father's okay."

"He's your father," Marcos said pointedly.

"Living in is necessary because of the time difference between here and London." Shannon quickly explained the circumstances, ignoring Marcos's disapproving glance and focusing on Wendy instead.

"Because of that six-hour difference, most of Oliver's

business will be conducted during the overnight hours," Shannon continued before Oliver could add anything. "As a toddler, Ollie can't be counted on to sleep through the night."

"We know all about sleepless nights." Wendy shot a teasing glance at her husband. "Remember when MaryAnne was that age?"

Marcos nodded but his gaze remained troubled.

For the first time, Oliver considered what Shep Singleton would think of his daughter living under the roof of a man he didn't know. Would he understand that it was a simple business arrangement? Or would he worry Oliver might take advantage of Shannon?

Shep had been pleasant and accommodating when Oliver had called to inquire about the house. A personal visit to the Singleton home appeared necessary. Oliver would introduce himself, explain the situation and allay the man's fears before Shannon moved in on Monday.

He was planning his strategy when his mum, Josephine Fortune Chesterfield, breezed through the door, a vision in pale blue silk. Her gray hair, arranged in a chignon, flattered her handsome face. "I'm here. The party can begin."

She extended both hands and moved quickly to him. "Oliver."

"You look lovely as always." He took her hands in his then bent to brush a kiss against her cheek.

"Good evening, Wendy. Marcos." His mother's curious gaze settled on Shannon. "You're Shannon Singleton, Shep and Lilian's daughter. Am I correct?"

"You have an excellent memory, Mrs. Chesterfield." Shannon smiled at his mother. "How are you this evening?"

"Josephine, please. I'm wonderful, now that my son and grandson have joined me in Horseback Hollow."

Ollie made a sound of displeasure when Oliver tightened his hold on the child's hand.

"There's my little darling." Without warning, Josephine scooped Ollie up into her arms.

Startled, the boy stiffened. His eyes widened and his bottom lip began to tremble. Oliver certainly didn't relish snatching Ollie from his mother's arms. But neither did he want his son to start crying and cause a scene in public.

He was rapidly sorting through options when Shannon stepped forward and stroked the child's arm, diverting his attention.

"Hey, Ollie," she said in a gentle, melodious tone. "Remember me from this afternoon?"

Apparently the child did remember. His trembling lips morphed into a wide smile and he extended chubby arms to Shannon.

Instead of taking him from his grandmother as Oliver expected, Shannon clasped his small hands in hers and jiggled them up and down. "Can you tell your grandma your puppy's name?"

Ollie smiled, showing a mouthful of drool and tiny white teeth. "Barn-bee."

"Is Barnaby a nice puppy?" Josephine shot Shannon a grateful smile before refocusing on her grandson, now content in her arms.

As the two continued their corgi conversation, Oliver touched Shannon's arm, drawing her attention to him. "Thanks."

She shot him a wink. "No prob."

Their gazes locked and that electricity she'd mentioned returned to give him a hard jolt.

Blast it all to hell and back. He was not so crass as to be attracted to the nanny. Okay, so perhaps he was...

intrigued. Shannon was different from the London social-ites he frequently took to the opera and sometimes to bed.

But *intrigued* didn't translate into action. Correction, *wouldn't* lead to action. Even if Shannon wasn't his em-ployee, Ollie and managing his business affairs were his top priority.

Shannon's eyes widened as Fortunes flooded the lobby, including Oliver's brother Jensen and his fiancée, Amber. "Why is everyone here? What's the occasion?"

"Mum decided to host a last-minute dinner party. She invited all the family in the area." Oliver smiled ruefully. "She didn't want to put my aunt out so she decided to have it here. She's a bit impulsive, but that's part of her charm."

"How fun. I admire spontaneity." A hint of wistfulness crept into Shannon's voice. "I'm not spontaneous. You miss out on a lot when you're always thinking things through."

"So true, my dear," Josephine interjected.

Shannon's cheeks grew pink. Clearly, she hadn't real-ized that his mother had eyes—and ears—in the back of her head.

"I was surprised to see you here this evening. I didn't know—" Oliver stopped, remembering. "That's right. You told me you had plans."

"I met some friends for happy hour." Shannon glanced over to the bar.

Oliver followed her gaze. A cowboy sat in the seat she'd vacated moments before, munching on nachos. Was the man someone she knew?

Oliver opened his mouth but shut it without speaking. Not his concern.

Strictly business, he reminded himself.

"It was a pleasure seeing you again, Josephine." Shan-non's use of his mum's first name earned an approving smile. "Enjoy your dinner party and your grandson."

Shannon shifted her gaze to Oliver, and when those brown eyes settled on him, he experienced another punch of awareness.

"Trust me." She lowered her voice to a conspiratorial whisper. "Go with the enchiladas. They're the best."

Unable to resist touching her, Oliver reached over and lightly squeezed her shoulder. "Thank you…for everything."

Shannon smiled and strolled off.

"I thought someone said we were meeting in the party room," a feminine voice said. "But the lobby works for me."

Oliver turned to find a petite dark-haired woman with an angelic face and a wide smile approaching him.

"You probably don't remember me from the other night." The young woman extended her hand. "I'm Gabi Mendoza. We—"

"He remembers you, darlin'." Jude Fortune Jones, another one of Oliver's Horseback Hollow cousins, stepped forward and pressed a kiss on the top of Gabi's head. "No man forgets you."

Gabi flashed her tall blond fiancé an indulgent smile. "Aw, thanks, honey. But Oliver saw a lot of new faces the day he arrived."

Though Oliver was exceedingly good with names and faces, Gabi was correct. With so many relatives to meet, including their spouses and significant others, he appreciated her courtesy. "We didn't have much of a chance to chat the other day."

"Tonight we'll get better acquainted over cowboy caviar," Gabi told him.

Oliver pulled his brows together, completely flummoxed. "Cowboy caviar?"

"It's not really caviar." Jude slanted a glance at his fiancée, who simply smiled cheekily.

"It's actually a type of dip," Gabi explained. "It contains
black beans, tomato, avocado, onion, cilantro and corn."

"Interesting," Oliver murmured.

Jude grinned. "Let's just say it's a whole lot more tasty
than those nasty fish eggs."

"Oliver has a discerning palate," Jude's brother Christopher Fortune Jones tossed out as he strolled past. "And
you, bro, are just a hick from the sticks."

Jude's eyes flashed, but then Gabi wrapped her arms
around his neck and pressed her nicely curved body against
him. "I like you just the way you are, sweetie pie."

Oliver couldn't decide if he'd just witnessed normal
sibling interaction or if there was more behind the tension
between the brothers.

"Oh my goodness." Gabi pulled from Jude's arms. "I
almost forgot."

The pretty Latina turned to Josephine, who still held
her grandson.

"I hope you don't mind. I asked my father to join us
tonight. Jude and I had planned to have dinner with him.
Then you called and—"

"Orlando is here?" Josephine sounded oddly breathless.

"He's on his way. I hope it's no trouble."

"No trouble at all." Josephine's free hand rose to smooth
her hair. "Orlando is always welcome."

Jude and Gabi wandered off to speak with Quinn and
Amelia.

"I need to freshen, uh, check on a few things." Josephine's long elegant fingers fluttered in the air, sending
diamonds flashing in the light.

"Would you like me to get everyone settled before we

leave?" Wendy asked Josephine as relatives continued to arrive.

"That would be very much appreciated." Josephine patted her niece's shoulder, even as her gaze remained fixed on the door.

"Everyone." Wendy spoke loudly above the conversational din. "The waiters have appetizers and beverages for you in the party room. The buffet is in the process of being set up. Please make your way down the hall."

"Thank you, dear," Josephine said. "I'm sorry you can't stay."

"Next time," Wendy began.

"Honey, we're late." Marcos took his wife's arm.

After offering Josephine a quick hug, Wendy hurried off with her husband and daughter, stopping for a second where Shannon stood speaking with a couple Oliver didn't recognize. Locals, he decided, noticing the denim and boots.

His mother surprised him by calling Shannon's name and motioning to her when she began to head out the door with Wendy and Marcos. When Shannon sauntered over, Josephine took one of her hands. "I fear I didn't make it clear—I'd love for you to join us."

"C'mon, Shannon, join us. Please." Gabi had returned. She slanted a glance at Oliver. "Shannon made me feel so welcome when I came to stay in Horseback Hollow last year after my father's accident."

Clearly, the two women were friends. Still, Shannon hesitated. "I don't want to intrude."

"You're not intruding." Oliver's gaze locked on hers. "You're very much wanted."

You're very much wanted.

What was there about the sentiment, said in that delightful British accent, that made her want to giggle like a nervous schoolgirl? The words echoed in her head, even as Shannon gestured to Rachel that she'd call her later. Her friend smiled and nodded, then refocused her attention back on the cowboy who was eating the last nacho.

While Ollie remained tightly clutched in his grandmother's arms, Shannon strolled with Oliver down a wide hallway to a large room that resembled the inside of a Mexican hacienda. It had arched doorways, stucco walls of bold red and spicy mustard and a tile floor that complemented the warmth of the walls.

Oliver slanted a sideways glance. "It was fortuitous, running into you here."

"Fortuitous for me." Shannon shot him an impish smile. "I'm getting dinner out of the deal."

"And I will have the pleasure of your company," Oliver said gallantly.

"You're going to be sick of me very soon," she teased with an ease that surprised her. "Underfoot practically 24/7."

"I'll be working a lot of hours," he said seriously. "Our contact will likely be minimal."

Shannon pulled back a scowl. He didn't have to sound so doggone pleased at the prospect. "Hopefully you'll carve out some time to play with Ollie."

Surprise flashed in his eyes. "Entertaining him, keeping him safe and tending to his needs will now be your job."

Before she could formulate a response, she was handed a margarita and Oliver was swept away.

Though Shannon hadn't done much socializing with the British branch of the Fortunes who'd recently arrived in Horseback Hollow, she'd grown up with Jeanne Marie's children. There were seven of them and they were all here tonight, as was Josephine's sister, Jeanne Marie.

Shannon mingled, accepting an empanada appetizer from a passing waiter before taking a seat at a table with Gabi and Kinsley Aaron. Kinsley was the outreach coordinator for the Fortune Foundation and engaged to Christopher Fortune Jones.

Since both women were set to be wed on Valentine's Day, bridal talk dominated the conversation and continued after they went through the buffet line and sat down with their plates of food.

Oliver stood across the room, caught up in conversation with his brother-in-law, Quinn Drummond. Back in middle school, Shannon had the hugest crush on Quinn. When she was thirteen she'd gathered the courage to ask him to a turnabout dance.

When both Quinn and Oliver turned to look at her, Shannon smiled and wiggled her fingers in a semblance of a wave, praying Quinn wasn't relaying to Oliver the awful story of how she'd awkwardly asked him out.

Abruptly she turned to Gabi and bared her teeth as her gaze flickered. "All clear?"

Gabi swallowed a bite of salad. "Perfect. Why?"

"Just checking." Shannon glanced at Gabi's chicken taco salad; heavy on romaine, light on cheese, no tortilla bowl. "How's the salad?"

"Delicious." Gabi smiled. "What about the enchiladas?"

"Truly out of this world." Shannon took another bite, savoring the taste. "You should try one."

The suggestion was out before she remembered Gabi was committed to eating nutritionally. Looking at her, it was hard to believe Gabi had needed a heart transplant when she was nineteen.

"This will fill me up, thanks." Gabi flashed an easy smile and gestured to where Oliver now stood speaking with his sister, Amelia. "Give me your take on Oliver."

Though she and Gabi were currently alone—Kinsley had joined her fiancé at another table—Shannon didn't immediately answer. "What do you mean?"

"You must like him well enough to go to work for him, to live with him."

"I think our *business* arrangement will work out well for both of us." Shannon chose her words carefully, knowing whatever she said stood a good chance of getting back to Oliver.

Jude was his cousin, after all. And Gabi didn't seem the type to have secrets from her fiancé.

"I'm asking what you think of him as a man." Gabi waggled a fork at Shannon. Her dark eyes sparkled. "Admit it. Doesn't that sexy accent make you want to swoon?"

"Who are you swooning over, Gabrielle?" Jude appeared out of nowhere to plop down in the chair Kinsley had recently vacated. "Before you answer, let me warn you that it better be me."

He lifted her hand to his mouth and kissed her knuckles.

"Sorry, Charlie." Gabi wrinkled her nose, her tone teasing. "Your cousin Oliver's accent has us both swooning. Isn't that right, Shannon?"

"That's a kick in the shorts." Though he tried to look stern, Jude failed miserably. Once he got the smile that kept trying to form on his lips under control, he turned and called out, "Oliver, get your ass over here."

Oliver merely glanced over at the sound of his name.

Jude made an impatient "come here" motion with his hand.

After a few final words to his sister, Oliver strode over.

"He was speaking with Amelia." Shannon had a sinking feeling she knew why Jude had summoned Oliver.

"Now he'll be speaking with us," Jude said, suddenly

all affable-cowboy charm. He reached over and pulled up a chair when Oliver approached the table. "Join us."

Oliver's brows pulled together.

Beneath Oliver's polished smile, Shannon saw signs of fatigue. Had everyone forgotten that he'd made a transatlantic flight with a toddler only days earlier?

"What can I do for you, Jude?" Oliver asked.

Shannon thought his eyes may have lingered on her for an extra heartbeat, but she couldn't be certain.

"You can stop making the ladies swoon."

Obviously perplexed, Oliver glanced over at Shannon for clarification.

She simply smiled and shifted her gaze to Jude. This was his bronc in the rodeo, not hers.

"These ladies—" Jude gestured to Shannon and Gabi "—are swooning over your accent."

Oliver ignored Gabi to focus on Shannon. Though she'd never been the wilting-violet, blushing type, heat rose up her neck.

"Actually, it was me." Gabi raised her hand like a schoolgirl eager to talk. "I adore your accent. Though I'm not sure the effect would be the same, can you teach me to speak like you?"

Poor Oliver.

Two lines formed between his brows. It was obvious he didn't quite know what to make of his cousin's soon-to-be bride or the plate of cowboy caviar someone shoved into his hand.

"Gabi's teasing you." Shannon spoke in a matter-of-fact tone and took a sip of the margarita.

"Oh."

"I'm in the mood for some dancing," Jude announced. "Mind keeping the ladies company while I get that started?"

"Dancing?" Shannon smiled. "On what dance floor?"

"That will be remedied momentarily," Jude said over his shoulder.

"Don't even bother trying to figure him out." Gabi's tone was filled with warm affection. The smile was still on her lips when she shifted her attention to Oliver. "I was surprised to see Amelia and Quinn here."

"Why?"

"Their baby is so tiny."

"I'm certain whoever is watching her has been cleared by Scotland Yard."

Oliver sat the plate of "caviar" down just as the sweet melody of a romantic ballad filled the air, followed by Jude's booming voice.

"I don't know about the other grooms-to-be, but with the wedding less than two weeks away, I need to practice my dance steps," Jude said.

"Give it up, Jude," one of his brothers called out. "Practice isn't going to change the fact that you have two left feet."

"He does not," Gabi muttered indignantly.

"Shut up, Chris," Jude shot back good-naturedly. "We're going to use this part of the room for dancin', so everyone put down your drinks and grab a partner."

"That's my man," Gabi said with pride. "A real take-charge guy."

Her take-charge guy returned to the table to pull her to her feet and lead her to the area he had cleared for dancing. They weren't the only couple. All around Shannon and Oliver, men and women were pairing up.

When Shannon saw a woman walk by with a toddler, it struck Shannon that she hadn't seen Ollie for a while. "Where's Ollie?"

"Mum is changing his nappy." Oliver grasped on to

the topic like a drowning man would grab a life jacket. "I couldn't pry him away from her even if I wanted to."

Do you want to, Oliver?

He looked at her so strangely that for a split second Shannon thought she must have spoken aloud. Until she realized his growing unease was because everyone who'd been seated at their table was now dancing.

Oliver pushed back his chair and abruptly stood. When he opened his mouth, Shannon found herself anticipating what it would feel like to be held in his strong arms.

"If you'll excuse me." His head inclined in a slight bow. "I must check on my son."

Oliver turned on his heel and strode off, leaving Shannon alone and, just as when she was thirteen, without a date for the dance.

Chapter Six

By ten the next morning, Oliver had fed his son, changed his nappy for the third time and was ready to get down to business. He placed Ollie in his car seat and set off for the Triple S ranch.

He called Shannon's father to make sure he'd be home, indicating he had something of a personal nature to discuss with him. When Shep had bluntly asked what it was, Oliver told him it was a matter best discussed in person. So here he was, on a bright and sunny Saturday morning in early February, headed over to clarify with a Texas rancher that he didn't have designs on his daughter.

Certainly Shannon intrigued him. How could she not, with eyes the color of rich, dark cocoa and a smile that pierced his reserve as easily as an arrow through marshmallow. Was it any wonder that last night he'd been seriously tempted to ask her to dance?

Oliver wheeled the Mercedes onto the highway, remembering how very close he'd come to asking her. But that, he thought rather righteously, was the difference between a strong man and a weak one. No matter how tempted he was to see what it would feel like to hold her in his arms, Oliver hadn't given in to temptation.

In fact, he'd walked away. Not because he couldn't handle the temptation but because he'd seen the way her foot tapped in time to the music and the longing way she glanced at the couples dancing. By leaving the table, he'd made it easier for other men to ask her.

Yet, when he'd watched his cousin Galen stroll over and Shannon had risen to take his arm, Oliver had felt a twinge of unease. He hoped his cousin was an honorable man.

Oliver couldn't help noticing Galen held her a little too closely when they danced. And why was he whispering in her ear? What could they be saying that was so secretive? It had to be a ploy to get even closer to her. And from what Oliver had observed, it worked.

Actually it was something Oliver might have done if she'd been in his arms. But Shannon was his employee. Not that a man couldn't dance with his employee. But he could never hold her close.

The last thing Oliver wanted was to mess up a good working relationship before it even began. Some women could handle a casual, meaningless affair. He had the distinct impression that Shannon wasn't like those women. In fact, she'd made it clear she wanted a business relationship only. He'd agreed. He'd given her his word. And a gentleman always kept his word.

Though right now Oliver didn't feel much like a gentleman.

Thoughts of Shannon occupied him during the rest of the drive to the Singleton ranch. By the time Oliver turned onto the long lane leading to the house, Ollie was fast asleep. Oliver stifled a groan at the sight of the boy's lolling head in the rearview mirror. He'd discovered if Ollie napped throughout the day, he often didn't sleep well at night.

But Oliver couldn't concern himself with that now. He would get through another night of little to no sleep with the thought that tomorrow night Shannon would be there to take care of Ollie. And Oliver would finally be able to get back to business.

For now, he had a different kind of business to attend to, and he wasn't looking forward to it.

Before confirming a time, he'd asked Shep if Shannon was home. According to Shep, she'd left early that morning to attend a "farmers' market" in Vicker's Corners and wasn't expected back until noon. By that time, Oliver's business should be concluded.

The Singleton home was a two-story with white siding, black shutters and a wraparound porch. The bushes on each side of the walk leading to the front steps looked like a sturdy variety with burnished red leaves and tiny thorns.

Oliver noticed the ceiling of the porch was painted blue, like the sky. Seeing the swing made him wonder if Shannon ever sat there and shared kisses with some lucky man while a full moon shone overhead.

Oliver chuckled at the fanciful thought and shifted Ollie's weight in his arms. Though his son was by no means fat, he was sturdy, weighing in at approximately a stone and a half. Not that easy to carry when he squirmed as he was doing now.

Having Ollie with him wasn't ideal but Oliver had brought some of the boy's favorite toys, so hopefully that would keep him occupied during the brief discussion with Shannon's father.

When Oliver reached the front door, he had Ollie stand beside him while he rang the bell.

The door opened several seconds later.

"You must be Oliver." Shep Singleton was a tall man in his late fifties with a thick thatch of gray hair and a lean, weathered face.

Dressing down for the occasion had been a smart move, Oliver decided. Though he considered this a business call, he hadn't worn his suit. Instead he'd taken a page from Jensen's playbook and chosen a pair of khakis and a polo.

Even with the concession, he felt overdressed compared with Shep's jeans and flannel shirt.

Because Shep didn't extend his hand, Oliver kept his own at his side.

"Come in." Shep motioned to him. "Lilian has coffee brewin' and she's cutting some slices of her blue-ribbon banana bread."

Oliver didn't think he'd ever had blue-ribbon banana bread. In fact he was fairly certain he'd never had regular banana bread. He considered asking how blue ribbon differed from regular, just for his own edification, but decided it wasn't important. Not when they had more important things to discuss.

He followed Shep into a foyer that was pleasant but unremarkable, with a staircase straight ahead and a parlor to the right. Because the older man's strides were long, Oliver was forced to pick up Ollie to keep pace.

The kitchen was as old-fashioned as the rest of the house, with appliances the color of avocado and a chrome kitchen table with a swirly gray-green top. There was an ornamental print on the wall with teapots and kettles of all shapes and colors.

A slender woman who reminded Oliver of her daughter, with warm brown eyes and hair the color of strong tea, turned to greet him.

"It's so good to finally meet you," Lilian said with a warm, welcoming smile. "When Shep told me you were stopping by, I hoped you'd be bringing this little guy with you."

Her gaze lingered on Ollie, and a soft look filled her eyes. She reached inside a clown jar and pulled out what looked like an oat biscuit. The questioning look in her eyes had Oliver nodding.

Lilian moved slowly to the child, who stood looking around the colorful kitchen with a wide, unblinking look of wonder.

"Hi, Ollie." She crouched down with the ease of a woman used to constant movement.

The toddler stared at her.

"Do you like cookies?" Lilian held it up in front of him, and when she was certain she had his attention, she broke off a piece and held it out to him.

A shy smile hovered on Ollie's lips. Still, after a moment, he reached out and took the piece from her hand, shoving it into his mouth.

"Ollie, what do you say to Mrs. Singleton?" Oliver prompted.

"Tank ooh," Ollie spoke around a mouthful of cookie.

Lilian ruffled his hair in a casual gesture and stood. "He's darling. Shannon has four younger brothers, so we're used to boys around this house."

"Four boys." Oliver almost cringed. He had a difficult time managing one. "That must have kept you busy."

"I'll say. For years I didn't know if I was coming or going. I longed for just a couple hours to myself. Even fifteen minutes." She laughed and a wistful look crossed her face. "Now I'd give anything to have that time back."

Her gaze dropped to Ollie. "Cherish every minute with your son. Time goes by so quickly."

Shep cleared his throat. "I told Oliver you had some banana bread for us. And coffee."

Lilian flashed a smile. "What's conversation without coffee and banana bread?"

Without realizing how it happened, Oliver was at the table with a steaming mug of strong coffee before him and a small plate containing delicious-smelling bread still warm from the oven.

He waited for Lilian to dispense the sterling, but when none was forthcoming and he saw Shep pick up the slice and take a bite, Oliver followed suit. When in Rome…

"This blue-ribbon banana bread is excellent," he told Lilian, making her blush.

"Last year it won a purple at the state fair."

Oliver simply nodded and smiled. He made a mental note to ask his sister about a "purple."

"Well, I'll leave you boys to your business." Lilian refilled their coffee cups before her gaze shifted to Oliver. "Being as it's such a nice day, I thought I'd air out some blankets on the line. Would you mind if I took Ollie with me? I promise I'll keep an eye on him."

Oliver hesitated. "He's wanted to stay close lately. Last night he didn't even want my mum to hold him."

Of course, his mother had unthinkingly swooped in, startling him. Still, Ollie had recently become cautious around people he didn't know. Other than Shannon. He'd taken to her right off.

"Do you mind if I give it a try?"

"Not at all." It would be easier to speak with Shep if he didn't have to keep Ollie occupied.

"Ollie." Lilian crouched down beside the boy, who still

held the scruffy yellow tiger he'd had when Oliver had picked him up from Diane's parents.

According to Diane's mum, they'd given the stuffed animal to Ollie when he was born, and it was a favorite of his. She'd had tears in her eyes when she'd relayed the story, Oliver recalled.

At the time, Oliver hadn't paid much mind to her. He'd been so angry with them for withholding information of Diane's death. For keeping his son from him.

"Would you like to go outside with me? You can take Mr. Tiger with you, if you like," her voice continued, low, calm and soothing.

There was something about the way Lilian spoke that reminded Oliver of Shannon. An intonation. Or a certain cadence in her speech. Not an accent, though the woman certainly sounded American. He finally concluded it was the warmth that wove through each word like a wool scarf on a foggy morning.

Whatever the reason, Ollie responded the same way to Lilian as he had to Shannon. Instantly and with no hesitation.

Lilian took his hand in hers. The two made it all the way to the door leading outside before they turned back. "Say, 'Bye-bye, Daddy. See you soon.'"

She demonstrated a wave for the child.

"Bye-bye," Ollie said in his high-pitched, sweet baby voice. "See you soon."

Oliver smiled, even though he noticed Ollie didn't call him "Daddy." He never did. Of course his vocabulary was rather limited, consisting of only twenty-five words. Still, if Ollie could say the dog's name, shouldn't he be able to say "Daddy"?

Once the back door banged shut, Oliver decided to get

right to the point. "I suppose you're wondering why I'm here."

Shep lifted his piece of bread. "I figure you're fixin' to tell me."

The older man bit into the bread, then washed the piece down with a swig of coffee. He leaned back in his chair and studied Oliver intently.

For a second Oliver felt like one of those young lads in films, meeting his girl's parents for the first time. Oliver had no personal experience in this arena. He'd been sent to a preparatory school when he was thirteen. Functions with suitable girls' schools had been prearranged. No parents involved.

"Your daughter has agreed to be Ollie's nanny while I'm in Horseback Hollow."

"She mentioned something about that the other night," Shep admitted.

Oliver felt a surprising surge of relief. "Then you don't have a problem with her moving in."

The mug of coffee Shep had lifted to his mouth froze in midair. He lowered it slowly until it came to rest on the table.

Unlike his daughter's, Shep's eyes were a piercing pale blue. Oliver felt the full force of his gaze punch into him.

"Move in. With you?"

"Not with me," Oliver clarified, keeping his tone conversational. "Into the house."

"Your house."

"Technically your house," Oliver pointed out.

"Don't give me any double-talk, boy." Shep's eyes narrowed and Oliver felt as if he were in the crosshairs of his father's foul temper once again.

Though Rhys Henry Hayes hadn't remained married to Josephine for long, it had been long enough for them to have two sons together, and for his father to make Oliver's life a living hell.

"Shannon will always be treated with respect when she's under my roof." Oliver met Shep's gaze with a calm one of his own.

As a young boy, Oliver had vowed he'd never be intimidated by any man ever again. "That's why I'm here. To let you know she will be my son's nanny. My employee. Nothing more. She's safe with me."

Shep's expression gave nothing away. He took a big gulp of coffee before he responded. "Shannon is twenty-five. As much as I'd like to, I can't make her decisions. But I will speak bluntly."

"Please do," Oliver said quietly.

"After what happened in Lubbock, after that incident, I don't feel comfortable with her being there with only a baby in diapers as a chaperone."

Oliver cocked his head. "What incident in Lubbock?"

"Oliver."

Shannon paused in the doorway, taking in the cozy scene with her father and Oliver at the table. She let her gaze sweep over the half-eaten pieces of banana bread and coffee mugs in need of refills.

"Your father was about to tell me about some incident in Lubbock," Oliver told her.

Despite telling herself not to react, Shannon felt her spine grow rigid, vertebra by vertebra. She shot her father a fulminating glance that, as usual, he ignored.

"Correct me if I'm wrong, but I believe that's my story to tell. Or not." Forcing a smile, Shannon shifted her attention back to Oliver. "It's not all that interesting. I had a boss who got a little handsy. It's over and done. I've moved on."

The back door clattered and seconds later, her mother

strode into the room, Ollie chattering happily at her side. "Shannon, honey. When did you get home?"

"Just walked through the door," Shannon answered absently, her mind back in Lubbock. She didn't like thinking of that time. It was in the past and she meant what she'd said to Oliver—she'd moved on. "Do you have any more banana bread?"

"It'll spoil your appetite for lunch," her father warned.

Some things never change, Shannon thought ruefully. But instead of being irritated, she found the knowledge strangely reassuring.

"You're eating it," she pointed out. "Won't it spoil *your* lunch?"

"Nope." Shep grinned and popped the last bite into his mouth.

Shannon rolled her eyes. "Oh, honestly."

Oliver's gaze traveled between her and her father, as if he found their simple exchange fascinating.

Out of the corner of her eye, Shannon saw Ollie run across the room to Oliver. He swung the child onto his lap with a welcoming smile.

Shannon's heart swelled. How could she have ever thought this man didn't care about his son?

"I hope the bread didn't spoil your appetite, Oliver. I'd love to have you join us for lunch." Lilian wrapped the rest of the loaf in plastic wrap. "We're having quiche."

Shep grimaced. "Aw, Lil, why not burgers?"

"Too much red meat isn't good for you." Lilian's argument was an old one, repeated daily. She shifted to Oliver. "We're also having a nice salad of dark greens with a balsamic vinaigrette I make myself."

"What happened to the good ole days of iceberg and Thousand Island?" Shep groused.

Lilian ignored the comment to focus on their guest. "If

you don't think Ollie would like quiche, I can rustle him up some mac and cheese."

Shannon expected Oliver to make some excuse to leave. Once again he surprised her.

"Thank you, Mrs. Singleton." He gestured to the now-empty plate before him. "If your quiche is as good as your blue-ribbon banana bread, I'm in for a treat."

"Splendid. And please, call me Lilian." Her mother smiled. "If you and Shep have concluded your conversation, why don't you take Shannon and Ollie out to the porch and check out the swing? It's a beautiful day and it'll give me a chance to clear the table and get ready for lunch. Shouldn't be more than a half hour or so."

Oliver rose and smiled at Shannon. "I don't know that I've ever sat with a pretty woman on a porch swing before."

Shep shoved back his chair. "I'll join you."

"Honey." Lilian covered the sharp tone with a laugh. "You're not going anywhere. You're staying right here and helping me."

"I can help you, Mother."

"No, no. Your father will help." Lilian turned to her husband and looped her arm through his. "Shep, sweetie, I think I may have a bottle of Thousand Island in the pantry after all. Why don't you look for it while Shannon and Oliver head outside?"

Shannon thought about telling her mother she knew exactly where to find the salad dressing, but kept her mouth shut. Her mother had it in her head that she and Oliver were going to have some time alone on the swing, and there was no getting around that.

Besides, Shannon was curious about what Oliver and her father had been discussing when she arrived. For that matter, she wanted to know exactly what had brought Oliver to the Singleton ranch this morning in the first place.

At this moment, she hadn't a clue. Oliver was a difficult man to figure out. Like last night at the dinner party. They'd been having a perfectly lovely conversation when he'd ditched her. Once he'd left the table, she hadn't seen him again all evening.

She'd enjoyed a couple of dances with his cousin, then headed out. Now she arrived home to find him shooting the breeze with her dad.

"Oliver." She looped her arm through his and shot him the same sugary-sweet smile her mother had offered her father only seconds earlier. "Let's swing and you can tell me what brought you all the way out here this morning."

Chapter Seven

Though it was only February, the outside temperature felt more like June. Thankfully there was a light breeze from the north and the covered porch shielded Oliver and Shannon from the worst of the midday sun. Shannon took a seat at one end of the swing and Oliver sat down with Ollie at the other.

Almost immediately, the child left his father's lap to scoot over to Shannon. He rested his head on her lap and she automatically began to stroke his soft brown hair. In seconds, his eyelids closed and he fell quickly asleep.

"He shouldn't be that tired." Oliver glanced down at his son with a worried frown. "He slept in the car on the way here."

"Little boys expend a lot of energy." Shannon smiled, then sobered as she remembered there was something they needed to discuss. She met his gaze. "Tell me why you came all the way out here today."

"To speak with your father."

Shannon curbed her impatience and merely lifted a brow. "About?"

"The comments Marcos made last night got me to thinking." Oliver shifted on the white lacquered slats. "I decided to reassure your father you would be safe and respected under my roof."

Shannon pressed her lips together and counted to five. "I am in charge of my own life, Oliver. Whatever goes on, or doesn't, under your roof is our business. Not my father's. Not my mother's. Understand?"

He stared at her for a long moment. "I see your point."

"I appreciate that your intentions came from a good place," she acknowledged. "But this is between us."

She wasn't sure exactly what all "this" encompassed, but for now it was simply the job and taking care of Ollie.

"You went behind my back." Shannon did her best to keep the hurt from her voice. After growing up in a family of men, she'd learned there was no quicker turnoff than to lead from emotion. "You never even mentioned you were considering speaking with my father."

"That's because it was something I decided last night."

"There were opportunities during the evening when you could have discussed your concerns with me," she said pointedly.

He reluctantly nodded, then surprised them both by reaching over and taking her hand. "Apologies. I overstepped."

She searched his gaze and saw only sincerity.

"Accepted." Shannon made no move to pull her hand away as the swing moved slowly.

"What happened in Lubbock?"

She blinked and jerked her fingers free. "I already told you."

"You said your previous employer got 'handsy.' That's not much of an explanation."

Should she tell him? If so, how much should she say? Even though it wasn't all that long ago, in Shannon's mind it was ancient history. She'd moved on. Still, it wasn't as if she had anything to hide, and if she didn't spill, she wouldn't put it past Oliver to do some investigating on his own.

"My last job was with a marketing firm in Lubbock. My direct supervisor, Jerry, was the CEO's nephew." Though Shannon did her best to keep her voice matter-of-fact, it shook slightly. She continued to stroke Ollie's hair and found the motion relaxed her. "He wasn't much older than me, but he was married with two kids."

Oliver made an encouraging sound.

Shannon felt the urge to get up and pace, but couldn't because of Ollie. The twist in her belly told her she wasn't completely over what had happened. Not fully, anyway.

"Jerry seemed nice at first, though there was something about him that put me on alert. Too many compliments of a personal nature, and whenever he was at my desk, he stood too close. I told myself I was just overreacting. At my previous job I'd worked with all women, so overreacting seemed plausible."

Oliver didn't speak, simply inclined his head in a gesture that seemed to indicate she should keep talking.

"Then he started touching me."

Oliver's head jerked up and a muscle in his jaw jumped. "Touching you?"

"It started out innocent enough—a hand on my shoulder while he leaned over to look at my computer screen, brushing back a strand of hair from my face." Shannon gazed down at Ollie's head resting in her lap. She swallowed past the dryness in her throat. "I told him the touching made me uncomfortable. But no matter what I said, he turned it around and made me wonder if I was being too sensitive. You know, making something out of nothing."

"He made you doubt your instincts."

"Yes. He didn't listen to my concerns, didn't acknowledge they were valid. I let the issue drop. That was my first mistake."

"What happened?" Oliver asked in a low, tight voice.

"One night, shortly before Thanksgiving, we were working late. I made a point to never be alone with him. It started out as four of us working on a campaign. The other two ended up leaving. I was almost finished so I stayed behind. That was my second mistake."

Without her quite realizing how it had happened, her hand was once again in Oliver's. The warmth of his strong fingers wrapping around hers gave Shannon the strength to continue.

"He—he pulled me to him, kissed me, told me his wife and kids were out of town and we'd have his house to ourselves. No one would ever know." Shame bubbled up inside Shannon. "He wouldn't let go of me. Finally I was able to jerk away. My shirt tore. I started crying."

"Bastard," she thought she heard Oliver mutter.

"I reminded him he was a married man. He laughed and called me a tease. But when I said I was going to his boss, he turned the tables again and accused me of coming on to him. Said he was shocked and appalled by my behavior. Then he asked who did I think his uncle would believe? Him, an upstanding family man and deacon of his church? Or me? A single woman who'd never complained about his behavior until now?" Shannon lifted her gaze to meet Oliver's. "I turned in my resignation without even giving notice. I returned to Horseback Hollow and put it all behind me."

Oliver's fingers tightened around hers.

She waited for him to say that she should have stood up for herself, should have at least told his uncle the story, but to her relief he didn't.

"I loved my job," she added. "It was hard to walk away. But I didn't see that I had any choice."

"You made the best decision for you."

"I did." Shannon felt herself relax and was sorry when Oliver released her hand. "Though it still makes me angry you went behind my back, it's probably a good thing you spoke with my father. He doesn't have a very high opinion of male employers right now."

"I meant what I said," Oliver told her. "You're perfectly safe with me."

Shannon could only wonder why she found his words more disappointing than reassuring.

When Oliver arrived home later, it was after two. By then Ollie was cranky and out of sorts. After changing his nappy, Oliver sat the boy down on the rug in the living room with his bricks, hoping a little quiet play would relax him.

But Ollie refused to be distracted or comforted. He knocked down the stack that Oliver had arranged, then picked up one and flung it across the room. When Oliver tried to put him down for a nap, he stood at the edge of the playpen and cried, rocking back and forth like a monkey in a cage as tears slipped down his chubby cheeks.

Though Oliver had some catching up to do on market indices, he lifted his son up and settled into the rocker with him. Every time Ollie pulled back, Oliver would bring him back against him. Finally the boy quit struggling, his hands resting on his shoulders as Oliver rocked him. Back and forth. Back and forth.

Oliver wondered if Diane had ever rocked Ollie. Or, for that matter, had Mrs. Crowder, his London nanny? This was a first for him, but he'd been desperate. As he felt his son relax against him, Oliver realized rocking was really quite nice. A connection. Between him and Ollie.

A connection that only served to remind him how much of Ollie's life he'd missed.

Not insisting on regular visitation had been a mistake. Just as Shannon not pressing charges against her boss had been a mistake. In his estimation the man shouldn't be able to harass an employee—hell, *assault* an employee—and get away with it.

Not only get away with it, but make her feel as if the whole thing was somehow her fault. That's why he hadn't added to her guilt by suggesting she could have handled the situation differently. She'd made the best decision based on where she was at the time.

Oliver closed his eyes, realizing he was more tired than he thought. Adjusting to a different time zone while having total care of a small boy had proved more difficult than he'd initially envisioned.

His respect for mothers and nannies had gone up a thousandfold...

Oliver awoke to a small hand pressed against his face. When his lids eased open, he found himself staring directly into Ollie's bright eyes.

"Up," Ollie ordered. "Get up."

The child could say "get up" but couldn't manage "Daddy"?

By the foul smell permeating the air, Oliver knew Ollie wouldn't simply need a nappy change. He'd probably need a bath, as well. His prediction proved correct.

It wasn't until Ollie was changed, bathed and fed that it struck Oliver that the child's schedule was going to be disrupted once again. Tonight was Amelia and Quinn's baby shower. He wasn't certain what to expect, but he assumed a gift was de rigueur. Thankfully, Oliver hadn't had a chance to give them the limited-edition Highgrove baby hamper he'd picked up at Harrods department store before he left London.

Though he wasn't sure if Amelia was still into organic supplies or not, the hamper contained not only a fully jointed antique mohair Highgrove bear, but an assortment of organic baby products created with a blend of oils to be calm and soothing to a baby's skin. The salesclerk had assured him the baby hamper was a popular gift for new mothers.

Diane had been a new mother once. Had she been as thrilled by Ollie as Amelia was by Clementine? Perhaps.

Oliver raked a hand through his hair. Their marriage had already been in trouble when Ollie was born. He'd dealt with the increased tension and Diane's unhappiness in the only way he knew how, by working even harder and giving her expensive trinkets. It hadn't been enough. Oliver expelled a heavy push of air, feeling the full weight of his failure.

He placed Ollie in the Pack 'n Play and watched his son pick up a toy truck with a squeal of delight.

He'd made so many mistakes…

Banishing the unproductive thoughts and emotions, Oliver motioned Barnaby off the sofa and headed for the shower. He'd never been to a couple's baby party. Gabi and Jude were hosting the event, held at his aunt Jeanne Marie's spacious ranch home.

By the time Oliver arrived, cars and trucks lined both sides of the graveled drive. He parked at the end of the long line. A truck immediately pulled in behind him.

He paid little attention, his focus on releasing Ollie from

his car seat. They were late and Oliver prided himself on being punctual. However, when he'd let Barnaby outside, right before they were to leave home, the dog had run off. Oliver had wasted precious minutes looking for the animal, who'd received a stern lecture once he returned.

"We're going to have to quit meeting like this."

He turned and there was Shannon, wearing a shirt and skirt the color of mint, her hair pulled back in a casual twist.

"You look amazing," he said.

"You don't look so bad yourself." Her gaze settled momentarily on his gray trousers and open-necked white shirt. "Let me hold your gift while you fumble with the car seat."

"Fumble is right." Oliver gave a laugh. "He's strapped in tighter than most astronauts."

Shannon stood close while he unbuckled Ollie. The light vanilla scent of her perfume was pleasing. "I should have realized you'd be here, what with Amelia being your sister."

"A sister who is a bugger about punctuality."

"We're not that—" Shannon glanced at her watch. "Eek. You're right. We are late. We need to hoof it."

She started down the lane toward the house at a surprisingly fast clip, the gifts hugged to her chest.

Oliver scooped up Ollie and headed after her.

They reached the house at the same time and climbed the steps to the porch in unison. Oliver rang the bell.

It was only seconds before the door opened and Jude waved them inside.

The gifts were lifted from Shannon's hands and Gabi directed Oliver to a temporary playroom set up at the back of the house. Several children were already there, along with two teenage child-care workers.

To Oliver's surprise, Ollie screeched in excitement and hurried over to pick up a plastic bat. Oliver only shook his head. His son's mercurial moods were a constant mystery. He told the teenage babysitter to come and get him if Ollie got scared.

As he didn't want to simply disappear—though the thought was tempting—Oliver walked over to Ollie and told him he was leaving and would be back soon. Ollie blinked, opening and closing his hand in the gesture Lilian had taught him. "Bye-bye."

Before leaving the room, Oliver reiterated to the young woman monitoring the door not to hesitate to retrieve him if Ollie turned fussy. He saw by the look on her face she'd written him off as just another overprotective parent. Especially considering Ollie was now happily banging the plastic bat like a drum on the floor.

His duty completed, Oliver hurried from the room and found Shannon waiting with two flutes of champagne.

She shoved one into his hand. "For you."

"Thank you." He took a sip and found the vintage very much to his taste. As they strolled down the hall, Oliver began to relax. "This evening may not be so bad after all."

"I'll ask how you feel after the games."

"Games?"

"Oh, yeah," Shannon said as they headed into the large double parlor where the guests were congregated. "You can't have a baby shower without games."

Oliver couldn't begin to imagine what kind of games she meant.

"There's the last couple," Gabi called out when he and Shannon entered the parlor. "We can get started now."

For a second, Oliver looked around to see whom she meant until he realized she was talking about him and

Shannon. He started to protest until he saw Shannon's friend Rachel had been paired with Quinn's elderly aunt.

Not that he minded being paired with Shannon for whatever games they would play; he simply didn't want to put her in an awkward position of everyone thinking they were a couple.

"What's the game, Gabi?" Shannon smiled easily, looking relaxed among this group of friends.

Even though Amelia was his sister and he was family, Oliver was clearly the outsider today. Though he was proficient at social conversation, he was rather relieved Gabi appeared ready to launch into the scheduled activities.

The first game was a baby word scramble. Each "team" was given twenty words where the letters had been scrambled. Oliver was, by nature, a competitive person. He quickly discovered Shannon shared his must-win attitude.

Sitting beside each other on an overstuffed sofa, they breezed through the first nineteen words. Then they reached number twenty.

"BELOTT." Shannon gazed down at the word. Her brows pulled together.

Oliver knew he should be studying the letters. But the simple task of focusing had become increasingly difficult with each word. He couldn't take his eyes off the side of Shannon's face, off the graceful arch of her neck, off the woman who took his breath away.

Her choice of attire for the evening only made it more difficult for him to concentrate. The shirt she wore was a thin fabric. If Oliver looked hard enough, he could practically see right through it to the smooth expanse of creamy skin and the lacy…

His mouth went dry.

"We've got eighteen," he heard Quinn's aunt announce to the room. "Two more and we win."

"One left," Amber said to Jensen.

Shannon leaned closer, as if she thought practically having her nose on the paper would unscramble the word.

All the closeness actually did was further scramble his brain until he couldn't think of anything but how good she smelled and wonder how good she'd taste.

"Twenty," Christopher called in triumph and high-fived Kinsley, then kissed her thoroughly to cheers and applause.

"The last one was the easiest," Kinsley said when she came up for air.

Oliver exchanged a glance with Shannon. She lifted her shoulders in a wordless gesture.

"What was it?" Oliver whispered.

"I have no idea," she said, her tone low and for his ears only. "But I'll find out."

"I'll pick up everyone's papers." Shannon jumped to her feet, collecting the paper and pencils.

She returned to Oliver's side seconds later. "You'll never guess."

He leaned close. "Tell me."

"Bottle."

He groaned. "How did we miss that one?"

"The question is how could we decipher *diaper genie* and fall apart on *bottle*." She laughed good-naturedly. "I guess you can't win 'em all."

As the evening progressed, Shannon discovered Oliver always played to win, whether it was "pin the diaper on the baby" or making a "baby" out of Play-Doh.

But all the Fortunes were competitive. It wasn't until they announced who'd guessed closest to the number of candies in the three-foot-high baby bottle that Oliver claimed his first victory.

"We did it, Shannon." His wide grin made him look years younger.

Actually, he'd done it. She'd wanted to go lower, but he'd convinced her to put the higher number on the guess.

By the time they got to cake and gifts, Shannon had almost forgotten this was a baby shower, an event she normally avoided like the plague. Mainly because it always reminded her she was still alone with no one special in her life.

Oliver stood across the room visiting with his sister when the babysitter appeared in the doorway holding Ollie's hand. The boy's face was tear-streaked. Drops of moisture glistened on his dark lashes.

"He wants his mom and dad," the girl announced to no one in particular.

"I'll take him." Shannon held out her arms and Ollie lunged toward her. She hefted him up and settled him on her hip. "Hey, bud, what's got you so upset?"

Ollie's only answer was to press his face into her neck.

"Looks like he's already halfway in love with you."

Shannon's heart gave a leap but her expression was nonchalant as she turned toward Rachel. "To whom are you referring?"

"Little Ollie. The kid has you in a death grip." Rachel leaned around Shannon and smiled at the boy. "Hi, Ollie. Remember me?"

Ollie burrowed deeper against Shannon.

"I guess I can't impress all the men." Rachel straightened and gave a little laugh. "By the way, it's totally not fair I ended up with Quinn's auntie and you got Oliver."

Shannon smiled benignly. "You've always told me life isn't fair."

Rachel thought for a second then grinned. "You're right.

I'm going to snag one of the leftover baby bottles. Want one?"

Shannon shook her head. The game where the goal was to finish a baby bottle filled with beer had been incredibly frustrating. Who knew bottles emptied so slowly? "No thanks. I've got my hands full right now."

"Later, gator." Rachel gave Ollie a cheeky grin then strolled off.

"Gator." Ollie lifted his head. "Gator."

"That's good, Ollie." Shannon thought for a second. "Can you say…Shannon?"

He stared at her. For a second his oh-so-serious expression reminded her of Oliver. Then he smiled and her heart melted. "Mama."

Shannon chuckled. "Sha-non."

"Mama," he repeated, flinging his arms around her neck.

Though it made absolutely no sense, tears stung the backs of her eyes and she hugged Ollie extra tight. He was so young to be without a mother.

"Amelia is ready to cut the cake." Oliver paused, appearing to notice Ollie for the first time. "What happened?"

"He wanted his daddy." Shannon continued to rub the child's back. "You were busy so we've been bonding. And he's fine now. Aren't you, bud?"

She tickled his ribs and the toddler giggled.

Oliver smiled. "He's pretty heavy. I can take him."

"He's fine." Shannon cuddled Ollie. "Amelia and Quinn sure received a lot of nice gifts for Clementine."

"They did," Oliver agreed, rocking back on the heels of his Ferragamo shoes.

She'd enjoyed watching Oliver mingle with his family in such a relaxed atmosphere. This was why he was in Horseback Hollow. To get reacquainted. To spend time with his sister and his new niece.

"I can tend to Ollie while you socialize." If she could take some of the pressure off him by watching Ollie tonight, she was happy to do it.

"I'm content where I am at the moment," he told her. "Except, I fancy a cake. And some ice cream. Shall I get some for both of us?"

"A man who knows the way to my heart," she teased.

His slow smile had said heart doing flip-flops.

"I'll take that as a yes." Oliver shot her a wink and everything inside her went gooey. "Be right back."

Shannon watched him cross the room to the refreshment table and realized in only a few short days, Oliver Fortune Hayes's happiness had become important to her.

The question was...why?

The reason, she decided, when he reappeared with a slice of strawberry cake in one hand and chocolate in the other, was one best pondered on a full stomach.

Chapter Eight

Spending his Sunday evening grocery shopping at the Superette was not the way Oliver envisioned ending his weekend. Especially after a baby shower had disrupted his normal activities last night.

Oh, whom was he kidding? Nothing had been normal since the day he arrived in Horseback Hollow. But he'd been hopeful that had been about to change. He'd planned on spending the evening preparing for his first full day of work since arriving in Texas. Then Shannon had brought up the serious lack of food in the house.

"What do you think about an asparagus and goat cheese frittata for dinner?" Shannon stopped in front of the dairy case. "I have a great recipe."

"If you're certain it's no trouble."

"No trouble at all." Shannon flashed him a smile. "I love to cook."

She placed a carton of eggs in the shopping trolley, an odd-looking contraption that resembled a red race car.

Though Ollie was strapped in, the boy didn't seem to mind. He happily turned the steering wheel in front of him.

As they went up and down the aisles picking out fruits and vegetables, bread and crackers, Oliver realized he and Diane had never gone to the grocery shop together. He wasn't certain she'd ever gone herself. She may have simply had one of the help handle the mundane task. Perhaps she'd called in the order.

Though Oliver wouldn't exactly call the excursion fun, it wasn't altogether tedious. In almost every aisle they'd run across one of his relatives or a friend of Shannon's. They'd talk for several minutes before continuing down the aisle. Then they'd run into someone else and another conversation would ensue.

The "quick" trip to the store was turning into quite an affair. Still, by the number of groceries in the basket, Shannon had been correct in her assessment. They had been seriously short on rations.

The truth was, he'd spent so much time making sure her room was ready that he'd given little thought to the food situation.

"Does Ollie like these organic food purees?"

Oliver stared at the two pouches she held up, one marked Sweet Potato and the other Blueberry. Had Ollie ever had these? Did he like them? Shannon might as well have asked him to name the ingredients in "blue-ribbon banana bread." "No clue."

Shannon tossed them into the buggy. "I have a friend in Lubbock with a little girl about Ollie's age. Her daughter loves them, so we'll take a chance. They're really good for a growing child."

He bowed to her wisdom. As the oldest of five and with friends who had children, she had the experience and knowledge he needed. Yet, it seemed he should know what food his son preferred.

By the time they reached the checkout lane, the trolley was full. He waited for the cashier to call for someone to assist her. But when Shannon began to drop items into the sacks once they were scanned, Oliver stepped up.

"You picked out the food," he told her. "I'll place them into the sacks."

Ignoring her dubious look, he attacked the task with gusto. His logical mind concluded heavier items should go at the bottom and he shouldn't place cleaning supplies next to food items. Shannon offered additional tips as she sorted the groceries into groups.

"I was a sacker in high school," she said when he gaped at her quick hands.

"You held a position while you were in school?" He paused, nonplussed, a bag of organic apples in his hand.

"Of course." She distracted a whining Ollie by having his stuffed tiger zoom toward him like an airplane. "When there are five kids in your family, if you want something extra you have to work for it."

Oliver simply nodded, though he couldn't relate at all to that logic. In his family there were six children. He and his brother Brodie were from his mother's first marriage. There were four children, his half siblings, from her second marriage to Sir Simon Chesterfield. Oliver felt confident all had received the same admonition growing up: excelling in the classroom was the only priority.

Once the groceries were stowed, he pointed the rental car toward home. As had become his pattern, Ollie fell asleep in his car seat. And when Oliver pulled into the driveway of the ranch house, Ollie woke up, all smiles and full of energy.

Oliver rounded the car to open Shannon's door, but she

was already out of the vehicle and releasing Ollie from his car seat. She helped the boy climb down, then turned to help Oliver with the groceries.

He held up a hand when she reached for a sack. "I will bring these inside. You can put them wherever you like in the cabinets."

"Okay." Despite her agreement, she snatched a small bag of produce. "I'll take this one in with me. That way you'll have one less bag to carry. Oh, and don't worry about Barnaby. Ollie and I will let him out."

With a sassy toss of her head, she strode to the door with Ollie on her hip and a sack of produce in her arms. She had a terrific figure. The way the denim hugged her backside brought a stab of heat and a plethora of lascivious thoughts.

Belatedly reminding himself that the woman he was lusting after was his employee, Oliver forced his gaze from her derriere and back to the groceries in the boot. By the time he'd brought all of the sacks inside and Shannon had put the food away, they were all hungry.

While Shannon whipped up the frittata, he put Ollie in the high chair and fed him leftover chicken from lunch, apples and a pureed pouch of sweet potatoes.

The boy ate with a single-minded determination Oliver couldn't help but admire. Though the cook had tended to Ollie's culinary needs back in London, Oliver found he enjoyed watching his son dive into the food and learning what he liked…and didn't like.

When Ollie finished eating, the sun had set and the serviceable kitchen took on a warm, pleasant glow. The unexpected sound of rain pattering on the roof only added to the ambiance.

"Looks like we arrived home just in time." Oliver pushed back the curtains. Rain fell in sheets and when the thunder boomed, Barnaby left Ollie's side to dive under the table.

Shannon moved to where Oliver stood and gazed out. The arousing scent of vanilla teased Oliver's nostrils. He wanted nothing more than to see if she tasted as good as she smelled. But if his nearness had a similar effect on her, it didn't show.

She stepped back and turned toward the stove. "I love the sound of rain on a roof."

I love being with you.

Considering that he'd already acknowledged enjoying her company, the sentiment shouldn't have surprised him, but it did.

The frittata, accompanied by a green salad, was soon on the table. Oliver brought out a bottle of Chablis, and once he'd poured them each a glass, he held his up in a toast. "To an enjoyable working relationship."

Her glass clinked against his. She smiled. When she took a sip, he felt a hard punch of awareness. Heat simmered in the air, and once their eyes locked he couldn't look away.

Shannon's eyes darkened until they looked almost black in the light. A splash of pink colored both her cheeks. When she moistened her lips with the tip of her tongue, Oliver nearly groaned in agony.

He wanted her. In his bed. On the floor. Heck, the kitchen table would do quite nicely in a pinch.

He wanted to strip off her clothes, touch her...

"Oliver."

Through his haze of desire, he became aware that she was speaking to him.

"Uh, yes?" His gaze remained focused on her lips, as full and lush as a ripe strawberry. He had no doubt she would taste just as sweet.

"I brought some snickerdoodle cookies with me. My mom and I made them earlier today. Would you like one for dessert?"

His foggy brain fought to process the words. Snickerdoodle? Had she really just asked if he wanted a cookie?

He opened his mouth to say he wanted *her*, not some damned biscuit, but instead found himself nodding.

"You won't be sorry." A pleased smile lifted those delectable lips. "They're delicious."

Oliver was already sorry. Sorry he had to settle for a biscuit instead of what he really wanted for dessert tonight.

After dinner, Oliver surprised Shannon by offering to clean up the kitchen so she could get settled. She immediately accepted the offer. Happy to have the time to get settled, Shannon fled to her room before Oliver changed his mind and decided he needed her to watch Ollie.

As she stood in the bedroom with the pale yellow walls and lace curtains, Shannon felt a twinge of unease. She hadn't realized how personal bringing her stuff into a man's home would feel. Though she and Oliver wouldn't be sleeping in the same room, she was supremely aware that his bed was just on the other side of the wall.

Shopping at the Superette had also felt intimate. Almost as if they were a couple, instead of just employer and employee. Part of it, she knew, was because instead of simply going in and grabbing a few things, they'd strolled up and down the aisle chatting with various friends and family.

She'd seen the look of surprise on the faces of the people they'd run across. Oliver must have seen it, too, because he made a point of explaining she was Ollie's nanny. Still, some had continued to look skeptical.

After all, Oliver was hardly treating her like an employee, laughing and joking and giving her almost carte blanche on choosing what they needed.

Then he'd surprised her by insisting on bagging the groceries. When they reached home, he carried the items inside. Had she even thanked him? She paused, a pair of lace panties in her hand, and tried to recall.

Though her door was partially open, a knock sounded.

"Come in," she said absently and turned.

Oliver stood in the doorway, an odd expression on his face.

It took her a second to realize he wasn't looking at her. His gaze was riveted to the black thong dangling from her fingers.

Lightning fast, Shannon whirled and dropped the scrap of lingerie into the drawer. She cleared her throat. "I was just unpacking."

"I saw."

She flushed.

"Ollie is in his cot." Oliver's gaze slid to the open dresser drawer. "I thought I'd take a quick shower but wanted to make sure you didn't need the facilities first."

Shannon shoved aside the thought of him wet and naked and her wet and naked with him. She shut the drawer. "I'm fine. I'll just be unpacking."

He gave a curt nod and turned to leave, but stopped when she said his name.

"Uh, hey, I just wanted to say thanks for everything." She waved a vague hand in the air, but his confused look told Shannon she needed to be more specific. "For putting fresh sheets on my bed. For having the house so clean and organized. For your assistance at the Superette. I didn't expect you to pack up the groceries or carry them inside."

His brows pulled together in puzzlement. "I've learned that taking care of Oliver and the home is a daunting task.

Be assured I shall attempt to lessen the burden on you as much as possible."

Shannon stared at him for a long moment. Who was this man? She thought she'd had a good handle on Oliver Fortune Hayes, but she was beginning to think she didn't know him at all.

Almost of their own accord, her feet crossed the room to where he stood. Without giving herself a chance to think, she placed her hands on his forearms and brushed a kiss across his mouth. "Thank you."

He visibly stiffened. "What's going on, Shannon?"

She took a casual step back. "I'm not sure what you mean."

"The kiss." A muscle in Oliver's jaw jumped. "You made a point of insisting we keep things between us strictly business. I agreed. I gave you my word."

Embarrassment heated her cheeks. She wasn't an impulsive person and had no idea what had gotten into her. "Technically that wasn't a kiss."

Obviously confused, Oliver cocked his head.

"Take your shower." She patted his cheek. "And trust me. If I ever do kiss you, *really* kiss you, you'll know it."

Over the next few days, Oliver and Shannon settled into a routine. There was no touching or kissing, but neither was ever far from his mind. He made a concerted effort not to dwell on such matters because he didn't want to screw up what was turning out to be an extremely satisfying business arrangement.

In the span of a few short days, Shannon had turned a small, slightly battered house into a home. The smell of baking bread often greeted him when he awoke. Ollie was always fed, bathed and entertained. Oliver didn't take any of this for granted.

The initial plan was for her to be off duty at five, but Shannon insisted he sleep until he woke. When he got up, supper would be waiting. She insisted she loved to cook and had discovered it was fun to make dinner for someone besides herself.

But this evening they wouldn't be eating at home. They'd been invited to her parents' house for dinner. When Lilian had called, Oliver had attempted to decline the invitation, but had felt sorry for her when she told him Shep had sprained his ankle and was making her life miserable. She needed company, a distraction for Shep.

Oliver suggested Shannon go alone but Lilian said quite seriously that her husband would behave better with another man in the house. Though he doubted Shep would be happy to see him, Oliver had reluctantly accepted the invitation.

Now he was faced with what to wear. He glanced into his closet. If he wore a suit he'd be overdressed. He pulled out a pair of dark trousers and a charcoal shirt. But when he saw his reflection in the mirror, Oliver realized he needed to go even more casual.

With one last longing look at his suits, he changed into a pair of jeans and a thin-striped cotton shirt. He pulled out a pair of leather dress boots. Ignoring his unease, Oliver reminded himself this was suitable attire for dinner at a Horseback Hollow ranch.

When he came out of his bedroom shortly before they had to leave, Oliver was surprised to see Shannon wearing a maroon dress with heeled boots.

"You look lovely…and I'm underdressed."

She grabbed his arm when he spun to head back to his room to change.

"You're perfect," she said with obvious sincerity. "You'll

put my dad at ease. You know he'll be wearing jeans and one of his flannel shirts."

Oliver narrowed his gaze. "If dinner is casual, why are you wearing a dress?"

Her cheeks pinked. "Mom got on me the other day about my appearance. She said every time she saw me lately, I looked more like a ranch hand than a young woman."

Oliver's gaze slowly slid down her figure, the curves nicely emphasized by the clingy fabric of the dress.

"You could never look like a boy," he said honestly.

She looked totally feminine and all too appealing. She wore a new scent, a sultry fragrance that reminded him of tangled limbs and sweat-soaked sheets.

"I like your new perfume," he said as he helped her on with her jacket.

The pink on her cheeks deepened. "Rachel helped me pick it out. There's going to be some new guys at the progressive dinner on Saturday. She says I'm never going to attract anyone smelling like vanilla."

"Progressive dinner?"

"It's where you have cocktails at one house, appetizers at another, salads at yet another, et cetera," she explained. "Jensen and Amber are organizing it all. I believe they're doing the entrée at their place."

Oliver lifted Ollie from the floor, ignoring his howl of protest. "Who are these new men?"

"Friends of Quinn," Shannon said absently, scooping up Ollie's tiger and handing it to his son. "That's all I know."

"I look forward to meeting them," Oliver said smoothly.

Shannon blinked. "I didn't realize you were going."

Oliver smiled. "Wouldn't miss it for the world."

Chapter Nine

"You actually took Oliver home for dinner?" Rachel gave a hoot of laughter, the sound so light and carefree that Shannon couldn't help but smile.

From his perch in the high chair next to their table at the Vicker's Corners ice cream shop, Ollie looked up from rearranging his Cheerios cereal. He garbled out a smattering of words.

Since the boy had eaten all but ten of the "Os," Shannon grabbed the Tupperware container from her purse and put a few more on the table.

"It wasn't so bad," Shannon said, recalling the evening that had started off a bit awkwardly but ended quite well. "Oliver loves my mom's cooking, and he and my dad talked horses. Apparently Oliver not only has a stable of Arabians at his country estate, he also owns a couple of racehorses."

"From what I've heard he's got big bucks. I'm sure he

owns a lot more than a few horses." Rachel leaned forward, resting her forearms on the table. "Has he kissed you yet?"

"No," Shannon answered quite honestly. "He's been a perfect gentleman."

She saw no need to add that *she'd* kissed *him*. Despite the havoc it had wreaked on her sleep, that brief one-time brush against his lips barely counted.

"Is he gay?"

"No, he's not gay, he's British." Shannon saw Rachel's lips twitch. She met her friend's gaze. "Sometimes when we're together, I can almost feel the heat between us scorch my skin, but he always shuts it down."

Rachel took a long, thoughtful sip of her soda. "Why do you think that is?"

"My fault. I insisted we keep things strictly business." For a second Shannon dropped her gaze to her hands, before focusing back on Rachel. "I still believe it's for the best."

"Seriously?" Rachel's disbelieving expression was almost comical.

"Yes, seriously. Think how awkward it would be if we hopped into bed together," Shannon pointed out.

"Honey, I'm betting the guy is fairly experienced in the bedroom. I don't think there would be much awkwardness."

"You thought he was gay."

Rachel dismissed this with a flick of her wrist. "I was just trying to get a reaction."

"Like you're doing now."

"Guilty as charged." Rachel sounded not at all sorry as she slurped up the last of her Italian soda.

"If we *did* have a physical relationship, then decide it's a mistake, I'd have to face him every day."

"You're a big girl. You could handle it."

"I don't know, Rachel. He's different from other guys I've dated. There's something about him that—"

"Mama." Ollie reached over and tugged on Shannon's sleeve, then repeated more loudly. "Mama."

Rachel gave an incredulous laugh. "Did the munchkin just call you 'Mama'?"

"It's his word for any woman." She turned to Ollie. "What is it you want, sweet pea?"

"Dink." He pointed to her malt. "Dink."

"You want a drink, sweet boy? What do you say?"

"Pease." Ollie batted his lashes. He had his father's charm in spades, Shannon decided, and let him sip from her straw.

"That kid has you wrapped around his little finger," Rachel said with a sly smile.

"I'm falling hard for both of them, Rachel," Shannon admitted with a heavy sigh. "And I can't seem to do a thing to stop it."

The one thing she'd done right, Shannon decided that Saturday evening, was not attend the progressive dinner with Oliver. When he asked if she wanted to go with him, she'd told him she planned to ride with Rachel.

She and Rachel had decided that in the ice cream shop several days earlier. Her friend insisted it would be good for Oliver to not take her for granted. From Shannon's perspective, it was all about making the two of them seem less like a couple. Not only in the mind of the community, but in hers, as well.

Oliver would soon be returning to England. Once he left, she'd likely never see him or Ollie again. She couldn't afford to get too attached.

"These Crazy Coyote Margaritas are de-lish," Rachel said, sipping hers.

"They're good…and strong." Shannon couldn't recall the last time she'd had a drink where the alcohol was so prominent. "We'd better pace ourselves."

"Let's pace ourselves right over to those two hunky cowboys Quinn invited."

"Doesn't that seem a bit bold to you?"

"The early bird gets the worm."

"Yeah, and the early worm gets eaten."

Rachel merely shot her a saucy smile. When she started across the room, Shannon hurried to catch up. Rachel looked adorable in her black skinny jeans and a color-block sweater. Shannon had chosen a wrap dress of emerald green but wondered if she should have worn pants tonight instead.

The two men speaking with Quinn were strangers. Shannon had heard through the singles grapevine that both were unattached and each owned large ranches in central Texas.

She and Rachel had almost reached the men, when she felt a hand on her arm. She paused but Rachel continued on without her, obviously wanting dibs on the cowboy of her choice.

"Fancy meeting you here."

Shannon turned and immediately found herself drowning in the liquid depths of Oliver's blue eyes.

"Hello, Oliver."

He looked terrific in dark trousers and a gray shirt. He smelled terrific. Not a scent she recognized but it was nice, very nice. And the spot where his hand now rested on her arm sent waves of heat throughout her body.

"You look lovely." His gaze traveled all the way down from her face to the tips of her heeled boots. "You should wear that color more often."

"I'll keep that in mind." Get off the personal, she told

herself. "How did Ollie do when you dropped him off at your mother's?"

Josephine had been thrilled when Oliver had asked her to watch Ollie overnight. It would be the first time the toddler had spent the night since arriving in Horseback Hollow. Though Oliver hadn't appeared concerned, Shannon was worried.

A troubled look appeared in his eyes. "He cried. I felt like a heel walking out the door and leaving him there."

"I wonder how he's doing."

"Better. I called before I came in. Mum said they were playing with his trucks." Oliver expelled a breath. "Bedtime may be difficult."

Shannon had gotten into the habit of rocking Ollie to sleep at night. She knew she should probably just put him in his crib—or cot as Oliver liked to call it—and let him cry. But he'd been through so much in his young life, and the closeness seemed to comfort him. "Did you tell your mother he likes to be rocked to sleep?"

"I did." His lips tightened. "I got the feeling she thought it unnecessary."

When someone took her empty glass and handed her another Crazy Coyote, Shannon accepted it automatically. "I hope she at least gives it a try."

"I hope so, as well."

"What are you two talking about?" Jude stopped beside them, one arm looped around Gabi's shoulders. "You look way too serious."

"Nothing important," Oliver said smoothly.

"Those Crazy Coyotes pack a punch," Gabi said to Shannon. "Watch yourself."

Shannon glanced down, surprised to find the second drink in her hand. "I will. But I'm safe anyway. Rachel is the designated driver."

"Rachel?" Gabi glanced curiously at Oliver. "You two didn't come together?"

"Nope," Shannon said, taking a gulp of her drink.

Gabi frowned. "How odd."

"Not so odd, sweetheart." Jude smiled. "Shannon works for Oliver. They're not dating."

Though she couldn't have said it better herself, for some reason the words stung.

The fact that Oliver merely sipped his glass of wine, his eyes dark and unreadable, only made it worse.

Time to seek out Rachel and those two gorgeous cowboys. Men who'd grown up in Texas and would *stay* in Texas. One of them was bound to be just the kind of man she was looking for.

But as Shannon crossed the room, she found her mind drifting to the two men she couldn't have, one a handsome charmer with dark hair and wicked blue eyes, the other a miniversion of the first, a little boy with a toothy grin who called her "Mama."

Oliver watched Shannon flirt and laugh with a tall blond-haired cowboy at every house on the progressive dinner circuit. The evening was coming to a close, and by the way the guy was looking at Shannon, baked Alaska wasn't the only thing he wanted for dessert this evening.

He'd started the evening with a glass of wine but had since switched to water. Not Shannon.

In addition to dessert, Christopher and his fiancée, Kinsley, had made a variety of after-dinner drinks available to their guests.

Not only had Shannon drank a couple of Crazy Coyote Margaritas earlier, she'd enjoyed wine with dinner and had another glass in her hand now. The cowboy, Oliver noted, had switched to coffee.

Though Oliver told himself Shannon wasn't his concern, there was something about the man he didn't like. When they'd been introduced, he'd noticed an arrogant immaturity, a meanness that he hid quite well behind a charming smile.

"Your nanny and the cowboy look like they're having a good time," Jensen observed, coming to stand beside him and noting the direction of his gaze.

"Her name is Shannon." Even as he spoke with his brother, his gaze remained focused on her. He saw her glance around as if searching for someone. "She's looking for Rachel."

"Rachel left. I heard her tell Kinsley she wasn't feeling well."

"She was Shannon's ride home."

"Rachel probably assumed you'd take her home." Jensen took a sip of wine, gazed up at his brother. "Or the cowboy."

Oliver's lips tightened. "I don't like the way he's looking at her."

"You mean like she's a piece of meat and he hasn't eaten in a week?"

"Excellent summation."

"What are you going to do about it?"

Oliver exhaled a ragged breath and turned away. "Nothing. Shannon's personal life is her business. Not mine."

That feeling lasted until it was time to leave and he headed toward his car. Most of the others had already left, but he'd stayed behind to speak with Chris about the work of the Fortune Foundation.

There was a shiny red pickup truck parked not far from his car. As Oliver drew closer to his car, voices resounded in the still night air.

He realized one of those voices was Shannon's. Oliver stopped and listened, his fingers on his key fob.

"I told you no."

There was frustration in her voice. Anger, too. And fear?

"C'mon, you've been teasin' me all night. No need to play the shy virgin."

"I don't want you to touch me. No. Wesley, stop."

Oliver saw red. Not even conscious of covering the last few feet to the truck, he jerked the door open and yanked the cowboy off Shannon.

Taken by surprise, the man fell to the ground with a hard thud.

"Are you okay?" he asked Shannon, her eyes too bright and her face pale.

She nodded, her lips trembling.

The cowboy was now on his feet, hands clenched into fists at his sides. "What the hel—"

Oliver took a step toward the man. He wasn't a street fighter but he had displayed a talent for boxing in his younger years. He resisted—but barely—the urge to tear the man apart. "When a lady says no, she means no."

The man's mouth turned sulky. "We were just havin' us a little fun."

"When a lady says no, she means no," Oliver repeated, his words like ice.

By now Shannon had scrambled from the car and moved so that she stood behind him.

"I don't have a beef with you." Wesley raked a hand through his shaggy blond hair. His gaze slid to Shannon. "Didn't mean no disrespect."

Oliver watched as Wesley turned, jumped back in his truck and roared off.

"There goes my ride."

Oliver whirled and gave an incredulous laugh. "You're upset he's not driving you home?"

"It was a joke." Shannon offered a shaky smile. "A poor one."

He extended his hand to her. "Let me take you home."

"He wouldn't listen to me." Her lips began to tremble in earnest now. Tears welled in her eyes. "I think if you hadn't come along, he might have…" She faltered, her breath coming in gasps. "He might have—"

Suddenly Oliver's arms wrapped around her and he pulled her to him, holding her tight while her tears drenched his shoulder. "He didn't. Shh. You're okay."

The words were soft and gentle, as soothing as the ones he said to Ollie when the boy cried. Thankfully, the man hadn't injured her. Or had he?

"Did he hurt you?" Oliver asked abruptly, holding her at arm's length, his gaze desperately searching her still-moist eyes.

"My wrist." She held up her right hand and he could see the red marks from pressure. "But no, I'm okay."

She trembled all over now; even her teeth chattered. "Could you hold me again? J-just for a s-second. I'm s-s-so c-cold."

"Certainly."

With great gentleness, Oliver wrapped his arms around her and held her close. Her body fit perfectly against his.

They stood there in the quiet, with the full moon shining overhead and the crickets chirping, until the trembling and the tears subsided.

She was the one who broke the connection, sniffling and swiping at her eyes as she took a step back. "I—I'm sorry."

"He's the one who should be sorry," Oliver said, a grim

note in his voice. "And he will be. I doubt Quinn will want to do business with him once he hears about this incident."

"Oh, Oliver, please don't tell Quinn." She lifted her pleading gaze to his. "I shouldn't have kissed him. It—it gave him ideas and—"

"You listen to me, Shannon Singleton, and listen carefully. There is no excuse for a man to force himself on a woman. You said no. You said stop. I heard you and he heard you, too. He chose not to listen."

"He wouldn't listen," she said morosely. "No one ever listens."

"Not people like him." Oliver pressed his lips together and fought for control over his anger. "I know his type. All charm and full of compliments, underneath cold calculation. He saw you, he wanted you, and by God he was going to have you…regardless of your feelings on the matter."

Shannon pressed a hand to her belly. "I feel sick."

Without warning, she sprinted to the bushes and was violently ill.

When she returned, looking pale as death, he handed her a precisely folded handkerchief.

A ghost of a smile lifted her lips. "Where'd this come from?"

"My pocket," he told her. "A gentleman never leaves home without a handkerchief."

His words had the desired effect of bringing a smile to her lips.

"I believe—" Oliver held out his arm to her "—it's time to head home."

She met his gaze. "There's nowhere else I'd rather be."

Chapter Ten

Shannon kept her eyes closed during the trip home. She couldn't believe what a mess she'd made of the evening. For a second, before Oliver had pulled Wes off her, she feared she wouldn't be able to stop him.

There had been something in the cowboy's gaze only seconds before Oliver had arrived that had chilled her to the bone. For a second white-hot terror resurfaced and threatened to overwhelm. Nothing happened, she reminded herself. Still, she shivered.

"You're shaking." Beneath the calm, well-modulated tone, Shannon heard the concern. "Shall I turn on the heater?"

"The temperature is fine." Even as she said the words, her teeth began to chatter.

Oliver shook his head. He pulled the car to the side of the country road. Reaching over into the backseat, he grabbed a jacket. "Put this on."

She didn't argue. Shannon shrugged into the cashmere coat and let the comforting warmth surround her. The exquisite softness coupled with the faint scent of Oliver's cologne that clung to the jacket soothed her jangled nerves. By the time they'd gone a couple of miles, the trembling stilled.

Oliver had been amazing; a white knight riding—well, more like running—to her rescue. He'd stood strong against Wesley, stared the cowboy straight in the eye and told him what he did—what he'd been about to do—was wrong.

Now, being with Oliver in the luxurious confines of the car with the strains of classical music playing on the radio, Shannon felt as if nothing could ever harm her. Not as long as Oliver was with her.

When they pulled into the driveway, relief washed over her. She was home.

Shannon wasn't sure exactly when she'd started thinking of the old ranch house as home, but it didn't matter. This was another place she felt safe.

"Thank you, Oliver." She unbuckled her belt and shifted to face him. "For everything."

He surprised her by leaning close and cupping her face in his broad palm. "I'll never let anything—or anyone—hurt you."

The fierceness of his tone was at odds with his gentle touch.

Her heart thudded against her chest so loudly it was a wonder he couldn't hear.

Or perhaps he did. Oliver's hand dropped away and he sat back. "Let's go inside. You've had a long day."

When he opened her car door, Shannon stepped out, slipping her hands into the pockets of the jacket.

His palm rested lightly against the small of her back

as they traversed the short distance to the house. Barnaby met them at the door, wagging his tail and offering several welcoming woofs before racing outside.

While the corgi's welcome had been loud and exuberant, without Ollie, the house seemed too quiet.

Seconds later, Oliver let Barnaby back inside. The corgi did his best to herd Shannon deeper into the house, but her feet remained firmly rooted in the foyer. She knew she was stalling, but couldn't bear the thought of going to her bedroom and being alone with her thoughts.

"How are Ollie and your mother getting along?" she asked, conscious of Oliver's concerned gaze riveted on her.

"Step into the kitchen and have a seat. I'll tell you everything I know." Oliver gestured to the table. "It's a fascinating tale."

The kind understanding in his eyes told her he knew exactly why she was hesitating. Her heart swelled in gratitude.

"I want to hear it all. He's been on my mind all evening." Right now, it felt good to focus on someone other than herself.

Oliver crossed the room, flipped on the lights in the kitchen and then turned back to Shannon. "May I get you a cup of tea? I have chamomile infusion. It has no caffeine. According to Amelia, drinking it before bedtime practically guarantees happy dreams."

Though Shannon's stomach was still unsettled, he looked so eager to comfort her, she couldn't refuse. "I'd love some."

As Oliver proceeded to fill the kettle, Shannon finally got her feet to move. She glanced longingly at the sofa, but her mouth held a foul taste.

"I'm going to freshen up a bit," she told Oliver.

"Take your time. The tea will need to steep."

She felt his gaze follow her as she headed to the bathroom. After brushing her teeth, she splashed her face with cold water and got rid of the raccoon smudges below her eyes. Obviously waterproof mascara wasn't the same as tear-proof.

Shannon pinched her cheeks to add color to the pallor, then sat on the edge of the tub and took off her boots and tights. Her legs were bare when she padded back into the living room. She hung up his cashmere storm jacket then took a seat at the table.

Oliver kept the conversation light until he handed her a steaming mug emblazoned with Don't Mess With Texas.

Wrapping her hands around the ceramic, she gave him a grateful smile while he sat across from her.

"You look as if you're feeling better."

"I am." Even as she said the words, Shannon realized they were true. She rested her elbows on the table and fixed her gaze on Oliver. "Now, tell me all about Ollie's evening."

"According to Mum, it was a bit of a rocky road at first. He kept crying out for 'Mama.'" Oliver's brows pulled together. "It's difficult for me to believe he meant Diane. From everything I heard, she hadn't spent much time with him those last few months. And she's been gone for some time now."

"He calls me 'Mama' sometimes," Shannon admitted. "I think it's a term he uses for women in general."

"I wasn't aware…" Oliver rubbed his chin. "That explains a lot."

"Did he finally settle down? Have fun?"

"Ah, yes, indeed he did." Oliver seemed to shake off whatever thoughts had pulled him away and refocused on her.

"Tell me," she prompted. "I want deets."

"Deets?" He lifted a brow.

She laughed. "Details."

"Ollie ate well," Oliver told her, sipping his tea. "Mum said he appeared to enjoy all the attention. He asked for Barnaby numerous times."

Hearing the sound of his name, the corgi rose from his dog bed, stretched and then moved to Shannon.

"Good boy." She patted his head and gave him a brief scratch behind his ears.

Oliver watched the interaction with interest, smiling when the dog finally left Shannon to mosey over to him.

"I checked with my mother right before I left the party. She said Ollie went to sleep—after being rocked, I might add—and was sleeping like an angel." Oliver's gaze took on a faraway look. "She told me many times how much she enjoyed having him over."

"Sounds like you may have a babysitter for life."

He lifted the mug of tea, appearing to consider the statement. "While I'm in Horseback Hollow, anyway."

Shannon's heart plummeted. It was so easy to forget that Oliver didn't belong here, to think this was his home. To imagine him being here forever. With her.

But he wouldn't be staying and putting down roots. In fact, by the first of April he'd be back in London. She'd likely never see him again.

It was something she had to keep in mind, or an April Fool's Day joke would be on her.

First thing the next morning Oliver called Quinn. He'd promised the sleeping beauty in the other room that he wouldn't tell Quinn what had gone on last night. And he kept his promise. But that didn't mean he couldn't let Quinn know that his potential business partner was a scoundrel of the first order.

While Oliver scrambled eggs and fried bacon, he issued his warning in words that had been carefully chosen prior to placing the call.

As expected, Quinn pressed for solid details. Oliver only reiterated if he was going into business with someone, Wesley should never be considered, no matter how perfect a partner he appeared to be on paper.

Oliver heard Amelia in the background telling Quinn that her brother rarely issued such warnings and they should heed it. He appreciated his sister's confidence and support. By the time he ended the call, Oliver felt certain he'd squashed any business deal between Quinn and Wesley.

"Good morning."

Oliver slid the phone into his pocket and glanced up. Shannon stood in the hallway, looking a bit heavy-eyed—but just as beautiful as always—in jeans, a long-sleeved T-shirt and cowboy boots. Her hair, normally loose around her shoulders, had been woven into some sort of complicated braid.

He rose from the table. "Would you like some breakfast?"

"I believe that's supposed to be my line." A smile lifted the corners of her lips. "But I have a different question for you this morning."

Intrigued, Oliver inclined his head. "What is it?"

"You like horses, right?"

"I do. Very much."

"I just spoke with my mother." Shannon shifted uncertainly from one foot to the other. "My dad's ankle isn't any better. It seems to be a pretty bad sprain."

"I'm sorry to hear it." Oliver was not only sorry for Shep but for Lilian, as well. It couldn't be easy keeping an active man like Shep Singleton down.

"The thing is, my parents ride every day. It's something they've done for years." Shannon crossed the room and picked a piece of crisp bacon from the frying pan. "Knowing Ollie would be at your mother's this morning, she asked if I would come over and exercise the horses. If we went together, both horses would get a workout. It wouldn't take long."

There had been a period, years ago, when Oliver had ridden every day. Once he moved to London, riding had been confined to visits to his country estate. He'd missed it, he realized.

"My mother said she'd like to keep Ollie all morning," Oliver mused.

"We'd easily be there to pick him up by noon."

Oliver thought, considered. There were things he needed to do to prepare for his workday. But he sensed Shannon needed a ride in the great outdoors more than she needed almost anything else.

He glanced down at his dark trousers and dress shirt. "Give me five minutes to change and I'll be ready."

Shannon reined the horse to a halt at the top of a hill that overlooked a large swath of her parents' property. Though the sun shone brightly, the temperature was in the upper sixties, perfect riding weather.

Beside her, Oliver sat easily on her father's horse, a spirited roan named Bucky. Right before he mounted Bucky, she'd plopped a black cowboy hat on his head.

He'd muttered a protest, but she knew it was only for form when he'd left on the Stetson headgear. Though comfortable outside, the sun could be intense to an unshielded head.

They'd ambled through fields, then galloped together down a well-worn path by the stream. When they'd reached the hill—okay, so it was more of a small mound—she enticed him to the top by telling him the view would be worth it.

"What do you think?" She relaxed in the saddle, gazing out over the valley where cattle grazed.

"Beautiful."

"That's what I think—" But when Shannon turned, thrilled he saw the peaceful serenity and beauty that many overlooked, she realized his gaze wasn't on the land, but on her.

Her face had to be dusty, her hat tipped back, and some of the hair that she'd woven into a side braid now hung loose against her cheek. Not to mention her eyes had to be puffy from last night. But the way he looked at her, well, she couldn't remember any man looking at her in quite the same way.

Her heart swelled until she thought it would burst from her chest. "Thank you."

A startled look crossed his face. "For what?"

"For being so nice to me."

"I don't understand."

"You were my knight in shining armor last night." Shannon refused to let embarrassment quash the words she desperately needed to say. "You saved me from an evil sorcerer. You comforted me. Not once did you make me feel stupid, though I had been very stupid."

"No," he said forcefully. "What happened was all on him."

"I just want you to know that I appreciated you coming to my rescue and being so…nice. If there's anything I can ever do for you, all you need to do is say the word and I'm there."

"Thanks is hardly necessary," he began. "I—"

"It's very necessary," she insisted. "I also realize what

you gave up to come here today. Being on horseback under the bright blue skies has made me feel better. You knew it would."

"How could anyone not feel better with all this beauty as far as the eye can see?" He gestured with one hand, though his gaze remained on her.

"You're a special guy, Oliver. I hope one day you find a woman back in London who can appreciate all you have to offer."

"This is the one," Rachel said with the authority of a seasoned shopper. "It's you."

Shannon studied the simple, yet sexy, black dress. All evening they'd searched for just the right dress for Shannon to wear to the Grand Fortune wedding ceremony Friday night.

When one Fortune got married it was a big deal. But when four Fortune siblings decided to tie the knot on the same day, the event took on epic status. The evening would be the talk of the year, no, the decade. Not just any dress would do for such a wedding.

The stores in Lubbock had an abundance of dresses in every style and color. A few had caught Shannon's eye enough to try them on. But none had jumped out and proclaimed, "I am the one."

They'd headed back to Horseback Hollow, empty-handed and discouraged. At the last minute they decided to check out a couple of boutiques in Vicker's Corners.

At boutique number two, they hit the jackpot. Amazed, Shannon gazed at her reflection in the triple mirror. "It makes me look positively skinny."

"Forget skinny. It makes your boobs look ginormous," Rachel said, and the sales clerk laughed.

"The dress is very flattering," the clerk concurred. "Is this for a special Valentine's date?"

"Actually," Shannon said, "I'm attending a wedding on Valentine's Day."

"Ah, *the* wedding. Wear that dress and your date won't be able to take his eyes off you," the clerk assured her before hurrying off to help another customer.

"She's right." Rachel relaxed in the dressing room chair while Shannon slipped off the dress. "It's perfect for the weddings."

Rachel's overemphasis of the plural made Shannon smile.

"Seriously," Rachel continued, "how often do you get one dress that will cover four weddings?"

Shannon slanted a glance at the price tag and tried not to wince. While the cost was definitely more than she wanted to spend, the dress *was* gorgeous. She thought about the clerk's words.

Would Oliver think she was lovely? Would he look at her—

"Especially four Fortune weddings."

Shannon reined in her thoughts. While she'd been daydreaming, Rachel had been chattering about the upcoming nuptials.

"I don't know about you," Rachel continued, "but I wouldn't want to share my special day with three other couples."

"It wouldn't be for me," Shannon acknowledged. "But I think the Fortune siblings must view this grand event as even more special because they're sharing it with the ones they love."

"I bet Jeanne Marie and Deke are celebrating."

Shannon raised a brow.

"Think about it, four weddings for the price of one," Rachel explained. "What a deal."

"For them maybe," Shannon said with a laugh. "I'm just grateful you agreed to go in with me on four gifts."

On Friday, at Jeanne Marie and Deke's sprawling ranch, four of their children would say their vows: Jude and Gabi and Chris and Kinsley, as well as Stacey Fortune Jones marrying Colton Foster and Liam Fortune Jones marrying Julia Tierney.

They'd had the large red barn on their property converted into a reception area. Outside, a huge stage had been constructed for the ceremony itself. Shannon had no doubt the quadruple wedding ceremony and reception would be a night to remember in Horseback Hollow.

"Did I tell you my parents are watching Ollie?" Shannon stepped out of the dress and handed it to Rachel.

"Your parents are such good friends of Deke and Jeanne Marie." Rachel placed the dress on the padded hanger, a look of surprise in her eyes. "I thought for sure they'd be invited."

"They are close friends and they planned to go." Shannon pulled on her jeans and tucked in her shirt. "But my dad's ankle is still bothering him. Because it's so difficult for him to get around, they decided to stay home."

Shannon reached down to pick up her bag. When she straightened, she found Rachel staring at her with a curious expression.

"What's wrong?" she asked her friend.

"I know we've planned to go together for ages." Rachel spoke slowly, as if choosing her words carefully. "But if you'd rather go with Oliver…"

"No. No way. I'll have more fun with you." The moment the words left her lips, Shannon wished she could pull them back. It sounded as if she was dissing Oliver, when nothing could be further from the truth.

She'd only meant to reassure Rachel their plans were solid and she wasn't doing a last-minute about-face.

"You're right. He may be hot but he's a little uptight." Rachel spoke cheerily, her good humor back. "Did you hear that all four of Gabi's brothers will be there? Orlando showed me pictures the other day. All I can say is, wow. Not a dog in the bunch. Tall. Dark. Hunky. They look like fun guys. We should consider hanging with them at the reception."

"Perhaps." Shannon did her best to summon some enthusiasm even though the only hunky man she wanted to hang with was Oliver.

Of course, Oliver would soon be an ocean away. She supposed it wouldn't hurt to consider other possibilities.

But even as the thought crossed her mind, Shannon knew she wasn't interested. There was only one man she wanted. Only one man she loved. And that man was the one who could never be hers.

Chapter Eleven

After making sure his tie was precisely knotted, Oliver strode down the hall. When he reached the living room, he came to an abrupt stop. For a second, all he could do was gaze at the vision of loveliness in black lace before him.

Shannon had bent over to give Ollie a toy. The angle gave Oliver an excellent view of her breasts—er, her dress. In his thirty-seven years, Oliver had seen his share of short black dresses. Cocktail parties, gallery openings and charity galas were filled with women wearing what many considered the classic party dress. Never had he seen one that took his breath away.

Though it didn't show an obscene amount of skin, something in the cut of the dress made Shannon's legs look longer, her waist impossibly tiny and her breasts…

His mouth went dry. When he cleared his throat, hoping to get some fluid to the area, she straightened and shot him a brilliant smile.

Then her beautiful eyes widened.

"Oh, my." She pretended to fan herself. "You're really rockin' that black suit, mister."

For the weddings of his four cousins, Oliver had chosen a slim-fit Armani, coupling it with a crisp white shirt and dark skinny tie. His favorite pair of Paul Smith black oxfords completed the outfit.

Though the phrase "rockin' that suit" wasn't familiar, the admiration in her eyes said she approved of his choice of attire.

"Your dress," he said, unable to keep his gaze from dropping to the lacy vee that showed the ivory swell of her breasts, "is…unbelievable."

"In a good way, I hope?" Though her tone was light, he saw concern in the brown depths of her eyes.

"You will be the prettiest woman there."

She gave a pleased laugh and lifted Ollie into her arms. "That's nice to hear, but with four gorgeous brides, I sincerely doubt that."

"The prettiest woman there," he repeated, happy her plans to attend with her friend had fallen through and she was his for the night.

A flush rose up her neck, but he saw his words had pleased her. She dropped her gaze to Ollie, who was attempting to pull the tiny silver necklace from her neck.

"Did you hear that, Ollie?" she asked the toddler. "Your daddy thinks I'm pretty."

With chubby fingers still wrapped around the necklace, Ollie lifted his gaze and stared at her for several seconds. He grinned.

"Pretty Mama," he said clearly, then repeated the words. "Pretty Mama."

Oliver stared, startled.

"I think you have another admirer," was the best he could manage.

"Yeah," she said with a self-deprecating smile. "I'm a big hit with the toddler set."

"He called you 'Mama.'"

"That's his go-to word for females," she reminded him.

Oliver didn't argue but he was fairly certain Ollie knew exactly who he was calling "Mama." He glanced at his watch. "We should leave."

"You're right. It's not going to be quick and easy getting away from my parents." Shannon offered a wry smile. "Be prepared. They'll want you to go through Ollie's bedtime routine in excruciating detail."

She never overstepped, Oliver thought. Shannon always made it clear Ollie was ultimately his son, his responsibility, not hers. The trouble was, Shannon was such a natural with him it was easy for him to forget.

Mrs. Crowder, his London nanny, was efficient and kind to his son. But Ollie had never called her "Mama." He wondered if the older woman rocked Ollie to sleep every night or sang silly songs with him. These were things Shannon did as part of the daily routine. Oliver made a mental note to pay more attention to those details once he was back in London.

On the drive to her parents' ranch, Ollie and Shannon sang a song about monkeys jumping on the bed. Actually Shannon did most of the singing, with Ollie occasionally yelling out "no more" or "monkey" several beats too late.

The foolishness of the tune coupled with the sound of his son's giggles made Oliver smile.

As Shannon had predicted, Shep and Lilian wouldn't let them leave until they'd been apprised of every nuance of Ollie's schedule. When they returned to the car, Oliver had no doubt his son would be well cared for during the evening.

"That was kind of your parents to offer to keep Ollie overnight." Oliver exited the long drive and turned the car in the direction of Jeanne Marie and Deke's ranch.

"My parents adore children." A tiny smile lifted her lips. "They can't wait to have grandchildren. Watching Ollie gives them a taste of what that will someday be like."

"Happy to be of service."

Shannon's expression turned thoughtful. "I'm glad you brought Ollie to Horseback Hollow. It's good he had this chance to get acquainted with your family and them with him."

Oliver realized with a sense of chagrin that he'd never thought of the trip in those terms. In his mind, coming to Texas had been about seeing Amelia and meeting his new niece.

"Thanks to modern technology, even after you return to London you'll be able to video chat with your mother and other family members," Shannon continued. "That way they can stay close to Ollie."

"Good suggestion." But Oliver found he didn't want to talk about leaving Horseback Hollow. Not tonight. "Do you like weddings?"

Shannon blinked at the abrupt change of subject but went with the flow.

"What woman doesn't? I enjoy seeing the dresses and the hair. I like seeing what kind of flowers the bride and groom chose and how they structured the ceremony." She paused for a second. "With four brides and grooms, I wonder how they decided everything. Majority vote?"

Oliver lifted a shoulder in a slight shrug.

"I can see the advantages of all of them getting married at the same time but…" This time, it was her turn to shrug.

"Not for you?"

"Never say never," she said with a little laugh, "but I don't believe it would be for me. Anyway, marriage is so far down the road for me it doesn't even bear thinking about."

Oliver slanted a sideways glance. "You'll find the right man."

Having Oliver mention her with another man in the same breath gave Shannon a bad taste in her mouth. "When you married Diane, you must have thought she was the right one for you."

Oliver's only reaction was a tightening grip on the steering wheel. "At the time, I was convinced we made an excellent match. We socialized with the same people, had similar interests and backgrounds. I thought she'd be happy if I gave her what she wanted. I was mistaken."

His lips clamped shut.

"What did she want?" Shannon asked quietly into the stillness.

"What most women want—a lovely home, designer clothes, jewels."

"I'd settle for a man who loves me," Shannon murmured.

Oliver continued as if she hadn't spoken. Perhaps he hadn't heard her. His gaze had taken on a faraway look. "She wanted a child, so we had Ollie. He was an infant when she began a relationship with another man."

"She cheated on you?" Shannon's voice rose, despite her efforts to control it.

"She left me for him." Oliver spoke in a tone one might use to report an expected change in stock prices. "They were together approximately six months when she replaced him with the man she was with at the time she died."

"It sounds as if she wasn't sure what she wanted."

"Perhaps." His expression gave nothing away. "All I know for certain was she no longer wanted me. I couldn't make her happy."

"I'm sorry." Impulsively Shannon reached over and squeezed his hand.

"It was the failure of our marriage that bothered me more than losing her," he said almost to himself. "Up until our divorce, I believed if I worked hard enough at something, I would be successful."

Shannon heard the disappointment in his voice. She knew what it was like to not live up to your own expectations. If only she could pull him close and comfort him as he'd comforted her not all that long ago.

"I never heard what happened to your plans to attend the weddings with Rachel." By the change in subject, Oliver made it clear the discussion of his failed marriage had come to a close.

Shannon understood that, too. She often did the same thing when the subject of Jerry and how she'd handled that whole situation came up.

"Rach is supergood with hair. A couple of the brides asked if she'd come early to help with final touch-ups." Shannon waved a dismissive hand. "She was concerned about leaving me in the lurch, but I assured her it was no problem. I told her I'd probably catch a ride with you. If not, there was always Wesley."

His gaze shot to her. "Surely you would not consider—"

"Not in a bazillion years." She made a face. "I just wanted to see if you were listening."

"I always listen to you."

He'd listened to her that night when that scumbag had attacked her. And Oliver had held her while she cried...

"I've decided if Wesley is there tonight—" Shannon swallowed her trepidation and forced a bright smile "—I'll simply ignore him. There'll be so many people that it shouldn't be difficult."

"He won't be there."

The words were said with such confidence Shannon had no doubt they were true.

"How do you—" Shannon frowned. "You promised you wouldn't say anything about what happened to anyone."

"You should know by now I'm a man of my word," Oliver said stiffly, appearing affronted. "I didn't mention your name or any specific incident. I merely told Quinn that Wesley was not the type of man he should have as a business partner or a friend."

Incredulous, Shannon could only stare. "He didn't ask why you felt that way?"

"Of course he did." A slight smile lifted Oliver's lips. "But he quit pressing for details when Amelia told him to trust me."

"Oh."

"I would never betray your confidence. Or my promise to you." Oliver slanted a speculative glance in her direction. "Enough talk about that. Did I mention my brother Brodie will be attending the wedding?"

"I don't believe I've met him."

"He's flying in for the ceremony." A look of fondness crept into Oliver's gaze. "Knowing Brodie, he'll return to London as soon as possible."

As if sensing her curiosity, Oliver smiled. "Brodie enjoys the finer things in life. This town would not be his cup of tea. Too small and too rustic."

Shannon pulled her brows together, trying to remember the family history. "Is he older or younger than you?"

"Four years younger."

"That means he's between you and Jensen?"

"Yes. Brodie and I are from our mother's first marriage. Jensen is from her second."

Shannon tapped a finger against her lips. "I knew Jensen's father had died and Josephine was a widow. Is your dad still alive?"

"No."

There was a wealth of emotion contained in the single clipped word.

As irritating as her father could be at times, Shannon knew she'd be devastated if anything happened to him. She reached over and placed a hand on Oliver's arm. "I'm so sorry."

"Don't be. He was a mean SOB who was not liked by most people, including his sons."

"Then I'm doubly sorry," Shannon said softly. "Growing up with such a father had to be—"

"I consider my mother's second husband, Sir Simon Chesterfield, my father. He was a good man. The best, actually." Oliver met her gaze. "You don't have to be related by blood to be a parent."

"I agree." For some reason Shannon thought of Ollie. She could easily love him as if he were her own. Heck, she was already halfway in love with the little guy.

As the car slowed, Shannon glanced out the window. "Oh my goodness, look at all the people."

A man Shannon recognized as working for the Horseback Hollow Sheriff's Department motioned for Oliver to turn into a large field that was now a parking lot.

White golf carts, festively decorated with ribbons and fresh flowers, zipped up and down the rows of cars, transporting attendees to where the ceremony would be held. The drivers—many of them locals—looked quite impressive in black pants, crisp white shirts and red vests.

Shannon wasn't sure how many carts were running but

had a feeling anyone golfing today would be walking eighteen holes.

She waited for Oliver to help her out of the cart, anticipating the moment he'd take her hand and she'd get to touch him—however briefly—once again.

To her surprise—and pleasure—the contact wasn't short-lived. Instead of immediately releasing her fingers, he entwined his with hers and retained the hold while they waited for the cart. Unfortunately, once they stepped inside the open vehicle, he released her hand. But she felt encouraged when he rested his arm on the top of the seat.

"I hear Jeanne Marie and Deke had the interior of the barn completely renovated for the reception and dance," Shannon said as the large red structure came into view.

"Mum told me the work has been going on for weeks." As they drew close, Oliver's gaze lingered on the large number of people waiting to be seated. "Apparently the carpenters just finished the outdoor stage where the wedding ceremony will take place earlier this week."

"It's fortunate rain stayed out of the forecast."

"I have no doubt there was a contingency plan in case of bad weather."

"I can't wait to see what everyone in the wedding parties is wearing." Shannon could feel her excitement build the closer the cart got to the drop-off point. "I heard each bride has two attendants, a maid or matron of honor and a bridesmaid."

"More than adequate."

Typical man, Shannon thought. She bet he'd had a whole slew of attendants at his wedding. From the little he'd told her, his ex-wife had liked the finer things in life. Shannon briefly considered asking for details, then tamped the impulse down almost as quickly as it had surfaced.

Right now she couldn't handle thinking of Oliver marrying another woman.

As if sensing her turbulent mood, Oliver took her hand. With a single touch her world, which for the moment had tilted on its axis, righted itself.

Sounds of a Bach concerto filled the air as the cart drew to a smooth stop. When Oliver took out his wallet to tip, the driver shook his head. "We're being well compensated for our services. Enjoy the ceremony."

Oliver took her arm to steady her as she stepped from the vehicle in her heels.

"Oh, my" was all Shannon could manage to say when her gaze fell upon the elaborate stage.

Shannon expected a simple raised wooden platform large enough to hold four sets of brides and grooms and a minister. She hadn't expected something that looked as if it had been carved from stone and borrowed from the Parthenon. Four fluted Ionic columns formed a semicircle, topped with an ornate frieze containing four vertically channeled tablets depicting hearts.

Two steps led to the stone platform. Four tall urns filled to overflowing with gypsophila and delphinium were strategically positioned on the stage. The heavy mass of the white flowers was accentuated by deep red roses.

In the center aisle leading to the "temple," a white tapestry had been placed, flanked by red rose petals. White wooden chairs lined both sides of the center aisle. The ends of each row held bouquets of roses and greenery.

"This is more elaborate than I imagined." Though there was no need to speak softly, Shannon spoke in a hushed whisper.

"It's a Fortune wedding." Oliver responded with a chuckle. "Prepare to be impressed."

Chapter Twelve

As the lovely strains of another piece of classical music from the string quartet filled the air, Shannon's eyes turned dreamy. "I take back what I said about not wanting to share my day with three other brides. If I could have this, I'd happily share the day with a dozen others."

Though Oliver could see how Shannon might be awed by the sumptuous arrangements, he thought how it paled compared with his wedding at Saint Paul's Cathedral.

Diane had wanted a formal, elegant affair, complete with trumpets and royalty in attendance. But the marriage that was supposed to last a lifetime had barely made it to the three-year mark. Diane bore her share of the burden for the failure, but he now realized that he did, too.

"Oliver."

His name, said in that cultured British accent, had him banishing any thoughts of the past and smiling even before he turned. "Brodie."

Though normally too much of a buttoned-up Londoner for public displays of affection, Brodie Fortune Hayes surprised Oliver by giving him a manly half hug with a thump on the back.

"Good to see you." His brother glanced around. "Where's the little guy?"

"Ollie is with a baby minder for the evening. A couple I trust."

"Undoubtedly." Brodie's gaze slid away to settle on Shannon.

"Brodie Fortune Hayes, I'd like to introduce Miss Shannon Singleton. Shannon is a friend. She's also graciously consented to help me out by serving as Ollie's nanny while I'm in Horseback Hollow."

"Miss Singleton." Brodie extended his hand.

"Shannon, please." She smiled and shook his hand. "I knew you were brothers the moment I saw you."

At six feet tall, both men were the same height, with brown hair and vivid blue eyes. Like Oliver, his brother was dressed in a hand-tailored dark suit. Though, in Shannon's estimation, Oliver was the more handsome of the two.

If Rachel thought Oliver was a true Brit, Shannon couldn't wait until her friend got a load of Brodie. The man gave new meaning to the term "stiff upper lip."

"If you're not sitting with anyone, perhaps you'd like to sit with us," she offered.

Brodie's brow shot up and his gaze shifted to Oliver.

Shannon felt herself color. She hadn't meant to imply she and Oliver were a couple. The question now was how to backtrack without making everything worse.

Oliver didn't seem to notice the faux pas. "Yes, Brodie, you must sit with us."

"You two are…together?" Brodie spoke cautiously, as if feeling his way through a minefield.

"Has the transatlantic flight addled your brain?" Oliver spoke with more than a hint of exasperation. "Shannon is standing right here. I just introduced her to you. Of course we're together."

Brodie let the subject drop, though Shannon was aware of his speculative gaze as an usher took her arm to escort her to their seats.

She was amazed how close to the front they were seated until she realized that, of course, they'd be near the front. Oliver and Brodie's cousins were being married today.

Shannon had to admit she'd grown so used to chatting with Oliver that it was difficult to stay silent. But, as they waited for the ceremony to begin, she bit her tongue each time she was tempted to share an observation or impression.

It had been a while since Oliver had seen his brother. She wanted to give him a chance to speak with Brodie without having her in the middle of the conversation.

As guests continued to be seated, Shannon struck up a conversation with Cisco Mendoza, one of Gabi's brothers, who was seated to her right. He was a handsome man with dark hair and eyes, and a charming smile.

She was laughing at something Cisco said when Oliver touched her hand.

"The processional is ready to begin," he said in a low tone for her ears only.

Feeling as if she'd been caught doing something wrong—though she wasn't sure what it was—Shannon shifted her attention.

The bridesmaids moved slowly down the aisle, in dresses ranging from deep wine to seashell pink. Shannon wondered if Oliver noticed the color of the groomsmen's boutonnieres matched the respective bridesmaids' dress color.

Soon it was time for the maids of honor and best men to make their trek down the aisle. When they reached the stage, little MaryAnne Mendoza appeared holding a white wicker basket filled with rose petals of every hue. The three-year-old waved to people she knew and flung the petals with great gusto on her way to the platform, making more than a few in the audience chuckle.

Finally, the audience rose and one by one the four brides began their walk down the aisle on their fathers' arms. Shannon thought Gabi's father, Orlando, looked incredibly handsome in his dark suit. Oliver's mother, Josephine, must have thought so too, because Shannon caught her giving the handsome Latino a second glance.

"They're all so lovely," Shannon whispered to Oliver as the last bride joined her groom at the front.

Oliver simply smiled and squeezed her arm as they took their seats.

Considering there were four brides and four grooms to keep track of, everything proceeded seamlessly. Shannon found herself especially moved by the minister's sermon. He urged the couples to continue to nurture the love they now shared and to move from a "me first" attitude to "us first."

The ceremony continued with the lighting of the unity candle. The recitation of vows made Shannon sigh. Each set was so very personal and unique to the couple saying them. Love wove through the vows like a pretty ribbon, bringing a lump to Shannon's throat and a tear to her eyes.

Soon the radiant brides and grooms were making their way down the aisle. Shannon had no doubt each couple would enjoy the blessing of a happy marriage.

As thrilled as she was for all of them, Shannon couldn't stop a stab of envy as she wondered if she'd ever find such happiness.

If she did, one thing was certain, it wouldn't be with Oliver. In a matter of weeks, he'd be back in London. The thought was a dark cloud on the sunny day.

It didn't help that Shannon felt like a third wheel strolling with Brodie and Oliver to the barn for the dinner buffet and dance. It was obvious—to her at least—that Brodie was puzzled by her presence, probably wondering why she was intruding on his time with his brother.

Catching sight of Rachel, Shannon seized the out. She tapped Oliver's arm. "I need to speak with Rach. I'll catch you later."

She ignored his puzzled expression and shifted her gaze to Brodie. "It was a pleasure meeting you. I hope you enjoy your stay in Horseback Hollow."

Then she was gone, disappearing into the crowd.

Oliver couldn't stanch a surge of irritation. It wasn't as if he expected Shannon to spend every moment of the reception with him. Though he *had* given her a ride and stepped up to be her escort when she'd been left high and dry by her friend Rachel. The same friend she was now scurrying off to meet.

"Your nanny is very attractive," Brodie said in a slightly bored tone.

"She's not my nanny—she's Ollie's nanny," Oliver snapped.

"No need to get testy." Brodie narrowed his gaze. "Are you falling for the cowgirl?"

"She's an employee," Oliver said pointedly.

"So, you wouldn't mind if I got something going?" Brodie raised a brow. "A quick shag might make my brief stay in this backwoods town more palatable."

Oliver rounded on his brother, barely resisted the urge to grab him by the lapels of his Hugo Boss suit coat. "Stay away from her, Brodie. Shannon is off-limits. Understand?"

Brodie merely laughed. "I knew you had a thing for her."

"What are you talking about? I've already told you she's my—"

"Employee. I heard that part. But I have eyes. I see how you look at her. When she was talking with that man on the other side of her, you looked as if you wanted to punch him."

"I'm merely concerned about my employee's welfare." Oliver's penetrating gaze dared his brother to disagree.

"Whatever you say." As they entered the barn, Brodie's cynical look eased. "Whoever was in charge put a lot of time and money into planning this reception. It might be tolerable."

This time it was Oliver's turn to laugh. "It's good to have you here, Brodie. Let's get a glass of champagne."

The reception was in full swing, the dance floor was crowded and Shannon still hadn't crossed paths with Oliver. But she'd connected with almost everyone else in the entire county.

She'd even done her part by helping Gabi's four brothers, Matteo, Cisco, Alejandro and Joaquin, feel welcome by introducing them to all the single women she knew.

They were a good-looking bunch who had all the women swooning. Moments earlier she'd been leaving the dance floor with Cisco when they'd run into Delaney

Fortune. She'd introduced the two, then hurriedly excused herself. She'd promised Galen Fortune the next dance.

She'd known Galen since childhood. He was her buddy. Because there was only friendship between them, spending time with him was always easy and comfortable.

"You're a good dancer," she told Galen. "How is it that I didn't know that about you?"

He maneuvered her around the crowded dance floor with quick, sure steps. "Another one of my many hidden talents."

Shannon smiled and caught sight of Oliver speaking with his mother at the edge of the dance floor. She waved but he disappeared from view when Galen spun her around.

"It's kind of weird, isn't it?" Shannon said, relaxing in his arms.

"What is?"

Her lips twisted in a wry smile. "Being single when everyone around you is getting married."

Galen's brows pulled together. "Some just aren't lucky enough to find the right person. Me, I'd rather stay single than settle."

"Me, too," Shannon said, relieved to hear she wasn't the only one who felt that way. "I can't imagine anything worse than—"

"May I cut in?"

A thrill ran down Shannon's spine. Oliver wanted to dance with her.

Galen stepped back. "Thanks for the dance, Shannon."

She smiled warmly at him. "Any time."

Before she could catch her breath, she was in Oliver's arms. She loved the way he smelled, a woodsy mixture of cologne and soap and maleness that had heat percolating low in her belly. She let the intoxicating scent wrap around her.

"You two looked quite friendly."

"Galen? We're buddies from way back."

"Did you ever date?"

"No." Shannon laughed. "He's like another brother."

Was it only her imagination, or did Oliver's shoulders relax slightly?

"Have you enjoyed the festivities?" he asked.

"It's been fun. I've danced a lot."

"I noticed. You seemed to have developed a particular affinity for Gabi's brothers."

"They're nice guys." She lowered her voice. "The women all think they're incredibly hot."

He stared at her for a long moment. "What about you?"

She wasn't sure what made her be so bold, but she let her fingers caress his neck. "Let's just say I prefer a different type of man."

His eyes darkened to stormy pools of blue and he surprised them both when his hand flattened against her lower back, drawing her up against the length of his body.

He held her so close she could feel the evidence of his desire against her belly. The hardness ignited the flame that had been simmering inside her for days.

Slow it down, she told herself. It might simply be the romance in the air that was causing him to react to her this way.

But she had to admit, whatever the reason, she liked having him stare at her with such blatant hunger in his gaze.

"My brother thinks you're hot," he murmured, twining strands of her hair loosely around his fingers.

It took Shannon a second to find her voice. "He—he's not my type, either."

"Who is your type, Shannon?" he asked in a husky voice.

There was a beat of silence. "I believe you know the answer to that question, Oliver."

Even as his mouth relaxed into a slight smile, he tightened his hold.

Shannon sighed with pure pleasure. Dancing with Oliver, being held so firmly in his strong, capable arms, was all she wanted, all she needed. Forget Galen and Brodie. Forget the Mendoza brothers.

Forget our agreement.

Shannon opened her mouth to tell him she'd been wrong to insist things stay strictly business. But as they dipped and swayed to the romantic melody, she found it impossible to think, much less speak. The world around her disappeared and all she knew was they fit together perfectly and she was right where she wanted to be…

Reluctant to give up the intimacy, she lost herself in the music, drifting on a cloud of pure pleasure until the jarring ring of his cell phone shattered the moment.

Shannon lifted her head as he slipped the phone from his pocket and glanced at the readout.

"Working on a Saturday night?" she teased.

"It's your parents' number."

Her breath caught, then began again. They wouldn't call unless it was important. A jolt of uneasiness went through her.

Oliver pressed the phone against his ear and talked with her mother as he maneuvered them to the far edge of the dance floor, where it wasn't so noisy.

"How high?" His mouth tightened into a grim line. "I'll be right there."

"What's wrong?"

Shadows played in his eyes, making them unreadable. "Ollie has a fever. One hundred and three." His brows knit together as he calculated. "Thirty-nine point four Celsius."

"Fevers that high aren't uncommon in a child his age."

"I can't stay." His gaze darted to the exit. "I can have one of my family members take you home."

"No need." Shannon snatched her bag up from the table where she'd left it earlier. "I'm going with you."

Chapter Thirteen

Oliver unbuckled Ollie from the car seat and carried him into the house, his strides so long and quick that Shannon had to run to keep pace. Once inside, he flipped on the lights with one hand and sat the boy down on the sofa. Barnaby immediately jumped up to sit beside him.

"Let the dog be," she told Oliver when his arm moved to swipe the animal off the sofa.

Confusion turned to understanding when the boy wrapped his arms around the corgi, resting his head against the dog's soft fur.

"I'll get the thermometer so we can recheck his temperature," Shannon told Oliver. Thankfully, after a recent trip to the store, she'd stocked the medicine chest in the bathroom with all the necessities. "Mom gave him some acetaminophen before we got there so it should start coming down."

"Stop," Oliver ordered, pushing up from the sofa. "You sit here with Ollie. He needs someone to comfort him."

Shannon moved to the sofa. She didn't argue, though she could make a good case that it should be his daddy comforting him rather than a relatively new nanny. But Ollie had taken to her from the start and now, even as she took Oliver's spot on the sofa, the child cuddled against her.

In less than a minute, Oliver returned with the temporal scanner. Shannon talked him through how to use it. A lethargic Ollie only whimpered.

Some of the grimness around Oliver's mouth eased at the readout. "One hundred and one."

Shannon exhaled the breath she didn't realize she'd been holding. "Better."

She brushed Ollie's hair back from his face and Barnaby licked her hand. The boy's eyes were closed now and his respirations were easy and regular.

"He's asleep," Shannon spoke softly, her voice barely above a whisper. She glanced up at Oliver. "Think we should try to put him in the crib?"

"Let's give it a few more minutes." Oliver sat on the other side of Ollie and the dog. His gaze lingered on her dress, a bunch of lace clutched between Ollie's fingers. "You can take my car if you'd like to return to the reception."

"Are you crazy? I'm not leaving Ollie."

Or you, she thought. His son's unexpected fever had clearly shaken Oliver.

Shannon brushed back a lock of Ollie's soft brown hair. Tears stung the backs of her eyes. Oliver wasn't the only one who'd been shaken. With his eyes closed and his skin so pale, Ollie looked so little, so defenseless.

"Children are such a responsibility," Oliver said quietly as he gazed at his sleeping child.

"And such a joy." Her heart rose to her throat. Shannon

realized she wasn't halfway in love with Ollie. She was totally in love with the little guy.

"You like children." Oliver's gaze never left hers. "The first time I saw you interact with him, I knew."

She nodded, feeling oddly embarrassed by the blatant admiration in his eyes.

"I've always loved children," she admitted. "Do you know when I was a little girl, I told my parents I wanted half a dozen kids when I grew up? Truth is, I'd still like a whole houseful."

As she'd hoped, the statement distracted Oliver from his worry. His eyes widened. "Seriously?"

"Yep." Shannon gave a little laugh, then lowered her voice to a confidential whisper. "Let's keep that our secret. Something like that gets out and any potential suitors will run screaming away into the night, never to be seen again."

He gave her a dubious glance. "You're kidding."

"I wish I were. Let me give you an example." Shannon shifted slightly and repositioned Ollie in her lap. "I dated this guy when I lived in Lubbock. We had fun together. Things were going well, until the subject of children came up. One night I said to him what I just said to you. You'd have thought I'd exploded a grenade under him."

Oliver cocked his head, his eyes bright with interest.

"His reaction made more sense when he told me he wasn't sure he even wanted kids...ever." Shannon expelled a breath and shook her head. "He called me once after that, but it was over. Now, if a guy asks, I just say I like children and hope to have a couple someday."

Oliver rubbed his chin. "Why not be honest?"

"I am being honest. I do like children. I do hope to have a couple. But having more would need to be something my husband wanted, too." Shannon gave a little laugh. "I have my doubts that I'll find any man who wants six."

"My mother had six," Oliver reminded her.

"Mine had five," Shannon said. "But I think things were different back then. Big families were more the norm."

"I don't know how they did it." Oliver glanced at his son. "Being a parent is exhausting."

"You even have household help," she pointed out.

"It's not only the physical care," Oliver said, almost to himself. "I'm organized and disciplined. Though I certainly don't know how I'd do it without a nanny and a housekeeper. But…"

He paused for a long moment then continued.

"Being a parent makes me feel vulnerable in ways I don't particularly like." His gaze lingered on his son. She saw the love in his eyes…and the fear. "I never thought I was capable of loving so deeply. It would kill me to lose him."

How had she ever thought Oliver was a cold fish or that Ollie was simply an obligation?

"That's the downside of caring for someone," Shannon said solemnly. "It makes you vulnerable. My grandmother used to say love isn't for the faint of heart."

She wasn't sure how the phrase translated into Britspeak, but from the look that crossed his face he got the gist.

"It can be frightening to have such intense feelings." Oliver raked a hand through his hair. "Especially when you aren't certain if the other person feels the same way."

Shannon was fully prepared to tell him Ollie wouldn't go to him so easily or let himself be comforted if there wasn't love and trust between them.

Then Shannon realized his gaze wasn't on his son, but on *her*. It wasn't Ollie's feelings he was wondering about, but hers. The knowledge gave her a subtle, pleasurable jolt.

She dropped her gaze to the boy, feeling warmth rise up her neck. "I think we can put him to bed now."

"Let me." Oliver rose, then bent over and carefully lifted his son from the sofa.

A second later, Barnaby hopped off the sofa, hitting the floor with a thud.

"While you get Ollie settled," Shannon said in a low tone, "I'll take Barnaby outside."

Oliver's brows drew together. "Stay close to the house and in the light. I heard howling out there."

"Coyotes." Her tone was matter-of-fact. The animals were a fact of life in the area. "They normally don't venture close to the house, especially when the floodlights are on."

"C'mon, Barnaby." She started toward the door, the dog padding behind her.

"Shannon."

She turned, raised a brow.

"Wait a minute. Once I get Ollie settled, we can take Barnaby out together."

"Sure. That'll work." Shannon didn't mind waiting.

Not because she was some wussy who couldn't stand being in the dark by herself, or because she was fearful of a few coyotes. But because it'd be nice to have the company. Especially on such a beautiful night when the moon was full and a plethora of stars filled the clear night sky.

Instead of remaining in the living room, Shannon followed Oliver into Ollie's room. She turned on the Mickey Mouse night-light and removed the stuffed animals from the crib.

Oliver laid the boy down, removing his jeans, shoes and socks with now well-practiced movements, leaving the child clad only in a T-shirt and diaper.

After checking the diaper, Oliver looked up. "Dry."

"Good. I know my mom said she'd changed him right before we got there, but still—"

"A soggy nappy would have awakened him for sure."

"Right. And what he needs right now is uninterrupted rest." After checking his temperature one last time, Oliver motioned Shannon out of the room.

"It's down another degree," Oliver confided, relief etched on his face.

"Good." Shannon squeezed his hand.

After they were a safe distance down the hall, Shannon turned to the dog. "It's time, Barnaby. Let's go outside."

The dog emitted a low woof and sped to the back door, his short legs moving surprisingly fast.

But speed disappeared once Barnaby was outside. The corgi took his time sniffing every bush and tree in the area. Though the night air had a bit of a bite, Shannon wasn't cold. Oliver stood beside her on the bricked patio and heat rolled off him in waves.

"I want to kiss you," he surprised her by saying as the silence lengthened.

Her stomach felt as if it had dropped three feet straight down.

"Then why don't you?" Even though her heart raced wildly, she spoke in the same matter-of-fact tone he'd used.

Oliver studied her for several seconds before he spoke, his steady gaze shooting tingles down her spine. "We have an agreement."

"I release you from that agreement," she said in a solemn tone. If she'd had a magic wand, she'd have tapped his shoulder for good measure.

Oliver shook his head. "You're still my employee."

Her heartbeat hitched. "I'm not."

"Unfortunately you are." He expelled a heavy breath but didn't take a step away. Instead Oliver moved closer.

Shannon recognized the signs. He was waiting, hoping, for her to convince him. Lifting her chin, she shook her head slowly from side to side, a tiny smile lifting the corners of her mouth. "You may be the one who signs my paycheck, but actually I work for Ollie."

For a second those blue eyes were simply astonished. "Ollie is a child. You can't work for him."

"I beg to differ." Her voice had taken on a playful edge. "He's my focus. So, technically I work for him."

"Let's say I accept that premise, which by the way is quite a stretch of logic. It doesn't negate the fact that if we begin an affair..."

Shannon held herself very still, firmly ignoring the unsettling flutter his words caused in her midsection.

"I thought we were talking about a kiss," she said with a studied nonchalance that deserved an acting award.

The look he shot her fried every brain cell she possessed, and then some. "We both know where one kiss will lead."

Yes, and Shannon wanted him so desperately it was a wonder she hadn't ripped his clothes off before now.

Not sure of the steadiness of her voice, Shannon settled for a jerky nod.

"This—" He paused, as if searching for the words. "Whatever happens would be a temporary thing."

Her heart performed another series of flutters. When she opened her mouth to say she didn't care, to say—

"I'm not looking for a relationship." She saw a flicker of challenge in his eyes. "And I won't be in Horseback Hollow that much longer."

Even with shadows playing in his eyes, making them difficult to read, she swore she saw regret lurking there. Nonetheless, his words were clear. He'd spelled it out, leaving no room for fanciful thoughts of happily-ever-after.

Though Shannon had grown up in a traditional home and had been taught intimacy was only coupled with love, and then only after marriage, this was her life and her decision.

She cared deeply for Oliver, she respected him and she was physically attracted to him in a major way. What would be the harm in stealing some moments of pleasure? Especially if they both went into an affair with eyes wide open.

Apparently misunderstanding her hesitation, Oliver reached over and squeezed her hand. His voice was soft, reaching inside her to a raw, tender place. "Refraining is the wisest course of action."

Yet, at his simple touch, sensation licked up her arm, down her breasts and on down to pool between her thighs. Heat simmered in the night air.

When he started to pull his hand back, she brought it to her mouth and placed a kiss in the palm. "Depends I guess on your definition of *wise.*"

His blue eyes darkened. "What are you saying?"

The intoxicating scent of his cologne wrapped around her senses. Her gaze met his.

"I'm saying I want you." Her eyes searched his. "I'm okay with it not being forever. I'm not sure I'm ready for forever, anyway."

"I don't want to hurt you."

She gave a little laugh, her pulse a swift, tripping beat. "Uh, correct me if I'm wrong. I believe it's pleasure—not pain—on tap tonight."

Still, he made no move toward her. "Are you sure?"

Shannon took a step closer, wound her arms around him and planted a kiss at the base of his neck, his skin salty beneath her lips. Then she lifted her face, and met his dark gaze with what she hoped was a sexy smile. "Very sure."

"Well, then…" He folded her more fully into his arms, anchoring her against his chest as his mouth covered hers in a deep, compelling kiss.

He continued to kiss her with a slow thoroughness that left her weak, trembling and longing for more. When his tongue swept across her lips seeking access, she eagerly opened her mouth to him, her tongue fencing with his.

The warmth in her lower belly turned fiery hot and became a pulsating need.

Barnaby's deep woof barely registered.

Another bark and the dog sprang. The unexpected impact of the solid body against the back of her knee knocked Shannon off balance. Only Oliver's strong arms saved her from a tumble.

"Barnaby." She dropped her gaze to the dog, who now sat at her feet. "What is your problem?"

"He's ready to go inside." Oliver's mouth skimmed the edge of her jaw. "It's a good plan."

Keeping a firm grip on her arm, Oliver opened the sliding glass door. The dog bounded inside, nails clattering against the hardwood, and made a beeline for Ollie's room.

With her fingers linked with Oliver's, Shannon followed the dog down the hallway. When Barnaby plopped down on the rug next to the crib, Shannon stepped around him to lean over the rail.

Oliver joined her.

"His cheeks aren't flushed anymore," he said, his voice filled with relief.

Shannon placed the back of her hand on Ollie's forehead. "His skin is cool."

She and Oliver exchanged a smile, then eased silently from the room. They stood in the hall and Shannon fought against a sudden wave of awkwardness and uncertainty. "I don't know about you, but I'm ready for bed."

"You took the words out of my mouth."

She tilted her head back, met his gaze. She'd never seen such beautiful eyes. Or such compelling eyes. Or eyes that had a weakening effect on her knees.

Oliver reached out and touched her cheek, one finger trailing slowly along her skin until it reached the line of her jaw. "I can't wait to have you in my bed."

Then, before she even had a second to breathe, his lips were on hers, exquisitely gentle and achingly tender. He took the fingers of her hand and kissed them, featherlight. "Unless you've changed your mind?"

"Race you there," she said and, with a breathless laugh, started to run.

Chapter Fourteen

Oliver caught up with Shannon just as she reached the doorway. She giggled like a giddy teenager when he spun her around.

"Caught you," he said.

"I let you catch me." How was it that standing here, both of them grinning like two fools, felt so right?

She'd had two other love affairs, one in college and one when she lived in Lubbock. While in both cases she'd had high hopes for a future with the guy, being with them had never felt quite right.

Now, here she stood beside a man who'd made it clear whatever they shared would be very short-term, and she had no hesitation or doubts.

Like now, having him scatter kisses down her neck felt natural and oh-so right.

"Hmm." Shannon tilted her head back, giving him full access to the creamy expanse of skin. "I love the feel of your arms around me."

"I love the taste of you." His lips continued their downward journey. Only when he reached the vee of her dress did he lift his head. "This dress drives me absolutely bonkers."

She gave a pleased laugh. For that one compliment alone, the dress had been worth every penny she'd spent. "Oh, so it's the dress you fancy, is it?"

Oliver chuckled, then kicked the bedroom door shut with his foot, reaching around her to lock it. "I fancy every part of you."

The sentiment, coupled with the wicked look in his dancing blue eyes, sent warmth sliding through her veins like warm honey.

"Locking the door seems a bit excessive," she said, her tone light and teasing. "Concerned about Barnaby doing some spying?"

"I don't want anything to disturb us," he said, then his smile turned rueful. "Except—"

Shannon didn't know what to think when he abruptly released her and strode to the bedside stand. When she saw him flip on the baby monitor, her admiration for him inched up another notch.

"Just in case Ollie needs us." In several long strides he was back beside her, pulling her to him.

"I must admit I find your concern for Ollie—" she leaned close to whisper in his ear "—incredibly arousing."

"I'll remember that." His eyes twinkled. "All I ask is you do your best to restrain any carnal urges while I'm checking his temperature or changing his nappy."

Shannon realized she was seeing a playful side of Oliver that up until now she'd caught only glimpses of. "This relaxed, fun side of you is also sexy."

"I'm beginning to think," he said, brushing back a

strand of hair that had fallen across her cheek, "that everything about me turns you on."

Shannon pretended to think for a second, then grinned. "Pretty much."

"We're going to take our time tonight. No rushing allowed." His expression turned serious. "That will be difficult, considering I've wanted to kiss you for a very long time."

"Well, what are you waiting for?" She lifted her face to him and placed her hand on his chest, toying with a button. She slipped it open. "What do you say? Let's get this party started."

Shannon felt her knees grow weak at the fire in his eyes. An answering heat flared through her, a sensation she didn't bother to fight.

"Oliver." She spoke his name, then paused, not sure what she wanted to say. Her eyes, which seemed to suddenly develop a mind of their own, zeroed in on the area directly below his belt buckle.

He chuckled, a low pleasant rumbling sound.

"Slow," he murmured, twining strands of her hair loosely around his fingers the same way he had when they'd danced earlier, "means keeping our clothes on a little while longer."

Shannon stuck out her lip and pretended to pout. The effect was spoiled by the smile that kept forming on her mouth. "I don't like this game."

"Oh, but you will." His voice was like a promise.

Shannon lifted her gaze and their eye contact turned into something more, a tangible connection between the two of them. Could he hear her heart pounding? How could he not?

"You're pretty full of yourself, mister," she managed to sputter.

Oliver winked. "That's a Fortune for you."

Shannon's laughter disappeared when his hands spanned her waist. He ran his palms up along the sides of her dress, skimming the curve of her breast, and she forgot how to breathe.

Her nipples stiffened, straining against the fabric toward his touch.

"You are so lovely," he whispered into her ear right before he took the lobe between his teeth and nibbled.

Shivers rippled across her skin.

Without warning, he shifted and pressed his mouth against hers. When his tongue swept across her lips seeking access, Shannon eagerly opened her mouth to him, her tongue fencing with his.

He tasted like the most delicious decadent candy she'd ever eaten. And she couldn't help wanting more.

Still, as he promised, Oliver didn't rush. He simply continued to kiss her. Testosterone wafted from him like an invisible tether, tugging at Shannon, keeping her feet anchored to the floor and her mouth melded to his.

The feeling of his mouth on hers was like nothing Shannon had experienced before.

She ached for him, desired him, with her entire being. The need quickly became a stark carnal hunger she hadn't known she was even capable of feeling.

"I want—" she whispered against his mouth, when they came up for air "—you."

"I'm not going anywhere," he said, his voice a husky caress.

"I want you naked." In a display of unexpected boldness, she pushed her hips against him, rubbing his erection.

"I planned to take this slow," he reminded her, his breath hitching. "Savor every moment."

"Plans have changed," she said. "Next time we'll go slow. For now, get naked."

"Heaven protect me from a bossy woman." But his eyes glittered and his clothes quickly landed in a heap next to hers on the floor.

She'd been hot only seconds before, but now, when his gaze shifted to her naked body and lingered, Shannon felt exposed and vulnerable. She almost embarrassed herself by trying to cover her most private parts with her hands... until she saw the stark desire in his eyes. Desire...for her.

To realize he wanted her as much as she did him was a heady feeling and a confidence booster. Her hands remained at her sides.

"You are...magnificent." He breathed the words and took her hands loosely in his.

"You're not so bad yourself." An understatement, but the best Shannon could manage at the moment. Broad shoulders, hard chest, lean hips, Oliver Fortune Hayes was every woman's fantasy.

Though a businessman, Oliver had a workingman's body, corded with muscle, lean and tan. Dark hair converged on the flat planes of his stomach into a line that...

She inhaled sharply and her knees suddenly felt weak.

Without warning, he scooped her up and carried her to the bed.

"Hey," she laughingly protested, "what do you think you're doing?"

"Something tells me you're going to be at your best horizontal."

The bed was soft and luxurious, and the tiny part of her brain still capable of rational thought registered the fact that he must have had a new mattress delivered.

Rational thought disappeared as Oliver settled beside her and once again began to kiss her. Not slow and easy as he had before but with a voraciousness that showed a mounting hunger.

The same hunger that was rapidly consuming her.

She could have cheered when his thumbs brushed across the tight points of her nipples. His stroking fingers sent shock waves of pleasure through her body.

"Oh, Oli—"

Whatever she'd been about to say died away on a soft little whimper as he found one sensitive part of her body after another. His hands continued to move, to search; touching, stroking, caressing until her heart pounded and she didn't even know her own name. All Shannon knew was she needed him to continue touching her.

"Your breasts are perfect," he whispered. "I need to taste you. Open your eyes."

Shannon opened her eyes. As she watched, he touched the tip of his tongue to the tip of her right breast. The combination of seeing and feeling brought her up off the bed and had her crying out in delight.

He smiled, then circled her nipple with his tongue before drawing it fully into his mouth. The gentle sucking had her arching against him. At the same time, his hand slipped between her legs.

She parted for him, catching her breath as he rubbed against her slick center. Then his head was moving down to where his fingers still caressed, scattering kisses down her belly.

The tension filling her body continued to increase exponentially with each warm, moist kiss against her bare skin until she stiffened, realizing just where those wickedly clever lips were headed. Part of her suspected what Oliver was going to do while the rest of her couldn't believe it was really happening. She'd heard…she'd read… but she never had…

His openmouthed kiss between her legs had her writhing in pleasure. He found her sweet spot and licked it over and over again until all she could do was dig her heels into the mattress and clutch the sheets with her hands.

How could it be she'd lived this long and had never known such pleasure existed?

"I want you inside me," she said even as her muscles tensed and collected and her breath came in ragged pants.

She didn't have to ask twice.

Oliver pulled away briefly and she heard the sound of foil tearing. Then he was over her.

She reached between them and guided him inside.

He was large and stretched her in the best way possible. Her legs swept around his hips as he began to move slowly inside her in a rhythm as old as time.

Shannon felt filled, yet the need—that all-encompassing need for him—propelled her to want more. She clung to him, urging him deeper.

The rhythmic thrusting grew faster. As she surged against the pleasure swelling like the tide inside her, Shannon heard herself groan, a sound of want and need that astonished her with its intensity.

Her blood had become a fire in her veins, her pulse throbbing hard and thick.

Seconds later, the orgasm ripped through her, hitting with breathtaking speed. Her entire body convulsed then released.

As she cried out, Oliver caught her mouth in a hard kiss.

He continued to thrust until every last drop of pleasure had been wrung from her. Only then did he take his release, shuddering in her arms and calling out her name.

For a moment he simply lay there on top of her, a sweet heavy weight. When he rolled off, she murmured a protest.

In answer, his arm slipped around her, not confining,

but comfortable. With a contented sigh, Shannon snuggled against his chest and discovered her head fit perfectly just under his chin.

He was warm and solid. A man she could hold on to, a man she could count on. At least for another few weeks...

Shannon fought to keep her eyes open.

"You kept your promise," she murmured before she fell into a sated slumber. "It was so very good."

Oliver waited until Shannon's breathing had turned easy and deep before he slipped from her embrace to check on Ollie. Even after he confirmed his son's fever had remained down and the child was resting comfortably, he didn't return to bed.

Instead he headed to the kitchen and poured himself a glass of whiskey. Sipping from a tumbler shaped like a boot, he stared into the darkness.

He'd had sex with a number of women, but tonight had been different. Shannon had touched a part of him that Oliver had always kept well hidden. From the time Oliver had been a small boy, his father had taught him to guard his emotions. Although the man had never struck him, Rhys Henry Hayes's tongue had been a potent weapon; sharp as a knife and capable of drawing blood.

His father had been fond of saying he didn't tolerate fools. To Rhys's warped way of thinking, a fool was anyone who cared too much and let it show. That included little boys.

Taking another sip of whiskey, Oliver thought of the words Diane had flung in his face the day she moved out. She'd accused him of being as cold as his father and told him it was no wonder she had looked for love elsewhere.

At the time, he'd shrugged aside the arrow that had been aimed to wound, concluding it was her way of excusing her own poor behavior. Now he wondered if there might have been some truth to the statement. Still, something had kept him from fully trusting his wife, and in the end Diane's duplicity had shown his instincts had been spot-on.

Shannon, on the other hand, was a different story. It would be easy to let her get too close, and that would be disastrous for all concerned. She was a small-town girl who loved living close to family and friends. Her home was in Horseback Hollow. His home—his life—was in London.

Her mind, her heart, the person she was fascinated him. Her body tempted him. She was the total package, and that's what made her so hard to resist, both in bed and out. That's what would keep him coming back for more. He knew there was so much more of this fascinating woman left to plumb.

The thought made him smile, remembering all he'd plumbed tonight—

Arms slid around his bare chest. "I hope that smile means you're thinking about me."

When Oliver turned, he found Shannon wearing one of his shirts, hanging open save for a single button. Her hair was a tangled mass of curls and her gaze was sloe-eyed and sensual.

He flipped the button open, then eased back the shirt and let it slide to the floor. His mouth skimmed the edge of her jaw, testing the sweetness of her skin. "You must be a mind reader."

She laughed softly and wound her arms around his neck, lifting her face for a kiss.

Though it hadn't been all that long since he'd left her side, it felt amazingly good to hold her again. To taste her. To smell her. He spread his hands over her buttocks and pressed her against his erection.

"Well, hel-lo there," she said, her eyes teasing.

He bent his head and kissed her softly on the mouth. "I haven't had nearly enough of you."

"You stole the words right out of my mouth."

"I love your mouth." Once again his lips closed over hers.

She kissed him back, and the kisses quickly became more urgent and fevered. Then abruptly she stepped back, swaying slightly.

He reached out and took her arm, concern deepening his voice. "Problem?"

"Just a couple shaky knees that aren't going to hold me up much longer." She grasped his hand, tugging and gesturing with her head toward the bedroom. "Remember, I'm at my best horizontal."

Oliver chuckled. Locking his hand around her elbow in a secure grip, he propelled her into the bedroom. Once the door was shut and locked, they tumbled onto the bed.

Though his body responded with breathtaking speed, this time, he took it slow. He wanted it to be perfect for her.

When the last shudder had left her body and she lay spent beneath him, Oliver held her close and savored the moment.

Still, his last thought before he joined her in sleep was that he had to keep up his guard. It would be far too easy to pretend he never had to let her go and start to believe this was exactly where he belonged.

Chapter Fifteen

Oliver pulled the rental car into the long driveway and mentally calculated the hours until he'd be able to leave. He couldn't use the excuse that their baby minder wanted them home early. Ollie was spending the night with Oliver's aunt Jeanne Marie.

Though he'd hoped to spend some quality time with his mother this weekend, Oliver never imagined it would involve attending something called a "card party" on a Saturday night. Especially a party held at the home of Shannon's parents.

The monthly event had been rescheduled from last weekend. Apparently too many of the "regulars" had wanted to attend the Fortune weddings, so they'd voted to move the card party back a week.

Oliver hadn't seen Shep or Lilian since the night of the wedding. Which meant he hadn't had to look in Shep Singleton's face since he'd begun shagging his daughter.

Though initially Oliver had told himself that what had happened after the wedding had been a one-time—okay, a two-time—thing, it had seemed so natural to go to her the next day. By Wednesday, a romp between the sheets had become a daily affair.

Of course, because of his crazy work hours, any love-making had to occur before midnight or after lunch. So far that hadn't been an issue. When he wanted something, he was pretty adept at making it happen.

And Oliver wanted Shannon Singleton. He wanted her with an intensity that continued to amaze him. It wasn't just physical. Shannon made him laugh and feel things he hadn't let himself feel in years.

Like with Ollie. Oliver hadn't realized it until she'd casually mentioned that she'd noticed he never told his son that he loved him.

"It goes without saying," he said, recalling his exact words. "I take care of him. I work hard to put food on the table and give him what he needs."

"He needs to hear the words," she'd insisted.

When he hesitated, she'd taken his hand and marched him into the living room, where Ollie had sat playing with his bricks.

"Tell him," she urged in a low voice.

Feeling incredibly silly, Oliver had crouched down beside his son. He opened his mouth, then closed it and cleared his throat. Why did something that should have been so easy come so hard to him?

"Ollie."

The boy looked up, his smile wide. He held up an *A* brick for Oliver to admire. "See."

"It's very nice." If Oliver had been alone, he'd have simply patted the boy on the head and stood up.

But Shannon stood there, looking at him with such

encouragement—and confidence—he couldn't back down. Not even with his father's words rolling around in his head.

It really wasn't a big thing, he told himself, just three little words. People said them all the time, even if they didn't mean them. But Oliver would mean them. He loved Ollie, more than he'd ever thought possible.

Just. Say. The. Words.

"Ollie." He gently touched the little boy's face and gazed into his eyes. "I love you."

The boy's smile was like a flash of sunshine warming everything it touched, thawing out a part of his heart that had been frozen for too long. Though Oliver was fairly certain the toddler hadn't understood what he said, Shannon had been right. He'd needed to say the words.

Oliver scrubbed the boy's head with his hand and then stood.

"Go ahead and play with your bricks." His voice had been thick with emotion and had shaken slightly. He'd felt foolish and more than a little angry that he couldn't seem to control the intense feelings welling up inside him.

Then Shannon had wrapped her arms around him and given him a big kiss. When she'd stepped back, the pride in her eyes washed away everything but joy.

"Earth to Oliver." Shannon's voice broke through his thoughts. "I think we should go inside."

Oliver pulled his thoughts back to the present. "I'm not looking forward to this evening."

"The fact that you pulled up and have yet to turn off the engine tells me you're still considering making a break for it."

She knew him so well. Why did he find the thought so disturbing?

"Forgive me if I don't want to spend a Saturday playing cards with my mother." His tone was curter than he'd intended.

Her cheery smile faded and she stiffened. "If you didn't want to come, you shouldn't have accepted the invitation."

"It's not just that," he reluctantly admitted.

"What then?"

"It's your father."

"My dad?" Her eyes widened then narrowed. "What has he done now?"

"I told him I wouldn't touch you when—"

"You've been doing nothing but touching me for the past week and in every possible place."

Just the words said in that throaty whisper had him going hard. He shifted uncomfortably in his seat.

"I'd promised him he had nothing to worry about." Oliver set his jaw in a hard tilt. "I assured him you would be totally safe living under my roof."

"I am safe living under your roof." Shannon reached over and wrapped her fingers around his hand.

The simple touch eased a little of the tension that held him in a stranglehold.

"You would never let anything bad happen to me. If someone broke in, you'd protect me. If I hurt myself, you'd tend to me." Her voice was low and soothing. "I *am* safe. The sex, well, that's something private between you and me."

Oliver frowned, realizing he didn't like hearing her refer to what they shared as *sex*. *Shagging* also didn't fit.

But that left *lovemaking*, and that didn't work either. There was warmth, there was caring, but love wasn't part of the equation.

"My father will never suspect," she assured him.

But halfway through the evening, when they were between games and Oliver had unconsciously slid his arm around Shannon's waist and she'd leaned into him, the look in Shep's eyes could have cut steel.

Oliver should have known better than to get too close to Shannon. Though he'd never been a demonstrative kind of man, she was very much the opposite. She was always finding excuses to touch him, and he'd discovered he liked it.

He'd also seen how it pleasured her when he unexpectedly reached over and took her hand or gave her a hug when she came in the door. It had seemed such a little thing to do to make her happy.

He'd also been more demonstrative with Ollie, and the boy had become more openly loving with him. Yesterday his son had even called him "Daddy" for the first time. Just recalling the moment brought a lump to his throat.

"When will you be leaving our little town, Oliver?" Shep asked pointedly during a brief conversational lull.

"Oh, Shep, must you bring up such a disturbing topic?" Josephine's brows knit together in a frown. "It feels as if Oliver and Ollie just got here, and now you're bringing up their departure."

"Can't ignore the facts." Shep took a swig of beer straight from the bottle. "Thought I heard you'll be returning to London in just a couple of weeks."

Beneath his arm, Oliver felt Shannon stiffen. They'd agreed not to talk about when he would leave, and Oliver inwardly cursed Shep for bringing up the topic. But the man's comment required an answer.

"Not that soon." Oliver kept his tone easy. "Closer to the end of March."

"Several weeks then, but not that long off." Shep shot a pointed look in his daughter's direction, as if making sure she was listening, before his gaze returned to Oliver. "You have a girl back home?"

"Pardon?"

"A girl. A woman you're seeing."

"No," Oliver said coolly.

"My son has been much too busy the past year to do much socializing," Josephine interjected. "His brokerage firm keeps him extremely busy, and now that he has Ollie to care for, I doubt there'll be much time for dating."

"Oh, I'm sure he'll find a few free moments now and then." Shep took another swig of beer. "Your son seems like the type to take advantage of every opportunity."

Oliver heard Shannon's quick intake of breath. If they'd been alone, Oliver would have had no hesitation in calling Shep on his comment. But the rest of those in attendance seemed oblivious to the conversation's undertones.

To make a scene would serve no purpose, he told himself even as his spine stiffened.

Oliver met Shep's gaze. They would talk, his eyes told her father, soon.

"Did I tell you Ollie has now started calling Oliver 'Daddy'?" This time it was Shannon who filled the silence. "It's so cute. He clearly says 'Daddy,' not 'Dada.'"

"Shannon called Shep 'Da' until she was three."

Shannon gave a little laugh. "Oh, Mother."

Lilian lifted her hand as if swearing an oath. "True story."

"Tell them what the boy calls you," Shep said to Shannon.

The slight pink across her cheeks deepened, but she acted as if she hadn't heard.

Josephine took a sip of tea, considered. "I believe 'Shannon' would be difficult for a child to say."

Shep opened his mouth.

"He calls me 'Mama,'" Shannon said, then quickly added, "I think it's what he calls all females."

"He calls your mother 'Lil,'" her dad said.

A lightning bolt flashed in Shannon's eyes. Oliver

couldn't believe her own father hadn't noticed his daughter's mounting irritation. Perhaps Shep didn't care. Perhaps he wanted to get a rise out of her.

Or perhaps this was his way of making a point. Steer clear of Oliver Fortune Hayes. He'll eat you up and spit you out and never look back.

Shannon pushed to her feet and flashed a smile that didn't quite reach her eyes.

"I'm really tired. Ollie was up a lot last night." She slanted a glance at Oliver. "I hope you don't mind leaving early."

"Not at all. It's embarrassing when your own mum trounces you." Oliver bent over and brushed a kiss against his mother's cheek. "May we give you a ride home?"

Josephine smiled and glanced over at Orlando Mendoza, who'd been her partner most of the evening. "Thank you, but I believe I have that covered."

Oliver and Shannon made their exit in record time. Once they were in the car, Shannon rested her head against the back of the seat and huffed a frustrated breath.

"My father was in rare form tonight." Her lips tightened. "No doubt about it. He's figured out we're sleeping together."

There was no reason to disagree. That fact had been very obvious. "You're his little girl. He's concerned I'm going to hurt you."

"I'm a woman, not a child," she snapped. "We both went into this with our eyes wide open."

Oliver didn't want to ask, but knew the question would fester if he didn't. "Any regrets?"

The anger fled her eyes, replaced with another kind of heat. She leaned over and brushed a kiss against his cheek. "Only that we're not at home right now so I can have my way with you."

* * *

The next week passed swiftly. Shannon kept her days so full she didn't have time to think. It was at night, when Ollie was in bed and Oliver was working, that her mind raced and she did nothing but think.

She thought about the fact that the Fortune Foundation would soon be choosing its new marketing executive. What would she do if the foundation offered the position to Rachel and not her? She couldn't continue to stay in Horseback Hollow and simply help out around the ranch. But the thought of returning to Lubbock filled her with dread.

But what weighed most heavily on her mind was the knowledge that each passing day brought her closer to the time when Oliver and Ollie would leave her and return to England.

Barely aware of the fragrant aroma of vegetables and meat cooking in the pot before her, Shannon automatically stirred the soup and blinked back tears.

This time spent with Oliver and Ollie had been the best of her life. Living under the same roof with Oliver had given her extra insight into the man behind the British stiff upper lip. He wasn't cold and off-putting as Rachel thought. He was a warm, caring man with a huge capacity for love.

At her encouragement, Oliver had become more demonstrative with Ollie. The increased openness was already bearing fruit. Ollie now ran to his father as often as he ran to her. And just yesterday, when Ollie had fallen on the rocky driveway and skinned his knee, his father had been the one he wanted to comfort him.

Oh, how she was going to miss them both. Shannon sighed and picked up the spoon.

She started to stir the soup again and felt a tug at her pant leg.

"Mama, up." Ollie stood beside her, arms held high.

Setting the spoon down, she lowered the heat even more, then stepped back and lifted the boy into her arms.

He smelled like soap and shampoo. Shannon wished she could hold him tight and never let him go. Instead she smiled. "Are you hungry?"

The little boy nodded vigorously. "Want ice cream."

"That's my boy."

Shannon whirled to find Oliver standing in the doorway, his hair mussed from sleep, Barnaby at his feet.

She glanced at the clock on the wall. "You didn't sleep very long today."

It wasn't even six and he hadn't gotten to bed—or rather to sleep—until noon. Ollie had been taking an extra-long nap and they'd been…occupied.

Oliver's normal pattern was to sleep until seven, then they'd have a late supper. She usually fed Ollie earlier, as the child preferred to eat smaller, more frequent meals.

"Couldn't you sleep?" she asked, when he didn't respond.

"Too much on my mind" was all he said, but she could see his expression was troubled.

Shannon set a now-squirming Ollie to the floor. He immediately ran to his father.

Oliver scooped him up and a smile lifted his lips. "You getting some loving from Shannon? Smart man."

The child turned his head and smiled at Shannon. "Mama give ice cream."

Oliver raised a brow, but there was laughter in his eyes. "Now I see what goes on while I'm sleeping."

"Give ice cream, Mama," Ollie repeated, pointing in the direction of the refrigerator.

Neither she nor Oliver paid any attention to the boy calling her "Mama." After the night they'd played cards, Shannon had tried again to get Ollie to call her by her given name—even a shortened version—but she'd had to concede defeat.

"Ollie may want ice cream," Shannon said easily, casting a playful glance at the child, "but he'll be getting yogurt."

Oliver grimaced.

"Hey," she told him, "it's healthy and it tastes good."

"I'll take your word on that." He sniffed the air. "Whatever is in that pot smells good."

"Homemade vegetable beef soup," she told him. "My mom gave me her old bread machine, so I made tomato basil bread to go with the soup."

"Sounds delicious."

"I thought we'd start off with a glass of wine and antipasto. Then a green salad, soup and bread." Shannon, who'd practically kicked and screamed while her mother taught her to cook, had discovered she actually enjoyed cooking…when she had someone to cook for besides herself.

Oliver swung Ollie through the air, and the boy erupted into giggles. When he set him down, Ollie began to protest until Oliver flicked on the television to a *Daniel Tiger's Neighborhood* rerun.

Mesmerized, the boy crawled up onto the sofa and Barnaby jumped up with him. Shannon got him a tube of yogurt and the child took it, his eyes firmly focused on the television.

"What do you say?" Oliver said automatically.

"Tank you," came the response from the child.

Oliver moved to the table and pulled out a chair. "I got another email from Diane's mother."

Ah, so that's what has him so troubled.

Shannon went to the counter where she'd placed two wineglasses and poured each of them a glass. She set the plate of antipasto on the table and took a seat opposite Oliver.

As she munched on an olive and sipped her wine, she thought back to when he'd received the first email. It had been right after the card party. Though he'd mentioned it in passing, she could see he was troubled by the contact.

She hadn't pressed, knowing he would tell her the specifics in his own time, or he wouldn't. As then, she had to resist the urge to push.

"She wants to video chat with Ollie. Says he's their only grandchild and they want to be a part of his life." Anger, at odds with the calm delivery, simmered in the air.

Unsure how to respond, Shannon took a bite of ham.

Oliver set down his wineglass and leveled a gaze at her. "They expect me to go out of my way when they couldn't be bothered to tell me about Diane's death. I had to hear about her death at a bloody cocktail party."

"I assume you asked why they hadn't told you when you picked Ollie up." Shannon kept her tone nonchalant, as if totally unaware of the hostility vibrating in the air.

"Celeste—that's Diane's mother—said she hadn't been thinking clearly. That her daughter's death had devastated her."

"Sounds…logical."

As if he'd finally found an outlet for his rage, Oliver pinned his gaze on her. "You're on their side. You think I should forgive them."

"I think—" Shannon carefully picked up another olive, though her stomach was so jittery she didn't dare put it in her mouth "—that losing a child *would* be horrific. It seems logical she wasn't thinking clearly."

"They had Ollie for two months." He shoved back his chair and jerked to his feet. "Two months without notifying me."

Let it go, Shannon told herself, *you're the nanny. This isn't your business.*

But even as the thought crossed her mind, she realized that she couldn't let it go. She cared for Oliver and for his son.

Ollie deserved to know his grandparents. And no good would be served for Oliver to harbor such anger. Still, how to proceed was the question.

Shannon took a long drink of wine. "What was your impression of Diane's parents? Prior to her death, I mean?"

He turned back from the kitchen window where he'd been gazing—or rather *glaring*—out into the twilight.

"Nice enough," he said grudgingly, as if it pained him to say the words. "Father is a barrister. Mother is involved in a lot of civic activities."

"Any other children?" she asked casually.

"Just Diane."

"Did you see her parents often after you were married?"

"At holidays. Occasionally they'd come to London and we'd go to the symphony or the theater."

"No backyard barbecues or card parties?" Shannon teased, relieved when he smiled.

"Not their cup of tea." His smile faded. "I can see where you're headed with this, what you're trying to do."

"Really?" She lifted the glass to her lips, but didn't drink. "Tell me. What is it I'm trying to do?"

"You want me to think about what they were like before, to give them the benefit of the doubt." He twirled the stem of the glass between his fingers.

"Someday Ollie will want to know about his mother. He'll have all sorts of questions. Who better to give him that information than her parents?"

His jaw jutted out at a stubborn angle. "They should have told me."

"Life is full of should-haves," Shannon said with a heavy sigh. "I should have confronted Jerry, but I didn't. Cut them some slack, Oliver. Not only for Ollie's sake, but for your own."

Chapter Sixteen

Shannon rested her head against the seat of Oliver's luxury Mercedes sedan and let the soothing tones of a Mozart piano concerto wash over her. As the car continued smoothly down the highway toward town, she slanted a glance at Oliver. Her heart tripped when he returned her smile then reached over to squeeze her hand.

She liked that they didn't feel the need to talk all the time. They'd both gotten comfortable with occasional silence. And she liked how when she did say something, Oliver listened to her, really and truly listened. Though Shannon still didn't know what he planned to do about the situation with Oliver's grandparents, it had been empowering for her to realize that he seriously considered her opinions.

Tonight she planned to simply sit back and enjoy her date with Oliver.

It *was* a date, she told herself. How could it be considered anything else?

Oliver had asked if she was busy Saturday night.

She'd said she was free.

He asked if she wanted to check out the recently renovated theater that had opened in Horseback Hollow.

She told him she'd love to see a movie.

While Horseback Hollow wasn't big enough to support a first-run theater—they had to go to Vicker's Corners or Lubbock for that—this week the local theater was running the classic *Back to the Future*. Shannon hadn't even been born when the movie had been made, but since this particular science-fiction comedy was one of her father's favorites, she'd seen it many times.

The thought of sitting in a dark theater with Oliver, eating popcorn and candy, perhaps even sharing a soda, made seeing the movie for what had to be the zillionth time very appealing.

Josephine had been desperate for what she had taken to calling her "Ollie time," so the boy was spending the night with "Nana," whom he now adored. Thinking of the vibrant woman brought to mind something Shannon had meant to bring up earlier.

"Have you noticed that lately your mother is always texting?" she asked Oliver after he parked and they started down the sidewalk of Horseback Hollow's main street.

Earlier when they dropped off Ollie, Josephine had been in the process of sending a text. Though Shannon's parents both texted occasionally, lately it seemed every time she saw Oliver's mother, the phone was glued to her hand.

"Mum likes technology," he said a bit absently. His eyes suddenly widened and a grin split his face. "Brodie."

Shannon hadn't seen much of Oliver's brother, although she knew he and Oliver had gotten together several times since Brodie had arrived in Horseback Hollow. From the few things Oliver had said, Shannon had the distinct impression his brother didn't think much of her hometown.

Brodie strode over. As always, he was impeccably dressed in a dark suit, his shoes shined to a high gloss. He cast a disapproving gaze at the jeans and cotton shirt Oliver wore.

"At least you're not wearing cowboy boots," Brodie said with a sniff.

"No," Shannon said with an impish smile, extending one foot so he could see her Tony Lama footwear. "I am."

A pained look crossed Brodie's face.

"We're going to view a movie at the cinema," Oliver told him. "Would you care to join us?"

"They're showing *Back to the Future*," Shannon added. "It's considered a classic."

A hint of a smile lifted Brodie's lips and then it was gone. It was as if he wasn't sure if she was putting him on or not. "I appreciate the invitation, but I have other plans."

"Would those plans involve Alden Moore?" Oliver lifted a brow. "I saw you coming out of the Hollows Cantina yesterday with him."

Shannon glanced at Oliver in surprise. He hadn't mentioned anything to her about his brother and Mr. Moore. Not that Oliver was required to tell her everyone he saw or spoke with during the course of the day. But Alden Moore was big news in Horseback Hollow.

The president of Moore Entertainment, Alden was the man charged with opening Cowboy Country USA, a theme park currently under construction at the edge of Horseback Hollow. The last Shannon heard, the park was scheduled to open Memorial Day weekend.

"The Hollows is one of the few places in town I can tolerate." Brodie gave a dismissive wave. "Thank heavens

I leave for London in a few days, where I can get some real food."

"What were you and Alden discussing?" Oliver pressed.

"Business. That's the only topic that interests me." Brodie shifted his gaze to Shannon, not missing the way his brother's hand circled her waist. "It appears you two are enjoying an evening out, leaving my nephew to fend for himself."

Oliver laughed. "Mum has him. Trust me, he'll be spoiled rotten by the time we pick him up tomorrow morning."

Surprise had Brodie's eyes widening. "You're leaving the tyke in her care overnight?"

"She insisted." Oliver's lips twitched. "You know how determined she can be."

"He'll be asleep by the time the movie is over," Shannon added. "We'd just have to wake him to take him home."

"Well—" Brodie inclined his head "—enjoy the cinema."

"Stop by before you leave," Oliver called after him.

Brodie nodded and continued to walk.

"Odd," Oliver said, almost to himself.

"What?"

"Brodie isn't usually so reticent." Oliver lifted a shoulder in a slight shrug. "It's of no importance."

He took Shannon's hand, a gesture that had come to seem so natural to him. Oliver assumed it was because there was a lot of touching going on at home.

Shannon's capacity for pleasure astounded him, as did his need for her. As their trust in each other had grown, they'd become even more adventurous in bed. Oliver had discovered that lovemaking could be passionate and intense but also casual and fun. Last night he'd even laughed aloud while tussling with her on the bed.

As they strolled down the sidewalk, under the glow of the streetlamps, they spoke of Ollie and Barnaby, of his mother and other family members. She didn't mention Diane's parents and he didn't bring them up either. Though he was becoming more reconciled to the idea of letting them be a part of Ollie's life, he wasn't quite there yet.

Once they reached the box office, he paid for the tickets. Shannon tried to pay for hers but that was never an option. He had invited her and he would pay.

Though the show was ready to begin, Shannon insisted she couldn't watch the movie without candy and popcorn. He hurriedly bought the refreshments and they found a couple of seats toward the back of the darkened theater. The place was only a third full, so there were plenty of choices.

"I love Junior Mints," Shannon whispered halfway through the show, popping another of the dark candies into her mouth.

The merest hint of chocolate remained on her lips. Leaning close, he ran a finger across her lips, heard her quick intake of air.

"Chocolate," he said, in response to her questioning look. "Your lips are sweet enough. They don't need any enhancement."

Instead of looking at the screen, where a truck of manure was being dumped on Biff's car, Shannon's gaze remained focused on Oliver. His groin tightened when she slowly ran her tongue across her lips.

Oliver had never condoned public displays of affection. But lately he found himself reaching for Shannon's hand or placing his palm against her back...simply for the contact and because the connection to her felt so good.

Taking her arm to steady her when getting out of the

car made perfect sense. Reaching out to grab her if she stumbled was totally appropriate.

Kissing a woman in a public theater? Unthinkable. But now, as Oliver's gaze lingered on Shannon's full, soft lips, he found he couldn't think of anything else.

Wait until you get home.

He'd never last that long.

Wait until you get in the car.

He'd never last that long.

Kiss her now. It seemed the best option. The *only* option. Societal rules be damned.

"Shannon," he spoke softly while his gaze traveled over her face and searched her eyes.

Was that harsh, uneven breath coming from her? Or him?

With great tenderness, Oliver brushed his fingers against her cheek then slowly lowered his head and closed his mouth over hers.

The kiss was warm and sweet and touched a place inside him that had been cold for so long. He heard sounds of laughter coming from the big screen but paid it no mind. All that mattered was him. And her. The closeness. The love.

The thought had him jerking back.

Even in the dim light, he could see the startled confusion in her eyes. Her lipstick was smudged from his kisses, the hair she'd intricately braided pulling loose.

Though his heart galloped in his chest, he casually gestured with his head toward the screen. "They're getting to the good part."

Since he'd paid little attention to the film, he had no idea what had happened or was about to happen. Neither did he particularly care.

Shannon gave a jerky nod and turned her attention back to the screen, but he sensed her puzzlement. When she straightened in her seat and leaned ever so slightly away from him, her withdrawal was like an ice pick to the heart.

Oliver slid his arm around her and pulled her close. When she relaxed and rested her head against his shoulder, his world that had tipped so precariously only seconds before righted itself.

He knew they were back to normal when she lifted the box of Junior Mints from her lap and offered him one.

Though Oliver wasn't a fan of the candies, he took one and realized when it hit his tongue that it tasted like her kisses. And he simply had to have another taste. The rest of the movie passed by unwatched.

Shannon blinked as they stepped from the darkened theater into the light. She looked, he thought fancifully, like a sleeping beauty waking up. *His* sleeping beauty.

Her lips were swollen from his kisses, her hair mussed. He hadn't been able to keep from slipping his fingers into the silky strands as their mouths melded together. And though they'd just stopped kissing when the credits had begun to roll, Oliver was seized with an overpowering urge to kiss her again.

Actually, he wanted to do a whole lot more than kiss her.

"Instead of going for ice cream in Vicker's Corners as we discussed, how about we go home and have…dessert there?" Though Shannon spoke casually, he recognized the look in her eye.

"Great minds think alike." He took her arm as they stepped out of the theater and onto the sidewalk.

Oliver resisted—barely—the urge to hurry her along. There was no need to rush. With his mum watching Ollie, they had all night.

"Oliver, what a pleasant surprise."

He pulled up short. "Amelia."

Looking young and carefree in a dress more suited to a college girl than a new mum, his sister quickly closed the distance between them. Quinn was with her, their baby bound to his chest in some kind of flowery fabric.

Oliver shot him a sympathetic glance.

Quinn simply grinned.

"What are you two doing out?" Oliver asked. The baby seemed far too small to be exposed to the cool night air.

"We could ask you the same question." Amelia's decidedly curious gaze slid from him to Shannon.

"We wanted to check out the new theater," Shannon said, then seemed to reconsider her words. "I mean, I wanted to check it out so I asked Oliver if he'd be interested in joining me. He said he was, so here we are."

She was chattering, Oliver realized, the way she tended to do when she was nervous. Why, he wondered, was she so nervous? And why was she making it sound as if he'd simply tagged along for the evening?

"It was very nice, wasn't it, Oliver?" she added, when no one spoke.

"It was very enjoyable." The only part Oliver remembered of the movie was the rolling credits, but the kisses had been exceedingly pleasurable. "What about you?"

"Wendy and Marcos wanted to see Clementine, so we stopped in for dessert."

Oliver resisted—barely—slanting a glance at Shannon. They had a different kind of dessert planned once they reached home. And he had no doubt he'd enjoy his more than whatever his sister and her husband ordered tonight.

"Where's Ollie?" Amelia glanced around as if expecting the toddler to jump out from behind a tree.

"He's with Mum this evening."

"Ollie is such a sweet little boy." Amelia's lips curved, her look one of fondness. "I was telling Quinn just the other day how much I wished you and Ollie would stay in Horseback Hollow."

"Am, you know that's—" Oliver began.

"Oliver was such a good big brother to me," Amelia told Shannon. "I couldn't have asked for better. I know our children are just cousins, but if Ollie grew up here, he'd be like Clemmie's big brother."

Amelia shifted her gaze back to Oliver. "Wouldn't that be nice?"

"Most certainly." Oliver knew his sister too well to argue. "But my home is in London."

"It doesn't have to be," Amelia said, her expression earnest. "Technology makes it possible for people to work from anywhere. Quinn and I watched an episode on the telly about that quite recently."

"Did you?" Oliver said, vaguely amused at the thought of his former jet-setting younger sister sitting at home watching the telly and discussing changing work habits with her rancher husband.

"You're conducting your business right now from Horseback Hollow," Amelia reminded him, as if she some-how thought that fact had slipped his mind.

"He is, but it's very difficult for him." Shannon spoke up for the first time since Amelia had started her discourse. "Because of the time difference, Oliver has to do all his work in the middle of the night."

"Granted, it's probably not ideal," Amelia conceded. "But if you wanted, you could make staying here work."

Once again, Oliver avoided arguing and simply agreed with his headstrong baby sister. "You're right, Amelia. If a person wants something badly enough, they can make it happen."

* * *

Though it was past midnight and Oliver had a lot of calls to make, he sat back in his desk chair, his mind on everything but stocks and bonds.

The words he'd said to Amelia—primarily to placate her—continued to haunt him. Three days might have passed, but he couldn't stop thinking about them.

He believed what he'd said. If he wanted something badly enough, he could make it happen. In his case, Oliver wanted Shannon.

Though he hadn't yet said the words, he realized somewhere along the way, he'd fallen in love with her. Here was a woman he could trust, a woman who cared for him as much as he did for her.

He'd learned a lot from his failed relationship with Diane. Oliver accepted part of the blame for the demise of his first marriage. Back then he'd showed his love the only way he knew how—by providing the material things she so desperately craved.

They'd had the house in the country, the one in London. He'd given her expensive jewelry and household help to make her life easier. But he realized now those were only things. He'd held back his heart. Or perhaps it was simply that his heart had been waiting for someone else.

Though he'd never say that aloud—it was much too Lord Byron-ish—he believed it. While it was still difficult for him to verbalize emotions, Shannon had taught him that actions had to be coupled with words.

That's what Oliver planned to do tonight. His fingers closed around the small jeweler's box in his pocket. When he'd been in Lubbock yesterday, he'd seen the perfect ring for Shannon in a small jewelry store's window.

A large marquis-cut diamond solitaire, comparable to

anything the Harry Winston jewelry company would carry, had caught his eye.

Oliver had never been a foolish man, or an impulsive one. He and Diane had dated for several years and he'd spent a lot of time considering whether he should propose. Only now did he realize that if he had to put so much thought into it—at one point he'd even drafted a list of the pros and cons—she hadn't been the one for him.

He'd settled, plain and simple. He'd been past thirty, he wanted a home and a family, and on paper they appeared well suited. But not once had Diane made his heart beat faster simply by walking into a room. Even worse, their house had never felt like a home.

With Shannon, Oliver could fully relax and be himself. No pretense, no posturing. She loved and accepted him as he was and, because he had her unqualified support, he wanted to be a better man.

She's never said she loves you.

The doubt surfaced and though he tried to brush it away, it kept returning to buzz around in his head, like a troublesome fly.

Oliver recognized this hesitation—knew the fear arose from those early years when his father had slapped down any talk or show of emotion.

It was no wonder his mother had left the man. Soon enough for Brodie not to have been tainted by his father's cold harshness, but not soon enough for Oliver.

But he'd gotten past that, Oliver told himself. Telling Ollie he loved him now came easier. And, once he said the words to Shannon, he vowed never to stop saying them.

In his mind, the only thing standing between them now was her affection for Horseback Hollow. But he felt confident of his ability to convince her she could find happiness in London with him and Ollie.

Tomorrow, he would confess his love. They would marry and meld their lives together.

For now, he had a business to run.

Oliver picked up his mobile phone and got back to work.

Chapter Seventeen

"I'm so happy you stopped by this afternoon." Shannon opened the oven door, releasing the delicious aroma of cinnamon into the kitchen. "Otherwise I'd have to eat this coffee cake all by myself."

"You've got Oliver," Rachel reminded her, sipping her coffee. "What time will he be up?"

Shannon lifted the pan to a cooling rack, then took off the oven mitts and tossed them to the counter. She glanced at the clock, saw it was just past four. "He didn't go to bed until almost two, so I don't expect him up until seven. Perhaps even later."

She saw no reason to mention Ollie had been taking a nap when his father had concluded his business dealings at noon. She and Oliver had taken advantage of the opportunity. Though Oliver had been in bed—with her—there had been no sleeping involved.

Rachel studied Shannon over the rim of her cup. "I thought you were supposed to get off at five."

Shannon dropped into the chair opposite Rachel. "Oliver would never get any sleep if I left so early."

Her friend clucked her tongue, reminding Shannon of her mother. "Some things never change."

The coffee cup Shannon had been raising to her lips returned to the table with a clatter. "What's that supposed to mean?"

"It means you let people run all over you."

For a second, Shannon was stunned. She wasn't sure how to respond. Could she have misheard? Transposed some of her mother's words into Rachel's mouth? "What did you say?"

"I meant no disrespect. I care about you." Rachel reached across the table and took Shannon's hands. Before speaking, she slanted a sideways glance where Ollie sat playing with his blocks, Barnaby supervising. "Think about it. Jerry comes on to you. Sure, you tell him you want none of it. But not forcefully enough to make him understand you mean business. He persists. Instead of filing charges or even threatening to, you ran away."

Heat flooded Shannon's face and she pulled her hands back. She rose and moved to the counter. Though the coffee cake was still too warm, she cut it anyway. It gave her something to do with her hands while her thoughts tumbled like clothes in an out-of-control dryer at the local Laundromat.

Though what had occurred at her previous job had happened pretty much the way Rachel described it, she *had* tried to speak with Jerry.

"I was forceful," Shannon protested. "I told him so many different ways to bug off, it wasn't even funny. But he didn't hear me. He didn't want to hear what I had to say, because I didn't matter."

"Now you're doing the same thing with Oliver." Rachel

leaned forward, resting her forearms on the table. "You set up parameters—like you're off at five every day—but then you don't hold him to them. He walks all over you, and worse yet, you don't seem to notice or care."

Ollie let out a shriek when his blocks came crashing down.

"Ollie, shush, your daddy is sleeping," Shannon said automatically, then refocused on Rachel. "What you said about Oliver, it's not like that between us."

"Of course it is. You just don't want to see it."

"You're wrong." A tightness filled Shannon's chest, making it difficult to breathe. "I want to help him out. I like taking care of Ollie."

Rachel's gaze searched her face. "You're in love with the Brit."

Shannon started to deny it, then decided why bother. Rachel knew her too well and would simply see right through her denial. She sighed. "I am."

Rachel inclined her head, her gaze speculative. "Does he love you, too?"

Ah, that was the question.

She thought about what Amelia had said, that if you wanted to make something work, you'd do it. She'd give up her life in Horseback Hollow for Oliver…all he had to do was ask.

But what is he willing to give up for you? To do for you?

Shannon frowned. Maybe she was a pushover. She shoved the troubling thought aside.

"C'mon, Shannon," Rachel pressed. "Be honest, with me and with yourself."

"It feels as if he cares," Shannon said slowly. "When he looks at me, there's this warmth in his eyes. When he touches me, there's heat but something more, something deeper."

"Heat. Warmth. You did it, babe." There was admiration in Rachel's voice. "When we made that bet, I thought for sure I'd win, but sounds like you heated up the iceberg. I owe you a drink."

Oliver paused in the hallway. He'd been jolted awake by the sound of Ollie crying out. But by the time his brain had cleared and he'd reached the living room, his son was happily playing with his bricks.

He'd intended to go back to bed until he heard Rachel's words. She and Shannon had a bet. A bet that involved him.

He clenched his stomach. How had he missed the signs? It wasn't as if this was a first. He'd been targeted before by women who wanted him for his stock portfolio and social position.

But Shannon hadn't been after his money. She'd done it simply for sport. Just to see if she could. And to his shame, she'd succeeded.

His father had been right, after all. A man who trusts was a fool.

Well, he wouldn't make that mistake again.

Though he returned to his bedroom, Oliver didn't sleep. Instead of the quiet candlelit dinner followed by a proposal tonight, once Rachel left, he would send Shannon on her way.

No one made a fool out of Oliver Fortune Hayes.

Not even the woman he'd been foolish enough to love.

Rachel left shortly after five and Shannon had just fed Ollie when Oliver walked into the kitchen.

"Hey, I thought you wouldn't be up for another two hours." She crossed the room to him, lifting her face for the expected kiss.

Instead, he brushed past her. Opening the kitchen cupboard, he took out the bottle of whiskey and poured himself a shot. He drank the amber liquid as if it was water and he was dying of thirst.

"Is something wrong?" she asked tentatively.

"Has Ollie been fed?"

"Just finished. He ate like a little piggy, so he's probably going to need changing soon." She shut her mouth before she could ramble even more.

Oliver was clearly upset over something, and all she could talk about was his son's diapers?

"What's wrong?" she asked quietly.

Though she longed to wrap her arms around him and hold him close, she stayed where she stood. It was as if he had this invisible force field around him warning of danger should one get too close.

"It's not working." He poured another shot, downed the contents of the glass again in a single gulp.

A cold chill slithered down her spine. "What isn't?"

"This." He gestured wildly, the empty glass in his hands. "You. Me. You taking care of Ollie."

"Wait a minute." Breathe, she told herself. Stay calm and breathe. "Things are good between us. Ollie is happy and I thought—" her voice trailed off slightly before she reined it back in "—things were good between you and me, too."

He turned and met her gaze, his eyes looking more gray than blue, and cold as steel. "I know about the bet."

"Bet?" She pulled her brows together. "What bet?"

"The one you made with Rachel." His fingers tightened around the glass until his knuckles turned white. "How you were going to thaw the iceberg, as you ladies put it. Well, congratulations. You may have won the bet but you lost the job. You're fired."

Shannon stared at him, trying to process what he was

saying. "That thing between Rachel and me was just a joke. When you first came into town, Rachel said—"

"I'm not interested in your excuses." His voice sliced like a knife through the air.

"I want you out of here in—" he glanced at his watch "—ten minutes."

For a second, Shannon thought she might faint. Or burst into tears. Instead she simply stood there, her body frozen in place.

This was all a simple misunderstanding, she wanted to say. But what would be the point? She'd tried to explain but he wouldn't listen.

Oliver didn't want to hear what she had to say. Because she didn't matter.

That was the one thing she hadn't been able to make Rachel understand.

That when you don't matter to someone, you might as well talk to the wind.

Fully aware that her unexpected appearance at the Triple S ranch would bring a ton of questions she preferred not to answer, instead of going home Shannon drove to Vicker's Corners. She rented a room at a quaint old Victorian B and B that had caught her eye when she and Rachel were shopping.

Last week, she'd hoped that before Oliver left town, they could carve out some time and spend the night here.

Well, she was here. But she was alone.

Shannon put her suitcase on the floor and flopped back on the bed, still dry-eyed. The tears were there, all balled up inside her. For now she was keeping them under tight control, afraid if she started crying, she might never stop.

Coming to a parting of ways was for the best, she told herself. Oliver would soon be returning to London anyway. By then she'd likely have her new job with the Fortune Foundation.

She tried to tell herself she'd been prepared for the fact that Oliver and Ollie would eventually leave, but she knew that was a lie. The truth was, she'd been secretly hoping Oliver would stay or ask her to go with him and Ollie to London.

Boy, had she been off the mark. He hadn't even cared enough to listen to her. No way was that love. Not the kind of love she wanted, anyway.

It was for the best, she told herself for the zillionth time.

When a stray tear slipped down her cheek, she hurriedly brushed it aside. She always felt like crying when she was tired. Perhaps, if she closed her eyes for just a second…

Shannon woke to sunlight streaming through the lace curtains. Groggy, she turned and saw that it was morning. The vintage alarm clock on the nightstand read 8:00 a.m.

The proprietress, a perky woman named Bea, had gone into great detail when Shannon had checked in about the lovely breakfast served daily between six and ten.

The last thing Shannon wanted to do was make small talk with strangers. She felt hollow and empty inside. But she refused to sit in the room all day and mope. She would visit her favorite Vicker's Corners café, the one that served the best granola pancakes in the entire state.

Even if the mere thought of eating made her stomach churn, she could sit outside in the sunshine and enjoy the fresh air. She would order a cup of their special coffee—a dark roast and chicory blend with steamed milk.

Feeling better now that she had a plan, Shannon headed for the shower. Minutes later, feeling decidedly more human, she pulled her hair back from her face with a couple of clips, grabbed a pair of jeans and a cotton shirt in heartbreak red—totally appropriate for today—and left the B and B via the back door.

The air held a crisp edge and walking briskly calmed her. It took her less than five minutes to reach the café. Though the café's outdoor seating was surprisingly full for a weekday, Shannon snagged a small wrought-iron table for two. She ordered pancakes—just in case her appetite came back—and coffee. She was scrolling through Facebook pages when her phone rang.

For a second her heart leaped. But it wasn't Oliver's name on the readout—not that she wanted to speak with him anyway—it was Rachel's. Better, she decided, and although they weren't on a FaceTime video call, she smiled. She'd read somewhere that even if you didn't mean it, a smile could be heard in your voice. "Good morning, Rach."

"Are you busy?"

"Not at all." Shannon smiled her thanks to the waiter who placed a steaming cup of coffee in front of her. "What's up?"

A long moment of silence filled the air.

"You haven't heard."

Shannon's heart seized. She set down the coffee cup with carefully controlled movements. "Heard what?"

Another few heartbeats. "I thought for sure they'd have called you."

Was it her parents? Oliver? Or, oh dear God no...Ollie? Her heart stopped, then began to gallop. The toddler was so quick, she didn't even know if Oliver realized how fast. If you didn't watch him every second, he could easily be hurt.

"Who?" Shannon's voice rose despite her best efforts to control it. "Tell me."

"Christopher Fortune."

Shannon's breath came out in a whoosh and she slumped back in her seat, relief leaving her weak. "Thank God."

"What did you say?"

"I said, that's great." But the moment the words left her lips, Shannon wondered why Christopher Fortune would be calling Rachel. She didn't have to wait long for the answer.

"I got the job." Rachel spoke quickly, as if she wanted to get it all out before she was interrupted. "In fact I'm at the Foundation office now. They have a bunch of employment forms for me to fill out."

"That's…wonderful. Fabulous news." Shannon did her best to force some enthusiasm into her voice, even as the realization hit. They'd hired Rachel, a woman with no marketing experience, instead of her. "I'm—I'm happy for you. Congratulations."

"You're probably wondering why they hired me and not you." Rachel's voice held a nervous edge.

Shannon paused. "Uh, maybe just a little."

The waiter delivered her pancakes and Shannon offered him a brief smile of thanks as her mind raced.

This didn't make sense. Sure, Rachel was pretty and smart, but so was she. And Shannon had three years of experience in the field. Christopher had been impressed by that fact, Shannon recalled.

"Well, I found out something that I think you need to know."

"I don't know, Rachel." Shannon expelled a heavy sigh. Did she really want to know that Christopher thought she'd blown the interview? Because what other reason could there be for her not getting the position? "What's done is done."

Rachel gave a disgusted snort. "How are you ever going to stand up for yourself when you insist on keeping your head in a hole?"

Shannon dumped some syrup on the pancakes. "Okay, tell me."

"The temp who's been working here is real chatty. She told me I almost didn't get the job because I didn't have the experience."

The piece of pancake that had been halfway to Shannon's mouth froze in midair. Her heart began to thud.

"She told me the other person they were considering got a bad reference from her previous employer," Rachel continued. "Apparently that swayed the decision in my direction."

"May I join you?"

Shannon looked up, startled, when a man's hand closed over the empty seat at her table.

Brodie Fortune Hayes may have asked Shannon the question, but he'd decided to join her regardless of the answer.

This morning, when Brodie had called his brother and asked Oliver if he wanted to check out how the Cowboy Country theme park was coming along, Oliver had nearly bitten his head off.

Something was clearly troubling his older sibling. When Brodie saw Nanny Shannon sitting alone, so far from home and without her little charge, he decided to do some investigating. While Brodie hadn't been able to get anything out of his closemouthed brother, he believed he'd have better luck with the woman.

Shannon covered the phone with her hand. "Sorry. Not in the mood for company this morning."

Ignoring her, he sat and motioned to the waiter for some coffee.

She shot him a venomous glance. He responded with a bland smile, pulling out his phone to check the stock reports. Oliver wasn't the only Fortune Hayes with a healthy portfolio.

"Jerry torpedoed me," Shannon muttered into the phone.

Brodie kept his gaze focused on his mobile unit, sensing she'd watch her words more carefully if she knew he was listening.

"It had to be that, Rachel. He's the reason I didn't get the job." Shannon breathed in and out, and Brodie watched in fascination as she fought for control. "If he thinks I'm going to let him get away with doing this to me, he's got a surprise coming. I—"

Shannon turned her back to Brodie and listened for several seconds.

"I don't think he'd physically harm me. I'll be fine, Rach. You told me to stop being a doormat…okay, maybe you didn't use those exact words, but that's what you meant. I'm just telling you. He's not getting away with this. Okay, bye."

Shannon set the phone down on the table and fixed her gaze on Brodie.

"Are you worried someone might do you physical harm?" Brodie demanded. "Is Oliver aware you might be in danger?"

"I'm not in danger." Her tone was as flat as her eyes. "Even if I were, I can take care of myself."

"Does Oliver know?"

"There's nothing to know. Besides, your brother and I aren't exactly on speaking terms at the moment."

"Oh?" Brodie lifted a brow and feigned surprise. "What happened?"

She hesitated for so long he wondered if he needed to ask again. But just as he opened his mouth to press a little more, she began to speak.

"You want to know? Well, I'll tell you. Oliver used some

ridiculous teasing bet I made with Rachel as an excuse to get rid of me. He couldn't even listen to my explanation. You know why?" Obviously the question was rhetorical because she plowed ahead, not waiting for his response. "Because I don't matter to him. He knows me. He knows my heart. But he doesn't care and he just wanted me gone."

Shannon jerked to her feet. "Thanks for breakfast, Brodie." She gestured to the waiter, who'd arrived to take the man's order. "He'll take my check, too."

Without a backward glance, she strode off.

Strange, Brodie thought, *yet very interesting.* He pulled out his phone to call his brother.

Chapter Eighteen

He had behaved abysmally.

For a man who prided himself on his integrity, it was hard for Oliver to admit that what his father had done—what he'd given the man the power to do—had caused him to overreact and treat the woman he loved in such a despicable manner. Shannon had seen through him. Her accusations had been spot-on.

He'd used the "bet" as an excuse to push her away, even though he knew in his heart she wasn't capable of such duplicity. It had been the move of a coward.

What he and Shannon shared didn't have anything to do with a wager. Even if their physical relationship had started that way—which he didn't believe it had—what was between the two of them, the closeness they shared, was one hundred percent genuine.

Oliver now faced the task of righting a very large wrong.

But he firmly believed the words he'd said to his sister;

that if a man wanted something badly enough, he could make it happen. He would win Shannon back. He would show her he could be the man she deserved.

He was on his way to the Triple S when Brodie called and relayed the puzzling conversation he'd overheard. Oliver pulled over to the side of the road. His mind raced as he put the pieces together.

"Daddy, cookie," Ollie called from his car seat.

"In a second, son," Oliver said, despite knowing he hadn't packed any biscuits. Even as he ordered Amelia's number to be dialed, he decided the tiger Diane's parents had given Ollie would have to do in place of a biscuit. He leaned over the seat and tossed the well-loved soft toy to him.

The boy squealed with delight and hugged the tiger to his chest.

Oliver stared thoughtfully at his son, at the toy given in love, then shifted his focus as the ringing stopped and Amelia answered. As he'd hoped, she had Rachel's mobile number. Another call confirmed his greatest fear. According to her friend, Shannon was already on her way to Lubbock to confront her former boss. And she'd gone alone.

Oliver dropped off Ollie at his sister's house, then attempted to ring Shannon again. She didn't pick up. He hadn't really expected her to and was once again on the highway headed to Lubbock.

His hands clenched the steering wheel in a death grip. If that sod touched one hair on Shannon's head, Oliver Fortune Hayes would make him sorry he was ever born.

The rental vehicle's GPS led him directly to a large office building of steel and glass in the downtown business district. The lack of parking in the area was of no concern to a Fortune. Oliver simply pulled the Mercedes sedan into a loading zone in front of the building and hopped out.

He barreled through the front door…and straight into Shannon.

He wrapped his arms around her, holding her so tight, she squeaked.

"Oliver, let go, you're crushing me."

Loosening his hold, he stepped back, studying her from head to toe. "Are you okay? Did he hurt you?"

"Who?"

"Your former boss. The one you came to see."

"I told him what I was going to do and I did it." For a moment, a smile of smug satisfaction lifted her lips. "I went to human resources and filed a sexual harassment complaint against him. Apparently the company takes such charges very seriously."

For a moment, it was as if yesterday had never happened. The connection, the warmth was still there. Had yesterday been a bad dream? Perhaps they would simply move forward, relegating his bad behavior to the past.

"You're a strong and brave woman." Oliver gave a little laugh. "Although, you may have taken several years off my life during the drive here."

For a second she returned his smile, then seemed to remember how things were between them. She took several very deliberate steps back.

It appeared forgiveness wasn't going to come so easily.

When Shannon turned abruptly on her heel and started walking, he followed.

She whirled and narrowed her gaze. "What is it you want, Oliver? Why are you even here?"

The coolness in her gaze sent a chill down his spine.

"I should think it'd be fairly obvious." He moved to adjust his cuffs, then realized he'd left the house in such a hurry he'd grabbed the nearest item of clothing. He looked down and saw he'd pulled on an old gray sweatshirt that Shannon had borrowed from her father the other night.

Though he tried to ignore the fact he was dressed like a country bumpkin, his confidence was shaken. "My brother called. I spoke with Rachel. I feared for your well-being."

She offered a tight smile, one that didn't come close to reaching her eyes. "As you can see for yourself, I'm quite fine."

"Well, I'm not quite fine. I haven't been since you left."

"You mean since you ordered me from your home? Since you fired me without even listening to me? When you didn't even give me a chance to say a proper goodbye to Ollie?"

That *had* been a mistake. His son had been distraught. All Oliver could think of to placate the boy was to tell him Shannon's mum needed her for a few days.

Oliver raked his hand through his hair. "We need to talk."

She opened her mouth, then shut it and considered. "There's a park just around the corner. I guess there are a few things I need to say to you."

Her tone wasn't promising, but he consoled himself that at least she was willing to hear him out. But when they reached the small green oasis and took a seat on an ornate metal bench beside an evergreen that had been cut to resemble a dragon, she lifted a hand when he started to speak.

"You had your say yesterday. It's my turn." Shannon lifted her chin, her brown eyes flat and cool. "You were completely out of line. You overheard only part of a conversation, yet you ran with it. I've spent a considerable amount of time thinking why a logical man such as yourself would do something so illogical."

She jerked to her feet and began to pace. "I concluded

you were scared of what had been building between us. You were looking for a way to run. That bit of conversation you overheard gave you the out you were seeking."

Oliver opened his mouth to respond but shut it when she glared and continued. "That may have made you feel all justified and righteous, but it was devastating to me. To have the man I loved think so little of me. Worse, I just took the abuse and slunk away. Well, no more. Shannon Singleton is no one's doormat. Not anymore. Not ever again."

Though her voice was steady, she was visibly trembling.

He stood and would have stepped closer, but once again she held up a hand. The coolness in her eyes was like a knife to the heart. And the worst of it was, he had only himself to blame for the distance between them.

Oliver cleared his throat. "First I want to say, I'm proud of you, Shannon."

"Well, doesn't that make me feel all warm and fuzzy inside."

The sarcasm had him raising his brows. "I mean it. I know what it took for you to come down here. You're right about my behavior. I was out of line last night. Please come home with me. And Ollie. It's where you belong."

"News bulletin. I don't belong anyplace where someone can order me out of the house when they get angry or scared or whatever." Shannon leaned over and picked up her bag, which she'd set by the bench, then straightened. "That's not a home, that's a job."

"Shannon," he called out when she headed to the ornate entrance gate.

After a slight hesitation, she stopped and turned.

"I'm sorry," he said.

She paused for the briefest of seconds, as if waiting for him to say more. After a long moment she gave a little laugh that somehow managed to sound incredibly sad. "Yeah, well, I'm sorry, too."

Before Oliver climbed the porch steps of the Singleton house, he cleaned off the bottom of his shoes. Who knew a walk through a corral could be so...unsavory?

Though it wasn't even ten in the morning, he'd already managed to cross two items off his agenda, as evidenced by the conciliatory email winging its way across the Atlantic to Diane's parents and his visit to the corral to speak with Shep.

His future father-in-law had been shocked when Oliver had shown up to ask for Shannon's hand in marriage. Actually, he thought, the man seemed vastly amused that Oliver wanted to marry a woman who wasn't even speaking to him at the present time.

Still, Shep had laughed and clapped him on the shoulder, telling him to "go for it." Oliver took that to mean he had the man's blessing.

Now came the hard part. After taking several deep breaths, he rang the bell.

Through the screen door, he watched Lilian approach. This time there was no broad welcoming smile, only a slightly wary one. Oliver didn't blame her. Shannon was her daughter and he was, well, the cad who'd hurt her.

"Hello, Oliver." Lilian glanced nervously over her shoulder. "I didn't expect to see you here."

"Mrs. Singleton," he said, reverting back to the more formal address. "I was wondering if you could fetch Shannon for me. I'd like to speak with her."

"Who is it, Mom?"

A second after he heard her voice, Shannon stood beside her mother and close enough to touch.

Oliver's heart slammed against his chest. She was

breathtakingly beautiful in blue jeans, a simple white shirt and bare feet.

Her eyes widened. "What are you doing here?"

Oliver met her confused gaze with a slightly unsteady one of his own. "I'm here to listen."

Shannon blinked. Her initial instinct had been to order him off the property. Until he said he'd come to *listen*. After she'd left the park, she'd thought of several other things she wanted to say to him.

In fact, she'd planned to call him today. She considered. For what she had to say, face-to-face would definitely be better.

"Okay, we'll talk." Shannon glanced at her mother. "Give us a few minutes."

Her mother's eyes softened. "Take as long as you need, dear."

Shannon stepped out onto the porch and, after a momentary hesitation, moved to the swing.

Oliver followed, taking a seat on the far end then swiveling to face her.

She had to admit he looked quite dashing in his dark suit, crisp white shirt and red Hermes tie. Once, when she told him wearing her favorite cowboy boots made her feel more confident, he'd sheepishly confessed he felt that same way about a suit and tie.

Her heart softened slightly. "You said you came here to listen."

He nodded.

"Well, then, I'd like to see Ollie." Shannon folded her hands in her lap, hoping he didn't notice the slight tremor. "I think it's important he understands I didn't leave because of anything he'd done."

"You can see him anytime you want," Oliver said. "Ollie has missed you. We both miss you."

The last was said so quietly, but with such emotion, that for a second Shannon found it difficult to speak. She took a moment to clear her throat. "I—I left a few things behind, too. Let me know when would be a good time to stop by."

"You're welcome anytime."

Tears stung the backs of her lids, but Shannon blinked rapidly and kept them at bay. "Okay, fine. Thanks."

He reached out as if he intended to take her hand but let it fall when she sat back.

"Is there anything else you want to say to me?" he asked.

Shannon thought for a moment, a task that was becoming increasingly difficult. His nearness appeared to have turned her brain to mush. Of course, five minutes after he left she'd likely recall a dozen things she wanted to say. "No. No. That was all."

"In that case, would you mind listening to me for a second?" When she opened her mouth, he lifted a hand. "If at any time you want me to leave or to stop talking, just say the word."

"Are you saying if I ask you to leave and never come back, you'll do it?" Though her insides shook like jelly, her voice came out steady.

"I can't promise I'll never come back." Oliver shifted in his seat. "You're too important to me to make such a promise."

"What do you want to say, Oliver?"

"You were absolutely right."

"About?"

"Deep down, I was fearful of allowing you to see how much you mattered to me. My father told me numerous times anyone who loves or shows emotion is a fool."

"You were married, Oliver. You'd taken that leap once before." Shannon's chuckle held no humor. "I'd have thought love would come easier to you the second time around."

"I was never able to give my heart totally to Diane." A red flush rose up his neck. "Since coming to Texas, I've come to believe my heart was waiting for you."

Shannon gaped. Never had she thought she'd hear such flowery prose come from Oliver's mouth. Yet he seemed sincere…if slightly embarrassed.

"I'm not proud of my behavior." His eyes closed for a second and she watched as he clenched and unclenched one hand. "When you walked out the door and drove off, I realized I'd been a berk."

"A what?"

"A—a fool." He gave her a lopsided smile. "You have my heart, you know. You will always have it." He reached over and took her hands in his. "Believe me. I love you. I trust you. Completely. Totally. Without reservation."

Tears welled in her eyes and slipped down her cheeks.

Oliver wiped them away with the pads of his fingers. "I'm sorry I hurt you."

"I love you, too." The emotion squeezing her heart made her voice husky.

"You realize Ollie and I are a package deal."

"I love Ollie." This time it was *her* fingers swiping at the tears that seemed determined to fall. "Your little guy stole my heart within seconds of meeting him."

"If we were to be together permanently, what is it you'd want, Shannon? Tell me what it is and it's yours."

Puzzled, she pulled her brows together. "What do you mean?"

"If we were married, where would you like to live?"

Married? Her breath caught. If they were *married*?

Shannon thought of how she'd insisted to Rachel she wouldn't wed any man unless he agreed to settle in Horseback Hollow. "What if I said I wanted to live in Horseback Hollow?"

"Then that's where we'll live," he said without hesitation. "I want you to be happy. If being here makes you happy, this is where we'll live."

"But your business," she protested. "The hours—"

Capturing her hand, he brought her fingers to his lips and kissed them one by one. "Don't worry. It won't be a problem."

He might be able to make it work, but she knew it'd be difficult not only for him, but for them as a family. Still, it appeared he was willing to make the sacrifice.

Because he loves me. Because he wants me to be happy.

Shannon loved her friends, her family and her little town. But there was a whole, wonderful—slightly scary—world out there she'd yet to explore. Was it fear that had made her so adamant about remaining in Horseback Hollow?

"Would we build a home in town? Or would you prefer living on a ranch? If you could pick," Oliver prompted, "tell me what your dream home would look like."

His blue eyes were focused on her. She had his full attention.

"In my perfect world—" she slid closer to him "—you'd have your arm around my shoulders during this discussion."

Before she'd finished speaking, Oliver closed the remaining distance between them and slipped an arm around her shoulders, pressing a kiss against her hair. "Better?"

"Much." The heat from his body mingled with hers and the coldness inside her began to thaw. "Actually, I'd like two homes."

He smiled. "That could be arranged. One in town, the other in the countryside, I presume?"

"Actually, I was thinking of one home here, the other in London. We could spend part of the year in England and the other part in Horseback Hollow. When Ollie is school-age, we might need to reconsider, but for now, that's what I'd like."

His brows pulled together. "Are you certain?"

"Yes." She kissed him on the lips. "Absolutely certain."

"Then that's what we'll do."

"Just like that?"

"Just like that." He smiled. "What about children?"

"What about them?"

"How many would you like?"

She hesitated.

"Be honest."

"Six," she said. "I've always wanted six."

His smile widened. "What a coincidence. That's how many I'd like, too."

"Seriously?"

"Seriously."

Tears flooded her eyes. "This is overwhelming."

"Oh, sweetheart, there's more."

"I don't know if I can handle more," she said with a shaky laugh.

It appeared, in this, he would give her no choice. Oliver rose, then dropped to his knee before her.

Shannon's breath hitched when he pulled out a velvet jeweler's box and flipped it open. The large diamond glittered in the sunlight. Smaller diamonds, but no less brilliant, surrounded the large marquis-cut stone.

"Shannon." He spoke her name softly, and in the quiet she heard the love, saw it reflected in his eyes.

"It's…it's the most beautiful ring I've ever seen."

His smile flashed and she knew her response had pleased him. He took her hand and focused those blue eyes directly on her as he began to speak.

"When I first saw you at the Superette, I was impressed by your kindness, your willingness to help a stranger find his way. Being around you, getting to know you, I realized just how special you are, and I began to fall in love." He squeezed her fingers. "If you count the days since we first met, we haven't known each other that long, but it feels as if I've known you forever. I've been waiting my whole life for you. Without a single doubt I know what we share is right and true and strong enough to last a lifetime."

It was quite a speech from a man not prone to verbosity. And she knew without a doubt the words came straight from his heart.

"Oh, Oliver." Joy sluiced through her veins. If this was a dream, Shannon prayed she'd never wake up.

"I promise no one will work harder to make you happy or cherish you more than me." His gaze searched hers. "And I will listen. Always. My life will never be complete without you beside me to share it. Will you marry me, Shannon? Will you be my wife and Ollie's mother?"

For several heartbeats, Shannon struggled to find her voice, to put into words all she was feeling.

"When I look into my heart, I see only you," she said finally. "I can't imagine growing old with anyone else. I love you so much. So yes, Oliver, I will marry you. And I'll be proud to be Ollie's mother."

Then the ring was on her finger. When he stood and pulled her into his arms, Shannon knew with absolute certainty there was no other place she wanted to be.

Not only for now, but for eternity.

Epilogue

The opulent hotel room on Buckingham Palace Road surrounded Shannon in a sweet cocoon of luxury. But the true treasure was the man sleeping beside her. She glanced at her husband, then at the large diamond solitaire on her left hand, now made complete by a wedding band.

Last week she and Oliver had tied the knot in Horseback Hollow, surrounded by family and friends. Two days ago, they'd flown to London, accompanied by her parents and brothers.

Oliver had insisted on paying for her family's trip to England and had gotten them all seats in first class. While in the UK, her parents and brothers were staying at his home in Knightsbridge. Shannon and Oliver would join them there at the end of the week.

She'd never thought she'd get her father on an airplane, much less out of the United States, but Shep had taken to England like a duck to water. Once he'd figured out how

to use the Tube, her dad had been unstoppable. For her
mother, this was the honeymoon she'd never had, but Oliver had waved aside her thanks, telling her that they were
family now.

His family had embraced her just as easily. Last night,
Brodie had hosted a reception for them, inviting not only
family but Oliver's UK friends and business associates
to celebrate their marriage at the swanky Savile Club in
Mayfair.

The best part of the evening for Shannon was having
the opportunity to get to know Brodie better. He wasn't as
uptight as she first thought. She'd come away from their
lengthy chat knowing she and Oliver's brother were destined to be good friends.

She was trying to decide whether to get up or go back
to sleep when she felt Oliver stir.

"Can't you sleep?" he asked, pushing himself to a sitting position.

"Just admiring the view." She glanced around the sumptuous bridal suite in one of London's premier hotels. "This
sure beats the B and B in Vicker's Corners."

"It's lovely here," he admitted. "I'm enjoying the view
myself."

She turned to see what part of the room had captured
his gaze. Was it the paintings? The mural on the ceiling?
Or the opulent fixtures?

Instead she found his gaze focused directly on her.

Her skin heated beneath his gaze.

"The B and B was nice, too," he said, offering her a
lazy smile. "I'll never forget that first night with my beautiful wife."

The images from their wedding day—and night—were
forever etched in a special place in Shannon's heart. There
were the vows they'd written and the scent from the or-

chids Oliver had had flown in because she'd mentioned once they were her favorite. Most of all, she'd never forget the look of love in his eyes when he'd seen her walking down the aisle on her father's arm.

"I like hearing you say 'my wife,'" she admitted. "Almost as much as I like saying 'my husband.'"

She snuggled beside him, her fingers toying with the hair on his chest. "Brodie mentioned last night he's taking full credit for us being together."

Oliver rolled his eyes and chuckled. "I don't know how he arrived at that conclusion, but it sounds like something my brother would say."

"Brodie is really very sweet." Shannon paused thoughtfully. "He's not nearly as stuffy as he first appears. I believe with a little help from the right woman..."

"You really think he just needs the right woman to warm him up?" Amusement ran through Oliver's voice like a pretty ribbon.

"I do."

"You know, I'm feeling a bit stuffy right now."

Shannon couldn't keep from smiling. "Is that code for you need some *warming up* yourself?"

"It is, indeed."

Oliver clasped her face gently in his hands, lowered his mouth to hers...then jerked back as the door to the bedroom was unceremoniously flung open.

Shannon gave a little yelp. "I thought we locked the door."

Oliver sat up straight, just in time to see his son race across the room, the nanny hot on his heels.

"Mama, Daddy," Ollie called out happily as he ran to his parents. "I come see you."

When he reached the bed, Ollie pulled himself up, then crawled over the covers, as quick and agile as a little monkey.

The drama continued when Barnaby appeared, zipping past the nanny, emitting deep woofs with each step. He reached the bedside and began to bark. Because of his short legs, the corgi required Shannon's help to make it to the top of the silk duvet.

"I'm so sorry, sir, ma'am. The little tyke got away from me." The distraught nanny's face was flushed and a strand of gray hair had come loose from her serviceable bun.

Though many relatives had offered to watch Ollie during their honeymoon, Shannon and Oliver had wanted the boy close, so they'd secured a suite and enlisted the help of Mrs. Crowder.

Ollie flung his arms around both parents, burrowing against them. He giggled as Barnaby reached him and began licking his face.

Nanny Crowder wrung her hands, obviously unsure if she should snatch her young charge and his pet out of his parents' honeymoon bed or simply beat a hasty retreat. "Oh, my. Oh, my. This will never do."

Oliver caught Shannon's eyes and they exchanged grins. It may have been a chaotic scene, at least to anyone unused to small boys and dogs, but this was his new reality.

He'd been blessed with a beautiful wife whom he adored, a son who brought joy to his life every day and a corgi that could always be counted on to liven things up.

"No worries, Mrs. Crowder," Oliver told the nanny, his heart overflowing with love and thankfulness. "This is all quite perfect."

* * * * *